"A superior collection ... Megan Abbott has _____ .d a talented list of contributors who deliver inspired performances."

> – **George Pelecanos**, *New York Times* best-selling author of *The Night Gardener*

"As a statement on contemporary noir and as a barometer of the culture, *A Hell of a Woman* tells the whole story and then some."

> – **Woody Haut**, author of *Neon Noir: Contemporary American Crime Fiction*

"Beautiful, bold and bloody – the dames in this collection rock, and when they do, heads roll. This anthology of compelling stories about members of the 'fairer sex' with a proclivity for deadly schemes is a must-read for all lovers of noir. Each story is a gem."

> – **Carolyn Haines**, author of *Penumbra* and *Fever Moon*

"The next time some jackass smirks and tells me that women can't write noir, I'm going to knock him upside the head with a copy of *A Hell of a Woman*. Megan Abbott, our leading Queenpin of crime, has assembled a powerhouse collection of noir by the best dames in the business. (And the stories by the dudes ain't half bad, either.) I've fallen hard for this antho, even though it's destined to clean out my savings account, sleep with my best friend and break my heart."

> – **Duane Swierczynski**, author of *The Blonde* and *Severance Package*

A Hell of a Woman

of a

Woman

An Anthology of Female Noir

Edited by
Megan Abbott

Foreword by
Val McDermid

Busted Flush Press
Houston, TX

A Hell of a Woman: An Anthology of Female Noir

Hardback, $26 (978-0-9792709-9-4)
Paperback, $18 (978-0-9767157-3-3)

First paperback printing, December 2007

Layout & Production Services: Greg Fleming & Jeff Smith

BUSTED FLUSH
PRESS
P.O. Box 540594
Houston, TX 77254-0594
www.bustedflushpress.com

Table of Contents

Hellcats, Madwomen and Outlaws

Appendix: Women in the Dark

An array of authors, booksellers, critics and film aficionados pay homage to favorite noir writers, characters and performers.

Foreword

by Val McDermid

I blame Raymond Chandler. I blame him for writing too well. Here's the thing with Chandler. He had a problem with women. Vamps, victims and vixens are the only roles he provided for us. And his perennial popularity has guaranteed that his twisted view of women would remain the template whenever the hard-boiled boys hatched a new tale of the mean streets. For years, we've been stuck in this gruesome girlie groove because of one man's screwed-up sexuality. (If you feel bold and foolhardy enough to disagree with my characterization of Chandler's perverse views on womankind, I refer you to the page-long diatribe against blondes in *The Long Goodbye*. It begins on page 89 in my edition. Oh, never mind. Just read anything the man wrote with a female character in it . . .)

It would have been so different if Hammett had taken pole position in the pantheon. Now there was a man who knew how to write women who take your breath away. Real women who were sexy in spite of the runs in their stockings or their smudged lipstick. Women who knew what they wanted and went after it. Even if meant ending up with an ice-pick in their chest. It's a lot harder to write grounded and rounded women, which is probably why the Chandler style won the day. Whores and madonnas are much easier to deal with than the bundles of complexity and cussedness we know women to be.

Twenty years ago, writers such as Sara Paretsky and Mary Wings began to redress the balance, demonstrating that women could be strong and resourceful, as smart-mouthed and capable of nailing victims as their male counterparts. The many followers who charged down the mean streets in their wake (myself included . . .) revealed a keen appetite among writers and readers for more women who knew their own mind and were prepared to do whatever it took to achieve their goals.

But that first wave of mostly feminist protagonists has largely receded now, leaving a high-water mark for a handful of women writers who have carved out an impressive territory that showcases how well women can run the game both as PIs and as cops.

Now there is another new wave, and this time what's breaking on the shore is scurf, not surf. A creamy curl of scummy water is the harbinger of 21st-century noir. The tide may have gone out on pulp fiction back in the sixties, but now it's back, led by a pack of writers whose appetite for darkness is matched only by their talent and their willingness to descend into the sort of lives none of us would want to inhabit.

One of the key differences between the old pulp fiction and the new noir is that this time it's not just the guys calling the shots. Women like Vicki Hendricks and Vin Packer are standing shoulder to shoulder with the men, just as merciless in their take on the underbelly. Because women are doing it, and because the men who are doing it spend their lives surrounded by women who are not victims, vamps or vixens, the female characters who populate these stories are a different breed.

These women are not ranking cops bucking the system to make their mark. They're not private eyes who have worked their way through the system so they can own their own businesses, be their own bosses. The first wave of hard-boiled female protagonists were essentially middle class. Their origins may have been working class, their politics of the left, but by virtue of the walls they had busted down to get where they were, they had moved up the social scale.

Most of the women we meet in *A Hell of a Woman* haven't jumped those barriers. These are the women who are normally swept into the dark corner of literature where they can be readily ignored. They're waitresses, hookers, illegal immigrants, addicts and grifters. Most of them are straight only in the sense of sexuality, and some of them can't even claim that. What they have in common is a refusal to become victims of their circumstances. These are women who are absolutely not taking anything lying down. Well, maybe temporarily, but only for as long as it takes to lull the men who would use them into a false sense of security.

Some of the writers in this anthology have been giving us pleasure for years, revealing here that they still have plenty of new tricks to show us. Sandra Scoppettone's classic twist in the tail, Ken Bruen's slice of warped life and SJ Rozan's poignant tale of love and determination all show their mastery of the short form.

There are brilliant gems too from writers who have just begun to demonstrate what they can do. Allan Guthrie, Charlie Huston, Donna Moore and Cornelia Read are among those featured here whose stories show a canniness and skill that's reflected in the handful of novels they've produced so far. I guarantee these samples of their work will have you running to the bookstore for more.

There are new voices too. Sarah Weinman, best known for her must-read blog at *www.sarahweinman.com*, and editor Lisa Respers France are proof of the truth of the mantra that reading is the best way to learn how to write. I can't wait to hear more from them.

A Hell of a Woman takes us on a journey into lives most of us can only imagine with a shudder. Lives of quiet desperation, easy violence, absent opportunities and grinding poverty. But the women at the center of these fictions are extraordinary. You wouldn't want most of them in your town, never mind in your house, but it's impossible not to grant them grudging respect and admiration for their smarts and their guts. This collection will make you squirm, but it will also make you smile. So load up your Mary Gauthier tracks and prepare to take a walk on the wild side.

Editor's Introduction

by Megan Abbott

"We're sisters under the mink."
— Debby Marsh (Gloria Grahame), *The Big Heat* (1953)

From the very beginning, noir fiction has given us memorable women. The gutsy and intrepid Anne Riordan, matching Philip Marlowe pace for pace in Raymond Chandler's *Farewell, My Lovely*. The stalwart and principled Effie Perine, to whom Dashiell Hammett hands over the final judgment on Sam Spade in *The Maltese Falcon*. Sylvia Nicolai and Laurel Gray, one a devoted wife, the other a vampish actress, joining forces to outwit the murderous Dix Steele in Dorothy B. Hughes' *In a Lonely Place*. James M. Cain's combustible sister duo, June and Dorothy Lyons, careering their way through *Love's Lovely Counterfeit*. Heartbroken and heartbreaking Helen Meredith in Charles Willeford's *Pick-Up*.

It is, of course, much easier to generate such a list if one begins with the femme fatales, the spider women, the remorseless vixens—from Phyllis Nirdlinger (*Double Indemnity*) to Elsa Bannister (*The Lady from Shanghai*), from Carmen Sternwood (*The Big Sleep*) to Charlotte Manning (*I, the Jury*), and on and on. And few could deny their visceral pleasure, the sight of Edward G. Robinson painting the toenails of the sullen Joan Bennett (*Scarlet Street*) or Barbara Stanwyck tossing her cigarette to the floor to finish off Fred MacMurray in *Double Indemnity*.

But the dark (and often darkly funny) stories in this anthology evoke a broader range of female characters, some expanding our ideas of women in noir, some reinventing the terms, some playing with the traditional icons, others smashing them outright. And what they all do is glory in their female characters' complexities, revel in their contradictions and celebrate their bravado. What they all do is give us arresting, complicated and pulsingly alive women.

The stories in *A Hell of a Woman* invite us into the world, and minds, of both the kinds of female characters who do frequent noir—the girl-Friday secretary, the moll—but are seldom given center stage, and the kinds of women who more commonly occupy only the fringes of noir or do not appear at all. She's the woman who pours your coffee at the rust-curled diner down the road. The one who delivers your mail with an enigmatic smile. She's the business-suited woman on the subway every morning with the forlorn smile and bitten nails. The pretty face you saw at the thrift store, gazing at that pair of vintage shoes from beneath a fringe of black bangs. And she's also the one who takes your ticket at the Cineplex without ever speaking, without even looking you in the eyes.

The women in these pages are climbers, dreamers, hustlers, holders of secret truths tucked close to their shuddering chests. They're both hardscrabble and manor-born, regal yet gutter-sprung. They're guileless and stout-hearted. They're steely and smooth as silk. They're love-riddled and heartbreakers. They're shopworn angels and stone-cold dazzlers, avenging angels and knights in shining armor. We have a boxing cutman with a fierce heart, a trailer park Madonna whom neither man nor nature can vanquish. We have a police detective with a wicked bluff and a housewife with hidden steel. We have one, two, three waitresses, dreamers all, and a milky-eyed recluse with a past darker than she can bear. We have a country girl, lashed with fear, finding her chance to make things right. And they all bear secrets heavy as this blue, sick world can hold.

After these women are through with you, though, there's more waiting. Flip a few pages and you will find an appendix in which writers, booksellers, critics and aficionados champion their favorite women of noir, for your perusing pleasure. There, you will find homages to women authors unjustly forgotten, rhapsodies to glorious and tough noir actresses, proclamations of devotion to beloved characters and enough recommendations to haunt your dreams for years to come.

Minxes, Shapeshifters and Hothouse Flowers

It's Too Late, Baby

by Annette Meyers

"Hey!" Fucking blinding light in her eyes.

She heard him say, "Who's the bird?"

Vernon turned so they were both looking at her. She didn't give a fuck about Vernon. He could look, but he wouldn't get much more, though she let him touch her tits once in a while so he'd keep her on. It was Brad Martin she wanted and he could do more than look. He was a fucking movie star and doing summer stock right here at the Sugar Mill Playhouse. Like the others in *Guys and Dolls*, he came in every night after the show for the burgers and booze. So he wasn't doing a lot of movies any more, he was still famous. People recognized him. If she was with him, they would recognize her.

"You mean Susie Rae?" Vernon rolled his eyes. "Summer help. Local kid. Wants to be a star."

"Nice piece of ass."

"Uh uh uh, jail bait."

"Oh, yeah. Aren't they all? Come on over here, kid, and let me have a look at you." He ground his cigarette out in the Cinzano ashtray. "I hear you want to be an actress."

She couldn't have planned it better. Summer job at the Seaside Bar, where the actors gathered after the show at the Sugar Mill Playhouse. Ten bucks a week plus tips. So what? She didn't mind putting out peanuts, emptying ashtrays, wiping down the bar, sweeping up. She was going to be one of them. She had to make connections. Knew she looked hot in her cut-offs, half her snazzy ass hanging out. She'd chosen the halter top two sizes down so her tits had to go somewhere. Yeah, she was the bird and she was ready.

Early afternoon was the best. The airport was busy. Lots of arrivals and departures. It was the arrivals she wanted, the baggage claim in particular. She hated to flatten her blonde curls with the cap, hide herself under overalls, but people would notice her otherwise. People always noticed how pretty she was. Pretty enough to be a movie star.

Last week she got lucky. Old lady, suitcase full of Salvation Army granny clothes. Susie Rae went through every pocket, and whaddaya know, wads of bills, fifty-three dollars in all, and under the cotton drawers, a change purse with diamond earrings and a flower pin with diamonds and sapphires.

She sussed out the area. Had to be quick 'cause she was parked in the wait zone. Okay okay. Woman in fancy fur, two kids. One kid took off. The fur yelled for one to watch the bags and went chasing after the other. Two suitcases. Nice ones with the LVs. The kid was playing some kind of game on a little computer.

"Your mom said for me to take the bags out to the taxis," Susie Rae said. "She'll meet you there."

He looked at her without really seeing her, perfect. No one paying attention. She picked up the bags and walked off. Out of there, whiz bang.

She drove home carefully 'cause it wasn't her car and her without a license. She always jacked Vince's Pontiac when he had a poker game going in the back room of the bar. Vince had no clue.

"Ma, Bobby took my ball and won't give it back!"

She slapped at the crawly fingers. "Get away, get away, how many times I told you not to wake Mama when she's resting."

"But Mama—"

"Take change from the bureau and get some ice cream." Susie Rae pulled the covers over her head and tried to go back to sleep. Didn't work. She put her feet on the floor, barely missing the stack of romance and movie magazines. Christ. What time was it? Shit, Jerry would be home screaming for his dinner. He always had to have his fucking dinner in the middle of the afternoon so he could be back in the city for rush hour.

That's what she was now, a fucking slave. How did it come to this? She inched her way over to the mirror. Married to Jerry Luskewski, a Polack cab driver, two kids, living in dump in Jersey City. All her plans.

She padded to the bathroom, peed, splashed water on her

face. It was a pretty face, even now. She pulled off her nightgown. Not a bad body either considering two kids. Tits still good, a little too much padding on the ass. But guys liked that, didn't they?

Brad had liked it all right. Yeah. It started okay. Brad Martin got her extra work on a couple of films being shot in the city. She even did a modeling job. Very sexy panties, topless 'cause her tits were outstanding, they said.

Brad took her around to a few parties. Called her Susie Bird. When he went back to L.A., he set her up with one of the guys on the trucks, Marco.

"You don't gotta do anything you don't want to," Marco said. "It's just a party. Lots of people in the business. Fifty bucks. You just walk around in some sexy silk underwear . . . You wanna play, it's up to you."

"Play?"

"You know, have a good time."

"Great. Can I keep the underwear?"

He thought that was a big joke so she laughed, too. He threw down his cigarette. "Why not? Here's the address. Get there at nine and ask for Brenda. There'll be other girls. Brenda'll set you up."

The joke was on her. Sexy underwear all right. The skimpy bra had the nipples cut out and the panties had no crotch. She got hot now, just remembering. Brenda put her in five-inch platform open toes, ankle straps. "You're gorgeous," Brenda said. "You can make a lot of money here."

Susie Rae posed in front of the tall mirror admiring herself.

"Remember, there'll be some famous people and they like to be regular guys. No names. Just go with the flow. What happens at the party stays at the party. Get it?"

She got it. It was her first orgy. The men wore tuxedos and skinny black masks like the Lone Ranger. There was champagne and caviar and sex. She'd been sore for a week afterward, but what a turn on. And she was a star. Brenda said when they called to reserve a place, they always asked if Susie Rae'd be there. She got big tips like five hundred once, perfume, a gold bracelet, which she hocked.

Ma had no clue, just that she made friends with another model and stayed in the city a couple of nights a week. Then only a month after her eighteenth birthday she got knocked up. Christ, she was having a life. What did she want with a kid? Brenda set up the abortion. Afterward, Susie Rae got in a cab, and who should be driving but Jerry. She was all weepy and stupid and blabbed too much.

Brenda never called again. Susie Rae found out about a week later the cops raided them. Close call for her, thanks to the abortion. Jerry started hounding her after that now that he knew where she lived. Boy, he sucked up to Ma, who kept yakking that Susie Rae should marry him, what with his good job and all. Her big mistake, she gave him a pity fuck, and wouldn't you know, she got pregnant again, and he told everyone and all of a sudden she was fucking married.

No way, José. No more lying around being depressed. She put on jeans and a t-shirt, went into the kitchen and got a big green garbage bag. She took her clothes out of the closet and threw them in the bag, cleaned her stuff out of the bathroom. The romance magazines went in her old backpack. She went through Jerry's pockets and the whole apartment picking up cash. Carole King's latest sang through her head. *It's too late, baby.* Oh, yes. Too late for Jerry, not too late for Susie Rae.

A door slammed. "Ma!"

"Get a garbage bag for yourself and one for your brother. Put your crap in them. We're going."

She dropped the kids off with her mother in Red Bank and took a bus to Atlantic City.

All she could see out of the cruddy window was the fire escape over the alley and the brick wall of the movie theater. No sweat. Easy walk to the casino.

She went right to the post office and rented a box. On her way back to her room, she passed a cheesy bar called the Golden Grill. Sign in the window said SINGER WANTED. Well, why the fuck not? She bought some Clairol extra-light blonde, went right back to her room, whiz bam, hello Marilyn. Got herself up in the slinky black dress she lifted at Loehmann's last year. Skip the underwear. Tits in your face. She got the job. So what if it was cocktail waitressing. The singer crap was a come on. The Golden Grill was a small-time mobster hang out, mostly bar, pizza and spaghetti restaurant around back.

"You got class, baby," Carlo Carlino, the greasy gumba who owned the dump told her, giving her ass a squeeze. "Let's see how it works out. Get to know the customers. We got celebrities coming in for a little quiet time when they get tired of the casino."

"Movie stars?"

"And singers. You know, like Frank."

"Wow. I'm good with people like that," she said. "You know Brad Martin? I went everywhere with him."

"Yeah, he used to stop in when he came to see his mother. Before she passed on." He made a half hearted cross sign. "I bet you didn't know he was from around here. Marty Bombano."

"You're kidding. He never said."

"I kid you not. So when can you start?"

"Tonight. How much?"

"Ten plus tips. You can eat here."

"Twenty."

"Fifteen and that's it."

"Okay."

"The last girl left her dress. It's hanging out back in the Ladies.'"

"What wrong with mine?"

"The customers don't like black."

She lay on her bed leafing through the movie magazines and newspapers she picked up at the market. She got so she could close her eyes, put her fingers on the page like a fucking fortune teller and they'd just jump off the page asking her to be part of their lives. Joey Anderson was the first. She went to the library and looked him up. What was there about him she could use? Career going nowhere. Boozing, breaking heads. No more mellow tones. No one would hire him except for short gigs in crummy lounges. She was in Atlantic City now, close to the big time. She bought stationery and began writing.

He was coming to New York to do a benefit for some disease no one ever heard of, staying at the Plaza. Someone throwing him a bone. His wife ran off with his business manager. 'Course she didn't mention this in the letter, just said how great she thought he was. Then told him her husband went off with their kid and the babysitter. She had a job in Atlantic City to pay for detectives looking for him. If Joey was ever in Atlantic City . . . she always had a nightcap in the Resorts bar around three a.m. after she'd finished her job. She had her picture taken by one of those boardwalk photographers and made copies. She slipped one in the envelope and mailed the letter to the Plaza.

She loved being on Joey's arm, meeting his friends. She needed different clothes for Nashville, like jeans and custom boots and spangled shirts. No big deal. Carlo owed her 'cause he got her cheap. Always crying the poor thing. What crap. His bank statement said otherwise. So she lifted a couple of his personal checks from the book in his desk drawer.

They were living in this trailer with Joey's bud, a drummer name of Gary Nowhar. Temporary. Weeks turned into months and she was getting really pissed about it when Joey just up and went off to L.A. to see about a job. "Gary'll look after you," he said. And that was it.

"Listen, Susie Rae, you want to stay, no skin off my ass, but I ain't no charity. I ain't feedin' you. 'Course I could take it out in trade."

For a while some of Joey's friends, the country guys, Jimmy, Chad, and Sonny, took turns taking her out to parties and stuff. "Keepin' her hot for Ole Joey," they said. After a while it petered out and she was left with no bread and Gary Nowhere.

She called Ma to ask about the kids. Maybe she could hit her up for some money. Especially now 'cause she was pregnant again.

"Where the fuck are you?" Ma said, in the bottle as usual.

"Nashville with all the country singers," she said. "They say I have real talent. I'm going to be famous."

"Oh, I'm sure," Ma said. "You calling me for money?"

"No, Ma. How are the kids?"

"Five fucking years and now you're asking about the brats you dumped on me? Jerry took them. He got a girlfriend good with them."

"Maybe you can send some pictures." She gave Ma the

address. "And maybe you could—"

"You ain't getting a fucking penny out of me, Susie Rae."

Susie hung up. Mean bitch. Me, I'm only trying to have a life. Jerry wanted the kids, he could have them. Better Jerry than Ma, for sure.

She made plans while Gary took it out in trade, fucking like a goddamn horse. When he went out, she lay in bed with movie magazines, making a list. The library in Nashville was better than Atlantic City. She rented a P.O. box, then wrote three letters. A soap opera actor, a little older, not a regular, on *General Hospital*. Another actor recovering from a bad motorcycle accident. The TV star Danny Diablo who lost his series a few years back, him having shot up his ex's Corvette.

It was raining when it happened and her without an umbrella, trudging back to the fucking trailer. She was stuck here with these hicks like some kind of sex slave. If one of her letters paid off, she'd be gone in a minute.

A car pulled up to the curb. "You wanna ride, girlie? You look like a wet chicken."

A Cadillac. Pink. Johnny Cash singing on the radio. The driver wore a baseball cap. His dark hair touched the collar of his shirt. A little rough looking, but he was smiling at her. "Come on, you can trust us."

"Us?"

"Yeah, my guy here. Charley. Say hello, Charley." He reached around and opened the back door for her. "Hop in. Where you goin'?"

She climbed in the back. She was soaking wet, hair plastered to the sides of her face.

"I'm Russ. You know Charley here." She heard the thunk of the doors locking.

Charley turned. Grinned at her. He was missing two teeth on the side. She knew him. He used to hang out at the Golden Grill. "Carlo sends his best," Charley said.

They fucked her up pretty bad, left her good as dead. And she lost the baby, which she didn't want anyway. Took her a week just to wake up. When she left the hospital, they loaded her up with

Percocet and Demerol and Tylenol with codeine, which she'd turn over for a quick buck.

The hospital chaplain found her a place to stay till she got better. Old Baptist lady named Minnie Moon in Murfreesboro, had a house out there. Getting a little frail. More like getting soft in the head, turned out. Murfreesboro was deader than road kill, for sure, though she could bus into Nashville when one of the church ladies came to take Minnie for her physical therapy.

Jimmy came around a couple of times. Once he took her out to Sonny's house where she could sit by the pool, but Sonny's dumpy wife didn't like her, and she never got to go back. Susie Rae was walking with two canes, being helpful as all get out to Minnie Moon, like going to the bank to cash her Social Security check. And for her trouble, skimming off a commission. Only right.

Susie Rae took a load of mail from her post office box, none worth shit. Just autographed pictures. One from Danny Diablo had a note: *sorry for your troubles*. She'd written to ABC. This envelope had a return address in Venice, California. She put it in her new backpack, wondering if it was from him or from some secretary. Took it out. It was from him. Had to be. Otherwise, why the return address? Yeah. Worth another letter.

She bought two romance magazines, and got a ride home with a fat geezer from Charleston, in Nashville to visit his grandson at Vanderbilt. Felt real terrible when she told him about her husband and little girl dead in the car crash, she there sobbing into his handkerchief, how the insurance lapsed, her trouble with her poor old senile mama and no money coming in and her not able to work till her legs healed. When they got to Minnie's house, he took a hundred-dollar bill from his wallet and pushed it on her.

The old coot coughed up a hundred dollars for her sad story. Wasn't that something? The romance mags were full of personal ads. Lonely hearts stuff. Next time she was at the post office, she'd have some ads to send off. And she'd take Minnie Moon's Social Security card and rent a new P.O. box in Minnie's name.

"Pretty girl lonesome after breakup looking for love again.

Need cheering up."

"Former model expert with toys wants relationship with nice man. Will travel."

"Young girl lost in small town, eager to learn, looking for good teacher."

Nothing. One dreary week after another, Minnie losing it day by day. The Baptist bitches came around often with food, so Susie Rae kept the mop and vacuum close enough to haul out when she heard a car stop. Look up from her cleaning and smile and thank them. They were so stupid. Poor and stupid. Wasn't going to be her. She was getting outa here.

Hell, some relative would turn up the minute Minnie kicked off and Susie Rae would be out on her ass. She'd better skim off a little more from Minnie's check.

First thing happened was a letter from Danny Diablo, answering hers. She wrote him that she was caring for the old lady who'd helped her recover but was now dying. Old lady's daughter was putting her in a nursing home and Susie Rae was about to lose her home. She didn't know what to do. Did Danny think she could get a job in L.A.? She'd been a model in New York before getting married.

"If you come out this way, give me a call," Danny wrote. "I have a few contacts." And whaddaya know, there was his phone number.

She didn't want to seem overly eager, so she didn't answer right away. She was going crazy. Getting herself off was not her idea of a good time. She bought new jeans, one size up from her old ones with the broken zipper, and cowboy boots and a white fringed shirt. She called Jimmy.

"You're out near the shooting range."

"I guess. I'm just dying to see you, Jimmy."

He came around in his old Ford truck and took her out for a drink.

"You got fat, Susie Rae," he said, jiggling the flesh spilling over her waistband.

"I'm trying to lose it so I can go back to modeling," she said. "I guess you won't like where most of my ha-ha fat went." She unbuttoned her blouse real slow.

He stared, rubbed his crotch. "Sheeet, girl. You are somethin.'" He paid for the drinks.

"Whaddaya think?" she said.

So Jimmy was good for her itch, and she calmed down a bit with regular fucking. And he bought her favorite, Carole King's "It's Too Late, Baby," which she played all the time on Minnie's old machine. But she didn't like doing it in the truck—too hard getting the jeans off and on. And they couldn't do it at Minnie's. They tried once and Jimmy had to hide in the closet when the Baptist bitches dropped in later than usual one night. Like they was keeping their eye on her. Jimmy said his wife, even though she was a cold one, wouldn't be too happy if he brought Susie Rae home.

Then one day Susie Rae opened the P.O. boxes and found both were jammed with letters. When she began pulling them out, a postal worker came and told her she could claim two more cartons if she had ID. She emptied the cartons into a grocery bag they gave her. On the way home she stopped to buy some file cards, more stationary and envelopes.

When she got home she emptied her backpack and spread the letters on her bed. Jesus.

From all over the country. Other countries, too, four from Germany. Two all the way from Russia. Six Mexico. 'Course no way was she going to spend more than she had to for stamps. She opened the top letter, postmark from Dayton, Ohio.

"Dear Sweet Little Minnie, Don't be sad. You break my heart. I'll take good care of you. I like small town girls. I'll show you the best time you ever had. Let me know when you can come (ha) and I will send you money for your ticket. Al Bosworth."

Money for a ticket. Money. She put the letter aside and opened the next one. Anaheim. More like it. Not that far from L.A. She'd already made up her mind she was going to L.A. to break into the movies. Danny Diablo would help.

"Dear Susie Rae, Toys are me. Take a look at this." Picture of him standing in front of his hog naked as a jaybird. A muscle-bound biker with a shaved head and a humongous cock. "Now that you seen my toy, let me have a look at you. Let's play." He'd written his phone number huge on the back and signed it "Boom-

Boom Adler."

She'd call him, for sure. Collect. If he took the call, she might squeeze some money out of him.

"Hello? Minnie? Susie Rae?"

That busy body Gracie Washington back again. She was here only yesterday checking up. Susie Rae gathered up her letters and shoved them under the bed.

"Be right there, Gracie. I'm in the toilet." Flushed the hall toilet as she passed. Christ, wouldn't you know the bitch was halfway up the stairs. "Minnie's resting."

"I want to see for myself, if you don't mind."

Gracie brushed past her. "Minnie, dear. Susie Rae, it smells in here. Minnie's wet herself. I thought you was using the diapers I brought."

So that's what her life had come to. Diapering a senile old bag. Soon as money started coming in, she was done.

Fifty-seven letters in all. Seven from women. What a yak. She was going to toss them, but ha-ha, dykes should get equal opportunity. She made up 3 x 5 notecards, putting the sucker's name on top, then each address and phone number, whether it was to Minnie Moon or Susie Rae and which ad each had responded to.

On another one of those boring times weeks earlier Susie Rae had explored Minnie Moon's attic. Trunks of crap, clothes mostly, corsets looking like from *Gone With the Wind,* or porn movies. Some old jewelry not worth much, and a lot of ugly furniture.

After she read through all the letters, she waited till Minnie went to therapy, then took the bus into Nashville. She walked around looking for the right place: a cheap touristy photography shop. Wasn't hard to find. Right next to a seedy movie house showing a porn flick. ARTISTIC PHOTOS BY JOHNSON, the sign said. Window so grubby you could hardly see the faded wedding pictures propped up in front. What you could see were amateurish girlie pictures. Probably sold porn in the back room. She needed pictures for her new pen pals.

A bell tinkled when Susie Rae opened the door. "Well, hi there," she said, sauntering up to the counter.

"What can I do you for, little lady?" He was a creepy little guy with a pimp mustache, hair slicked down in a comb-over to cover his bald spot.

"I want my picture taken," she said. She began unbuttoning her shirt. "Maybe we can make a trade."

"Oh, yeah? Come into my studio."

She began answering the letters, tucking in her new photo, saying how much she loved his/her letter and how no relationship would work for her without sex. She'd like to meet, but she was going through a bad time now that her dear daddy had died and her stepmama had taken all his money and then kicked her out of the house. She needed a hundred, two-hundred dollars to rent a place. Had a waitress job all lined up but wouldn't be able to start without a place to live. If he/she could help her out with even a twenty, she would pay it back when they met. Fifty letters, wrote till her hand was swollen, and wasn't easy either, what with Minnie moaning in the next room.

She was flush: Cash she'd skimmed off Minnie's Social Security these last three years, which wouldn't be there any more now Minnie'd passed, and the contributions from her pen pals. Collected her mail, closed down the P.O. boxes, and caught a bus to Memphis. Checked into the Hilton with a Visa card she'd lifted from Gracie Washington. Stayed just long enough to pick up a nice wardrobe and get herself back in shape.

Two weeks later, Gracie Washington bought a plane ticket to L.A.

Danny Diablo was older than she thought, but she was remembering him from the TV variety show from twenty years back. Maybe close to fifty and wrinkled. Even had grown-up kids. Had the same Marine haircut, but it was white now. Still, everybody knew him and she liked that. Liked going out with a celebrity.

She moved in with him until she found herself a cheap furnished room in Hollywood—she liked the sound of that— where she could keep her business. And she got right back into the swing. Rented P.O. boxes, one for her, one for Minnie, and

one for Gracie. Made her laugh just thinking about it. Gracie
sure was kinky. Just loved phone sex. Knew all the right things
to say. Maybe she would send some of the mail Gracie got back
to Gracie herself in Murfreesboro or better, give one of the guys
Gracie's phone number. She would have a nice old heart attack.

"Was you had her picture in the paper with Danny Diablo?"
Susie Rae squinted at the man on the stool next to her. She'd
seen him around always giving her the eye like he was undressing
her. Well, why not. He had a crude edge, kinda like Jimmy, but
better looking. "So what?"
"Give the lady a refill," he told the bartender. "I been watchin'
you."
"Don't I know it."
"You ought to be careful, pretty young thing like you." He
patted her thigh.
She let his hand stay where it was, making a hot spot on her
thigh. "Whaddaya mean?"
"Danny's cool. He's usin' you, is all."
"For what?"
"Shtuppin.'"
"You ever think maybe I'm using him, too."
"You could get better sex from yours truly, believe me." He
took his hand from her thigh and held it out to her. "Name's Zak
Walker."
She took his hand, leaning in to him. He had a smell, beer
and cigs. "Susie Rae Anderson."
"Real pleasure, Susie Rae. How about a demonstration?"
"I'm pregnant." She smiled. "I could use a friend."
Zak whistled. "Danny's?"
"Well, shit, whose else?"
"Don't kid a kidder. Said I been watchin.' You been screwin'
around with the Sterling kid. And by the way, Roger Sterling
didn't leave his kid a pot to piss in."
"He'll marry me."
"Who, Danny or the Sterling kid?"
"Danny."
Zak howled. "Good luck tryin' to get anythin' out of Danny.
He's a tightwad. Has his first dime. I know."

* * *

She took a cab to the house but he'd changed the locks and wouldn't let her in. Her two suitcases were on the porch.

Who the fuck did he think he was? She banged on the door, raising all hell, screaming, "Danny, baby." He opened the door, pulled her inside, and gave her a smack on the side of the head, knocking her down. She was crying and screaming, sniveling snot.

"I know what you are, you crazy bitch. I had you followed. You want Danny Diablo's baby. This one's not mine."

"It's ours," she said. "It was an accident."

"Get rid of it," Danny said. "You're a liar. You promised me this wouldn't happen. You did it on purpose."

"I want it."

"I don't."

"I'll get my ma out here and she'll watch it. You don't have to have anything to do with it."

"I'll call you a cab." He opened the door and pushed her out.

She sat on a suitcase, sniffling. Her cell phone rang. "Yeah? Hey."

"Minnie, you said you're in town. I can't wait."

"Who's this?"

"Charley . . . you know, Cucumber Charley. Don't tell me you forgot."

"Charley baby, I'm in L.A. seeing to some family business and my poor dead Gary's pension check went astray. I miss you so much."

She named the baby Danielle Diablo and had the hospital send the bill to Danny. He refused to pay it and demanded a paternity test. Joke on him, the kid was his. She demanded child support and got a lawyer. Him kicking and yelling like a stuffed pig. Yeah, until he got a look at little Danny. Then he melted. They went to Vegas and quick as that, she was Mrs. Danny Diablo. She moved into the house, which was as good as hers now.

Now he butted his nose into everything. Criticizing. Saying she was not a good mother. And that Ma, who came out to L.A. to live with them, was a crazy falling-down drunk. Well, even if she drank a little too much, she never fell down and she never dropped little Danny either.

Not a day passed without screaming and yelling. Sometimes it got so bad, Susie Rae hid out in her little furnished room in Hollywood.

"He even has his pig daughter June come around when he's out so she can check up on how I care for his precious kid. Like he forgot he wanted me to get an abortion."

"You're still Mrs. Danny Diablo. Isn't that what you wanted?" Zak said, getting them refills. He was easy and she'd taken to meeting him for a drink and a buddy fuck more and more lately.

"Yeah, but a lot of good it does me. He plays poker with his guys, comes home drunk, throws party invitations in the garbage. I have to fish them out and go by myself. And shit, yesterday he starts talking about a divorce. Fat chance."

"Hold him up." Zak signaled for another round.

"Fucking A I will. He wants little Danny, like I'll just turn her over to him. I love little Danny."

"Sure you do."

"He's going to have to pay through the nose to get her."

Zak smiled. "You go, baby."

"He's taking me out for our anniversary tonight, to Monillo's."

"Red sauce place for gumbas."

"He loves the place 'cause they treat him like he's still a celebrity."

She had the veal piccata and he ordered his usual, ziti a la Siciliana and a bottle of cabernet. He was being nice. Never even brought up the divorce or little Danny. He had the pianist play her favorite, "It's Too Late, Baby."

He wasn't drinking. She was on her third glass when he got up to go to the john and stayed a long time.

"What's with you?" she said, when he came back, face white as his hair.

"Let's go home." He put a credit card on the table, which was really crazy 'cause he had this thing about paying cash for everything.

He was so shaky he held onto her on the street. "I don't know why you parked so far from the restaurant," she said. "What the hell is valet parking for?"

It was a cool night but he was dripping sweat. He unlocked the passenger side and she got in. "Forgot something," he mumbled, closing her door and heading back down the street toward the restaurant.

"What're you talking about?" She stuck her head out the window and hollered after him, but he didn't turn around. He was acting weird. She settled back in the seat. It was so fucking dark on this part of the street. He'd parked right behind a dumpster.

Where the hell was he? Stuck her head out the window. "Hey—"

Fucking blinding light in her eyes.

High Yellow

by Libby Fischer Hellmann

Patricia Thomas' mama said everyone needed a fixer in their life, and from the moment she met Desmond McCauley, Patricia knew he would be hers.

She stepped down from the streetcar at Connecticut and Calvert into a wall of September heat so heavy and humid you could carve big chunks out of it and swallow them whole. Despite its pretensions, Washington, D.C. in 1957 was a sleepy Southern town where summer didn't end until October. Even Congress had the sense not to come back until then.

She tried to keep an unhurried pace as she walked the three blocks to Oyster School. She didn't want to sweat on the first day of school. She'd dressed carefully in a crisp, black and white sleeveless outfit she snagged in Hecht's bargain basement. She'd ironed starch into it, but in this heat it wouldn't last. She was wearing black pumps, and carried a little black bag. Her thick, dark glossy hair, good hair, was held back with a wide red band.

As she rounded the corner, she nodded coolly at the Negro man who stepped to the side and doffed his hat. Afterwards she savored the little thrill that ran through her. Likewise when she stopped into Peoples' Drugs for a comb, and the woman at the cash register with chocolate skin made sure their hands didn't touch when she dropped Patricia's change in her palm. With her dark hair and eyes, pale skin, and delicate features, Patricia was passing. She looked like an exotic beauty—maybe Oriental, maybe Italian—but definitely not colored. High yellow, they called it.

Patricia remembered asking Mama if the father she never knew had been white. She recalled how her mother's lips tightened as she shook her head. "He was just a light-skinned no-good nigger who ran out on us first chance he got." Mama, a Southerner with skin like brown ochre, had spent years scrubbing floors, ironing shirts, and cooking meals for the Friedmans, a white family who lived near the school. They kept telling Patricia that she and Mama were part of the family, but that was just white folks' talk, Mama said. An excuse to have Mama babysit their kids when they went to Mexico every winter to get away from it all.

Mama would laugh at all Mister Friedman's jokes, put up with the Missus's mood swings, and never said anything about the empty booze bottles under her bed. Every year they would take the streetcar down to 9th and G to buy the Friedmans a box of Velati's caramels for Christmas. Good thing, too. Turned out Mrs. Friedman was her first fixer. It was through her that Patricia got her job teaching first grade.

Which was how Patricia came to believe in fixers. "Look at me, sweetie-pie," her mother had warned. "Don't end up like me. You got the right cards in your deck. Play 'em. Whatever it takes, you make life better fo' yourself." Once Mrs. Friedman intervened on her behalf two years ago, after Patricia secretly bought her a few bottles of gin, she understood. She definitely wanted a better life, and she'd do anything to make it happen. Oyster School was just the beginning.

Now, as she mounted the steps to the school, she let out a hot breath. The first week would be the usual confusion of learning the children's names, assigning desks, and figuring out what they knew. Oyster School was in a white neighborhood inhabited by government officials, ambassadors and long-time Washington residents. There was talk of expanding the school's boundaries to include the coloreds and poor whites who lived across the bridge, but the school board kept putting it off.

Still, Patricia loved her students. She patiently taught them how to sound out letters, and she would clap her hands when they figured out the words to "See Spot Run." She giggled when they correctly added six bananas to four apples, and told them they would have a fine fruit salad. Her students liked her, too. She wasn't elderly and frumpy like Miss Murray, who wore gloves every day because she was allergic to chalk. Or Miss Finkel, whose manner was so stern it sent chills through everyone, even the principal. She was Miss Thomas. Fresh, young and lively. She was their fixer.

But when Desmond McCauley walked in, his shy little son clutching his hand, Patricia felt a jolt. Maybe it was his wide appealing face, his blond hair slicked back with Bryl Creem. Or maybe it was the way he politely greeted her and had his son, Franklin, do the same. Or maybe it was his wintry blue eyes, so utterly lacking in deception.

Whatever it was, she wondered if he felt the same spark when they shook hands. She thought his eyes widened just a little, and his expression took on a more observant cast, as if he was seeing her—really seeing her. She looked into those eyes and let her hand rest in his just an instant too long. Then she squatted down to assure Franklin they would be great friends and that school would be loads of fun.

Once she was able to coax a shy smile out of the boy, she stood up slowly, and stretched to show Desmond her long legs and slim waist. Desmond smiled, a flush swimming up from his neck to his face. "I can't thank you enough. We just moved here, and Franklin doesn't have many friends."

"Where did you move from?"

"Cleveland, Ohio."

"Nice place, Cleveland." Patricia said, as if she'd just been there last year. "Now, don't you worry, Mr. McCauley. I'll take good care of Franklin."

Desmond swallowed. "Thank you, Miss Thomas."

* * *

A month later, the hot scrim of summer still hung in the air. But Patricia knew anticipation was mounting, just like she knew the season would eventually burn itself out.

The day it finally happened had been routine. The children had spent the last hour working on colors and writing down "blue," "red," and "yellow" next to dabs of paint. Afterwards Patricia prepared to dismiss them for the day.

Usually Mrs. McCauley came to pick up Franklin. Like her husband, she was blond. No wonder Franklin was flaxen-haired. Today, though, both parents came to the school, Mrs. McCauley two steps ahead of her husband, as if she was embarrassed to be seen with him. Patricia watched as she corralled Franklin, who was playing with Henry Deutsch near the jungle gym. Franklin was settling in well. He was quiet, but well organized and methodical for a six year old. Mrs. McCauley retrieved Franklin's plaid book bag and hurried him across the playground.

"We'll see you after your meeting, then." Mrs. McCauley said to her husband, inclining her cheek for a kiss.

Desmond pecked her cheek, gave his son a hug, but made no effort to leave. "Aren't you coming?" his wife asked.

"I'll just grab a cab, dear. I want to talk to Miss Thomas. About Franklin," he added.

His wife nodded and disappeared. Desmond hovered at the edge of the playground while other parents collected their children. As if by tacit agreement, they didn't speak until all the students were gone.

She turned around. "You're still here." She pronounced it as if she'd just become aware of it that minute.

He nodded and looked at the ground.

She crossed her arms. "So. You wanted to talk about— Franklin?"

Desmond studied his hands, flipped them over, then back again. She thought of washing the children's hands before lunch. Drying them on those rough brown paper towels.

"Actually," he faltered. "I— I was hoping—well—would you like to have a drink?"

Patricia stared at him. "A drink?"

His forehead, cheeks, even his ears turned crimson. Must be all that pale skin. "Well, perhaps a cup of tea?"

Patricia tilted her head. He was watching her. She smiled. "A cocktail would be just fine."

As they crossed Calvert Street to the Shoreham Hotel, a fragrance she couldn't quite identify hung in the air. Good scents lingered in this part of town. The late afternoon sun gilded everything in hues of gold. There was no litter on the streets. Even the traffic was muted.

* * *

They spent an hour in the hotel bar, drinking cocktails and listening to Eddie Fisher crooning through discreetly placed speakers. The Shoreham was one of the most elegant hotels in Washington with an outdoor swimming pool, an enormous high-ceilinged lobby, and the Blue Room, a night club that attracted the best entertainers in show business.

Desmond seemed just as shy as his son, and Patricia carried the conversation. During the first round of drinks, she amused him with stories about her students. During the second round she pumped him gently about his marriage. Lorraine was sturdy Midwest stock from Omaha, he said. They met at Ohio State and fell in love, but their marriage was more an accommodation these days, he admitted. Best friends who lived together. "You know what I mean?"

She lost interest in him sexually, Patricia thought. Aloud, she replied, "More than you know."

By the third round, Patricia told him she was looking for a new job.

"I thought you loved teaching." Des wiped his forehead with a white handkerchief.

"Oh, I do. But I want to do something bet—I think I'm capable of more."

"Like what?" Desmond asked, picking up his cue.

"A government job. Working with international issues. Better pay, lots of travel, more responsibility." She eyed him. "I want to make a difference. Do something for my country. You know what I mean?"

"Yes." A tiny smile played around his lips. "I see."

Patricia leaned forward. She noticed a sheen of sweat above his lip. "What do you see?"

Desmond swallowed. Patricia lifted her index finger to his lip and gently stroked the sweat away. Then she ran her finger over her own lips, opened her mouth, and inserted her finger.

He stammered and cleared his throat. "I—I might be able to help, you know."

"Is that so?" Patricia smiled lazily, although she already knew he could. She'd checked Franklin's file in the office one day during lunch. She knew exactly where Des worked and what he did. Even who his boss was.

"What do you do?" She took her finger out of her mouth and wrapped her hand around her drink.

Desmond's eyes followed the track of her finger. "I'm an—an assistant secretary in the Commerce Department's International

Trade Administration," he said. "I help protect U.S. businesses from unfair pricing by foreign companies and governments."

"Well now." Patricia feigned surprise. "That sounds right up my alley." She smiled coyly. "If the right opportunity ever pops up, I hope you'll think of me." She met his eyes with an appraising look.

"Yes. I might be able to do that."

She twirled the little umbrella that had come with her drink, then put it down and inched her hand across the table. Her long, slender fingers were topped by pink nail polish she'd applied last night. It didn't take long for Des to cover her hand with his own. She let him massage the back of her knuckles.

Ten minutes later, he took a room under the name of Richard Dudley. Patricia came up in a separate elevator. She had hardly walked through the door before he tore her clothes off and threw her down on the bed. She let him do what he wanted. He was like a man who'd been starved, and it was over quickly. Then she taught him a thing or two.

* * *

Moths played around the hotel lamp as she rolled on her stockings two hours later. Des was lying on the bed, smoking a cigarette, looking spent but quite pleased with himself. His blond hair was tousled, but his pale skin glowed like girls in love were supposed to. She gazed at his chest, which was curiously hairless, and his torso, slim except for an ever-so-slight paunch. His was the body of a successful man, a man on the way up. She snapped her stockings to her garter belt, then twisted around to stroke him. He moaned, stubbed out the cigarette, and pulled her to him. She unsnapped her stockings again and sank back on the bed.

The hum of traffic down in Rock Creek Park drifted through the open window an hour later, bringing with it a welcome breeze. Des lit another cigarette, and set the ashtray down on his chest. She watched it rise and fall with his breath.

"I've never had a woman like you," he said softly.

She smiled, watching blue smoke curl up over their heads and disappear.

"You're magic. We're magic." He moved the ashtray and nuzzled her leg with his lips. "You've revived something in me I thought was gone forever. I thought—I thought—well, it would never happen again."

Patricia felt a ripple as his mouth slid down her shin. "Honey, I could see that from the first time we met."

"What about you?" He asked hesitantly. Was I—was it good for you?"

"You were the best, sugar. A giant of a man. Never had anyone better."

* * *

The Negro elevator operator eyed her but kept a respectful silence as Patricia descended to the lobby. She was used to people staring at her, but there was something telling, almost bold in his look. Was her dress unbuttoned? Did he know she'd been having sex all evening? Or was it something else, the thing that some colored people picked up without being told? Was he a spotter? No, spotters were generally fair-skinned Negroes. Still, she felt like slapping his face for having the audacity to challenge her.

The breeze had disappeared by the time she caught the bus, and her legs stuck to the seat as she rode across the Calvert Street bridge. "Across the bridge" was a euphemism for the other side of the tracks. Most high yellows lived in Portal Estates off 16th Street, but Patricia lived across the bridge. During high school she'd gone on a few dates with a boy from Portal Estates— Clarence, his name was— but after his mother met Patricia's brown-skinned mother and discovered where they lived, Clarence stopped calling. Patricia didn't care. Across the bridge was just temporary.

By the time she got off the bus, it was almost midnight. She walked the two blocks to her house on Lanier Place. As she unlocked the door, she heard her husband's voice.

"Where you been, baby?"

She went into the front room. She'd met James at Howard University. Mama had just died, and she was lonely. Patricia didn't have a lot of friends: the whites kept her at a distance, the colored girls hated her because she looked white. James had light skin that passed the brown bag test, but with his wooly black hair and Negroid features, he would never be high yellow. Still, he wanted to take care of her forever and, at the time, Patricia didn't have the strength to resist. He was a good man: honest and hardworking. But he was boring, and even his job as manager at Hahn's Shoes wouldn't get them where Patricia wanted to go.

"I've been job hunting, Jimmy."

"From three in the afternoon till midnight?"

"I left your dinner in the oven."

"I don't want dinner. I want you."

"And I want us to have a better life." She spared a brief glance around the front room, with its shabby furniture and faded curtains. "So we can move out of here. Find a nicer place." She looked at him. "Don't you want that too, sweetie-pie?"

"I want us to have a baby, Patsy. Isn't that the best job in the world?" He grinned. "Come upstairs, baby doll. We need to practice."

She shot him a look.

He changed the subject. "So where you lookin' for that new job?"

* * *

The weather eventually cooled, the leaves fell, and the gray of November descended. Patricia didn't notice. Her afternoons and evenings were full of Des. They met twice a week at the Shoreham, once in a while at the Sheraton Park. Between the passion and sex, Patricia mentioned the new job as often as she could. Des said he was working on it.

Over time Des emerged from his shell. His smile grew broader, his step more assured. Between the sheets, too, he developed into a sensual, giving lover. It made him happy when Patricia climaxed, so she made sure she did. In fact, he was turning out to be the best lover she'd ever had, and Patricia was half in love with him. She couldn't figure out why his wife didn't want him, but she was thankful she didn't.

One afternoon just before Thanksgiving, Patricia rushed from school to the Shoreham. A conference with an anxious parent had made her late. She was just crossing Calvert Street, watching the wind whip leaves into tiny eddies above the ground, when she sensed someone following her. She stopped and turned around. No one was there. She shook it off and hurried to the hotel.

After their lovemaking, Des lit a Winston and cradled the ash tray on his chest. "I have something to tell you, Patricia."

"What's that, sweetie?" She snuggled in close and ran her fingers across his milky skin. That was another thing she liked about him. There was almost a delicacy to his body.

"We're going to Havana the week after Thanksgiving," he said. "For a conference."

"Havana, Cuba?"

He nodded. A vision of casinos, men in tuxedos, and women in long gowns flashed through her mind. Her fixer had come through. She snuggled in. "Oh, baby. This is wonderful. When do we leave? I have so much to do."

He pulled away and stubbed out his cigarette. "Patricia, I think you misunderstood. Lorraine is coming with me to Havana," he said softly.

"Lorraine?" He wasn't making sense.

"She—she wants us to spend time more together. She's noticed we've grown apart. She wants—she's talking about a second honeymoon after the conference."

Patricia froze. If she stayed absolutely still, the words he'd uttered wouldn't count, and they could start fresh. From the beginning. She didn't move a muscle, but nothing happened. Then Des looked at her with such a sad, wistful expression her stomach flipped over.

"What—what about Franklin?" she managed to ask.

"Lorraine's mother is coming from Nebraska to take care of him."

Patricia swallowed. "But Des, this isn't—"

A loud banging at the door cut her off.

They both sat up, startled. "What's that?" Des frowned.

"I don't know."

The banging persisted. Between the knocks were muffled thumps, as if someone was throwing themselves against the door. Patricia and Des exchanged anxious looks. Hotels had notoriously flimsy locks. Then a raw voice shouted. "You in there, baby? If you are, open this door."

Patricia felt her jaw drop.

Des didn't notice. "What the hell?" He reached for the phone. "I'll take care of this."

But Patricia stayed his hand. Wrapping the blanket around her, she jumped out of bed and stared at the door, as if she could see through to the other side. "No, don't, Des. Let me take care of it."

"Are you crazy, Patricia?" Des picked up the phone but didn't have the chance to call, because Patricia ran to the door and opened it wide. James stumbled into the room. He nearly lost his balance, but righted himself and looked around. Patricia wrapped the blanket more tightly around her. Her heart was pounding so fast and hard she could hear it in her ears.

James started toward her, rage spinning off his face. "What the hell . . . ?"

Patricia backed away, terrified.

Des jumped out of bed. "You. Stop right there!" He shouted. "Before I call the policc!"

James ignored Des and kept going toward Patricia.

"Did you hear me?" Des yelled.

James's response was to pull out a knife.

"No!" Patricia gasped. "Put that away!"

But James waved the knife. The blade gleamed in the lamplight. Patricia recognized it—it was the kitchen knife she used to de-bone chicken and fish. As he closed in, she backed up until she hit the edge of the bed and fell across it. James kept advancing, brandishing the knife above their heads.

Suddenly Des appeared in her field of vision. He jumped James from behind, caught his arm, and twisted it. James lost his balance and fell on Patricia. As he did, the knife slipped out of his hand and skittered across the carpet. Des bent down and scooped it up faster than Patricia would have thought possible. Lunging forward, Des plunged the knife in James' back.

James raised his head and looked at Patricia in surprise. Patricia was surprised, too. She wouldn't have thought Des had a chance in a match-up against James. Her husband had to be four inches taller and thirty pounds heavier. But there Des was, stabbing James again and again, like a madman, his face a frenzy of fury. James looked like he wanted to say something but couldn't quite form the words. Then his eyes rolled up, and he fell forward.

Finally, it was quiet. Patricia disentangled herself from her husband. Blood gushed through his jacket and pants, staining the bed sheets, the spread, the carpet.

Des stared at James, at Patricia, at the knife. "He was going to kill you," he whispered.

Patricia kept her mouth shut.

Des hesitated. Uncertainty flashed in his eyes. "You saw, right? He was going to kill you. Maybe me, too."

For one brief moment, Patricia didn't know what to do. She saw her life careening out of control, away from her government job, her job as a teacher, even her life with Des. She was terrified. Then something occurred to her. She could fix this. All it would take was a little work. She fought back her fear.

"Yes. I saw, Des." She nodded her head. "I saw the whole thing."

"Well, then . . ." Des let his voice trail off. A violent shudder ran through him. He went to the phone and lifted the receiver.

Patricia ran over and snatched the phone away. "What are you doing?"

"I'm calling hotel security."

"No. You can't."

He reached for the receiver. "Of course I can. He was going to kill us. This was self defense."

"No. It's—he—" Des tried to grab the receiver, but Patricia kept it away from him. "Wait. Think about what you're doing, Des."

"What's to think about? The man is dead. We need to report it. He was—" Des stopped. "You opened the door. Why did you do that? What the hell was going through your mind?"

"I—I don't really know. I just wanted to stop the banging. I thought—"

Des's face grew pinched with anger. "If you hadn't opened the door, this might never have happened." He squeezed his eyes shut. Another tremor shot through him. He seemed to be struggling for control. He opened his eyes. "It doesn't matter. Give me the phone."

"No, Des. Think what will happen when it comes out you

were here in the hotel room. With me."

"That doesn't matter." He sounded stoic. "You don't play around with death."

"Are you prepared to lose your job?"

"My job?"

"If this gets out, it'll be all over the papers. There'll be lots of publicity. The Commerce Department won't be happy that one of its assistant secretaries is making news. They'll get rid of you, just like that." She snapped her fingers. "And what's Lorraine going to do when she finds out?" Des started to speak, but she cut him off. "She'll throw you out, Des. She probably won't ever let you see Franklin."

Des paled.

"I know what it's like to grow up without a father. Don't do this to your son."

"No, Patricia. You're wrong. It's not like—"

"Listen to me, Des." She held the receiver close to her heart. "We can fix this."

"No. We have to take responsibility."

She ignored him. "You registered under a fake name, right? Paid cash as usual?"

"You know I did."

"And I came up the back stairs." She nodded more to herself than to him. "This will work." She put the phone down, went over to James's body, and started rolling his pockets.

"What are you doing?"

"There's no one who can prove we were here."

"The desk clerk knows what I look like."

"Honey, you look like every other white man who ever checked into a hotel under an assumed name."

Des stared at her. But he didn't pick up the phone.

Patricia reached into James's pants pocket and pulled out his wallet. "It's okay, baby. I'm gonna fix everything." She extracted James's driver's license and glanced at it briefly.

"Who is he?" Des's voice cracked.

She looked at Des, then back at the license. "Why do you care?"

"I want to know his name."

"It's better if you don't. He's just a colored man."

Des frowned.

"Tell me something. How hard do you think the cops are gonna work to find the killer of an unidentified colored man?"

"I—I don't know."

"Well, I do." Patricia slid James's driver's license back into his wallet and dropped it into her purse. "Not hard at all."

Des swallowed.

"Des, you can never speak of this again. Never. Understand?"

He hesitated, then gave her a brief nod.

"That's good, honey. Now let's wash up and get out of here."

Patricia went into the bathroom and ran the hot water so long that it steamed over the mirror above the sink. She wiped a small circle in the middle and peered at her reflection. "Another thing, honey. I think you'd best postpone that trip to Havana."

* * *

Patricia checked the *Post* and the *Star* every day, but there was nothing about an unidentified colored man found dead at the Shoreham. When a week had passed, she put out the word that James had left her. She didn't know why, and she didn't know where he'd gone, she told her neighbors. She was disconsolate, of course, so miserable that she'd decided to move. There were too many painful memories here. She was going to give up teaching, too. Someone had kindly offered her a new job at the Commerce Department. In the International Trade Administration. Patricia packed her things and said sorrowful goodbyes. She moved to an apartment in Cathedral Mansions off Connecticut Avenue on the "right" side of the bridge.

The first few months, Des was more dependent on her than ever. There was a primitive, almost violent quality to his lovemaking, as if killing James had somehow filled Des with her husband's life blood. He had never been more virile or passionate. Through it all, though, he was true to his word. He never spoke of James. In fact, he never spoke much at all.

To make up for his silence, Patricia talked about the future they'd share, once he left Lorraine. She was careful never to overlook Franklin and always made him part of the tableau:

"And then you and I and Franklin will drive to Luray Caverns. We'll have to make sure Franklin brings a sweater. It gets cold down there."

It wasn't until winter dissolved into spring that things changed again. Des lost his ardor. Oh, he would come to the apartment and make love to her, but his passion had faded. What had once been spectacular sex became mechanical. By the time the dogwoods were at their peak, Des told her it was over.

"I can't do this any more, Patricia."

"Do what, sweetie-pie?"

"Every time I'm with you, I see that dead colored man. I need to make a clean breast of it. I'm going to tell Lorraine and go to the police. I'm prepared to take responsibility. I was the one who killed him. But I'll keep you out of it. I promise."

Patricia laughed harshly. "I don't think so."

"I figured you'd say that, but I've made up my mind."

"Have you told anyone yet?"

"No."

"That's good."

He inclined his head. "Why are you so opposed to doing the right thing?"

Patricia sat down daintily in the new Louis XVI chair she'd bought at the fifth floor furniture department at Hecht's. It was a far cry from the bargain basement. She took a breath.

"Because that wasn't just any dead man, sugar. That was my husband, James."

Des froze. "What?"

She repeated what she said.

Confusion spread across his face. "But he was a—a Negro."

"That's exactly right. He was. And so am I. You ever heard of the phrase 'high yellow'?"

Des's mouth fell open. He stared at her for a long time. She saw him take in her dark hair. Dark eyes. Her pale skin. Saw comprehension dawn in his eyes. His face grew hard. "My god. I've been screwing a nigger."

"Yup. And you killed one too, honey. Two facts you'd best keep to yourself, don't you think?"

Des's eyes went dead, losing any flicker of emotion. His coldness was so unnerving Patricia went into her bathroom and quietly closed the door. The silence lasted so long that she flinched when the door to the apartment finally slammed.

* * *

Patricia dressed the next morning in a new red dress from Woodie's. Strolling to the bus stop, she was aware of eyes watching her from behind the shades of nearby homes. She lifted her chin. She was a good-looking woman. No sense hiding it. As she rode the L-4 downtown, she started to map out her plan. Des's boss seemed like a nice man. She took out her compact with the tiny mirror and checked her make-up. It would do. After all, her mama always told her she needed a fixer in her life.

The Kiss of Death

by Rebecca Pawel

When Paco announced a birthday dance for the fat jerk with the sweaty hands I almost fell off my chair. In the world of New York *milongas*, birthday dances are a rare mark of honor and affection. (If you're a newbie, a *milonga* is a gathering where people dance tango. It's also a type of dance.) I've never had a birthday dance, and when my birthday rolls around I'm always torn between envy of those who merit dances, and fear that I'd make a total idiot of myself. See, the way a birthday dance works is the host of the *milonga* takes the microphone and clears the dance floor. Then he (or she) announces whose birthday it is, and invites everyone to dance with the honoree. In effect, the birthday dancer gives a three-minute improvised performance in front of everyone, with a series of random partners.

Obviously, only the best and boldest dancers have the courage to go out and dance under those circumstances. Usually, they're dance teachers, or old *milongueros* from Buenos Aires who've danced the tango for decades and move as easily as they breathe. That was why it was a surprise when (after welcoming everyone to the *milonga*, and making a couple of announcements of upcoming events) Paco announced a birthday dance for the fat jerk with the sweaty hands.

He didn't call him that, of course. What he said was, "And now we would like to celebrate our friend Brandon's fiftieth birthday." I didn't know who "Brandon" was at first, although I'd known him by sight for years. I'd just always thought of him as the fat jerk from tango. New York has a thriving tango scene. You can go out dancing seven nights a week if you want to (and if you have no other life). But the community of dancers is fairly small, and all the regulars pretty much know each other by sight. Exchanging names is only something you do with people you like, and no one liked the fat jerk, so he was pretty much always identified as "the guy with sweaty hands," at least by the women, who were the ones who knew what his hands felt like. He always held his partners' right hands so tightly they were sore after a couple of dances, but he almost had to do that, because his hands were so sweaty that a woman's hand would have slid out of his grip otherwise. (I knew one woman who said she wouldn't dance with him when she wore a light-colored dress because his right hand would leave sweaty palm marks on her back.)

Let me make this clear: although it isn't pleasant to dance with someone who has sweaty hands, the tango community is pretty tolerant. We've all danced with nice people who are never going to be great tango dancers because they have hunched backs, or pinched nerves in their arms, or simply aren't that coordinated. I even danced a couple of dances with an older gentleman who had some sort of tremor (it could have been Parkinson's, but I didn't ask). No one liked dancing with Brandon (a.k.a. "sweaty hands") because he was a jerk. He ignored the subtle rules about tango dancing: you don't invite a woman to dance if she is deliberately avoiding eye contact with you; you don't ask someone much more advanced than you are to dance (or if you do, you apologize and explain that you are a beginner hoping to learn); when your partner says "thank you," you accept that as a dismissal. He also ignored the unsubtle rules of tango, the most obvious one being: you don't use the dance as an excuse to grope your partner, nor do you hug her and give her a sloppy kiss after the music has ended and she has said "thank you." (Three dances is the minimum number for courtesy before switching partners. Saying "thank you" after two dances is abrupt, and saying it after one dance is the equivalent of saying "drop dead." Brandon Sweaty Hands had been known to squeeze his partners against him after a definite two-dance "thank you" with the words "You're welcome, sweetheart.") He coupled these charms with a blithe disregard for time and tempo, and a fondness for leading his partners into dramatic dips and lunges (the better to squeeze them) that tended to make him careen into other couples. This made him a danger to others on crowded dance floors, so the men weren't crazy about him either.

Most of the experienced dancers on the New York tango scene knew Brandon and avoided him. He was one of the very few people I invariably refused to dance with, although he'd finally gotten the message after I'd turned him down three or four

times, and stopped asking me. He generally preyed on beginning
dancers (the younger and prettier the better), who were still naive
enough to buy his shtick about tango being "the dance of love"
or "all about passion." (The passion was his excuse for holding
his partner very tightly even—or especially—when he had an
obvious erection. And for planting sloppy kisses on her cheek at
the end of the dance.) He also occasionally managed to dance
with some of the women from Argentina, who were generally
very good dancers and very beautiful, but who presumably didn't
realize he was a jerk since they were foreigners.

And *this* was the guy who elbowed his way out onto the
center of the dance floor, grinning like one of the larger and
stupider breeds of dog when Paco said, "Will Brandon please
take the floor? We would like to invite all the ladies to dance with
Brandon. *Música, maestra.*"

I thought at first that it was a mistake, or that Brandon was
mugging in the spotlight, which God knows he was conceited
enough to do. Even when the lights went up, and I heard the
first notes of "*En el Café Domínguez,*" I thought that the *other*
Brandon would show up at any moment, maybe making his
way from the little knot of professional dancers clustered around
the DJ's table, leading one of better *tangueras* to the floor. But
Brandon Sweaty Hands just stood there grinning, until Natalia
glided up to him. He grabbed her like a drowning man grabbing
a lifesaver, and started to—well, dance might not be the right
word. Move around the floor, holding her very tightly.

Natalia is over six feet in heels, and looks like a slightly sexier
version of Penelope Cruz. She teaches the beginner tango class,
and one of her students once memorably said to me that she
"moves like a panther." Even Brandon couldn't make her look
ungraceful, although she didn't look exactly comfortable with
his nose wedged in her cleavage. (The height difference between
them was unfortunate.) I thought maybe he was taking private
classes with her, and that she had arranged this dance for him
as a treat.

But then, as Brandon dragged Natalia along the floor, Giselle
stepped out to take her place. Brandon didn't particularly want
to let go of Natalia, but he couldn't complain about Giselle as an
exchange. She is as fair as Natalia is dark, and all petite curves

and dainty movements like a little bird. She is also one of the best dancers in New York. Brandon gave Natalia a final squeeze. She leaned down and kissed him warmly on the cheek, and then he twirled her out of his arms and grabbed Giselle, who snuggled into his arms, until his grip tightened so that she hardly had room to breathe much less snuggle.

After about eight bars, Yasuko replaced Giselle. And then Nzinga flowed up and nudged aside Yasuko, and then Rachel slid an arm around Brandon's shoulders, and freed him from Nzinga, and finally Beatriz took over from Rachel. One after the other they stepped out to dance with Brandon Sweaty Hands, moving like swans, like gazelles or like tigers; like the similes for beauty in all the world's cultures. They were some of the best tango dancers in New York, and they were also all very beautiful women. And Brandon embraced all of them as hard as he could, and released each one reluctantly. And each of them kissed him as affectionately as if he were a lover, or a best friend, or a really good tango dancer. Beatriz even kissed him on the lips at the end of the song. Brandon made damn sure the kiss was lingering, whatever her intention might have been.

Everyone applauded, since that's the convention at the end of a birthday dance, or any performance, but the applause was a little bewildered. I don't think I was the only one who couldn't figure out what the hell was going on.

I left the *milonga* not too long after that. I'd been on call at the hospital, and had come straight out to dance because after a shift that long I felt that I deserved a treat, but I couldn't sleep in the next morning, and I knew I'd pay for it if I stayed until the last dance. I wasn't tired yet, although I knew that I would be soon. When I come from dancing I've got a natural high, and just disappearing into the subway is awfully depressing, especially on warm summer nights. So I decided to walk a few blocks before getting on the train.

I love heading up Eighth Avenue after one a.m. The yuppie cafés and "nice" restaurants look ghostly with only dim lights on and the chairs all piled on the tables as if they were elementary school classrooms. The lines outside the clubs are pretty short too. (Don't you believe that New York has a night life. You want to see places that are open late, check out Madrid. Or Ghent, in festival time.) The only things open besides clubs are the all-night Korean groceries, and you're left with the "Nice Catch!" ads for gay.com, the public service announcements about crystal meth on the lighted phone booths, and the audience for both groups of ads: young men out on dates. There's not much traffic except for taxis, and the occasional lumbering bus, but there are plenty of people on the streets. Occasionally there'll even be a woman or two sprinkled in among a group of friends. A straight woman alone is invisible then, and she can check out a lot of eye candy.

I usually stop at the Korean grocery on Twentieth to get something to drink. It's a funny atmosphere in there. The grim part is the fluorescent lighting, and the man behind the counter, who's been there God knows how many hours, sacrificing sleep for the American Dream. Then there's the glitter; the clubbers and party goers, in their skintight outfits (me included, I suppose), plunking down $2.50 for about three swallows of a designer iced-tea. And then there's the occasional homeless person, shaggy and disreputable looking, frequently muttering to his personal voices while he redeems bottles, or plunks down carefully hoarded change in exchange for a sandwich. I don't know what you'd call that. Sleaze? Spice? A disgrace to a civilized nation? You tell me.

I was coming out of the grocery with a bottled Frappucino at about a quarter to two when I heard someone yell, and the kind of thump sound you get when a car hits something. There was a dark car sitting in the intersection that had pretty obviously just run into a cab that had tried to do an illegal right turn on a red light from the left lane. The driver of the car hopped out and started cursing loudly enough to make it clear that he wasn't hurt.

The cab driver hopped out too. "Call an ambulance!" he yelled. "My passenger, he needs to go to the hospital!"

"You make a fucking turn from the left lane I'm not surprised!" The other driver was still pretty annoyed. "You could have fucking killed us, motherfucker!"

"He say 'go to 68th Street' then he say 'no, go to hospital now!'" protested the cab driver, whose English was deteriorating under the stress. "He say he can't breathe. I hurrying so he can get to the hospital. Someone call 9-1-1," he appealed to the crowd that had gathered prudently on the sidewalk, some yards from the stopped cars.

"I'm calling the fucking cops!" The other driver snapped.

"You fucking not look where you going!"

A young white man, wearing a sleeveless shirt that showed off biceps that wouldn't have disgraced one of the models in the gay.com ads stepped out into the zebra, and bothered to look in the back of the cab. "You okay, buddy?" He opened the door, and leaned in. Then he backed out, looking scared, and made a bee-line back to the sidewalk. "Hey, Jules," he spoke to a slender guy with a mustache, who looked vaguely European. "Call an ambulance. I don't think that guy's breathing." He turned to the crowd of onlookers. "Anybody know CPR?"

"I do," said the part of me that was still running on a pleasant adrenalin high. The sane part of me that knew I had just come off four hours of dancing and a twelve-hour shift managed to make me shut my mouth before I blurted out something stupid about being a doctor. It's one of the first things you learn: good samaritans can't get sued. A doctor can always be guilty of malpractice.

I headed out into the street, the center (for once) of a circle of male eyes, and leaned into the cab. I almost cracked my skull on the roof pulling back. It was Brandon Sweaty Hands.

My first, slightly hysterical thought was that it would be just like Brandon to fake his death to see if there might be a woman around to give him CPR. I actually got as far as wondering whether he knew that CPR involved a good chance of broken ribs as well as the kiss of life, or whether he'd decided that with all his excess body fat his ribs had a nice cushion and the risk was worth it. Then realism set in. The light in the car wasn't very bright, but I was used to seeing Brandon in low-light conditions, and there was no way he was faking being that flushed. His face, always fat, was swollen to positively grotesque proportions, and any distinction between chin and neck had disappeared. When I ripped open his shirt, I saw the tell tale hives. It looked like a textbook allergic reaction; pseudo-anaphylactic shock. *Bee sting*, I thought, noting that the cab window was open.

He wasn't breathing, but it looked to me like there was damn all that artificial resuscitation could do. He needed a shot of epinephrine. I reached across his body, and grabbed the tote bag on the seat next to him, hoping that he was carrying an anti-allergy kit. It was unlikely he'd have a reaction this severe the first time he was stung, and if he knew he was allergic, he might be smart enough to take precautions.

It turned out that he wasn't that smart. The bag held his dance shoes, his wallet, and his keys. That was it. I was glad to hear the siren announcing an ambulance. When it pulled up, wailing, a minute or so later, I told the EMTs what it looked like, explained that he didn't have an epinephrine kit on him, and then got out of the way and let them do their thing. They thanked me but didn't ask me to stick around, and my pleasant high was wearing off and turning into exhaustion, so I headed up to the subway at Twenty-Third Street, and got on an A train uptown. I wondered a little if the EMTs had been able to resuscitate Brandon, but not enough to keep me awake when I finally got home.

My very mild curiosity about the fat jerk with the sweaty hands was satisfied two days later, by my roommate, Kathy. "Hey," she said, looking up from the trashy tabloid she pretends that she only uses as a coaster for her coffee mug every morning. "Did you know this guy? Brandon Williamson III?"

I'd never known his surname, but I could only think of one Brandon I knew. "The fat jerk!" I said. "Why's he in the paper? Is he dead?"

Kathy gave me a look that suggested that I was much too disturbing to contemplate so early in the morning. "How'd you know he was dead?"

I explained my brief post-tango encounter with Brandon, and a little about why I thought of him as "the fat jerk." "Was it a bee sting?" I asked.

Kathy shook her head. "Peanut allergy. And he obviously was an idiot as well as a jerk. It says here he knew he was allergic but didn't carry an epinephrine kit except when he was traveling."

"Except when he was traveling?" I echoed, puzzled.

"'Williamson's wife, Nicole, said that her husband was careful to let everyone in his immediate circle know about his allergy." Kathy read aloud. "'He warned everyone to keep peanuts away from him,' Mrs. Williamson said. 'And people listened when Brandon told them things. He didn't want to carry the kit because he was afraid of seeming like an invalid.'" Kathy snorted. "Newsflash, Einstein: New York is not arranged for your personal benefit." She shook her head. "Honestly, there's a sucker dies every minute."

"Mmmm," I said, not paying attention. Something was bothering me. Kathy fulminated for a while on people who were walking public health risks (she's in an MD/PhD program, and her thesis is about MDR-TB, so it's a subject dear to her heart), and I made appropriate noises. Finally, she looked at her watch, squeaked, gulped her coffee, and ran.

I looked at the paper she'd left behind. There was a coffee ring on the article about Brandon Williamson III, but the text was still legible, and the photo was clearly Brandon, wearing a suit, and a shark-like smile. It turned out that he'd been a partner in some law firm that I'd never heard of, and had lived with his wife and son on the Upper West Side. He was fifty-two (I couldn't help thinking how typical it was that he'd shaved a couple of years off his age for his birthday dance), and described as "a devotee of ballroom dancing." He had known about his allergy to peanuts for over thirty years, and had refused to carry an epinephrine kit except when traveling, in spite of several earlier attacks, the last one ten years ago, when he had picked up his son from a playdate where the boy had been eating peanut butter and jelly sandwiches.

The newspaper said that doctors had said there was no way of knowing exactly how and when Brandon might have come in contact with the allergen that triggered his death. The paper described his death as "a tragedy" and had a side-bar with statistics and symptoms of peanut allergies, along with hotlines to call in case of attack, and websites with further information for concerned parents and relatives of sufferers.

I read the story three times. It didn't say anything about Brandon being a jerk with sweaty hands who spent his evenings groping women young enough to be his daughter. And it didn't say anything about the young woman who had volunteered to give him CPR before the ambulance arrived and then melted away into the night. I realized that I was glad about that.

I'd be lying if I said that Brandon Williamson's death haunted every waking moment for the following week. A three-year residency in internal medicine gives you enough experience with the deaths of strangers that you don't lose too much sleep over them. And I was pretty busy. But now and then, riding the train, or shopping for groceries, or doing laundry, I'd find myself thinking about him. About how all the New York tango regulars felt about him. About how he'd relied on telling everybody very loudly about his allergy so that no one would bring peanuts near him. And about the orange wrappers in the garbage can of the ladies' restroom at the *milonga*. I'd noticed them because they showed up so brightly against the white paper towels and white plastic of the can.

I'd thought even at the time that it was odd to see them there. Generally *tangueros* don't eat candy while they're dancing because it gives you bad breath, and when your face is that close to someone else's, it's not courteous to breathe chocolate at them. Most *milongas* have an open can of Altoids at the entrance, and people may pop other breathmints of their choice, but not candy. Besides, nothing ruins lipstick quicker than chocolate. Especially soft chocolate, like the kind in Reese's peanut butter cups. But someone had gone through five or six packages of peanut butter cups that evening. There had been some kind of empty plastic jar in the trash can too. It hadn't had a label, and I wouldn't have sworn to its shape after only a glimpse a week earlier, but thinking back it looked awfully like an empty jar of Planter's Peanuts.

I went out dancing again the following week. The milonga was the same as always. People chatted about work, or their families, or upcoming classes and workshops. People danced. No one mentioned "our friend, Brandon" who had died a week ago, on his fifty-second birthday. Some of my favorite partners were there, and I danced with them. As always, I felt myself getting less tense as I danced. There's something very relaxing about a dance that basically involves a gentle hug.

Natalia was DJ for the evening. After a while I went over to the DJ's table and sat next to her. She smiled a greeting, programmed the laptop that's connected to the speakers, and then stood up to give me a kiss on the cheek. "*¿Cómo estás?*" she asked. She knows that I live in Washington Heights, and that I try to practice my Spanish whenever I can.

"*Muy bien, gracias, ¿y Ud.?*" I answered automatically.

"*Muy bien.*"

She smiled, but didn't say anything more. I tried to think of a graceful way to bring up the topic. "Are there going to be any birthday dances tonight?" I asked in English.

"I don't think so." She didn't seem ruffled. "Unless it's your birthday?"

"Oh, no. I always enjoy watching them though." I paused, and then tried again. "I was kind of surprised last week that Brandon got one. He didn't seem . . . quite the type for it."

"I think he enjoyed it though." Natalia was serene.

"Yes. Nice in a way. He died a few hours later, did you know?"

"I saw something in the papers. I wasn't sure if it was the same man."

"The loving husband and father," I agreed. "And devotee of ballroom dancing."

She laughed. "Tango isn't *ballroom* dancing."

"And as to loving husband . . ." I trailed off.

She met my eyes and we grinned at each other. She looked like a contented panther. "I'm sure he loved his wife," she purred. "I think he loved every woman he could get his hands on."

"I wonder who ate those peanut butter cups before his birthday dance," I said softly.

Natalia became serious. She turned away from me, and began intently arranging the next set of songs on the laptop, her profile absolutely still. When she spoke, it was in Spanish, and very quiet. "A lot of Argentines have come here for work, since the crash there, you know? I send home fifty dollars a month, and for that my parents and my little brother can eat. But I'm lucky. I'm legal. It's hard to get a green card nowadays, with all the worry about terrorism. And our *friend* Brandon . . ." She paused. "Our friend Brandon was a lawyer. He might have promised a few girls who were here illegally that he could help them with the INS. In exchange for . . . certain favors, if you understand me."

I sat there for a while, listening to the music. I thought about how I feel poor because I'm going to be paying off my student loans for the next ten years. Brandon's son might be poor that way. It's a lot different from fifty dollars a month feeding a family poor. "I guess I won't ever know who ate them," I said finally. "It's a shame. I'd like to shake her hand."

Natalia turned her face toward me and smiled. Crying would have ruined her eye makeup, but her eyes were very bright. "We would have shared them with you," she said. "But you're always so shy. You never go out on the floor during birthday dances."

I blushed. "Well, I'm not that good," I murmured.

"Yes." she said. "You are."

Eric came up just then, and asked her to dance. She gave him her hand, and I watched them move out onto the crowded floor. Giselle and her boyfriend were dancing near them there, and Rachel and Jorge were across the room. Yasuko was dancing with a German guy whose name I can never remember. I enjoy watching really good Argentine tango. The dancers move like panthers. Or like lionesses, the only cats who are not solitary, prowling the savannah, defending their pride.

Blue Vandas

by Lynne Barrett

I studied botany. I like to think I'm still someone who observes, following nature down her strange pathways. Certainly what I have to say is more truthful than much of the trash written after the murder of Cage Danvers, when my sister, the actress known as Doro, was first caught in the great search-light of scandal.

Some facts: My sister is not, technically, a dwarf. A dwarf must be under four feet tall and Doro is 4'6". Through some genetic grace she's delicate and disdainfully pretty, with none of the dysplasia from which many true dwarves suffer. Though at some angles her head looks large for her body, this is characteristic of movie stars, perhaps something they're selected for, the famous faces. She's a sport on the O'Malley family tree, a wild mutation, nature's idea of fun. Perhaps she is a throwback. Our father says that his great-grandmother, back in Ireland, was tiny and believed to be a witch.

By two, I was taller than my older sister, feeling, always, wrong. For me, her first fan, she set a measure I could never fit. Our father saw her as frail and damaged. Our mother thought her willful, which she was. At nine, she refused growth hormone taken from the pituitaries of the dead, which turned out to carry Creutzfeldt-Jacob disease. Now we know about prions, but then the doctors could only acknowledge the truth of Doro's instinct that it was Something Dangerous. When synthetic growth hormone became available, she was a teenager and defiantly herself. At seventeen, she demanded that they send her to California, where she would find an agent and a drama coach. They refused, but she went anyway, right out of high school, cursing them because they wouldn't help. So she became, in B movies and guest spots on TV: Doro, the dwarf starlet. Not, technically, a dwarf. But as I say, everyone out here is careless with the truth.

Snow spun outside the Ludlow Arboretum greenhouse, where I was tending Professor Blaufelt's Hinoki cypress hybrids, when she herself, Doro, called up to ask, Could I come out for a week or so if she paid for the ticket? Would I like that?

I called home to say I'd be working intensively on my thesis. "I'll be totally inaccessible," I said. "That's good," Mom said. When I asked why, I got grim silence. Then she said, "Well, Annie, I guess you should be warned, we hear Dorothy's trying to locate you. She's been calling neighbors." "I haven't seen her in seven years," I said, which was true enough. "You're a good girl, Annie," she said. "What does she want with you?" "Search me," I said. I soothed my conscience by packing notes on bio-diversity, forgotten varieties of roses and their lost perfumes.

And now, here I was, I could hardly believe it, sitting with Doro by the pool at Cage Danvers' party, waiting for the appearance of the famous old beauty, Pamela Taft, on a blue and gold day we might have in June in New England if we were lucky. The lawn rolled from the pool down towards bright formal gardens I wanted to explore. For now we held good positions, on teak deck chairs with a view of the arcade at the back of the house, where cameras and mikes were set up to record remarks about the reissue of Danvers' early film, *Intrigue in A Minor*. The big white tent set up for food still had its flaps down. Guests, milling around, eyed it hungrily.

"Everyone's so thin," I said.

"Because of the camera," Doro said. "Even the famous fat people are thinner than you think."

She looked tiny in her lounge chair, but not childlike. She wore a dress made of leather tatters, knotted here and there, showing golden skin. Sandal straps wrapped her ankles and her tawny hair floated in the warm breeze. She said her agent had her holding off commitments because she was up for the part of a Bond girl, and she hoped there might be action on a script about a Civil War spy dwarf. "Next year," she announced, "I'm going to be big."

I looked down at myself, stretched the length of the lounger. Five foot seven and going slowly nowhere in the Ludlow master's program for garden design, which amounted to indentured servitude on my professors' projects. I couldn't leave without being clobbered by education loans, so I sketched dream gardens, waiting. "How is it you've always known what you wanted?" I asked Doro.

"It's like a door appears—" She arranged her hands in front of her. "And you have to open it and go through." She caught my expression. "You've never felt that?"

I shook my head.

"You have to understand what the world is. You sell yourself to stay alive. People try to hold themselves apart, but what you really are, you have to sell that." She looked at her hands. "Maybe the door is really a mirror. You have go towards yourself. Do you see what I mean?"

"Yes," I lied.

"Stop hiding away at school. You can move out here, be my personal assistant while you look around. What do you say?"

"I'll think about it." I couldn't imagine explaining to my parents that they'd lost me, too.

Her hands became white butterflies. She waggled her fingers at friends.

"There's Cage Danvers," Doro said. A tan old man, with something painful and valiant in his posture, as if he had to fight to keep his spine so straight, moved through the crowd, greeting people. His brown and blue plaid shirt and khaki pants had an equestrian air.

Doro filled me in. In the late '50s Cage Danvers got his start directing memorably gritty noirs, then produced twenty years of TV detectives and amassed real estate and influence. Now on the board of GC Pictures, he was a Wise Man; the real money people took his advice. Doro cited projects he vetoed—none of which, of course, I ever heard of, since they didn't happen because Cage Danvers said no.

He moved in our direction. "Okay—*now*," Doro said. She got up from the lounge chair with an impossibly sexy motion and shook her tatters into graceful place.

"You go ahead. I wouldn't have anything to say."

"Oh, it's like a funeral. Everyone says the same thing. You've always been a fan."

She stepped forward, smiled up at Cage Danvers, and introduced me.

"A pleasure." He had a deep, echoing voice I didn't expect. This, his pale gray eyes, and his very high tan forehead might explain his reputation for wisdom. I mumbled admiration for his garden.

He turned back to the house, shaking hands. As he reached the arcade, Doro clutched my arm. "*Pamela Taft.*" And here she was, coming through the French doors, in a pale blue dress and amethysts. I'd seen pictures of Pamela Taft all my life—her famously carved cheekbones and sweep of moon pale hair. They stood side by side in the lights and Pamela Taft gave the cameras bright teeth, aqua eyes, the lift of her shoulders that drew attention to the famously deep cleft between her breasts, while Cage Danvers made a speech about the 40th anniversary remastering of *Intrigue in A Minor*, how the premiere Monday would benefit film restoration, his pleasure in being with his old friend again. Right now Pamela would be doing interviews, so we should enjoy ourselves and meet her later. He gave us a wise smile and gestured towards the tent.

Out paraded waiters with trays of drinks. "Should we eat?" I said. It was past dinnertime back home. Doro led me through the crowd, which formed happy clusters, drinking champagne or Calistoga. Whenever Doro slithered by people dropped back to look at her, so I saw she had a natural advantage in a crowd. You had to step away a pace to take her in.

Near the tent, she said to go ahead, she had people to talk to. I worked through the mob at the buffet, grabbing sushi, strawberries, and some kind of tiny crepes. I came out among munching, murmuring strangers. At the back of the garden, beyond tall hedges, sunlight struck the copper roof of an outbuilding. I carried my plate down the path until I reached a bench of mellow old wood, its arms carved into lions. It was set so you could gaze up towards the house, but I leaned over the back, looking at the flower beds in increasing amazement. Tall spikes of foxglove, delphiniums and campanula. My God, hollyhocks. An English cottage garden in full bloom. How did they do it? Los Angeles must be zone ten, maybe zone nine, hot, dry, nothing like rainy England. These were the biggest foxgloves I'd ever seen, tiger-spotted pink and salmon. Maybe they weren't real? With a glance over my shoulder I stepped into the garden, my flats sinking into rich, damp mulch. Yes, real. Each plant was tagged, I saw, with a copper ID. Digitalis purpurea, Althea rosea, Delphinium Consolida Blue Cloud. Labels dangled from the foliage like jewelry. I heard a low hiss. Water. Even as I identified it, I felt cool liquid seep into my shoes. Crouching, I saw the green plastic capillaries of a watering system, tiny hoses running to the roots, and others wired up on stakes to cast a fine mist. The garden was one constant trickle. Impressed, I stood up. A man sat sideways on the lion bench with legs stretched out, watching me and calmly eating sushi from my plate.

He was beautiful. Sad. Big nosed, curly headed, wearing old jeans and an ivory polo shirt. Everything reeled, shifted, realigned around him. Yes, I know that's a crazy thing to say, but it's what happened, though I told myself it might be jet lag.

"I guess this was yours," he said. "Excuse me. Come on, we'll share." He swung his legs off the bench to make room.

Breathless, I sat beside him and took a crepe filled with a delicious salmon cream. Chewing, glad for the excuse not to speak, I looked down. My black leather flats, the only shoes I owned that weren't sneakers or boots, were soaked. I took them off. My white New England feet were turning rose on top with sunburn. I tucked them under me.

He said, "Can I ask what you were doing?"

I explained about the watering system, its perfection, what it must have cost.

"Well, he's got the money," the man said. "You're an actress?"

I shook my head.

"Don't tell me. You write screenplays."

"Never thought of it."

"How odd," he said. "What are you?"

I saw in front of me, just as Doro had described it, the little door. "I'm a gardener," I said airily. "Garden design, special projects. Back East. I'm here visiting my sister. She's an actress."

"Somebody had to be," he said.

"Who are you?"

"Oh, I'm Oz," he said. "The great and terrible."

I didn't laugh, though I got the idea I was supposed to.

"Paul," he said, "Paul Ferris. Third-generation Hollywood.

Deals in my genes." I didn't laugh at that either. What was happening seemed deadly serious to me. "You should see my yard," he said. "It's a mess."

"How would you want it to look?"

"I don't know. Not flowery."

"You know the Japanese say an all-green garden is the most subtle."

"Really?" he said. "Interesting."

I was about to launch into theory, but a woman walked up, greeting him, an older lady in a long simple burlap-looking dress, her gray hair pulled back into a braided knot.

He stood to meet her so I did too. "Marie," he said, "I didn't know you were here." I stepped into my soggy flats and made a move to get away, but he said, "Marie Bergeron, this is—"

"Annie O'Malley," I put in quickly.

"She's a gardener."

The woman nodded politely. I was jealous of her, for knowing him. I was glad she was old and weathered.

"I wasn't sure you'd be here," he said, "though I know we contacted whoever we could find."

"Of course I came," she said. "Don't you know I'm very sentimental?"

"Marie was in Cage's movie." Paul Ferris turned to me. "*Intrigue in A Minor*. My father was his cameraman."

"He was a sweetie," Marie said.

"He died when I was twelve," Paul Ferris said to me. "Cancer. A lot of them are gone, from that movie. Walter Stacey."

"Mike Shaw, too," Marie said. "Cancer. Might be the government's fault. We filmed that on-the-lam sequence downwind of the testing grounds. But you know, we all smoked then."

They were silent for a moment and I heard the silvery motion of water among the roots of the English flowers. "So it'll be a small reunion," said Paul Ferris, and Marie broke into a laugh of true amusement. Her face had lovely planes.

"Marie was married to Cage," he explained to me.

She said, "I was an early wife. He used to marry, but he got cautious. I don't think he'd risk losing this place in a divorce. This was his dream house, even back then."

"What have you been doing?" Paul Ferris said.

"I moved out to the desert for the peace, but maybe it's too peaceful. Because here I am, like an old warhorse. You'll have to keep me in mind." She reached into one deep pocket and pulled out a leather case, handed him a card.

"I'd be happy to," he said. "I didn't think you were working."

"Well, I haven't been because . . . what do they offer me, anymore? I might have to go on one of those soaps and be the old buttinsky, you know, the interfering aunt." She turned to look up towards the house. "Pam's out again. Looks marvelous, doesn't she?" Marie Bergeron put her hands above her head and stretched. Her big sleeves fell gracefully away from her thin arms.

"Does Cage know you're here?" Paul Ferris said.

"I haven't spoken to him yet."

"Come on," he said to her, taking her arm. They began moving up the walk. I tagged along. As we reached the pool, I said, "I could take a look at that yard of yours." But he just nodded, said, "We'll do that," and led her off.

Doro, coming down the walk, smiled at them. I watched him disappear into the throng around Pamela Taft, as my sister clicked swiftly to me. "You genius," she said. "How did you do *that*?"

I said, "Huh?"

"No," she said. "Don't even tell me you don't know who that was."

"Cage's ex-wife. And Paul Ferris."

"Marie Bergeron went to Europe and made films with all the famous depressing directors," she said. "Paul Ferris is an executive of GC Pictures *and* he has his own production deal."

"He's nice," I said.

"Oh my God." She gurgled with laughter. "We've got to get to work on you."

Manicured, pedicured, salt scrubbed and massaged, with copper highlights in my tea-colored mop, I felt oddly new Saturday evening when we left Doro's apartment building at the foot of the Hollywood Hills, driving off in her specially adapted Audi. Perhaps I would have resisted, but I'd met Paul Ferris, so I'd let her buy me the slinky black rayon tank and pants, the sandals in which I trotted after her into the parties for which she'd lined up invitations, each promoting something or other in this pre-Oscar season.

At one party, Doro introduced me to Jeff Chang, screenwriter of her early movie, *Voodoo High School*. He was a bit shorter than me, though his thick black brush cut gave him an inch. For intangible reasons, it seemed to me likely he was gay. Not for the first time, I wondered about Doro's sex life, something she never mentioned. He shouted at me about the convolutions of *Miss Thumb*, the novel about the Civil War spy dwarf. The rights, bought by an independent, were acquired by an Italian producer whose bankruptcy left his assets locked up in GC Pictures's vaults. If one of Jeff's projects hit, if Doro made a splash as a Bond girl, perhaps they'd have the clout to extract it. Just as someone handed me another blue Margarita, Doro came back and said no one was here and we should move on.

As we moved from the obscure to the semi-famous, I entered a dark tunnel of voices and names. I grabbed fresh rolls with warm duck, a tiny cup of cool yellow soup. At a private home I saw the shrimp crepes from Cage Danvers', so I figured we'd reached that level. I had champagne and watched the door for Paul Ferris.

At this event Doro scored an invitation to a party up on Mulholland, at the house of a famous actor. Here people were frankly drunk and all I could find to eat was tortilla chips, but my sister assured me this was the most exclusive blast of all. Then she disappeared. Men were watching basketball on TV, in a room with no light on. Out back, a woman was making out with the bartender. The dumb stoned look on people's faces was just like college. So what if the faces were famous? I decided I would refuse Doro's offer to be her assistant and go home.

I went outside and sat on a wall at the head of the long driveway full of cars. Newcomers had to park further down the perilous road and walk back. I recognized a best supporting actress nominee in a gold satin dress. She went in, and I yawned, wondering if I dared drink beer on top of all the other stuff. Then a green sportscar pulled up and out got Paul Ferris. He had on a brown sweater and holey jeans. He jingled his keys, looking around for a place to park. I gave him a fond inebriated wave.

He said. "The gardener. O'Malley. What's your sister's name? I tried to look her up, see if I could find you."

"She dropped the last name. She's simply Doro."

"She's that tiny one," he said.

"Right," I said. "D.O.R.O. Rhymes with Zorro, not Thoreau."

"That her line?"

"No, it's Dad's. He disapproves. Did you really try to find me?"

"I did," he said.

I had a stupid smile on my face. I felt an overpowering sexual embarrassment, sure this man knew more about me than I could stand to know myself.

"You said you might want to take a look at my garden. It's quite a mess."

"Do you want to fix it up?"

"I like that Japanese idea. Something meditative."

"Anything can be done, if you know how," I said, with all the bravado I could summon. "I've been considering some projects out here."

Don't go off with strangers they tell you, all your life. But no one explains how attractive the stranger can be, how irresistible. We were in the car and winding along Mulholland before I thought to worry—and then I really only worried that he wouldn't like me enough. He let me use his car phone and I left a message on my sister's cell, saying who I was with, as lightly as I could.

Unfamiliar with the geography, I understood just ridge and canyon, till we pulled into a garage where I could see the shape of another car covered with canvas. His house was built from the lip of the hillside downward,. We entered the top level, which had the living room and kitchen, then wound down a spiral staircase into a dark room—a bedroom?—and out onto a deck. The city cast light up into the sky, far brighter than the slim edge of new moon. He took my hand and led me down some stairs. We stepped onto dry crackly stuff, not grass, something dusty and aromatic, like sage. The hillside fell away below us in a dark tangle of brush.

"Well," Paul said, "I guess you can't see very much at night.

Take my word for it, it's all gone wild. It was planted, groomed, in my parents' time."

I breathed in eucalyptus and some kind of pine. "I'd need to test the soil, look at the structure. And there are microclimates in these hills, depending on which way you face and how much moisture gets here." I'd been reading up, did I mention?

"That's interesting." He went back inside and turned on a lamp, so I saw this was not a bedroom but an office, with blond leather furniture and a big glass desk. "Want a drink?" he said.

"Water."

"Ah," he said. "Good girl." He went up to the kitchen. I listened to him pad around, the clink of bottles, ice chunking out of the fridge. My body felt hollowed out with anticipation and I told myself to breathe, to think. He came down with a beer and a big glass of water for me, but before I could taste it he kissed me and then we got tangled up together on the blond leather couch. "You're cute," he said. It sounded like a lie, but I liked it. I held my arms up and he pulled the black tank over my head. He went into the bathroom to get a condom.

Then things got odd. We sweated, we grappled. Basically, he couldn't do it. He pulled away. "Sorry, sometimes this happens the first time I'm with someone," he said.

I said it didn't matter and tasted the sweet part of his neck. It cheered me to hear he was thinking of this as just the first time.

"Could be the antidepressants," he said. We lay together naked on the couch, looking at the ceiling. The ceiling, I noticed, sparkled. When I moved my head, the sparkle shifted.

He said, "Maybe it's throwing me that you're not an actress. You could be, you know."

"Not me."

"Hey, I'd help you. I'll get you lessons if you're scared."

"No, I'm not an actress," I said. But he was panting. So I said, "Not me. But my sister— there's this film she's dying to do that's tied up, somehow, in your company." I told him what I knew about the saga of *Miss Thumb*.

"The Civil War?" he said. "Battle scenes? Big budget?"

"I imagine it's more behind the scenes. She's a spy. I think there's a circus. P.T. Barnum, when was he?"

"Hmmhmmm," he said. "Can't hurt to find out." He walked

over to his desk, beautiful and slow moving, naked except for the condom. He called somebody's voicemail and gave orders that by Monday he wanted to know the status of the project. He walked back to me, stiff, and before you knew it, we were doing it just fine.

Once in the night I heard him talking on the phone. But early in the morning, when I was wide awake on East Coast time, he was asleep. I went into the shower: gray stone, with many knobs. I spun one and water shot at me from the sides so I jumped around laughing, but when I came out, he had a pillow over his eyes.

I pulled on clothes and went outside. I'd studied up on the Sunset zone system, which allows for West Coast complexities. Up here—Zone 22, coastal canyon—rainfall mattered most, and which way cold air would drain in winter, how hot it got when the Santa Anas blew. Downhill overgrown eucalyptus had cast off branches. Cement and chicken wire at the bottom caught what might tumble onto the road below. A hollow on the south side of the house, before the land dropped away, looked like the place that had been cultivated in the past. I squatted and ran my fingers through this alien dirt.

Paul came out and handed me a tumbler of orange juice. "What do you think?" he said.

"Do you know the English say it takes six years to make a garden?"

"That's ridiculous," he said. "Who has that kind of time?"

"Money can replace time," I said, trying not to hear Professor Blaufelt scream. "Here, anyway. This is a magic climate. Plants from South Africa and Asia find new destinies hidden in their genes. But you have to be careful what you plant. And water matters. Do you mind if I do some research on what would work here?"

He nodded. "Good," he said. "But not now. I have to go to work."

"On Sunday?"

"Lots cooking. I'll take you home."

Driving, he pointed out Griffith Park, where, he said, Cage Danvers' TV shows had often ended with chase scenes. "That and parking garages," he said.

"You don't like him," I said.

"He can be difficult."

"But you're celebrating his movie."

"The film's good, my own dad's work for Cougar Films. Anyway, we've made money on video releases, and now DVD, from the Cougar film library. GC was Grantham Pictures before it merged with Cougar, thirty years ago. Now there's a corporate structure above us—gas and wine and soybeans."

I really didn't know what he was talking about. Palm trees flicked by, reminding me of the souvenir pendant my sister sent me when I was sixteen, palms silhouetted on iridescence, lovely and unreal. In Hollywood, before we turned up Argyle, I noticed a girl and two boys, sharing coffee. Street kids. Transplants from somewhere. I wondered how it was for my sister when she first came out here. Magic dirt, though: she'd somehow done all right.

I said, "I'll be at the *Intrigue in A Minor* premiere, tomorrow night. Will you be there?"

"Oh sure," he said. "My budget's paying for it."

Monday I was on duty as Doro's PA. For the premiere, she'd had made a fitted sheath of black satin, very plain. Blue vanda orchids were to twist up the bodice, across one shoulder and down the back. The seamstress had made a line of small, nearly invisible black satin loops through which I threaded plastic tubing, capped off at the waistline front and back. Not wanting any leakage, I barely dampened cotton and pushed it through the piping with straws. Orchids keep well anyway.

She'd had her hair done in the morning, up, simple. After she had the dress on, I inched up the side zipper and worked around her, inserting vandas in tiny holes in the plastic, petals overlapped to hide the hose. I thought of Cage Danvers' capillary watering system.

All that mattered was how she'd look walking in. She had wangled as her escort a strapping young actor who'd be in a GC Pictures summer action film. She hoped their striking image would garner time at the microphones, possibly a photo in *In Style*, publicity worth all expense.

I realized this outfit had made her think of me, and call me in. I was to go along, riding in the studio hired car, carrying extra flowers in case any fell out. I would be, I teased, not bodyguard but body gardener.

"I love that," she said. "Body gardener!"

I knelt in front of her and took another vanda from the big florist's box, and smiled.

Indeed she got attention on the red carpet. The orchids made the jewelry around look hard, as flowers do. She wore soft pearl earrings, and I'd pinned one spray on her clutch purse. Next to the tall young man in a tux she shimmered, her body tiny, fey.

As PA, I followed behind, in my black duds, carrying a saddlebag-size purse. With others of my kind, I sat in the back. Paul was up front, a world away. Someone from the film preservation society praised Cage Danvers, who introduced Pamela Taft, and Marie Bergeron, looking years younger in a blue satin pantsuit, and an old man who had been the bad guy's henchman. All stood up, to applause, and then Danvers thanked lots of people, and the movie played. The leading man, Walter Stacey, had been in one of Danvers' detective shows before he died. In the film I noticed the careful lighting of Pamela's breasts, their precise form in three-quarter view. And I saw Marie's young grace as the tomboy in the mountain town where the hero sought the secret while being chased. The way she was struck into femininity by him, the way she sacrificed to save him, knowing that he was oblivious—all this hurt me, I have to say, so I felt the film had power although I didn't really follow all the turns. There were a lot of scenes with mirrors and moody jazz in dark bars. The camera's eye was Cage Danvers, but also Paul's father, odd to think of.

On the way out, there was another photo op for celebs to praise the movie and a bunch-up of people waiting for their cars. When I got near Paul, he stepped away—I saw him—then turned back to me and Doro. I introduced them. "You look lovely," he said to her. "I think you got our boy here some attention."

Doro smiled and turned flirtatiously in front of him. But all I could see was the way he was leaving me. I stepped after him. "What's the matter?" I said, walking beside him.

"I found out about that project of hers. We own it, but I can't do anything with it right now."

"Why?"

"There was some interest, but Cage Danvers nixed it, wrote notes about how expensive it would be, large cast, locations, no star connected to it. The corporate guys listen to him. I've got ideas about that, but . . ."

"What ideas?"

"I can't talk about it here," he said.

"I have every confidence you can pull it off," I said.

But he looked at me with an eyebrow raised, doubting me, doubting himself.

"But what I really want—"

Is you, I didn't say.

"—is to show you what I've come up with. Look." I pulled my notebook out of my shoulder bag and fanned it at him. "I'd, I'll put in a meditation garden on the south side where that hollow is. With a pool. With fish. Some big flat stones around it. And then the hillside, where it drops away, needs to be thought of vertically, like a Japanese print." I tried to sound sure. "To make a fast change, right now, I can bring in dwarf cypresses in pots, then start landscaping."

"A Japanese print?" he said. "How quickly can it be done?"

He was listening. I just wanted him to take me home with him, you understand. But I knew he wouldn't trust a personal reason.

"It would be—to do it fast would be expensive," I said. "And I'd need to get started right away, talking to you, ordering plants. I'd need a budget. It would be a really big break for me to do this, get me started out here." I could feel his attention heat up. "Very important for me," I said. Which it was.

And he nodded. "Come along. "

"I have to tell my sister—"

"Well, go take care of it," he said, "Make it quick."

Doro was waiting for the car. I said, "Listen, I have to talk to Paul. He wants to, I mean—"

She said, "Good girl. Tell him *Miss Thumb* is terrific."

"Oh," I said, "about that. He said Cage had blocked it, but he has some plan . . ."

"Who blocked it?"

"Cage Danvers. He said it was big budget and no stars."
"Oh," she said.
"But Paul might be able to do something . . ."
I saw Paul getting into a car and I ran.

We talked under the stars, about the melancholy calm of Asian gardens and how as a boy he used to shoot hoops up here, alone. We made love where the pond would be. When I woke up in the night, he'd carried me inside. I heard him pacing upstairs, his voice saying, "Every plant has its shadow," but that was something I had said so I sank back through layers of dream. And I was a happy sleeping woman till the phone rang at four a.m.

"He shot himself?" Paul said. "No? Damn. Yes. Okay. We'll need a statement . . ."

"Come on," he said to me. Holding the phone in one hand, he opened his closet with the other and pulled out a suit. I shook my clothes on. They were in sad shape. In his closet I saw an array of linen shirts. I gestured, and when he nodded I grabbed one, wrapped it around me, tied it, and followed him out while he told me that had been the studio, alerted by the cops, the cops alerted by the neighbors, the neighbors alerted by the water flooding downhill out the back of Danvers' property, his watering system turned on full force, Danvers found dead, shot in the heart, and the news about to break.

"I was trying to get rid of him," he said. "But not this way." We got in the Mercedes he called his business car, and drove down to Beverly Hills where Cage Danvers' house was blocked in by police vehicles. Satellite trucks were positioning themselves. He shook his head and turned around.

"Drop me at my sister's," I said.

"I might need you," he said, "as an alibi. It's known I was fighting with him over control of the studio. I've been talking to new buyers for it, Japanese." He smiled at me. "I wanted to entertain them in my garden."

He turned again. "We'll go to my office. It's better if the police talk to us there."

And so he took me to the GC Pictures corporate building. Feeling badly dressed and foolish, I went with him to his office on the third floor. There was a large TV turned on. I won't go into all the people there. The important thing is that the studio had contact with the police—in fact detectives were already in Cage Danvers' office down the hall—and so we knew, before it emerged on TV, each bit of news:

Cage lay dead beside the pool.

Naked from the waist down.

And in the pool floated blue vanda orchids.

A test helps you take a test, I was taught, the way a question is framed, informative. I tried to learn more from the police than they did from my answers.

Had my sister planned to be at Cage's after the benefit? I had no idea.

How long had they been involved? Again, no idea.

The maids said she had been there quite a bit, and knew the alarm code. Did I have any idea when she got home?

"I was with Mr. Ferris," I said, "I just don't know. I called her cell and her apartment a while ago but got no answer."

"All night with Mr. Ferris?"

"Yes."

They left that alone. They were talking to him separately.

"Did she have a gun?" No idea.

"A .45?"

I had no idea what a .45 would look like. I thought, if she had a gun, it would be a derringer.

Was I aware that Cage Danvers owned her apartment building?

I was aware of nothing but the danger she was in. Could my sister have killed him?

I remembered the extra orchids wilting in my purse. But they didn't look in my purse. Just as I was Paul's alibi, he was mine.

Was he telling them that Cage Danvers blocked the project she wanted?

Later, a different detective came in. "Your sister says she and Cage Danvers were very close."

I thought, but he blocked her movie? Then I thought: so they've found her and she's safe. I said, again, "I don't know. She didn't confide. I just came out a few days ago. I knew she admired him." Could this cause any trouble?

They went away and let me be with Paul. We picked at

sandwiches and watched TV. Helicopter shots showed the tiled roof of the house, tarpaulins over the ground around the pool. The tent from the party was gone. The lawn shimmered and in the English garden flowers toppled in muck. On some passes, I could see the copper roof of the back building, and the whitewashed glass of an attached shade house. No orchids remained in the pool—all gathered up, I supposed, as evidence.

I said, "I don't see why Doro would have turned the water on. Or even have known how to."

Paul said, "I don't see how she could have held a .45."

I said, "Did they say anything about the trajectory?" He shook his head. "Because if she shot at him, she'd have to shoot upward, wouldn't she?"

"She could have stood on a bench. Or he could have been kneeling."

"Thanks."

And then there she was, on television, being released by the police, accompanied by her lawyer, Doro dressed in simple shirt and trousers, composed and pale. "The police have questioned me about my relationship with Mr. Danvers and of course I've given them every assistance. I am devastated by his death. He was my advisor and my friend, and I loved him. I'm sure whoever did this will be caught."

Shouts from the journalists were cut off by the lawyer leading her away.

Shots of her the night before, alluring in the dress. Cage, gallant but old. Doro's statement again. Shots of the dress, close up on the vandas. Shots from *Intrigue in A Minor*, which seemed irrelevant.

"Good publicity?" I said to Paul. He shook his head. I was not sure at that moment whether we were friends or enemies.

I called her cellphone and left another message and this time she called back. "I can't go home," she said. "You either. The media's there."

I explained to Paul. "Where should she go?"

"Tell them to drive in this direction for now," he said and went off to confer. He came back. "They can drive in, we'll change cars, and take her to a hotel in a while. The one where we have Pamela?" he said to an assistant.

"Pamela Taft wasn't staying at his house, then?" I said. A vagrant hope I'd had.

"No, we brought her here from Carmel and put her up as part of the PR. You look tired," he said, but I wasn't. I was wired.

Soon Doro came in, carrying a suitcase; she'd had the forethought to pack before she went to the police. She shook hands with Paul and said, "I had nothing to do with this."

I said, "What happened, then?"

"After I was dropped at home, I got my car and went over. He'd said to. I usually saw him late at night at his house. He loved his house. But he wouldn't let me live there—it would lead to palimony, he said. And it was better if our relationship wasn't known."

"You and Cage? You were lovers?"

She rolled her eyes. "What do you think?" she said.

"I don't understand," I said. "You wanted to do *Miss Thumb* and you didn't know he'd stopped it?"

"No, but when I asked, he said when I was ready he'd untie it, and he'd see that it was funded, but I wasn't enough of a name yet. Meanwhile he'd fixed it so no one else would get it."

Paul hmmmhmmmd ambiguously.

"So you were fine with that?"

"I was upset, but he said I'd done well at the premiere and he liked the dress, so I did a little striptease for him and . . . you know. Then I went inside to get cleaned up and to rinse out the dress. I'd stupidly tossed it in the pool instead of the other way. I'm sure the chlorine ruined it. When I heard the shot, I ran out of there, out the front door, drove home wrapped in a bath towel. I brought in the towel. Best I could do." She stretched and yawned. She seemed utterly relaxed.

"Who else was there? " Paul asked.

"I don't know," she said.

"Do the police believe you?" I asked.

"Why wouldn't they? I told them everything. We've had a relationship for years. He was guiding my career but then, too, I was guiding his. I suggested the remastering of his first film, as a campaign to get him more artistic respect."

Paul hmmmhmmmd again.

"We were good, I thought," she said.

I thought she was crazy. I looked at Paul. He said, "My assistant is going to take you to a hotel for now. They can keep the press away. Be back in a minute." He left.

I said, "Why didn't you tell me?"

"I would've eventually," Doro said. "If you were working for me, you'd have had to know."

"How, I . . . uh," I said, uncomfortably. "You and he?"

"I'm completely normal, you know," she said. "Physiologically."

"I know. But . . ."

She laughed. "It's good to be small. And young and fresh. And tough. I don't see why you're judging me," she said. "How are you any different?" She cast a glance around Paul's office.

And I thought of how far I'd come in a few days. Mooch, easy lay, fake landscape gardener, hussy. "You're right," I said.

"It's a good thing you hooked up with him," she said. "I need some corporate protection."

I was surprised when we went out to find it was bright daylight.

"What time is it?" I asked Paul.

"About two thirty," he said. "We'll follow them to the hotel. Come on."

I said, "You're being very kind to her."

"It's better if she's under wraps than having her out making who knows what kind of statements." He drove for a bit in silence.

"Are you saying she did it?" I said.

"I don't think you're sure of her yourself."

I sighed.

"There were probably other things going on in Cage's life," he said. "Let's leave it to the cops."

At the hotel, Doro was settled down with room service, watching herself on TV. "Miss Taft called," Paul's assistant said, before leaving. "She'd like to talk to you. Her room's right down the corridor."

In her kaftan, Pamela Taft looked heavier, but still far from her age. "I would've flown home today, but it wasn't possible. The police had a little chat. You know I never had anything to do with him personally. Not my type. I loved your father," she said to Paul. "You're very like him." She leaned forward and damned if he didn't glance into that loose cleavage. I wanted to cuff him.

"I can't believe Cage is dead," she said. "Just last night he was on top of the world. Marie and I were talking about how unpredictable life is, but this—"

"Marie?" he asked.

"That was sweet of your PR people, to put her up here. After she showed up at the party, I asked them to. She didn't expect it. Always the modest one, Marie. We had a good time chumming around this weekend, reminiscing, talking about our aches and pains. We had a drink last night after the show. Then she went to bed; she had to drive back to the desert early."

"Aches and pains?" I said.

"You'll see, you young things. I'm lucky, just some wheezing. Poor Marie had, well, more serious problems, but I gather she's fine now. It's essential," she said, "your health. Anyway, darling, I'll be out of here as soon as the police say I can go, all right?"

In the hall, Paul said, "Do you want to stay here or come home with me?"

"Maybe you should stay here too," I said. "What if the press gets onto the corporate angle?"

We went down to the front desk and I got a load of how the clerk kowtowed to him as he got us a suite and added it to the corporate booking.

I asked, "When did Marie Bergeron check out?"

The clerk glanced down, then up. "She hasn't."

We looked at each other. "What's her room?"

"Right across from the one your people took a while ago."

We walked fast back to the elevator.

"What are we thinking?" he said.

"Well, she was his wife. I don't know."

He tapped on her door. There was no answer. "Marie," he said. "It's Paul Ferris. Are you here?"

A voice said, "Just a minute," and she came to the door. She was wearing the loose burlap dress, and her hair was down in gray twisted locks. She took a step back, and we went in.

The television was on behind her. Close up on flowers bobbing in water. I blinked. The orchids weren't blue vandas, but purple dendrobiums, some kind of faked-up TV shot, the real evidence being unavailable.

Paul said, "Pamela thought you'd checked out."

"I could have, couldn't I," she said. "Just driven off and gone on home to the desert. No one would even have thought of me."

Paul said, "Marie, I don't understand."

"No?" she said. "Why would you?"

I noticed that the mini-bar was open, brandy in a glass.

I said, "Why did you go to Cage Danvers house last night?"

She chuckled.

I shivered. I said, "You know my sister's in terrible trouble. His lover."

"You think so?" she said. "I got her *out* of terrible trouble, if she only knew."

"How did you get inside?" Paul asked.

She shrugged. "Through the back, the plant house, the conservatory, as he liked to call it. Horrible snob. There were always keys back there, on a hook. I lived there, you know. Hasn't changed that much, really. That's how I got in the day of the party. Your people hadn't found me," she said to Paul. "I crashed."

"But you were welcome," he said.

"And you saw him with Doro?" I tried to haul us back to the point.

"I was young when he first got hold of me. He said to her what he'd said to me: When you're ready, I'll let you, you'll have your chance. But I was never ready, not in his view. Years went by before I realized, and left him, and found I could get no work here. He'd blocked me."

"So you went to Europe," Paul said. "And you were wonderful."

"Yes, I'd do anything a director wanted. He'd taught me that. I worked, overworked till I cracked and then retired, that's the nice word for it."

"But after all this time, why kill him now?"

"Oh," she said, "it was the *movie*. Seeing what I had then. And those lovely young people. It made me . . . sentimental."

"When you went out," I said, "you turned on the water?"

"It was on. I threw a couple of hoses out there and turned it up all the way. Had some idea of erasing my footsteps, of going off in the middle of nowhere to chuck this—" And she pulled the gun out of her pocket.

Paul reached out and put his hand on her wrist and squeezed. So brave, I thought.

"Don't be silly. I'll drop it," she said, and did so. It clunked on the carpet. I jumped. Paul stooped and swept it up. "I decided I wouldn't miss this. I came back here. I felt the need of a bracer. Or two. Then I waited to see what would happen. I thought someone would come. I wouldn't be . . . forgotten."

"No, not at all," he said. "Let me make a call." Paul kissed her cheek. He pulled out his cell phone, handed me the gun.

I'd never held one before. It was heavy, ugly. "Where'd you get this?" I said.

"Always have it in the car," she said. "In case of snakes. Or men."

Paul made arrangements for a discreet surrender. But the police, let me tell you, leak. Because when she arrived with the studio lawyer, the media thronged and she was photographed looking wild in her elegant, rough dress. And then they began showing pieces of her films.

My sister was furious.

"Days and days and *days* it would have played out," she said.

"But you were going to be arrested for murder," I said.

"Oh my God," she said. "No I wasn't. I knew I didn't do it. Was she standing there the whole time in the petunias admiring my technique? The old bitch."

"But maybe Paul will go ahead with *Miss Thumb* now."

"Bet you they find it's not worth the budget. I'm not big enough yet. Oh, I miss Cage, he knew best." And she wept, but it was such pretty weeping I wasn't surprised when I saw it later on TV. Because after all they hadn't had enough of her. Not nearly.

And when I called my parents, they were so frightened by what they'd been seeing, they agreed it would be better if I stuck around to watch over her.

I rented an SUV and drove to Paul's. "You still want a garden, sir?"

"The Japanese game company are coming in as major

stockholders. Yes, I need it *now*."

"I'm your gardener," I said, and I proffered him my first business card. I walked around the side of the house and began to measure the place where we'd made love. I didn't know how to be with him, so I was brusque.

He followed. "Did you think I'd done it?"

"No," I said.

"You could have said you were asleep, didn't see me for a while, and put me in a fine fix."

"No," I said, "Don't be grateful about that. It never crossed my mind. I brought you an estimate," I said. "Just for the preliminary work. Am I hired?"

"Sure," he said. "I'll sit up here and watch you dig."

"I'll hire a crew," I said. "But I can do some private digging."

He hugged me, but he sighed.

"I love you," I said.

But he looked at me with a certain sad resignation. "Sure, baby," he said. "You love your sister."

Served Cold

by Zoë Sharp

Layla's curse, as she saw it, was that she had an utterly fabulous body attached to an instantly forgettable face. It wasn't that she was ugly. Ugliness in itself stuck in the mind. It was simply that, from the neck upwards, she was plain. A bland plainness that encouraged male and female eyes alike to slide on past without pausing. Most failed to recall her easily at a second meeting.

From the neck down, though, that was a different story, and had been right from when she'd begun to blossom in eighth grade. Things had started burgeoning over the winter, when nobody noticed the unexpected explosion of curves. But when summer came, with its bathing suits and skinny tops and tight skirts, Layla suddenly became the most whispered-about girl in her class.

A pack of the kind of boys her mother was usually too drunk to warn her about took to following her when she walked home from school. At first, Layla was flattered. But one simmering afternoon, under the banyan and the Spanish moss, she learned a brutal lesson about the kind of attention her new body attracted.

And when her mother's latest boyfriend started looking at her with those same hot lustful eyes, Layla cut and run. One way or another, she'd been running ever since.

At least the work came easy. Depending on how much she covered up, she could get anything from selling lingerie or perfume in a high-class department store, to exotic dancing. She soon learned to slip on different personae the same way she slipped on a low-cut top or a demure blouse.

Tonight she was wearing a tailored white dress shirt with frills down the front and a dinky little clip-on bow tie. Classy joint. The last time she'd worn a bow-tie to wait tables, she'd worn no top at all.

The fat guy in charge of the wait staff was called Steve and had hands to match his roving eye. That he'd seen beyond Layla's homely face was mainly because he rarely looked at his female employees above the neck. Layla had noted the way his eyes glazed and his mouth went slack and the sweat beaded at his receding hairline, and she wondered if this was another gig she was going to have to try out for on her back.

She didn't, in the end, but only, she realized, because Steve thought of himself as sophisticated. The proposition would no doubt come after. Still, Steve only let his pants rule his head so far. Enough to let Layla—and the rest of the girls—know that he'd be taking half their tips tonight. Anyone who tried to hold anything back would be out on her ass.

Layla didn't care about the tips. That wasn't why she was here, anyhow.

Now, she stood meekly with the others while Steve walked the line, checking everybody over.

"Got to look sharp out there tonight, girls," he said. "Mr. Dyer, he's a big man around here. Can't afford to let him down."

He seemed to have a thing for the name badges each girl wore pinned above her left breast. Hated it if they were crooked, and liked to straighten them out personally and take his time getting it just so. The girl next to Layla, whose name was Tammy, rolled her eyes while Steve pawed at her. Layla rolled her eyes right back.

Steve paused in front of her, frowning. "Where's your badge, honey? This one here says your name is Cindy and I *know* that ain't right." And he made sure to nudge the offending item with clammy fingers.

Layla shrugged, surprised he picked up on the deliberate swap. Her face might not stick in the mind, but she couldn't take the chance that her name might ring a bell.

"Oh, I guess it musta gotten lost," she said, all breathless and innocent. "I figured seeing as Cindy called in sick and ain't here—and none of the fancy folk out there is gonna remember my name anyhow—it don't matter."

Steve continued to frown and finger the badge for a moment, then met Layla's brazen stare and realized he'd lingered too long, even for him. With a shifty little sideways glance, he let go and stepped back. "No, it don't matter," he muttered, moving on.

Alongside her, Tammy rolled her eyes again.

Layla had the contents of her canapé tray hurriedly explained to her by one of the harassed chefs and then ducked out of the service door, along the short drab corridor, and into the main ballroom.

The glitter and the glamour set her heart racing, as it always did. For a few years, she'd dreamed of moving in these circles without a white cloth over her arm and an open bottle in her hand. And, for a time, she'd almost believed that it might be so.

Not any more.

Not since Bobby.

She reached the first cluster of dinner jackets and long dresses that probably cost more than she made in a year—just for the fabric, never mind the stitching—and waited to catch their attention. It took a while.

"Sir? Ma'am? Would you care for a canapé? Those darlin' little round ones are smoked salmon and caviar, and the square ones are Kobe beef and ginger."

She smiled, but their eyes were on the food, or they didn't think it was worth it to smile back. Just stuffed their mouths and continued braying to each other like the stuck-up donkeys they were.

Layla had done this kind of gig many times before. She knew the right pace and frequency to circulate, how often to approach the same guests before attentive turned to irritating, how to slip through the crowd without getting jostled. How to keep her mouth shut and her ears open. Steve might hint that she had to put out to get signed on again, but Layla knew she was good and he was lucky to have her.

Well, after tonight, Stevie-boy, you might just change your mind about that.

She smiled and offered the caviar and the beef, reciting the same words over and over like someone kept pulling a string at the back of her neck. She didn't need to think about it, so she thought about Bobby instead.

Bobby had been the bouncer in a roadhouse near Tallahassee. A huge guy with a lot of old scar tissue across his knuckles and around his eyes. Tale was he'd been a boxer, had a shot until he'd taken one punch too many in the ring. Then everything had gone into slow motion for Bobby and never speeded up again.

He wore a permanent scowl like he'd rip your head off and spit down your neck, as soon as look at you, but Layla quickly realized that was merely puzzlement. Bobby was slightly overmatched by the pace of life and couldn't quite work out why. Still plenty fast enough to throw out drunks in a cheap joint, though. And once Bobby had laid his fists on you, you didn't rush to get up again.

One night in the parking lot, Layla was jumped by a couple of guys who'd fallen foul of the "no touching" rule earlier in the evening and caught the rough side of Bobby's iron-hard hands. They waited, tanking up on cheap whiskey, until closing time. Waited for the lights to go out and the girls to straggle, yawning, from the back door. They grabbed Layla before she had a chance to scream, and were touching all they wanted when Bobby waded in out of nowhere. Layla had never been happier to hear the crack of skulls.

She'd been angry more than shocked and frightened—angry enough to stamp them a few times with those lethal heels once they were on the ground. Angry enough to take their overflowing billfolds, too. But it didn't last. When Bobby got her back to her rented double-wide, she shook and cried as she clung to him and begged him to help her forget. That night she discovered that Bobby was big and slow in other ways, too. And sometimes that was a real good thing.

For a while, at least.

"Ma'am? Would you care for a canapé? Smoked salmon and caviar on that side, and this right here's Kobe beef. No, thank *you*, ma'am."

Layla worked the room in a pattern she'd laid out inside her head, weaving through the crowd with the nearest thing a person could get to invisibility. It was a big fancy do, that was for sure. Some charity she'd never heard of and would never benefit from. The crowd was circulating like hot dense air through a fan, edging their way up towards the host and hostess at the far end.

The Dyers were old money and gracious with it, but firmly distant towards the staff. They knew their place and made sure the little people, like Layla, were aware of theirs. Layla didn't mind. She was used to being a nobody.

Mr. Dyer was indeed a big man, as Steve had said. A mover and shaker. He didn't need to mingle, he could just stand there, like royalty, with a glass in one hand and the other around the waist of his tall, elegant wife, looking relaxed and casual.

Well, maybe not so relaxed. Every now and again Layla noticed Dyer throw a little sideways look at their guest of honor and frown, as though he still wasn't quite sure what the guy was doing there.

Guy called Venable. Another big guy. Another mover and shaker. The difference was that Venable had clawed his way up out of the gutter and had never forgotten it. He stood close to the Dyers in his perfectly tailored tux with a kind of secret smile on his face, like he knew they didn't want him there but also knew they couldn't afford to get rid of him. But, just in case anyone thought about trying, he'd surrounded himself with four bodyguards.

Layla eyed them surreptitiously, with some concern. They were huge—bigger than Bobby, even when he'd been still standing—each wearing a bulky suit and one of those little curly wires leading up from their collar to their ear, like they was guarding the president himself. But Venable was no statesman, Layla knew for a fact.

She hadn't expected him to be invited to the Dyers' annual charity ball, and had worked hard to get herself on the staff list when she'd found out he was. A lot of planning had gone into this, one way or another.

By contrast, the Dyers had no protection. Well, unless you counted that bossy secretary of Mrs. Dyer's. Mrs. Dyer was society through and through. The type who wouldn't remember to get out of bed in the morning without a social secretary to remind her. The type whose only job is looking good and saying the right thing and being seen in the right places. There must be some kind of a college for women like that.

Mrs. Dyer had made a big show of inspecting the arrangements, though. She'd walked through the kitchen earlier that day, nodding serenely, just so her husband could toast her publicly tonight for her part in overseeing the organization of the event, and she could look all modest about it and it not quite be a lie.

She'd had the secretary with her then, a slim woman with cool eyes who'd frozen Steve off the first time he'd tried laying a proprietary hand on her shoulder. Layla and the rest of the girls hid their smiles behind bland faces when she'd done that. Even so, Steve took it out on Tammy—had her on her back in the storeroom almost before they were out the door.

The secretary was here tonight, Layla saw. Fussing around her employer, but it was Mr. Dyer whose shoulder she stayed close to. Too close, Layla decided, for their relationship to be merely professional. An affair perhaps? She wouldn't put it past any man to lose his sense and his pants when it came to an attractive woman. Still, she didn't think the secretary looked the type. Maybe he liked 'em cool. Maybe she was hoping he'd leave his wife.

At the moment, the secretary's eyes were on their guest. Venable had been free with his hosts' champagne all evening and his appetites were not concerned only with the food. Layla watched the way his body language grew predatory when he was introduced to the gauche teenage daughter of one of the guests, and she stepped in with her tray, ignoring the ominous looming of the bodyguards.

"Sir, can I interest you in a canapé? Smoked salmon and caviar or Kobe beef and ginger?"

Venable's greed got the better of him and he let go of the girl's hand, which he'd been grasping far too long. She snatched it back, red-faced, and fled. The secretary gave Layla a knowing, grateful smile.

Layla moved away quickly afterwards, a frown on her face, cursing inwardly and knowing he was watching her. She was here for a purpose. One that was too important to allow stupid mistakes like that to risk bringing her unwanted attention. And after she'd tried so hard to blend in.

To calm herself, to negate those shivers of doubt, she thought of Bobby again. They'd moved in together, found a little apartment. Not much, but the first place Layla had lived in years that didn't need the wheels taken off before you could call it home.

He'd been always gentle with Layla, but then one night he'd hit a guy who was hassling the girls too hard, hurt him real bad, and the management had to let Bobby go. Word got out and he couldn't get another job. Layla had walked out, too, but she went through a dry spell as far as work was concerned, and now there were two of them to feed and care for.

Eventually, she was forced to go lower than she'd had to go before, taking her clothes off to bad music in a cheap dive that didn't even bother to have a guy like Bobby to protect the girls. As long as the customers put their money down before they left, the management didn't care.

Layla soon discovered that some of the girls took to supplementing their income by inviting the occasional guy out into the alley at the back of the club. When the landlord came by twice in the same week threatening to evict her and Bobby, she'd swallowed her pride. By the end of that first night, that wasn't all she'd had to swallow.

Even Bobby, slow though he might be, soon realized what she was doing. How could he not question where the extra money was coming from when he'd been in the business long enough to know how much the girls made in tips—and what they had to do to earn them? At first, when she'd explained it to him, Layla thought he was cool with it. Until the next night when she was out in the alley between sets, her back hard up against the rough stucco wall with some guy from out of town huffing sweat and beer into her unremarkable face.

One minute she was standing with her eyes tight shut, wondering how much longer the guy was going to last, and the next he was yanked away and she heard that dreadful crack of skulls.

Bobby hadn't meant to kill him, she was sure of that. He just didn't know his own strength, was all. Then it was his turn to panic and tremble, but Layla stayed ice cool. They wrapped the body in plastic and put it into the trunk of a borrowed car before driving it down to the Everglades. Bobby carried it out to a pool where the 'gators gathered, and left it there for them to hide. Layla even went back a week later, just to check, but there was nothing left to find.

They stripped the guy before they dumped him, and struck lucky. He had a decent watch and a bulging wallet. It was a month before Layla had to put out against the stucco in the alley again.

How were they supposed to know he was connected to Venable? That the watch Bobby had pawned would lead Venable's bone-breakers straight to them?

A month after the killing, Venable's boys picked Bobby and Layla up from the bar and drove them out to some place by the docks. Bobby swore that Layla wasn't in on it, that they should leave her alone, let her go. Swore blind that it was so. And eventually, they blinded him, just to make sure.

Layla thought she'd never get the sound of Bobby's screaming out of her head as they'd tortured him into a confession of sorts. But even when they'd snapped his spine, left him broken and bleeding on that filthy concrete floor, Bobby had not said a word against Layla. And she, to her eternal shame, had been too terrified to confess her part in it all, as though that would make mockery of everything he'd gone through.

So, they'd left her. She was a waitress, a dancer, a hooker. A no-account nobody. Not worth the effort of a beating. Not worth the cost of a bullet.

Helpless as a baby, damaged beyond repair, Bobby went into some institution just north of Tampa and Layla took the bus up to see him every week for the first couple of months. But, gradually, getting on that bus got harder to do. It broke her heart to see him like that, to force the cheerful note into her voice.

Eventually, the bus left the terminal one morning and Layla wasn't on it.

She'd cried for days. When she'd gotten word that Bobby had snuck a knife out of the dining hall, waited until it was quiet then slit his wrists under the blankets and quietly bled out into his mattress during the night, there had been no more tears left to fall.

Layla's heart hardened to a shell. She'd let Bobby down while he was alive, but she could seek justice for him after he was dead. She heard things. That was one of the beauties of being invisible. People talked while she served them drinks, like she wasn't there. Once Layla had longed to be noticeable, to be accepted. Now she made it her business simply to listen.

Of course, she knew she couldn't go after Venable alone, so Layla had found another bruiser with no qualms about burying the bodies. And, once he'd had a taste of that spectacular body, he was hers.

Thad was younger than Bobby, sharper, neater, and when it came to killing he had the strike and the morals of a rattlesnake. Layla knew he'd do anything for her, right up until the time she tried to move on, and then he was likely to do anything *to* her instead.

Well, after tonight, she wouldn't care.

She slipped out of the ballroom but instead of turning into the kitchen, this time she took the extra few strides to the French windows at the end of the corridor, furtively opened them a crack, then closed them again carefully so they didn't latch.

By the time Layla returned to the ballroom, the canapés were not all she was holding. She'd detoured via the little cloakroom the girls had been given to change and store their bags. What she'd collected from hers she was holding flat in her right hand, hidden by the tray. A Beretta nine millimeter, hot most likely. As long as it worked, Layla didn't care.

A few moments later someone stopped by her elbow and leaned close to examine the contents of the tray.

"Well hello, *Cindy.*" A man's voice, a smile curving the sound of it. "And just what you got there, little lady?"

Thad, looking pretty nifty in the tux she'd made him rent. He bent over her tray while she explained the contents, making a big play over choosing between the caviar or the beef. And underneath, his other hand touched hers, and she slipped the Beretta into it.

"Well, thank you, sugar," he said, taking a canapé with a flourish and slipping the gun inside his jacket with his other hand, like a magician. When the hand came out again, it was holding a snowy handkerchief, which he used to wipe his fingers and dab his mouth.

Layla had made him practice the move until it seemed so natural. Shame this was a one-time show. He would have made such a partner, someone she might just have been able to live her dreams with. If only he hadn't had that cruel streak. If only he'd touched her heart the way Bobby had.

Poor crippled, blinded Bobby. Poor *dead* Bobby . . .

Ah well. Too late for regrets. Too late for much of anything, now.

Layla caught Thad's eye as she made another round and he nodded, almost imperceptibly. She nodded back, the slightest inclination of her head, and turned away. As she did so she bumped deliberately into the arm of a man who'd been recounting some fishing tale and spread his hands broadly to lie about the size of his catch. He caught Layla's tray and sent it flipping upwards. Layla caught it with the fast reflexes that came from years of waiting crowded tables amid careless diners. She managed to stop the contents crashing to the floor, but most of it ended up down the front of her blouse instead.

"Oh, I am *so* sorry, sir," she said immediately, clutching the tray to her chest to prevent further spillage.

"No problem," the man said, annoyed at having his story interrupted and oblivious to the fact it had been entirely his fault. He checked his own clothing. "No harm done."

Layla managed to raise a smile and hurried out. Steve caught her halfway.

"What happened, honey?" he demanded. "Not like you to be so clumsy."

Layla shrugged as best she could, still trying not to shed debris.

"Sorry, boss," she said. "I've got a spare blouse in my bag. I'll go change."

"Okay, sweetheart, but make it snappy." He let her move away a few strides, then called after her, "And if that's caviar you're wearing, it'll come out of your pay, y'hear?"

Layla threw him a chastised glance over her shoulder that didn't go deep enough to change her eyes, and hurried back to the little cloakroom.

She scraped the gunge off the front of her chest into the nearest trash, took off the blouse and threw that away, too, then rummaged through her bag for a clean one. This one was calculatedly lower cut and more revealing, but she didn't think Steve would object too hard, even if he caught her wearing it.

She pulled out another skirt, too, even though there was nothing wrong with her old one. This was shorter than the last, showing several inches of long smooth thigh below the hem and, without undue vanity, she knew it would drag male eyes downwards, even as her newly exposed cleavage would drag them up again. With any luck, they'd go cross-eyed trying to look both places at once.

She swapped her false name badge over and took the cheap Makarov nine millimeter and a roll of duct tape out of her bag. She lifted one remarkable leg up onto the wooden bench and ran the duct tape around the top of her thigh, twice, to hold the nine in position, just out of sight. The pistol grip pointed downwards and she knew from hours in front of the mirror that she could yank the gun loose in a second.

She'd bought both pistols from a crooked military surplus dealer down near Miramar. Thad insisted on coming with her for the Beretta, had made a big thing about checking the gun over like he knew what he was doing, sighting along the barrel with one eye closed.

Layla had gone back later for the Makarov. She didn't have enough money for the two, but she'd been dressed to thrill and she and the dealer had come to an arrangement that hadn't cost Layla anything at all. Only pride, and she'd been way overdrawn on that account for years.

Now, Layla checked in the cracked mirror that the gun didn't show beneath her skirt. Her face was even more bland in its pallor and, just for once, she wished she'd been born pretty. Not beautiful, just pretty enough to have been cherished.

The way she'd cherished Bobby. The way he'd cherished her.

She left the locker room and collected a fresh tray from the kitchen. The chefs were under pressure, the activity frantic, but when she walked in on those long dancer's legs there was a moment of silence that was almost reverent.

"You changed your clothes," one of the chefs said, mesmerised.

She smiled at him, saw the fog lift a little as the disappointment of her face cut through the haze of lust created by her body.

"I spilled," she said, collecting a fresh tray. She felt every eye on her as she walked out, smiled when she heard the collective sigh as the door swung closed behind her.

It was a short-lived smile.

Back in the ballroom, it was all she could do not to go marching straight up to Venable, but she knew she had to play it cool. The four bodyguards were too experienced not to spot her sudden surge of guilt and anger. They'd pick her out of the crowd the way a shark cuts out a weakling seal pup. And she couldn't afford that. Not yet.

Instead, she forced herself to think bland thoughts as she circled the room towards him. Saw out of the corner of her eye Thad casually moving up on the other side. The relief flooded her, sending her limbs almost lax with it. For a second, she'd been afraid he wouldn't go through with it. That he'd realize what her real plan was, and back out at the last minute.

For the moment, though, Thad must think it was all going according to plan. She stepped up to the Dyers, offered them something from her tray. The secretary still hadn't left his side, she saw. The girl must be desperate.

Layla took another step, sideways towards Venable, ducking around the cordon of bodyguards. Offered him something from her tray. And this time, as he leaned forwards, so did she, pressing her arms together to accentuate what nature had so generously given her.

She watched Venable's eyes go glassy, saw the way the eyes of the nearest two bodyguards bulged the same way. There was another just behind her, she knew, and she bent a little further from the waist, knowing she was giving him a prime view of her ass and the back of her newly-exposed thighs. She could almost feel that hot little gaze slavering up the backs of her knees.

Come on, Thad . . .

He came pushing through the crowd nearest to Venable, moving too fast. If he'd been slower, he might have made it. As it was, he was the only guy for twenty feet in any direction who didn't have his eyes full of Layla's divine body. Venable's eyes snapped round at the last moment, jerky, panicking as he realized the rapidly approaching threat. He flailed, sending Layla's tray crashing to the ground, showering canapés.

The bodyguards were slower off the mark. Thad already had the gun out before two of them grabbed him. Not so much grabbed as piled in on top of him, driving him off his legs and down, using fists and feet to keep him there.

Thad was no easy meat, though. He kept in shape and had come up from the streets, where unfair fights were part of the game. Even on the floor, he lashed out, aiming for knees and shins, hitting more than he was missing. A third bodyguard joined in to keep him down, a leather sap appearing like magic in his hand.

There was that familiar crack of skulls. *Just like Bobby . . .*

Layla winced, but she couldn't let that distract her now. Her mind strangely cool and calm, Layla stepped in, ignored. The fourth bodyguard had stayed at his post, but Layla was shielded from his view by his own principal, and everyone's attention was on the fight. Carefully, she reached under her skirt and yanked the Makarov free, unaware of the brief burn as the tape ripped from her thigh.

The safety was already off, the hammer back. The Army surplus guy down in Miramar had thrown in a little instruction as well. Gave him more of a chance to stand up real close behind her as he demonstrated how to hold the unfamiliar gun, how to aim and fire.

She brought the nine up the way he'd shown her, both hands clasped round the pistol grip, starting to take up the pressure on the trigger, she bent her knees and crouched a little, so the recoil wouldn't send the barrel rising, just in case she had to take a second shot. But, this close, she knew she wouldn't need one, even if she got the chance.

One thing Layla hadn't been ready for was the noise. The report was monstrously loud in the high-ceilinged ballroom. And though she thought she'd been prepared, she staggered back and to the side. And the pain. The pain was a gigantic fist around her heart, squeezing until she couldn't breathe.

She looked up, vision starting to shimmer, and saw Venable was still standing, shocked but apparently unharmed. How had she missed? The bodyguard had come out of his lethargy to throw himself on top of his employer, but there was still an open window. There was still time . . .

Layla tried to lift the gun but her arms were leaden. Something hit her, hard, in the centre of her voluptuous chest, but she didn't see what it was, or who threw it. She frowned, took a step back and her legs folded, and suddenly she was staring up at the chandeliers on the ceiling and she had to hold on to the polished wooden dance floor beneath her hands to stay there. Her vision was starting to blacken at the edges, like burning paper, the sound blurring down.

The last thing she saw was the slim woman she'd taken for a secretary, leaning over her with a wisp of smoke rising from the muzzle of the nine millimeter she was holding.

Then the bright lights, and the glitter, all faded to black.

The woman Layla had mistaken for a secretary placed two fingers against the pulse point in the waitress's throat and felt nothing. She knew better than to touch the body more than she had to now, even to close the dead woman's eyes.

Cindy, the name tag read, even under the trickle of the blood. She doubted that would match the woman's driver's license.

She rose, sliding the SIG semiautomatic back into the concealed-carry rig on her belt. Two of Venable's meaty goons wrestled the woman's accomplice, bellowing, out of the room. She turned to her employer.

"I don't think you were the target, Mr. Dyer, but I couldn't take the chance," she said calmly. She jerked her head towards the bodyguards. "If this lot had been halfway capable, I wouldn't have had to get involved. As it was . . . "

Dyer nodded. He still had his arms wrapped round his wife, who was sobbing, and his eyes were sad and tired.

"Thank you," he said quietly.

The woman shrugged. "It's my job," she said.

"Who the hell are you?" It was Venable himself who spoke, elbowing his way out from the protective shield that his remaining bodyguards had belatedly thrown around him.

"This is Charlie Fox," Dyer answered for her, the faintest smile in his voice. "She's *my* personal protection. A little more subtle than your own choice. She's good, isn't she?"

Venable stared at him blankly, then at the dead woman, lying crumpled on the polished planks. At the unfired gun that had fallen from her hand.

"You saved my life," he murmured, his face pale.

Charlie stared back at him. "Yes," she said, sounding almost regretful. "Whether it was worth saving is quite another point. What had you done to her that she was prepared to kill you for it?"

Venable seemed not to hear. He couldn't take his eyes off Layla's body. Something about her was familiar, but he just couldn't remember her face.

"I don't know—nothing," he said, cleared his throat of its hoarseness and tried again. "She's a nobody. Just a waitress." He took another look, just to be sure. "Just a woman."

"Oh, I don't know," Dyer said, and his eyes were on Charlie Fox. "From where I'm standing, she's a hell of a woman, wouldn't you say?"

Housewives, Madonnas and Girls Next Door

The Chirashi Covenant

by Naomi Hirahara

There were Alice Watanabe's deviled eggs, lined up in diagonal lines on her white ceramic serving plate, Betty Shoda's potato salad mixed in with a smidge of her secret ingredient, *wasabi*, and Dorothy Takeyama's ambrosia, peeled orange slices with coconut flakes.

Next to the hostess's ham was a wedge of iceberg lettuce with Green Goddess dressing dripping from the sides. Not a surprise—Sets Kamimura hated to cook and always took the lazy way out. The rest of the women knew this but would never say anything to Sets, even in jest.

And finally, in a huge round lacquerware container was Helen Miura's *chirashi*. The women were amazed by Helen's handiwork. Each piece of vegetable–carrot, *shiitake* mushroom, burdock root–was uniformly cut and mixed in with the rice like scattered tiny leaves and twigs blown by the Santa Ana winds. Others may have used a grater or a Japanese *daikon suri*, but Helen was a master with the knife. Her father had been a fisherman in Terminal Island before the war and Helen, being the oldest, was in charge of cleaning the catch he brought home for dinner. Her mother worked in the tuna cannery, so Helen was destined to get things done.

In the ice box was a vanilla cake, which had been purchased at a Japanese-American bakery on Jefferson Boulevard in the Crenshaw area of Los Angeles. Written in thick pastel icing were the words, "Japanese-American Court Reunion" and below "10-Year Anniversary."

In 1941, these seven women had ridden on a float in a parade down the streets of Little Tokyo. Yoshiko Kumai, who was hosting the reunion, had been the queen, but everyone knew that Helen was the most beautiful one of them all. Even today, with her thin frame despite having a baby girl two years ago and her long legs, she captured second looks from men of every color and income bracket.

But what Helen lacked was charm. She didn't smile easily; even in the all the photos with the rest of the court she never showed her teeth. Helen and Yoshiko, both twenty year olds at the time, stood together at the Yamato Hall in Little Tokyo, waiting for the winner's name to be called. Yoshiko groped for Helen's hand, her own hand moist and warm. Helen's hand remained limp and cool, and when Yoshiko squeezed, Helen did not reciprocate.

Even though Helen hadn't won the 1941 beauty contest, she had won life's competition so far. She had married Frank, probably the most eligible Nisei man in the Manzanar War Relocation Center. By all counts, the insurance company he had started for the resettled Japanese Americans was headed for success.

"I just don't know how you do it, Helen," said Alice. "I'm always embarrassed to make *chirashi*, because I know how beautiful yours comes out."

"It's nothing, really. Just a lot of chopping and cutting. You need to start off with a good knife."

The conversation then quickly turned to children and the Japanese American women's club that three of them belonged to. While the women giggled and laughed, Helen grew more distant.

"I'll be right back," she excused herself, taking her clutch purse with her.

When Helen was nearly out the back door, Sets pressed two fingers to her mouth and then mimed blowing smoke from her lips. "Ta-ba-co," she commented to the others, with a wink.

* * *

Helen took a package of cigarettes from her purse. She had started smoking just recently. Frank didn't approve, of course, and his mother had been aghast to find her smoking in the backyard of their rented Boyle Heights wood-framed house. No matter how much Frank and his mother commented on her smoking, Helen refused to give it up. She needed something of her own.

"Hello." On the other side of the low fence stood a *hakujin* man in a suit. He was clean-cut and handsome with a large open forehead. A William Holden type.

Helen lit a cigarette with a lighter she had purchased in a department store in Little Tokyo.

A young white couple emerged from the back door of the next door neighbor's house. The woman was visibly pregnant. "We love it, Bob. It's perfect," she said. They then noticed Helen on the other side of the fence. Helen could feel their enthusiasm wane immediately.

"You'll love the neighbors," the man who had greeted Helen said enthusiastically. Almost like he meant it. "Ken was in the U.S. Army, fought over in both Italy and France, I think. Works for the city as a draftsman. He and Yoshiko have two children. They're good people. Go to a congregational church not far from here."

"That's nice," the pregnant woman said weakly. She was disappointed, Helen could tell. Her picture-perfect world was shattered. Helen knew what that felt like.

"Don't worry," Helen spoke up. "There's not too many of us living on this block. Give us ten years, it might be a different story. But you will have moved out by then."

The couple exchanged glances and looked down at the lawn. "Well," the pregnant woman said a little too brightly, "let's take another look at the laundry room." The couple surveyed the backyard wistfully, as if saying goodbye for good before returning to the inside of the house. The man in the suit remained outside.

"I think that I might have cost you a sale," Helen said without any regret.

"Well, good riddance, then. Ken and Yoshiko are good people. Anyone would be lucky to have them or any of their friends as neighbors."

Helen was surprised. She had expected to be met with anger.

"Bob Burkard." The man walked to the low fence and stuck out his hand. Helen hesitated. She moved her lit cigarette from her right hand to her left to better shake hands. She murmured back her name.

"Are you in the market for a new home?"

"What do you mean?"

"You look hungry for a new house." The agent then laughed. "I can tell these things. In my job, you need to be observant." Frank had said the same thing in his line of work. He was constantly selling, but in a comfortable, non-threatening way. Usually by the end of his sales pitch, his customers thought it was they who had approached him for insurance.

"Not here," Helen said. Not Montebello, a few cities east from where they lived now. Montebello was a growing suburb, but it was inland. Helen hated to be landlocked.

"Where, then?"

"The ocean."

"Ocean? Do you mean Sawtelle?"

Helen almost burst out laughing. Alice Watanabe had represented the Sawtelle area in their beauty pageant. Unincorporated, it drew a cluster of Japanese-American nurseries and small shops just a stone's throw away from the Veteran's Administration Hospital.

"Not Sawtelle. Pacific Palisades. Malibu. Right by the ocean."

The agent didn't even blink. Helen was impressed.

"I grew up near the water," she offered up more.

"Where?"

"Terminal Island."

"The military base?"

"It wasn't always the military's."

Helen snuffed out her cigarette on the Kumais' cement patio floor and turned to go back inside.

"Wait," Bob called out.

Helen took a few steps into the soft grass again, restaining the pointy heels of her pumps.

Bob handed Helen his business card. "Call me at my office. We'll see what we can do."

* * *

Helen had told Frank her dream to live in Pacific Palisades months ago.

"Dear," he said, refolding the Japanese-American newspaper that was delivered to their rented house every afternoon. "That's impossible."

"They can't keep us away. Not anymore, right?" Helen readjusted the embroidered doily on the middle of their dining room table.

"It doesn't matter what the Supreme Court says. Remember what happened to the Uchidas in South Pasadena—they had to be interviewed by all the neighbors. Do you want to go through that? Get their seal of approval? I don't want to be where I'm not wanted."

"Who cares what they want? How about what we want?"

"It's too far. I need to be around Japanese people. They are my customer base, our livelihood. Someplace like Gardena is a better bet for us. And what would Mama do in Pacific Palisades? She needs to be close to Japanese people, too."

Helen said nothing. She went outside and smoked two cigarettes right below her mother-in-law's bedroom window.

* * *

Helen had absolutely not wanted to get married in camp. She hated the idea of being imprisoned with other Japanese Americans on her wedding day. Frank's bachelor friends had agreed to move out of their barracks so that the newlyweds could have a proper honeymoon night, but Helen refused to go along with it. If Frank insisted that they get married in Manzanar's mess hall with tissue paper flowers, Helen would force him to spend their first night together in a bumpy mattress next to his widowed mother's, only separated by some hanging wool blankets.

"We need to get out of here," she told Frank. "Let's apply for special clearance." She brought back bulletins about work in Detroit and Chicago.

But the answer was always the same. "What about Mama? At least in camp she has her friends nearby."

Helen thought everything would have changed when Japanese Americans were allowed to move back to the West Coast in early 1945. But Mama would live with them and they had to be close to Little Tokyo.

Then came the birth of Diana. When Helen looked down at

her perfectly formed daughter, this mini-human being that both she and Frank had created, Helen knew that she had a renewed purpose in life.

"I won't let anything happen to you," she had whispered in her daughter's ear. "You will have everything life has to offer."

* * *

Despite their earlier conversations, Helen told Frank that she was going to be looking for a new house. Frank was busy with work after all. "You should use Jun. I have his office phone number somewhere." He rifled through the layers of paper on his desk in the corner of the living room.

"There's an agent I met through Yoshiko," Helen said. "I think I'd rather use him."

Frank shrugged his shoulders. "Just don't sign anything."

The next day Helen kissed Diana's forehead and left for Bob Burkard's office in Montebello. Bob's hair seemed freshly combed and the scent of his cologne was so strong that it tickled Helen's nose.

They drove in his new Studebaker towards the beach.

"Who's watching your daughter?" he asked.

"My mother-in-law."

He showed Helen two homes and then drove her back to his office. This routine continued for four days straight.

On the fifth day, Bob parked his car in a dirt lot overlooking the ocean. "I brought us lunch," he said, taking out a blanket and picnic basket from his trunk.

Helen thought it was strange for a bachelor to own a picnic basket. "You've never married?" she couldn't help but to ask him after eating one of his egg salad sandwiches.

"Came close," he said. "It's just taken me some time to meet the right woman."

"So you're picky."

"And what's wrong with that? It's the rest of your life, right? You want to get that right."

Tears came to Helen's eyes. She knew that she was being silly.

"What did I say?" Bob became flustered and fished a handkerchief from the breast pocket of his suit. "I'm so sorry. I didn't mean anything by it." Before Helen could stop him, he was wiping her tears with his handkerchief. He then rested his hand on her cheek. "You are a remarkably beautiful woman. Do you know that, Helen?" With that, he kissed her. Helen had never been kissed by a white man before.

On their silent drive home, all Helen could think about was, *what have I done?*

* * *

The picnics continued the next day and then the next. Bob's kisses quickly moved from her mouth to her neck, down to her breasts and beyond. Helen knew what she was doing was wrong. That she would be punished someday.

"*Hausu sagashi*? Mama asked when she returned from one of her expeditions with Bob.

"Yes, house hunting," said Helen, feeling grains of sand in her panties.

"Really," she said in Japanese, not looking convinced of it at all.

* * *

Helen wasn't sure if Mama had spoken to Frank about her long hours away from the house and their daughter. Frank, for all his earnestness, wasn't the type to deal with a problem directly. Instead he usually found a solution through a side door.

"I found it," Frank reported one evening upon returning home. "A beautiful house. It's in Gardena, but southern Gardena. Not that far from the ocean, and when you breathe hard, you can smell salt air, really."

Frank even had a photo of the property. A single-story wood framed house, which didn't look that different from the property they were renting.

"What are those?"

"Oil derricks. But you can pretend that they are towers. The Eiffel Tower."

In the past, Helen would have been amused by her husband's fancifulness.

"So, what do you think?"

Gardena was at least thirty miles away from Bob's office, even further from their spot in Malibu. Helen said nothing.

"You'll love it, dear. Really. It'll grow on you."

* * *

"I'm moving to Gardena. Frank's bought a house," Helen told Bob over the phone while Mama was bathing Diana.

"Gardena?"

Helen nodded. "I won't be able to see you anymore."

"Why?"

"I can't be driving all the way to Montebello. Diana will be ready to go to school soon. I need to spent more time with her."

"Well, then, I'll find us a meeting place down there."

"In Gardena?" Both Helen and Bob knew very few secrets could be hidden there.

"Listen, I've found the perfect house for you in Malibu. It's just come out on the market."

"It's too late, Bob."

"It's never too late. I'll show it to him. He can always sell the Gardena house. He'll fall in love with it, really."

"But why? It's not like I'll be able to see you in Malibu much."

"I want you to be happy."

Bob was being ridiculous, and Helen was angry that he couldn't accept the inevitable. Their affair couldn't last. Diana was getting fussy from her long hours away from her mother. Helen had to bury her feelings. She had practice, but obviously *gaman*, perseverance, was a new concept for Bob.

That Thursday evening, Frank didn't come home for dinner. He hadn't called and Helen was becoming worried. She called Frank's secretary at home and was told that he was meeting a real estate agent on the westside of town.

At nine o'clock, the phone rang. "Is this Mrs. Frank Miura?" A male voice that Helen didn't recognize.

"Yes."

"This is the sherriff's department. There's been an accident."

* * *

Helen was surprised that Frank's mother wanted to come with her to the coroner's office. Helen told her to stay with Diana. "Mama, it will be better if you stay behind."

"This is your fault," Mama said in Japanese.

Helen's legs had been shaky to begin with, but now she felt like her knees would buckle underneath her.

"You told him that you wanted to move near the water. He only wanted to make you happy."

* * *

The coroner had warned Helen that she might not recognize her husband. His body had been severely battered from the rocks. It had been fifty-foot drop, after all.

His neck was twisted; his beautiful face now raw and torn. Helen thought that his nose was missing, but she saw that it was instead flattened into a pulpy mass.

His ears were still intact, and Helen checked behind his left earlobe, and sure enough, his mole was there. She studied his hands. His fingers were stiff but his nails were still well manicured, a little squarish at the top.

It was definitely Frank.

Later a police officer sat down with her and asked Helen what her husband was doing on a cliff in Malibu.

"I'm not sure. His secretary told me that he was there to look at a house. A new house that we were thinking of buying." Helen's voice shook. Should she mention Bob? She wasn't sure it had been Bob. But it had to be him.

"Yes, we found the address in his pocket. The real estate agent, in fact, was the one who discovered your husband's body. Do you know a man named Bob Burkard?"

* * *

The police car parked in front of their rented house and Helen got out, her hands still trembling.

She thanked the officer, and the car slowly disappeared down the street. Before she got to the stairs, someone pulled at her arm.

"How dare you come here?" Helen said to Bob.

He pulled her into some pine trees framing the side of the house.

"You killed him," she declared.

Bob shook his head. "I didn't even make it on time for our appointment. He had fallen by the time I had arrived. I was the one who called the police."

"I'm going to tell the police about us." Helen was ashamed that she had not been more revealing during the police interview. All she mentioned was that Bob had been their agent. Purely business.

"That we were having an affair? What do you think that will do to your daughter? People will talk. You'll be implicated, you know."

Bob was right. Tongues would wag. Helen Miura was having an adulterous affair with a white man. Diana would be shunned by the parents of her peers. Her family shamed. And if something happened to Helen, who would take care of Diana? Mama couldn't do it on her own. Helen's parents were too old, and Helen's siblings had their own children to raise. Helen knew what it was liked to be one of many. She didn't want that to happen to her Diana.

"I'll wait for you. Even a year. In respect of your husband's death."

Respect? Helen felt like screaming, tearing Bob's hair out. *I know what you have done.* She wanted to spit in his face, but she used all her rage to manage a slight smile on her lips.

* * *

That night Helen lay in their double bed by herself. The doctor at the Japanese hospital had dropped by some sleeping medicine for Helen. Something to stir into hot water. But Helen didn't want to sleep. She didn't deserve to sleep.

Helen reached out for the crumpled sheets Frank had slept in the night before. She planned to never wash them. Instead she would save them in a box so that she could periodically go and smell her late husband.

She wrapped the sheets around her legs and stared at Frank's pillow. There were a few loose hairs coated with oil.

She felt now that Frank, in his death, could see everything. He could see her deception, the romantic trysts in Bob's car and on the beach.

"I'm so sorry, Frank," she whispered. And then she knew what she had to do.

* * *

Helen's parents had an old family friend, Kaji-*san*. Kaji-san, a Japanese immigrant like Helen's father, had been a fisherman as well. He was *rambo*, rough. A lot of Terminal Islanders had been that way, cured in the sun and salt water. But Kaji-*san* not only had callused hands but a callused face, dried up crevices like earthquake faults.

After the war, Helen's relatives had taken the old bachelor for a while before he got back on his feet and opened a Japanese restaurant in Little Tokyo. To everyone's surprise, Kaji-*san* succeeded and before long, he had even purchased a boat that was docked at Pierpoint Landing in Long Beach.

Kaji-*san* felt indebted to Helen's family, so much so that they even stopped going to his restaurant because he never took their money. But Helen needed a favor now, and Kaji-*san* was, of course, more than willing to comply. Deep down inside, he had questions and concerns. Helen had lost some weight—she was thin to begin with, but now her high cheekbones were even more prominent and defined. Frank's death had definitely taken a toll on her, but Kaji-*san* knew that Helen would never do anything rash. She wasn't that type of woman.

Helen arrived at the empty restaurant three hours before her appointment and let herself in the back with Kaji-*san*'s key. She needed the extra time to get ready.

Bob came early, too, fifteen minutes early. Helen could tell from the flush in his cheeks that he was excited. She even let him give her a peck on her cheek. That much she could tolerate.

Helen had him sit at the wooden counter and served him a piping hot cup of green tea.

"I've never had green tea before." He sipped carefully and then grimaced. "Bitter."

"You'll get used to it. This tea is expensive; you'll insult me if you don't finish it."

By the time the teacup was empty, Bob's head rested on the wooden counter. Helen went to the kitchen and put on her rubber gloves. And then rolled out the wheelbarrow.

One time she had been out on the fishing boat when her father had caught a bluefin tuna. It had been a magnificent fish, almost six feet tall, almost three hundred pounds. It took three men to handle the fish. The fish first needed to be stunned. Helen's father used one of her brother's baseball bats. This time Helen used Frank's.

The fishermen found the soft spot in the fish's head and then pushed a spike in its brain. Helen was amazed how easy it was to kill a huge fish like that. It shuddered as if it was hoping for another chance for life and then became limp.

There was a method to cutting a bluefin tuna. You first needed some time to bleed the fish so that its sheen would still be maintained. And then go right to the internal organs in the gilling and gutting of the fish. Later you would cut the fish's meat into chunks and sell them by the pound.

Helen could skip many of the steps she had learned as a child. The most important tools here were the knife and the mallet. She was thankful some family friends had watched over her father's tools while they had been in Manzanar.

After Helen was done, she carefully packed different parts of Bob in three different suitcases and cleaned the cement floor of Kaji-*san*'s kitchen. She had brought extra bottles of bleach for the task. She then drove to Pierpoint Landing and took Kaji-*san*'s motorized fishing boat as far as she could, and dropped each suitcase into different parts of the ocean. The water was black as the ink of an octopus, and for a moment, Helen imagined a huge sea monster emerging from the darkness and tearing her, too, into shreds. But her mind was only playing tricks on her. After closing her eyes hard and reopening them, she found that her fear had disappeared.

* * *

Shortly thereafter, Helen, Diana and Mama moved into

the wood-framed house in southern Gardena. Next door was a flower farm and packing shed.

"That Miura widow is a cold one," the flower grower's wife said to her husband as they were bunching up flowers at night to get ready for the two o'clock morning drive to the Flower Market in Los Angeles.

The flower grower, Tad, just nodded, so that his wife would be under the impression that he was listening.

"Never says hello. She was on one of those beauty queen courts back in 1941. But she wasn't the queen. Too stuck-up for the judges, I think."

Tad grunted. He wasn't one to spread stories. But he knew who she was. One day when he was driving back from the flower market in the morning after the children went to school, he saw her in the middle of his snapdragon blooms, next to one of the oil derricks. She was screaming and crying; at first he thought that she had been injured. When he slowed his panel truck, she straightened her hair and rubbed the smeared makeup from below her eyes.

"You okay?" he asked from his open car window.

She stared back at him, her eyes shiny like wet black stones. She then spoke, her voice barely audible above the rhythmic squeak of the derricks. "Are any of us?"

Tad's panel truck remained idling as the widow slowly walked back into her house and closed the door.

The Token Booth Clerk

by Sara Gran

People come by all day and it's *two tokens, one card, gimmie one, buzz me through the gate.* Sometimes they don't say anything at all, just push their money through the slot and grunt and wait for me to push their tokens out from the other side.

It ain't any better at home. Next door are Mr. and Mrs. Kawalski. They're why I need ear plugs. Every night and every morning a fight. Two or three o'clock at night he comes home drunk, there's one fight. At seven in the morning she's got to get him up for work, and there's another one.

The couple on the other side are just as bad. Young. They've got two cats who cry all the time like babies. They say hello, goodbye, how are you doing. They cook. Once I found one of their stupid cats wandering on the stairs, and when I brought it back the girl was so grateful she gave me a little hug and asked me in for a cup of coffee. I said I had to go to work or something. That night I got home and there was a bottle of Scotch, all wrapped up in fancy paper, sitting in front of my door with a card that said thank you for saving our precious kitty or some bullshit. The Scotch tasted good, though.

Your grocer, the guy you buy your cigarettes from, the waitress who served your breakfast, the schmuck who did your taxes —they all come down to take the subway. And not one of them knows they've seen you before. One of the guys, a black guy on the night shift, a real loudmouth, he told me once his own mother-in-law came down and didn't even say a word. No one sees you, no one says hello, which is probably for the best. Because as soon as one of them does start talking about the weather or their government check that's late or the doctor's office they're going to, you just grit your teeth and wish to God you could have another grunter.

After the thing with her cat, though, the girl next door recognized me in the booth, for the first time, and after that she always stopped to yap away like we were best friends. She used to take the bus to her old job, but now she's got this new job, which is great and so super and really very fulfilling, and she can take the train, which she likes so much better, because when it rains who wants to wait for a bus, and yap yap yap yap yap. Even when she had a weekly card and didn't need to come to the booth she made a big production of waving and saying hello.

One night I wake up because there's screaming so loud, it must have woken up every schmuck in the building. At first I figure it's the drunks next door and I put a pillow over my head, the ear plugs are already in, but it doesn't let up, it gets louder, and it's different than usual this time.

It was the couple on the other side.

All kinds of high pitched shrieks and crying, and then the door SLAMS and she's running down the stairs in shoes with wood heels. The shoes echo in the halls and I hear them for days.

The next night, even with my frozen food in front of the television, I knew something was different, and it was different for good. She wasn't coming back. No cats crying. No cooking sounds, no cooking smells. Just the TV, and the smell of something burned in a microwave oven.

It's not like I missed her. It was nice to go to my booth and not have to wave back at her stupid little wave and to come home and not have to answer *Oh how* are *you* in the hallway. After a few days went by with no waves, no smiles, no crying cats, I started to think about it. About how happy I was she was gone. How nice it all was, and where she might be now, who she might be bothering now. I thought I remembered her saying that they, she and the guy she lived with, had just moved here, and her family was all still back in . . . Missouri? Mississippi? Montana?

A week went by and I saw the guy, her boyfriend or husband or whatever. He was still living next door, and he looked so down, with circles under his eyes—I was going to ask him and then I didn't even want to bring it up. We just grunted, and I saw it all pretty clear; without her, he was just another grunter. So at least now I wouldn't have to make bullshit conversation with him in the hallways, either.

Well, it was all better without her, no question there. Where had said she was from? Tennessee? Tallahassee? Toronto? Now of course she could have gone back there, wherever it was, but I didn't think so. Not after all that talk about her *wonderful* new job that was *just* what she had always dreamed of. I couldn't imagine her going back home after that.

And so I was thinking about her a lot. Thinking how good it was to have the building back the way it had always been, just the Kawalskis screaming at night, no home-cooked-meal smells coming from next door, no fucking kittens crying all night. It was just like it had always been. Except you wonder. In this city, nine million people, eight and a half million of them out to take something from you, you start to wonder. As little as you have, maybe it's a penny—well, there's eight and a half million motherfuckers out there who want that penny.

That was the problem. All those people after her pennies, and her being such an idiot—I would go home at night, and it was like every sound I heard, it wasn't her, and every smell I smelled, it wasn't her. Until everything wasn't her, and that was all it was: not her.

We have these days. They're called personal days. It's like sick days, but you don't have to pretend to be sick to use them. I had some days coming so on Sunday night I called in personal and I packed up a few bottles of soda and some sandwiches and I got on the train. I figured the train was a good bet because once in her yapping she let out that only one train, the L, goes to where she works, and no bus, so even if she was someplace else in the city, at some point she'd be transferring to the L to get to work.

For three days I rode the train. Of course, I got off from time to time to use the men's rooms in the station, but I didn't want to leave too long. Out to Rockaway, in to Eighth Avenue and back. Five times a day.

Halfway through the first day I realized, I had to come up with a system. If I stayed on one car the whole time it wouldn't get me anywhere, because she could easily be one car over and I wouldn't know. I had to get the whole train covered at least once, better twice, before we got to the stop where her job was. But it didn't make any sense running up and down the train the whole time either. First of all, I'd tire myself out too easily. Worse, it would always seem like the second I left one car she'd get on it, and I'd be wasting my time. So the system I came up with was this; walking around slowly, taking it easy, from the end of the line until close to her work. Then, the two stops before her work, I'd try to cover the whole train. One stop would have been better, but it wasn't enough time for the whole train.

Sometimes I switched trains, breaking the system, thinking she was on the train just behind me. Always thinking she was on the train just behind me. It wasn't very likely to see her at three, four, five in the morning, but the train runs all night and I wasn't sure what kind of work she did; nurses, doctors, waitresses, even some kinds of secretaries, which I thought she was, work at night sometimes, or maybe since she was alone now she'd be going out at night. So there was no use in taking any chances.

I thought I saw her everywhere. Every time I saw hair that color or shoulders that size I'd go over to take a look, but it wasn't her. It was never her. But so many of them could have been her. And it was like every fucking con artist on the train was looking for her too, but if they couldn't find her, they'd settle for one of these other girls. I would imagine a man like that finding her and I would know she was on the train somewhere. I would just know it. But the whole fucking train would be full of people who weren't her. And then I would be sure that now she was in the car I had just left, so I would rush back and still, it wouldn't be her.

Until it was. Towards the beginning of the fourth day I got off to use the men's room. It was the last stop I would have expected to see her, a low-down neighborhood way on the West Side. She was just leaving through the turnstile and I only saw her from behind, just for a second. It was a little after nine o'clock and there was still the late rush hour crowd. But this time I was sure it wasn't my imagination this time. It felt different. I was sure.

I caught up with her at the top of the stairs, almost at the street. I hadn't seen the sun for three days and it was brighter than I remembered.

"H—hello." My voice cracked. I hadn't used it for a while.

She turned around. She looked the same except there was a little something new around her eyes that I didn't like at all. She looked older. She looked kind of tired.

It took her a minute to place me, and she smiled, just like we were best fucking friends or something, just like she used to. "Oh, *hi*! How are you? Are you working over here now?"

I didn't know what to say, so I nodded. "Just for today. It's a temporary—I'm filling in for another guy." I let myself think for a minute. "You don't live in the building anymore?"

She shook her head, still smiling, still smiling, but her face was all different. "No, I moved out. I'm in Midtown now. I've got a studio, it's a fortune, but it's great to be in the city again."

"You like it there?" I asked. "In your new place? You're, you know, happy and everything?"

She nodded and opened her eyes wide. "Oh yes. Everything's great, actually. I switched jobs, too—again! Well, not yet, but next month. I'm going to be working from home, freelancing."

"Oh." I didn't know what that meant.

"How have you been?" she asked.

"Me? I'm okay. Can't complain," I answered. "So everything's good?"

She nodded again, still smiling, and now that something was gone from around her eyes and her face was just like it used to be. Just stupid and happy and eager like an animal. When I saw that, it was like things fell into place. Like a piece had been fit into a jigsaw puzzle or I'd put a check in the bank or I'd just eaten a steak dinner. It was like things were the way they were supposed to be. As bad as they were, at least they were in place, the way they were supposed to be.

"Okay," I said, and I smiled too. "Well, you be careful. You be careful."

"Okay," she said. "I promise, I will."

I went home, and I never saw her again.

The Big O

by Vicki Hendricks

My ass was tired of driving, and I welcomed the sight of the dented, mildewed trailers on the east side of Lake Okeechobee. Miles of trailer parks with single- and double-wides stretched down the road on the side by the lake, a few of them tidy, landscaped Florida retirement villages, but discarded refrigerators and broken down cars were the landmarks of my interest. I needed the worst rubble-strewn lot and the cheapest tin can I could find.

Some months earlier, Merle and me had made a Sunday drive up from Miami to check out what we figured was an affordable lakeside resort. When he saw the layout, Merle said he'd rather pitch a tent in the Everglades, but I took note. It was a place where anybody could get lost, and I had it in the back of my head that I might need to do that soon.

It only took me a few months to stash some bucks and finance an old car. I'd managed to dodge the punch the night before and lock myself in the bathroom till Merle passed out. It wouldn't be the first time I'd left a man, far from it, and usually for less reason than I had now. My threats had lost all effect in the three years Merle and me'd been together, and I didn't want Chance toddling around a household like that.

I knew it would be rough. My dreams of making it as a fashion model were all dried up, and I lived for the nights, the high I could depend on with Merle, alcohol, drugs, and sweaty rough sex. Yeah, I'd miss 'em. They were my only relief from the boredom and bad luck that were all life ever had to offer. It took discipline to keep pushing Merle's appetite for my pussy out of my mind. He was hot shit. But I was determined. I had dreams for Chance—his name was no accident. He was the possibility for me to redeem my luckless life. I had to break out of my old habits before he was old enough to absorb his asshole father's anger into his sweet baby brain.

I was in my area, trashy trailer parks scratching bottom. Splintered wood, dead palm fronds, tarpaper, shingles and scrap metal waited for pickup, mounds of trash sprawling over the properties. Last year's hurricane litter would soon be this year's projectiles, crashing through windows, killing people. Not that I cared about people in general, just Chance. I reached behind me and stroked his soft little foot.

Hell, if it was my trash, I'd have just left it there too. That's the way I was, always dragging my ass, till teeth were in it. I couldn't say shit about anybody else. I fit right in.

I drove down the strip, reading names that would've been attractive if I'd seen them in the Yellow Pages. Lakeside Haven, Quiet Waters Retreat, Jenny's Big O Fish Camp, Water's Edge RV—sure, there was water, a canal that flowed behind the trailers, but the fifteen-foot dike behind the canal, surrounding the lake like an Indian burial mound, didn't give a peek at Lake Okeechobee. The berm, as they called it, kept the lake from drowning thousands at every hurricane, like I heard happened in the Twenties, when the water flowed over farms. Even so, I wondered how all these tin cans had made it through the last hurricane season. I pictured them in a big blow, rolling and bouncing into each other, corners smashed and contents banging around like pebbles in a rock tumbler. I'd seen the wreckage of a trailer park near the coast, a few homes untouched through sheer luck, amid fifty or more smashed and resting on their sides, soggy insulation hanging out in clumps. But here were many survivors, thank god—cheap, crusty boxes, perfect housing for an unemployed, alcoholic single mother.

The Big O. I liked the nickname for Lake Okeechobee for obvious reasons. No more big "O's" from Merle though. Too bad.

Chance started to crank up with some whining in the back seat. Not to blame him, he was barely a toddler, a year old, and had been strapped in for hours. I glanced at my watch. Pretty soon time for him to nurse. I couldn't think about that for long or I'd start to leak.

I was low on gas, food, and money, and needed a sweet deal on the spot. No time for jawing with scraggly old farts who expected to glare at my tits for free. I slowed to a crawl and scanned the windows, seeing plenty "For Rent" signs, all crappy places, but still above my finances.

The "Touch of Clapp"—Class—Trailer Park sign caught my eye. I had to laugh. Local vandals had a sense of humor.

Just past it was the office, a single-wide with rusty awnings and ugly as the rest. For a person who reads men way better than books, the scrawled white letters sprayed on the glass sliding door, Merry Xmas, Dudes!—at least six months old, or maybe a year and a half—told me this was the right stop. Maybe the good-ole-boy manager was the one with the sense of humor, and I didn't mind that either.

Nursing was handy in more ways than one. I pulled off the road beside a huge pile of trash, and unbuttoned my shirt—one, two. I'd hold back on button number three for now.

I stuck Chance on my hip and crunched across the gravel and dry sticks to the door. I could hear a baseball game on the TV. I put Chance's little hand inside my shirt, and he started to knead like a kitten. I chewed my lip, he was so cute.

 I knocked. A dog barked, and a tall shadow flickered past the slit in the curtains. If this didn't turn out to be a straight, single, long-haired, druggie white boy, thirty to forty, I swore I'd turn lesbian.

The door opened. My sexuality was safe.

"Back off. Back off," he said and pulled a white-headed bulldog aside with his collar. The dog stopped barking and snuffled and snorted at my knees.

I tucked my chin a little so I could bat some lashes and look up at the dude with my big blue eyes. Chance was pawing my breast, exposing mucho skin, as if on cue. "I'm interested in a rental," I said.

The guy glanced at my tit. He was a young forty—or an old thirty-five. A hunk of blond hair fell over his eye, and the smell of beer, cigarettes, and slight B. O. drifted into my nose. I was in my element. He patted Chance on the head with a muscular arm tattooed to the wrist and smiled. The tattoo-to-tooth ratio wasn't looking good, but I couldn't afford to be choosy. Teeth were never a priority in the style I was accustomed to.

"Cute little sucker," he said and reached for Chance's tiny hand, partway down my shirt. Mr. Tattoo's thumb brushed the poking nipple, sending a chill down my chest, and I knew the hook was set perfect.

"I've got a single-wide, fully equipped with furniture and kitchen utensils for $400 a month, including utilities. It's got a leak in the plumbing so the bathroom floor is rotted in the corner, but the rest is tight. I'd want two months up front, one for the deposit. Need to have it cleaned first, if you're interested."

"I need a place right now," I said and nodded toward Chance. I licked my upper lip slowly. "I'm short on cash. How about . . . if I do the cleaning myself?"

"How short are you?"

"I've got almost a month. Gotta keep a few bucks for food till I find a job. Then I'll catch up."

"Not much work around here."

"I'm fast and cheap. I can always find something." Chance started to whimper and stretch my shirt lower. I bit my lip. "C'mon, pal. That rust bucket is sitting there empty. I'll improve it for the next tenant."

The dude studied my tits, searching for his answer.

"Give me a chance." I felt my face light up in a smile. I always got a good feeling when I used my baby's name. Chance was all sweetness and innocence.

I pulled back my shoulders to make my chest stand out proud. I winked.

"I can put you in there, if you give me $400 and clean the place. When you get a job, I'll add on twenty-five bucks a month until the deposit is paid."

"Three-hundred is all I've got. C'mon. You're not going to rent that place this time of year. Everybody's gone before the mosquitoes can carry them away."

"You'll have to owe me the rest then. I'll give you a month and see how it goes."

I stuck out my hand. "Candy," I said. "Pleased to meet you."

"Jimmy," he said and shook on the deal. He pointed to the dog that had dropped down drooling. "Spike."

The trailer was the worst on the lot, but it had a little air-conditioner with a burn-holed Lazyboy under it, so Chance and me settled right in. I looked around at the cheap paneling and dirty carpet while I nursed him. I wouldn't be able to let him loose. Lucky I had his playpen and swing in the trunk. I just hoped there weren't bed bugs or other nasties to bite his sweet skin. I couldn't wait to get started on the cleaning. I could see a dead roach on the countertop from where I was sitting, and the bathroom was bound to be moldy as hell.

Life was exactly as I expected at the trailer park. A month later, having moved into Jimmy's place, I felt like I'd been there for years. I raised up from his sunken mattress and glanced in the mirror, then dropped back on the pillow. My eye was swollen and purple as a ripe eggplant. I looked down at Jimmy sleeping. With his mouth closed, tattoos covered by the sheet, and that blonde hair, he seemed enough like an angel so's I almost believed that he was sorry for the punch, even before he said it. He wasn't quite as cocky as Merle, because he just plain wasn't as cocky, but his was big enough. Leastwise, my asshole wasn't sore. And so far, he hadn't asked me for any money.

Jimmy yawned and dropped his arm across my chest. I was rock hard with Chance's breakfast and it hurt. "Fuck!" I pushed him away.

"Oh, sorry, darlin'. Lemme kiss it and make it better."

He grabbed my arm and nuzzled into my left breast before I could dodge him. The touch of his lips on my nipple let down the flow and he laughed and tongued at the warm spray as it wet his mustache. "I thought there was only one hole," he said. "You've got yourself a sprinkler head."

I tried to knee him away, but he was too close to get any force behind it, and he had me pinned in a second and clamped his face onto my nipple, slurping hard and cutting with his few teeth.

"Stop it!" I yelled. "Get your rotten mouth off me!"

My voice woke Chance in his pen in the living room, and he was whimpering. I tried to worm away, but Jimmy had both my arms in control while he drained my sweet milk. His erection pressed into my thigh, and all I could think of was poor Chance, hungry and scared out in his little crib, while Jimmy wheezed and sucked. Finally, Jimmy broke off to breathe. I had his allergies to thank.

He swung over on top of me and stuck his cock in. I was wet despite myself. He was busting to come, and the strokes filled me up to a fine tightness. I beat him by a few seconds with a groan and a hot gush, and he pumped on out. His weight eased down on top of me, but I pulled loose and made my escape. Chance was bawling loud by this time. I headed to the shower to scrub off the cigarettes and beer before I offered him what milk was left. I could fill him up on baby cereal and strained bananas, but I felt guilty as hell. I'd done wrong hooking up with Jimmy in the first place. I wanted to bash out a few of his teeth—which wouldn't leave him with any. I decided right then that I was gonna pay him back for being such a motherfucker.

Anger ate on me all week, until one morning while I nursed Chance. I looked into his clear blue eyes and caressed his powder-soft cheek and shiny hair, almost transparent, like corn-silk, and thought, what am I doing? He was all the motivation I needed to form a plan. Besides teaching Jimmy a lesson, I needed money. With money, I could forget the losers and have my chance—I smiled—to be a good mother. I'd thought about getting a job, but that wouldn't leave me any time for my boy. It was a vicious cycle that only strong action could break.

I knew Jimmy ran a drug business locally and had his stash in a heavy safe cemented in the floor of the Ted's Shed behind the trailer. Running the park didn't bring in enough to cover his daily habits, so he'd found a way to skip the middle man and make a profit besides. I'd heard him on the phone enough to know the code, and I walked out to the shed with him a few times when he went to get the money for his deals, but he always shut the door in my face. I knew it was a keyed safe, because he kept that key on his person, and hid it good when he slept. From the looks of the nylon bag he'd bring out of the shed, there was major cash-flow. He was only living in a dump because he was used to it. He'd grab a gun from an end table drawer in the living room. It was .38, just like the one my uncle let me shoot when I was a barely a teen.

My eye had turned from ripe eggplant to green by then, so I had to get moving before the evidence disappeared. Besides that, after the milk incident, I could hardly fake enough affection toward Jimmy to keep myself around. I let him plug me, telling him I had a sore throat to stop his slobbery kisses, but I couldn't keep it up much longer.

I couldn't think of any way to get the money, except by pure force. That was where Merle came in, dynamite on a half-inch fuse, bold as shit. He wasn't any kind of father material, but he didn't know it. He was bound to be frothed up like a rabid dog already, since I snuck off and took Chance. That energy could be put to good use.

I remembered one day shortly after the little tyke was born. I was taking a putrid diaper off him, wiping pea-colored shit off his little red butt, and Merle came into the room drinking a beer. He just stood there with this look of wonder. I knew what he was feeling. I always had to bite my lower lip on the inside to keep from bursting with love. We both swore an oath that we'd eat baby-shit rather than let anything happen to our little guy. That choice never came up, but I knew I could use Merle's strong feelings to help Chance and me lose both those losers for good. I'd taken enough shit off men. Come to think, I'd taken abuse from every man I ever knew. There was nothing to recommend any of them—except their parts. I needed to get past that.

It took some guts to give Merle a ring. I was sweating a puddle in the payphone booth.

"Hi," I said.

"Where the fuck are you?" he hollered. "Where's my son?"

It was five-thirty and he had a good start on Happy Hour. Working construction, he sometimes took off early on a Friday.

"We're fine, thanks."

"The cops are looking for you. It's illegal for you to take Chance and run off like that."

"I didn't think you'd notice."

"Fuck."

"Merle, listen, I'm really sorry. I made a big mistake. Is there any chance we can patch it up?" I smiled and wondered if he could hear it in my voice. "For Chance's sake?"

"Come back and we'll talk."

"I can't. I'm up by Lake Okeechobee. The car's broke down and I'm broke. I can't get a job because there's nobody to watch Chance, and I owe the trailer park dude a bunch of money." I took a breath and made my voice sound pitiful. "He already beat me up once. You should see my eye. I'm scared."

"Oh, you're fucking him."

I heard something—like a beer bottle—hit the terrazzo floor and shatter. "Merle, sweetie, I just want you back. I want our little family together again."

He was cussing so loud I had to hold the phone away. I knew he considered me his property. I got goose-bumps thinking how he always said he loved me to death.

Finally, there was a pause in obscenities. "I'm coming up there to take care of my son."

"I need you inside me, baby," I added, using a little gravel in my voice.

"Didn't I tell you I'd kill you if you left me?"

"That wouldn't do either of us any good," I said.

He grumbled something, and then said he could get to the park around noon. I said I'd meet him at Butch's Fishcamp and Backyard Bar. Nobody knew me there, and I didn't want him driving into the Touch of Clapp so's his car could be identified.

That morning I saw the weather report that a hurricane was headed our way, Beryl. She'd been off in the Gulf but switched course and now they expected her to cut straight across the state, anywhere between Clewiston and Okeechobee. The whole lake was in the red cone of warning, and I was glad I was getting out. I didn't want to be near the Big O, even though the berm was supposed to hold it.

I had to walk down to Butch's because I didn't want Merle to catch me in a lie right off about the car, so I put a cap on Chance and smeared the sunscreen thick on us both. It was sweltering outside and I knew the bar must be half a mile from The Clapp. Jimmy had drove to Lake Wales to pick up some trailer parts, or so he said. I figured he was making a drug run. He was always gone most of the day, taking Spike with him, and came back high, so it was good timing for the setup.

Merle walked into the bar right at noon. I saw him first. His mouth was hard and his eyes mean, but when he looked at me with Chance in a highchair, he couldn't hold back a grin. I felt a big one slide over my face too. He sure was pretty, with his square jaw clean-shaved, and construction muscles bulging. It looked like the beer belly had tightened up some too. I had to get over all that.

He stared at Chance and me like we were the Madonna and

Child.

"Hey, Merle."

His face hardened, but I knew I still had power over him. He moved close and stuck out his finger so Chance would grab it.

"What the fuck's the matter with you?"

"Nothing. I'm better now. That last punch you threw me loosened up my brain. I thought I could really leave you, you know."

He hung his head, and I figured that was as big a sorry as I was going to get for all the abuse, the motherfucker.

He sat down in the booth next to me, and I gave him a kiss. He squeezed my thigh under the table hard enough to remind me that it was time to get down to business. I told him the story about Jimmy nursing off my tit and showed him the eye, which was a rainbow of colors by then. I watched his neck get red. He considered himself a protector of women and children, even though he was just as likely to break my nose as look at me. He couldn't wait to go over there and rip Jimmy a new asshole.

I waited to spring the drug money idea on him, since it involved murder. We ate some cheeseburgers and he had some beers. Didn't take long to loosen him up.

"You know, Merle, that asswipe deals drugs on the side—to high school kids. He's got a safe in his shed just full of money. I sure worry about Chance when he's a teen, with those kinds of guys around. He's got no morals whatsoever."

Merle looked over at Chance, and I could see he was thinking. His brain was hard and soft at the same time.

"It would serve him right if somebody got ahold of that stash," I told him. "Jimmy's not any asset to the world."

"You got any brilliant ideas?"

I shook my head. "Not sure. He keeps the key to the safe on a chain around his neck. I think he even wears it in the shower."

"He don't trust anybody."

We had another beer and then the weather report came on the TV at the bar. Beryl was strengthening and still moving in our direction. It was only a Category One so far, but all mobile homes were on mandatory evacuation.

"Better start packing up, all you guys in the double-wides," the bartender hollered. "Beer cans are gonna roll!"

There was excitement in the air, even though hurricane prep was a major pain in the ass. "Hmm," I said. "I wonder what asshole Jimmy does for a hurricane."

Chance started to fuss. He had a big mess of wet crackers crumbled on his tray, but I knew what he wanted. "Let's go out in the truck and crank up the AC. I can tell you my idea while I feed Chance."

It was a simple plan. We'd knock out Jimmy in his trailer and leave him for the hurricane. He was a dumb enough fuck that nobody would question his decision to stay. We'd whack him with a piece of wood so when the trailer got tossed around it would be a natural injury, like a shelf or a table got him. If that seemed unlikely to happen, we'd pull his body out on the ground after dark so it looked like he got hit by flying debris.

"I heard that some guy died last year when he stepped outside for a smoke and a tree limb hit him. Probably happens all the time."

"I bet his wife wouldn't let him smoke in the house," Merle said. "Sounds like something you'd make me do." He laughed. Then he stopped. "You're talking murder, Candy. You know that."

"So, what? He's a scumbag. Without him, the world will be a better place. I bet you already killed somebody in your life for less reason."

He didn't answer, so I figured it for a yes.

I knew I was a pretty picture feeding Chance with my shirt unbuttoned and my tits loose and sweaty. I gave Merle a slow smile and put his hand part on Chance's cheek and part into my cleavage. "We need a fresh start and there's nothing like a pile of money to help us get along." I stretched my neck to give him a long kiss and tongued and sucked at his mouth until I figured the bargain was sealed. There were people in the world just a cunt-hair away from murder. You only had to know how to spot 'em. It was my job to get Merle and Jimmy together.

"There shouldn't be any suspicions," I said. "I don't have any friends here, and it would make sense if I never came back after the hurricane."

"What about the time of death?"

"I don't think they'd know that close, if you knock him off

late Sunday."

"This is my job?"

"You're the man, darlin'. We'll turn the AC down low so he stays cold until the electricity cuts off—if it does."

"We can't stay in there when the hurricane comes."

"So, we put the money in a suitcase and head to the shelter. It's easy."

We set the time for the deed at 9 pm, so it would be dark, and everybody else would be gone, but we'd have plenty of time to get the money and get out before Mother Nature dealt us her blow. In my mind, it would be enough time for me to shoot Merle besides.

Merle went off to a motel for the night since he couldn't be seen back at The Clapp. I walked home to sweat it out with Jimmy and set him up for Merle's arrival.

"He's a maniac, I'm telling you. If you got a gun, you better get it ready so you can scare him off. I don't know how he found me, but my best friend called this morning. He might already be headed this way."

"With a hurricane coming?"

I shrugged. "He's a mad dog."

"Maybe you oughta just leave. I'm not in any of this."

"He's out for you too."

"Christsakes, why? How could he know anything about me?"

"I bet he got a P.I. That's all I can think."

"Cock-sucking motherfucker."

Sunday morning, people were cranking down their awnings and clearing out. By mid-afternoon there was a solid river of traffic going north and about half that flow headed south. I guess it depended on where the friends and relatives lived. Since Beryl could change course, especially when she made landfall, neither direction was safe because you might be driving straight into her path. You run out of gas and the stations are shut down, you're pretty well fucked.

I would have liked to got moving, though. I was nervous for Chance, knowing we had to stay late, but the shelter was a few miles away in the high school and we were still only looking at a Cat One. I went ahead and put Chance's porta-crib and swing in the trunk and packed the clothes and some bedding for me.

Jimmy said he had lots of hurricane prep to do at the park, checking the augers for the tie-downs, moving porch furniture and other junk. He was working on a cooler of beer at the same time, so I didn't have to worry that he'd be headed out early. Everything was going just right. I wore dishwashing gloves when I got the bullets out of his .38, so only his prints would be on there. I waited to make supper late, cooked Jimmy a few hotdogs. I figured I'd put a couch pillow over the gun barrel the way they do on *The Sopranos* when I shot Merle, just in case there were still cops around. Under the sound of the wind whipping and rain drumming, the crack of the shot could be anything.

It would be easy to make it look like Jimmy shot Merle, and then let the hurricane take care of the rest of the evidence. I'd leave a small amount of money in the safe, and nobody would know anything was missing. Later, when the cops tracked down where Merle came from, they'd figure Jimmy shot him in a fight over me. It wouldn't be no surprise to anybody, and I'd squeeze out a few tears when they told me.

I had Chance asleep in his stroller in the back bedroom, and it was eight-thirty when Jimmy stuffed the last half of his third hotdog into his mouth and pointed his beer bottle toward the road. "I think your friend decided to hunker down at home, just like I thought."

"No friend of mine. Might be all the hurricane traffic slowed him down. You got that gun handy in case, don't you?"

"Always got it handy, babe." He cocked his head toward an end table, and I knew the gun was still in the drawer where I'd found it and put it back that afternoon. He took his beer, rousted Spike off the couch, and punched on the remote. "I don't want to leave Spike and go to that disgusting shelter until I have to. Maybe you should leave with the kid now."

"I'd rather wait for you," I said, but I was starting to worry about the storm. The flow of traffic outside had dwindled to almost nothing, so every time I saw headlights my heart started to pound. I wanted to get it done, but I didn't. I knew Jimmy was no match for Merle, especially if he was pointing an empty gun, but chance was always unpredictable. I smiled.

The wind was loud through the trees, and I was almost gonna take Jimmy's suggestion. Let Merle take care of him and just get away. Finally, lights swung past the window. The sound of tires pulling off the road set me on the edge of my chair. I didn't need to fake being nervous. "That's him. That's Merle. I knew it."

Jimmy sat up and motioned me to stay in my seat. The engine was shut off, and footsteps crunched on the drive. He'd parked behind my trailer, like I'd told him. I grabbed Spike and held him, but Jimmy didn't notice.

The knock was soft, just like I'd said to do.

Jimmy slid open the drawer and took out the gun. He walked to the door and opened it a crack.

"You got something of mine in there. You know what I mean?"

Jimmy pulled up the gun to show it to Merle through the crack. "You get off my property while you still can."

Merle ripped the door out of Jimmy's hand and threw himself into the room, the door banging closed behind him with the wind. Jimmy pulled the trigger, once, twice. His face drained and he flung the gun toward Merle's head. There was a flash of a two-by-four and Merle had him on the floor, out cold, his forehead bloody. I was sitting on Spike, who was barking his head off.

"Whack him again," I yelled. "Make sure."

Merle bent over and gave him a couple more hard ones in the same spot. The gun was on the floor next to me and I slid it under the sofa with my foot.

Chance started to whimper in the bedroom. I shoved Spike into the bathroom and slammed the door. "Key's in his jeans' pocket. You get it, and I'll get Chance. Meet you in the shed."

He picked up the bloody two by four. "I better put this in the truck so we can toss it."

"Good idea," I said. I was thinking that I had to remember to bring it back.

He went outside, and I took the gun into the back bedroom. I had to change Chance's diaper, put on the plastic gloves, and reload the bullets. When I brought Chance out to the living room, the body was laying there just the same, but Merle must've got the key off him and went to the shed. It wasn't a pretty sight in front of me, the dead body and ugly green shag carpet soaking up blood. I put Chance on the couch and hid the gun behind the pillow. Chance reached for the shiny gun, but I pulled him away in time. I didn't want to mix up any baby fingerprints with Jimmy's.

The trailer wobbled and squeaked in its tie downs. Once Merle got back into the trailer there'd be no reason to poke around, just shoot and go. I was spooked by the sound of the wind and the bad reputation of these metal coffins.

Merle was taking too long. I wasn't sure whether it was safer to carry Chance with me or leave him inside, but I stuck him on my hip and tore out of there. It was wild outside, garbage cans already rolling around, branches whipping by. I shielded Chance with my arm and ran to the shed. The door was closed and for a second I thought Merle had snatched the money and left me, but when I yanked it open, he was zipping the overnight bag.

"You didn't take it all, did you?"

"No, I left a pack of twenties and two Ziplocs full of crack, so everything looks normal. No sense trucking that shit around anyway." He hefted the case, weighing it in his hand. "I don't know how much this is, but several of these packs are hundreds."

"Give me a look."

He unzipped the top and picked out a pack of hundreds, flipping the bills close to my face. There was only one dim light bulb in the shed, but I could see a couple more packs of money in the top of the bag.

"You were right," Merle said. His eyes were big with excitement. "We're rich." He grabbed my hand as I reached toward the bag. "Why the gloves?"

"I been doing some cleaning up."

"Wiped my prints off the door?"

I nodded. "Okay, let's put the key back around Jimmy's neck. It's getting crazy outside." I was too freaked to be happy. I still had to commit murder and escape the storm with my baby.

I followed Merle back into the trailer and put Chance in the corner of the couch. Merle knelt down by Jimmy with the key, wiping it on his shirt, putting it back in Jimmy's pocket. I picked up the pillow and the gun behind it.

Merle was shaking his head. "What if the hurricane doesn't break this sucker up? The cops'll know it's murder. Moving this asshole outside won't work either because the blood's in here."

"I never thought of that," I said. I had the gun pointed at him from behind the pillow. "Jeez, what should we do?"

I didn't wait for an answer, just squeezed the trigger. I hadn't done much shooting before, but being close, I hit him in the chest, and he fell backward, dropping the bag, oozing red down the front of his shirt. Chance was screaming bloody murder and Spike was barking like a maniac, but I stood over Merle and gave him one more to the head to make sure. Clumps of gray jellyfish stuff spattered onto the wall. It hit me then, what I'd done. Chance was still bawling hard, but I had to race into the bathroom past the dog to puke. I'd been so caught up in the planning, none of it seemed real until then.

I splashed my face and ran back to Chance just in time before he could fall off the couch into the mess of Merle and Jimmy. I grabbed him and hugged him tight. "Don't cry, sweetie," I told him. He was scared by all the noise, and maybe the scenery. I wished I could explain how it was all the best for him in the long run.

Spike was sniffing around Jimmy, and I felt real bad about that. He was really a nice dog, but there was nothing to do but shoo him out the door. He'd have to find a safe place to hide while Beryl passed over.

I put the gun in Jimmy's hand and closed his fingers. If the trailer went, everything would be tossed around messing up the evidence. Even if it didn't, it would seem that Jimmy revived long enough to shoot Merle—like happens in the movies. There was only a few minutes between their times of death. I doubted I'd be a suspect, since I didn't have a motive to kill either of them—except that they were men. The cops wouldn't think of that one. Merle, on the other hand, was well known for his temper, and Jimmy was a drug dealer with a gun, besides the money and crack in his safe.

Chance wailed, rain pounded the aluminum roof, and the trailer creaked and shuddered. There was a snap and crackle in the roar, like Rice Krispies, that I recognized as all the tiny dead branches popping off trees from the force of a gust. I'd seen and heard that before, in my last hurricane experience. Those heaps of rubble from last year must've been scattering too, all projectiles looking for a head to smash. The lights went out. I set Chance back on the couch and felt my way outside to the pickup for the bloody two-by-four.

When I ran back inside to toss it on the floor, Chance was so quiet, I thought he'd fallen off the couch and knocked himself out. I started to panic, but I felt for him and there he was. I prayed he wasn't traumatized. I held him to my chest, grabbed the bag of cash, and dashed to the car.

I held my breath as I drove, dodging branches and trash cans, all kinds of unidentified debris. Now, according to the radio, Beryl was up to a Cat Two, and the outer bands were already hitting the Big O. The berm was expected to hold, but there could be small breaks and minor flooding.

I laughed when I saw the high school with lights still on. "We made it, baby love. You're my lucky Chance!" I parked in an area blocked from the wind by buildings and took a deep breath. God finally sent good fortune flowing my way. He helped those that helped themselves.

There was nobody outside, and I couldn't resist a peek at the money. I hoisted the bag onto the seat. It was heavy. With all those hundreds, there should be enough to cover years of cheap living until Chance started school. One thing I knew was how to live cheap. I wouldn't skimp on Chance though. I'd buy him some fancy educational toys. He would love the one where you touch an animal, like a bear, and he growls and says "bear."

I laughed, just thinking about the fun we'd have, and unzipped the bag and pulled out a pack of bills. I flipped through them. A hundred on top—but the rest was ones! I reached back into the bag for more, only found two, and they were all singles. I dug down. Old newspaper and cans of beer from the floor of Merle's truck. My head boiled with rage and I thought the top might fly off. "Damn you, you cocksucker!" I screamed out loud to Merle.

Chance started to cry and I had to shut up and swallow it down, but I never wanted to kill somebody so much in my life. It was frustrating, since fucking Merle was already dead.

I dropped the packs of ones and turned the key. I had to go back. I pulled out from between the buildings and into the wind. Big chunks of wood and metal were flying around now, and that's just what I could see in the headlights. I tromped the gas and turned onto the road. Something slammed into the side window and flew off. The glass broke into tiny beads that splattered inside the car. Rain poured in. Chance screamed like I'd never heard him before. I looked close, but couldn't see any blood. It was pure terror. I let out an angry roar at the wind and pulled back between the buildings. I couldn't risk the drive. If something happened to Chance, all the money in the world would be worthless to me. I pulled back into the sheltered spot. I doubted I could go back for the money after the storm. I'd be seen and become a suspect for sure.

I couldn't stop my tears as I bundled Chance into a blanket and carried him inside the building. I didn't even have enough money to rent a sleazy trailer. With my usual luck, I was in the same damn place where I started, except for I'd learned a lot about murder. I'd took right to it.

Lights were bright inside. The auditorium was packed, mostly old people and Spanish speaking families. I found a cot, sat down, and adjusted my shirt to settle Chance with a nipple, calming him and trying to stop my own sniffling. I wasn't showing much tit, but I felt eyes on my chest.

I glanced across the room. There was a looker all right, big guy in a cowboy hat, legs spread, sitting on a folding lounge chair, shuffling a deck of cards. He looked free and open to suggestions. I felt a juicy twinge. The Big O that I hadn't had for a while came into my mind and slid over me. Those jeans were snug and I liked the boots. I was too tired to think much farther.

I let my head hang, watching Chance, his feathery lashes on his cheeks, suckling like an angel. My plan had failed, but at least his father was out of the picture—no more worry about violent assholes as role models. I tilted my head up and winked at the cowboy. Maybe I still had a chance at the money if this guy would help me out. I smiled.

As I relaxed and drifted off, I saw the Big O rushing over the berm and felt the cold water pour over us. It was like being caught under a wave, but I knew I was dreaming, so I didn't struggle. My luck was changing. I just had to hold my breath till the sun came out.

School Girl

by Lisa Respers France

April 25, 1987

Dear Diary,

I have to work out a good hiding place for you. I will try to write everyday but I won't make any promises because I am busy with housework, cooking, schoolwork, finals coming up. The usual crap.

If Terrell ever found out I was keeping a journal he would bug out. "Don't commit nothing to paper," he constantly tells the guys who work for him. He likes to throw out phrases like that because he thinks he is so deep, but I know he heard somebody say that in a movie. Probably one of those gangster flicks he always watches. If I have to suffer through *Scarface* one more time, I swear to God I am going to throw up.

The movie is one of Terrell's favorites and he even has the stupid Al Pacino poster. Too bad the mob doesn't let black people in because Terrell would love to be a mafia don. I told him that selling crack doesn't make you a kingpin; it just makes you a criminal. He slapped me for saying it and I made my eyes well up with tears. He got all apologetic and wrapped me in a bear hug. "You are my special baby," he whispered in my ear.

He bought me a novel the next day as a way of saying he was sorry. He knows reading is my favorite thing in the whole world so he got me some dumb romance, thinking it would make me happy. I think romances are stupid, but I smiled and squealed and threw myself into his arms. I would much rather have a James Baldwin or a Toni Morrison, but Terrell knows nothing about literature. I'm not sure he has ever read a book.

I average about a book a week. I want to be a writer one day. I've never told anyone that, but my teacher, Mrs. Simms, figured it out. She teaches AP English and she asked me to stay one day after the bell rung. I'm pretty quiet in class and I get good grades so I wasn't sure what it was all about. "Jane," she said as she reached into her desk for something flat wrapped in a plastic bag.

"I want you to have this. I sense that there is a great deal within you that you would like to express. Perhaps this will help." Inside the bag was this purple hardcover book, slightly larger than a paperback. I traced the spine with my forefinger and opened it to see blank, lined pages. "What is it," I asked, curiously. "It's a journal," she said, smiling. "Consider it an early graduation present. You can write your thoughts, or poetry or anything that comes to mind. You can write whatever you want. Just write."

So, here goes.

April 28, 1987

Dear Diary,

I came up with an idea of how to hide you. I used an old book cover to fool Terrell into thinking it's a textbook. He never goes near my school stuff because he HATED school. The teachers treated him like an idiot yet they passed him year after year so he must not have been but so stupid.

A little bit about me: I am seventeen years old, 5'7", light brown skinned, shoulder-length dark brown hair that I usually keep pulled back in a ponytail and sort of skinny. Kids used to call me "Plain Jane" on account of the fact I am. Not ugly, just kind of non-descript. People usually don't notice me and I like it that way. That's why I was so shocked when Terrell and I first got together.

I had never seen him before, but apparently he was pretty well known because later girls I didn't even know started approaching me to ask it was true that he was my man. I attend the oldest all-girls public school in the country and when the final bell rings, our parking lot is usually crawling with car loads of boys from other schools that cut class just to come watch us be dismissed. They hoot and holler, whistle and beg for phone numbers. It's so retarded. Anyway, the buses line up directly in front of the building and I was waiting for mine when Terrell and his friend Jay sauntered up to me. Terrell is almost six feet tall and he grinned down at me. "You got enough stuff to carry, little girl?" I looked around to see if anyone else was near by. "I'm talking to you, sweetheart. What is all that in your book bag?" I practically whispered the word. "Books."

Jay barked a laugh. "Can I carry that for you?" Terrell made a move to take the nylon bag and I snatched it back. "Leave me alone." I pivoted and almost tripped over my size nines trying to jump on my bus, which by now had pulled in to its usual spot. I thought I'd never see him again, but he was back the next week. He was leaning up against a black Sterling with dark tinted windows that was idling in the bus lane. "Get in," he said. "I don't know you," I sputtered. "I'm not getting in your car." "How else are you going to get to know me," he asked me with a grin. "Okay, if you won't let me give you a ride, tell me where to meet you so we can talk. I just want to talk to you." "I'm headed to the mall," I said. "To pick something up. I'll meet you at the pizza place on the second floor." I started walking away, heading toward my destination, the bus stop that would take me to the mall. "Hey," he yelled after me. "What's your name?" "Jane," I called over my shoulder.

I'm still not sure why I did it. Maybe it was because no guy had ever approached me before. Or perhaps I just liked the way he looked, leaning so confidently against his ride, all cocoa-brown fineness in his street uniform of a black Nike sweat suit with sparkling white tennis shoes. I expected rap music to be blaring from his car stereo, but Whitney Houston was belting out "I Want to Dance with Somebody." He was cute, he was older and he wanted to talk to me. TO ME!

Later, he confessed he had liked the fact that I had run from him. It made him want to protect me, he said, because I seemed so scared and vulnerable. I think what really happened was that Jay gave him such a hard time about me dissing him that Terrell felt compelled to save face. That first day, he did most of the talking, bragging about himself. He was twenty two, self-employed and rented his own house. He had moved to Baltimore from New York when he was fifteen and gone into the messenger service business with his uncle. He traveled a lot for work, he said—New York, Virginia, Washington, D.C., Delaware. He made deliveries via car and enjoyed the driving because it gave him time to think.

I was hesitant to give him my phone number because I lived with my aunt and she was a trip. Me and her have never gotten along. My parents were killed in a car accident when I was twelve years old and I had lived with Aunt Trudi ever since. They were traveling back from North Carolina where my father had been looking for work. It was my mother's idea since my father wasn't exactly the most industrious man and my mom thought a fresh start was what we needed. They had been together since she had gotten pregnant with me when she was sixteen and he was eighteen. My mother was beautiful and smart and funny and my father hated her for it. He was brutal and thought nothing of smacking us around when he felt like it. She was reading *Jane Eyre* in school when she got pregnant and that's how I came to have my name. We were best friends, more like sisters. She doted on me and my father didn't like it. "You think giving her some white-girl name is going to make her better than us," my father would yell at her sometimes when they argued. "The girl is half retarded and doesn't know how to do anything. Just keeps her nose buried in books all day. What is she good for?"

He once caught me reading under the covers with a flashlight after he had sent me to bed. I was immersed in the *Little House on the Prairie* series at the time and I used to think how I wouldn't have minded the harsh life on the frontier if Pa Ingalls could be my father. He always had time for his daughters and he played the fiddle for them and pulled Laura on his lap to cuddle. When my father opened my bedroom door to find me wrapped up like a glow worm instead of sleeping, he used the flashlight to whack me upside my head.

My mother protected me as best she could and would send me to the library a couple blocks from our house to keep me out of my father's way. We lived in a poor neighborhood so the reading selection wasn't great, but I loved it anyway. Teachers always wrote on my report cards that I had the best vocabulary in the class and I knew that was from the hours I spent living in the other worlds reading afforded me. I would come home and tell my mother stories based on what I had read and she would listen while she cooked dinner or ironed clothes. "I can see the story in my head when you tell it baby," she said. "You should tell your daddy these stories sometimes." But the one time I tried to tell him, he turned the television up to drown me out.

I lost them both on Interstate 95 when my father fell asleep at the wheel and the car slid into oncoming traffic. They had left me behind with Aunt Trudi, my father's oldest sister, and

I discovered I was an orphan by her shaking me awake at three o'clock in the morning asking whether I knew if my parents had insurance policies. Trudi was the most money-hungry person I knew and was not to be trusted. My grandmother used to say that she was so trifling she would steal the grease out of a biscuit if she could. I later found out that before my early morning wakeup, she had taken my house keys and high-tailed it to our apartment to snatch whatever she could of value before the rest of the relatives descended. She even wore my mother's best suit to the funeral.

I was still living with Trudi when I met Terrell because she insisted I stay there once she found out about the monthly social security checks I would be receiving until age eighteen. Suddenly, she was my guardian and I was crammed into a bedroom with her three brats in a two-bedroom apartment she shared with her nasty boyfriend, Charles, who was always leering at me. I only escaped from her because of Terrell. But that's another story and my hand is getting tired so I am going to go for now.

May 4, 1987
  Dear Diary,
  I never explained how I came to live with Terrell. I was fifteen when we met and we would go on dates and talk on the phone sometimes. Trudi didn't like it and things were getting rough at the house. "You think you grown now 'cause you got your fast tail out in the street chasing after some boy," she spit at me one night after I had come in from seeing a movie with Terrell. "You turning into a slut, just like that mother of yours." Before I even realized what I was doing, I had my hands around her throat and we were tumbling onto the living room floor. She outweighed me by more than a hundred pounds so it wasn't long before I was pinned under her and our screams brought Charles running downstairs. "This whore done tried to kill me," she gasped, as Charles helped her up from the floor. I scrambled backwards crablike to make sure I was out of her reach. "Get out of my house," she screamed. "You are good for nothing. Get out NOW."

  I paged Terrell from the payphone down the street and he came to get me. I had scratches on my face from where Trudi had gouged me and I was crying. Terrell was steaming. He took me to his place and I have been living with him ever since. Trudi cooled down after a few days and when we came to pick up my stuff she tried to get me to stay. The fear that someone would report that I was no longer living with her and end the flow of support the government was paying clearly weighed on her mind. "You can't just take her away," she whined. "I'm the only family she got." Terrell stared her down coldly and whipped out a knot of money from his back pocket. She licked her lips when she saw it. "I'm her family now," he said. "You have any problems, you come see me. I can make it worth your while if don't nobody find out about this here 'arrangement' we got."

And that's how I got to move out almost on my own at fifteen. No one bothers us because just about everybody knows who Terrell is and what he does.

May 12, 1987
   Dear Diary,
   Some of the girls at my school can't stand me. I have nice clothes and jewelry and Terrell drops me off at school and picks me up in the Sterling every day. I can buy whatever I want for lunch and if I had any friends, I could even treat. Most days, I sit at a table by myself in the seniors' lounge and read a book while I'm eating. I hear some of the other students whispering about me behind my back and one girl even straight up asked me if my man was a drug dealer. I just stared at her until she walked away. It had taken me a couple of weeks to figure out what Terrell really did. He would stay up all night and go to sleep early in the morning. His pager was forever going off and he would be out the door at all hours.

   Then there were the guns. I mistakenly kicked an open shoe box out from under Terrell's side of the bed and there they were, two shiny handguns nestled in a t-shirt. I had seen guns before, you don't grow up in my neighborhood and not, but there was something about having them under the bed I was sleeping in. As if I had been resting all this time above two snakes, coiled, and ready to strike. Terrell found me examining them and I thought he would get mad like he sometimes did. I had caught more than one slap for being "in his business." But this time he didn't get angry. "Sit next to me, babe," he said, patting the place on the bed beside him. I nestled in the crook of his arm as he wrapped my right hand around one of the guns. "Feel that," he said. "That's power. You like that?" I said nothing as I stared at the weapon. "What do you need this for," I asked. "Jane, don't be stupid. You know what I do and why I need it." He quickly wrapped the gun back in the shirt and shoved the box under the bed again. From then on, he would have me carry his gun sometimes when we went out. He hardly ever conducted business around me, but sometimes I would go with him when he had to meet people and he would either leave me in the car or I would sit around and talk to the other guy's girlfriend. "This way if I get popped, I'm not carrying. Plus, you're a girl and underage so the police won't do anything to you," he said.

Gradually, I got used to carrying it and the weight started to feel comforting.

May 18, 1987
Dear Diary,
I got home from the hospital this morning at three a.m. My jar is wired shut and I have a concussion. Terrell dropped me off at the Emergency Room and told me to tell whoever asked that I was jumped by a bunch of girls. He's no stranger to the Maryland Department of Corrections and said he couldn't risk being there when the cops came.

It all started yesterday with a phone call. An admissions officer from University of Maryland called and Terrell got the message on the answering machine. She had tried to reach me at Trudi's house and that dumb heifer gave the women our number. Terrell and I had argued before about me applying to colleges. His plan was that after graduation, we would get pregnant. Like it really would be both of us sitting around with a fat belly. He had even started a "baby fund" after I moved in and it was up to $20,000, stuffed in socks and hidden in the closet. I tried to convince him that my guidance counselor had practically forced me to fill out applications because of my grades, but in reality, I had been taking advantage of the fact that my mail went to Trudi's house to apply to colleges in Maryland, Virginia and Boston. I'm not sure if I even thought about what I would do if accepted.

Terrell was livid. BAM, he socked me in my jaw as soon as I got into the car and we were a far-enough distance from the school building. He hustled me, cheek swelling, into the house and the beating continued with Terrell yelling so loudly that I thought my ears would pop. "What do you think, you are going to go off and leave me?!?!? That I would let you leave me? You think you are going to meet some college boy that is going to do for you everything I have done for you? Take care of you like I have?" The last thing I remember is his pounding my head into the dining room floor. When I came to, Terrell was cradling me in his arms, trying to revive me with a damp wash cloth, the moisture mixing with the tears that were careening down his face and splashing on to mine. "I'm so sorry, baby. I'm so sorry." I didn't understand the pressure he was under, he said. He had been having some problems with another crew and his boys weren't earning like they had been, he explained. He was convinced that some of them were considering defecting to the other gang and now I was trying to leave him too. We both skidded in my blood as he helped me out of the house on the way to the hospital.

June 3, 1987
   Dear Diary,
   It seems like years since I have written, but really it's only been a couple of weeks. So much has happened that I don't even know where to begin. I was coming home from a follow-up doctor's appointment and some guys grabbed me right off the street. They threw me in a van and pulled a pillowcase over my head. At least, I think it was a pillowcase because I could smell the sweat that still lingered on it and feel the seam on the top tight against my scalp. Everything was dark and the heat was unbearable.
   I must have passed out from fear or lack of oxygen because when I came to I was in a basement. The whitewashed walls gleamed in the late day sun and it was cool belying the humid day. I was on a cot, my hands restrained in front of me with some type of twine. I sat up, swinging my legs in front of me and noticed for the first time a dreadlocked man sitting on the steps opposite the cot. He was holding a stick which he used to tap on the ceiling. Almost immediately I heard feet on the floor above

us. Three more men came down the steps and the one in the lead approached the cot while the others scattered around the mostly vacant room. They all wore loose linen clothing and sandals and had dreadlocks. The one before me sported a neat goatee and had the longest locks, reaching almost to his waist. They were tied back with a piece of something that I couldn't see and for a moment I wondered if it was with the same type of twine which now encircled my wrists. "You are awake," he said softly, a lilting accent making it seem as if he were singing the words. "Don't worry, mahn. We mean you no harm." "Who are you," I asked through clenched teeth, trying to keep the tremor out of my voice." "I am a man with a problem," he said. "A problem your boyfriend has caused. Why do you speak with this closed mouth?" I parted my lips so he could see the wiring that was soon to come off. "Bring her soup," he said to no one in particular. One of his minions left to do his bidding. "I am Trevor," he said. "You are in my home."

"What do you want with me?" "You will be our guest until we have completed a bit of business we have with Terrell. He has been informed that you are safe but as of yet has refused to negotiate. But he will." I shuddered to even think what he meant by that. "The food you are bringing me," I asked. "Is it goat's head soup?" "Ahhhh," he smiled. "What do you know of goat's head soup?" "My mother was Jamaican," I said, and I began to tell him a tale I had read. I spoke of her longing for home and how she drank so much ginger beer to settle her stomach when she was pregnant with me that she swore that as a newborn I screamed bloody murder unless I got a bottle of it diluted with water. I reminisced about the beaches I saw through her stories and family members I had never met but who we had sent money to. This auntie who needed surgery and this cousin whose son was being harassed by the police who were demanding to be paid off. I explained how I continued to try and help, doing what I could in memory of my mother. By the time I finished speaking, Trevor was crouched down next to me with his eyes half mast and the light was fading.

"You must go back one day," he said, softly. "For your mother." "There is something I can do for you," I replied. "What might you be able to do for me," he said, standing. I motioned for him to crouch back down again and come closer so that I could whisper in his ear. He leaned back and looked at me. Something flickered in his eyes. "You would do this," he asked. "I would," I said. "For family."

June 15, 1987
    Dear Diary,
    Today is graduation, but I don't think I will be going. I am staying close to home in case the police have anymore questions. A few days ago Terrell threw a graduation party for me at Druid Hill Park. I guess he still felt bad about my jaw and everything, so when he asked me what I wanted for graduation I told him I would love to have a cookout in the park. Now that my jaw was healed, I could finally eat and I was looking forward to it. We set up right near the Reservoir and the parking area looked like a luxury car lot with all of Terrell's friends' rides. We had three grills going and we even invited Trudi and her family. A huge boom box was tuned to a local R & B station and the smell of marijuana floated beneath the aroma of ribs and chicken. I sat close by Terrell with my purse in my lap while his boys cooked the food. He was reaching for a Miller's in one of the coolers when the three cars cruised by.
    I'm not sure if anyone else saw the dreadlocks when the tinted window on the Mercedes whispered down, but I knew their instructions had been to spray high and if they happened to hit a dealer here or there, so be it. The shooting seemed to go on forever as some of my party guests pulled their own weapons to fire back. My hand was in my purse and whipping out my surprise for Terrell before he had a chance to go running from the picnic table. He never even stopped to shove me out of harm's way. In the midst of the mayhem, I ran towards the Reservoir. On the way, I did manage to pass right by Trudi who was crouching near a bush.

    Everyone has called me brave with the way I am holding up, having lost both my boyfriend and my aunt in a vicious drive-by. My strength, I tell everyone, has come from knowing that Terrell would want me to go on to college and do well. Thanks to the $20,000 baby fund and the bonus Trevor paid me, I will be able to make Terrell proud.

Gold-Diggers,
Hustlers and B Girls

Nora B.

by Ken Bruen

She had a mouth on her.

Jesus, like a fishwife.

And mean with it?

You fooking kiddin?

She'd slice your skin off with three words.

I was a cop, out of the Three Seven in those days.

Man, we'd do the night shift

Give me

Your scumbags

Your dopers

Your skels

Your preds

The zombies

Had 'em all and twice over.

They came out of the fucking sewers, menacing, feral and lethal

And lemme tell you, we were ready for em . . . . no fucking innocents there.

We had a stone simple rule.

Fuck 'em first.

We did.

Always.

Our Sarge, half wop, half Mick and deadly, he'd go,

"Bring em down, fast, don't let em ever . . . . and I mean fucking ever, get up, got that?"

We did.

Did we fucking ever.

My wife had run off with some carpet salesman and if I'd had the energy, I might have cared.

Got a free carpet though.

Nice Persian job, I piss on it every chance I get, which is most mornings after the usual boilermakers with the guys.

First though, we clocked off, we went over to May's, diner

Eighth and 28th.

There is no May, it was owned by a Polack hardass who wouldn't give you the time of day if you paid him.

Our kind of guy, he never charged us neither and we kept an eye on the joint. He was the cook too, did hash browns, eggs over easy and bacon like your mother might have, if she'd ever been sober.

How I met Nora, the guys had been yapping about this Irish broad who'd been working there a time, I missed her first two weeks as I caught a knife in the gut from a domestic. The guy, he caught the fucking hiding of his life, you gut a cop, better have more than a small blade.

But it put me in the hospital for four days and then I had some time coming so I went fishing.

Like fuck.

I went to the OTB and the track.

Lost me whatever savings I might have had.

You might say, I came back on the job, a wiser, more cautious guy.

You might say shite.

I was meaner, more violent, more intent than before and lemme tell you, I was no Mr. Nice to start.

So, me and Richy, we're heading for the diner and Richy says, "Wait till you get a load of Nora."

"The fuck is Nora?"

Like I gave a flying fuck.

Richy, he was a small guy, but he had my back and he was real good in the close-up stuff, a guy got in his face, he lost his face.

Think I'm kidding?

But here he was, sounding kinda . . . . goddamit . . . . shy?

He said, "Jeez, Joe, she's like . . . . I dunno, special, I'm thinking of you . . . . know, mebbe asking her out, a drink or something?"

I gave him the look, but the poor bastard, he was . . . . . what's the word . . . . smitten . . . . or better, fucked.

I cuffed his ear and he didn't even notice.

We went into the place, got our usual booth at the back, watch the exits, yeah, cop stuff.

And there she was.

I felt something move in my heart, like a melting. Ah Jesus, I'm not that kind of guy, but a jolt and I hadn't even had me my caffeine yet.

She was small, red hair, green eyes, nice, nice figure, real built but not showy with it, she knew what she had, didn't need to push, pretty face, not spectacular but there was an energy there, you found it hard to look away. She had her pad out, and of course, the coffee pot and without asking, filled our coffee mugs, cops, you gotta ask? She smiled at Richy, said,

"Tis himself."

He smiled like a love-struck teenager, I wanted to throw up, then she leveled those eyes on me and here was the goddamn jolt again, asked,

"And who is Mr. Silent here?"

Richy blurted out about me being his partner, how I'd been in the hospital and she cut him off, asked me,

"Cat got your tongue, fellah?"

Something had, I had a million put-downs, couldn't bring one to mind, I put out my hand.

Jesus.

She looked at my hand, laughed, said,

"Tis shaking hands now is it, my my, aren't you the polite devil."

Fucking with me.

She said to Richy,

"Usual?"

He nodded like an idiot and to me,

"What about you, gorgeous, you able to eat?"

I mumbled something about having the same as Richy.

She gave that smile again, said,

"Christ, what a surprise."

And took off.

Richy was almost panting and I swear, he had a line of sweat above his eyes. He asked,

"Isn't she something?"

I wanted to bitch slap him, but I went with,

"Got a mouth on her, I'll give her that."

He had his Luckies out, lit one with a shaking hand, hard to believe that back then you could smoke anywhere, he persisted,

"But you like her, don't you, I mean, she's hot, isn't she?"

Fuck yes, I felt the heat offa her the moment she rolled up to us and I knew I was in some sort of serious bind, had to bite down, keep my cool, said,

"Whatever . . . . so you going to the ball game Sunday?"

She was back, balancing the plates with easy grace, put them down, gave me a look, asked,

"You have a touch of Irish in yah, haven't yah?"

I wanted to put more than a touch of Irish in her, right there, right over the mess of eggs, bacon and linked sausages. I said,

"Second generation."

She blew that off like it was horseshit, said,

"And a house full of harps and Irish music, fecking sad."

Left us to our food.

Her voice, the real deal, the soft lilt, those gentle vowels, you could have her cuss at you all day and still want more of that sound.

I gulped some coffee, it was bitter, black burned my tongue, just the way I liked it, like my fucking life.

We don't get a bill, we leave a fat tip on the table, that's how it works, Richy left a twenty and seeing my look, he pleaded,

"I'm gonna ask her out, can you give me a minute?"

When he went to ask her, I switched the twenty for a five . . . . no point in madness.

I waited in the prowl car, the radio squawking and my head full of her, she was dancing across my heart . . . . fuck and fuck.

I lit a Lucky, tried to figure out what the hell had just happened to me.

Richy came back, shit-eating grin all over his dumb face, said,

"She said yes, can you believe that?"

I said, as I put the car in drive,

"Guess the twenty did the trick."

I didn't have to look to see the disappointment on his face, like his school project had been trampled on.

Tough.

The next couple of weeks, Richy was gone, signed sealed and fucked. He was taking Nora to fancy restaurants, clubs, buying her shitloads of jewelry, clothes, and crackin on about her, till I went,

"Shaddthefuckup."

He didn't.

He couldn't.

Where was the money coming from and it took a lot of moola.

Richy had grown up with wiseguys and now he was on the pad. He'd hinted I might like me some of the action till he saw my face and I could tell, deeper and deeper in the hole to these scum, he was going.

He was my partner, what could I do, watch the disaster take shape and get ready to annihilate him.

I watched.

One evening, I was sitting in the Mick bar, down a block from the precinct, fuming, the constant simmering rage in barely reined leash. I had me a Jameson rocks, Guinness back, and it wasn't my first. Someone slipped onto the stool beside me and I got the whiff of that perfume, swoon stuff.

Heard,

"'Tis himself."

I turned to face her and my damn treacherous heart skipped some beats, those eyes and that Irish coloring and she had lips, you wanted to run your finger, gently across them and kiss them till they bled. She was wearing a tight dress that had to be against some law, least one that protected fools like me. She asked,

"So will himself buy a girl a jar or have I to beg?"
She had a double Old Grandad, Bud back. I asked,
"You're not gonna drink an Irish brand?"
She gave me a look, her eyes half lidded, said,
"Sure I'm in America, I can have the other stuff at home, wouldn't I be stone mad not to try yer drink?"
She put a cigarette between those gorgeous lips, waited and said,
"So Mr. Grumpy, ate yah going to light me up?"
Jesus.
I did and she held my hand as I did so, I swear, I had a tremor in me fingers and she said,
"Christ fellah, calm down, I'm not going to bite yah . . . . yet."

An hour later, I was buried to the hilt in her, sweating and groaning and howling like a lunatic and she goaded,
"Ride me like yah loved me."

After, her head on my chest, I asked,
"What about Richy?"
She was pulling at the hairs on my chest, said,
"Tis a bit late to remember him now."
I sat up, that hair-pulling, the sucker hurt, said,
"So you'll finish with him?"
She laughed, asked,
"Are ye mad entirely, he's loaded and I love money."
I tried for some decency, not that I know much about it, said,
"He's my buddy."
She began to massage my dick, asked,
"And how do you treat yer enemies?"

Another month of me fucking her twice a week, Richy buying her more and more shit, getting deeper in the hole and one evening, over a few brews, his face a riot of agony, he said,
"Joe, I'm in trouble."
I thought,
"You've no fucking idea, pal."

I said,

"Spill."

Deep, huh?

He drained his fourth bottle, now, he hit the Jameson, hard, said,

"I owe some guys and I can't meet the vig, never mind the freaking principal and Nora B, she's wanting more and more."

I echoed,

"Nora B . . . . what's with the B?"

He was puzzled, said,

"Jeez, I never asked . . . . beautiful, I guess."

Bitch, I thought

I said I'd see if I could maybe help him out.

Right.

The following Monday, Richy had his kids, and against my better judgment, I went back to Nora's place, always, we'd used my pad, we were deep in it when the door opened and there was Richy, his face a mask of stunned bewilderment. Nora, cool as an Irish breeze, slipped out of bed, naked, said,

"How 'as your day dear?"

He was reaching for his piece when she shot him in the head, twice, said,

"I just wouldn't have been able for all that whining he'd have done . . . . you?"

I was too shocked to speak and she said,

"Let's make it look like his shady friends got fed up with him, you can fix it to look like that, can you sweetheart?"

I could and I did.

And worse, I was part of the team that went after the wiseguys.

Nora disappeared, taking every cent Richy had stashed under the bed, she left me a note,

Joe a gra
I'm tired of policeman, ye are too serious.
I was thinking of getting some sunshine,
so if you're ever in Florida, look me up.
Tons of kisses,

Nora B.

'Course, she wasn't in Florida or anywhere else I could find her. She just seemed to vanish.

The years went by, and I managed to retire with most of my pension, and a cloud over my whole career.

Most nights, I sit and listen to that Irish wailing music, they give free razor blades with it, and I see Richy in my dreams, always with that lost look.

A few days ago, I heard from an old cop buddy, there was a hot joint up on the west side, run by a hot Irish broad, she had the most stunning red hair he said . . . . and get this,
green eyes.

I got the knife from a guy in a bar, and soon as I finish the next Jameson, I'm gonna take a stroll up there, after I chop off that red hair, and before I sever the jugular, she's gonna tell me what the fucking B stands for

It's like, been . . . . bugging me.

Bumping Uglies

by Donna Moore

"Hey! That's *my* fucking bag, you fat junkie bitch." Nice mouth on her, for all her expensive gear and fancy-looking Prada handbag. The handbag that was now in *my* possession as I legged it across the concourse of Central Station. Serves her right for putting it down on the seat beside her. Everyone knows that Central is like a well-stocked buffet of Glasgow's junkies, pickpockets and lowlifes. I considered it teaching her a lesson.

I could hear her stilettos pecking away like a crow on steroids as she tried to run after me. I wasn't worried that she would catch me—the shoes were too high and her skirt too tight. As I dodged startled passengers hurrying for their trains, I heard a shriek followed by the thwack of a bony Versace-clad arse hitting concrete. Excellent. Now I just had to avoid the cops. Half of Strathclyde's finest hang around Central Station. It's an easy way of meeting their arrest targets for the month. Just nip into Central and huckle a few likely characters—the nylon shell suits and Burberry baseball caps are a dead giveaway.

There are plenty of exits out of the station and, within seconds, I was down the stairs and out onto Union Street.

"Fuck's sake, hen . . ." The Big Issue seller I slammed into spun like a bearded prima ballerina.

I raised my hand in apology but didn't turn. "Sorry pal." I didn't stop until I got to the Clyde where I stood puffing and wheezing for a while, wondering if I was going to throw up. Running is not my forte. My chest is too big and my lungs are too wee. It was quiet by the river at this time of day and I sat on a bench and emptied the contents of the handbag out beside me, giving each item the once over before laying it down on the flaking blue paint of the bench.

First out was a wallet containing five crisp twenties, some loose change, gold credit cards and a handful of store cards— Frasers, John Lewis, Debenhams. Mrs Gillian McGuigan— according to the cards—certainly treated herself well. Then there was a top-of-the-range mobile phone with a diamante-studded G hanging from it. Tacky. Enough MAC cosmetics to stock a stall at The Barras, an appointment card for hair, nails and sunbed at The Rainbow Room and a couple of letters. She lived in Bothwell, and she would certainly fit in there amongst the footballers wives and ladies who lunch. High maintenance and flashy.

I opened the mobile phone and thumbed through the messages from oldest to newest. There were a couple from female friends and one or two from someone called Stewart. Since they were of the "Need loo rolls" and "working late, c u at 9" type, I assumed that Stewart was the poor, long-suffering Mr. McGuigan. Probably had to work late to keep his wife in bling.

Most of the texts were from Tom. "Wear the red basque on Friday," "Kate at sister's this weekend. Can u get away?", "Can't live without u. We need to do something about K and S" and "Seeing lawyer Thurs." It looked as though poor Kate and Stewart were in for a shock.

There were a couple of texts from someone called Billy. The most recent read, "One hit £10k, cd do both for £15K." Billy might be the solution to the problem, but if he was a lawyer, he was pricing himself out of the market. I checked the rest of Gillian's received texts and moved on to the sent box. They told quite a story. It would appear that the shock for Kate and Stewart was of the "shot in the head and dumped in the Clyde" sort rather than the "I now pronounce you ex-husband and wife" sort. Still, it was nice to know that "buy one, get one half price" extended as far as contract killings. I assumed that even taking into account the cost of the hitman, Gillian stood to make more as a widow than she would as a divorcee.

As I sat with the phone in my hand, pondering the best course of action, it rang. I might have guessed. The woman *had* to be my age at least. Nearly forty and she had a Justin Timberlake ringtone. The screen said "Home" so I flipped it up and answered.

"Gillian McGuigan's secretary. How may I help you?"

"You can fucking *help* me you cheeky fucking skanky whore by letting me rip that greasy ponytail out by the fucking roots you bitch. I want my bag back."

"Ouch. I'm hurt. Not all of us can afford to go to the Rainbow Room you know. I wonder what it is that Tom sees in you . . . your bleached blonde hair? Your orange sunbed tan? Your hatchet face? Your shrill voice with its extensive vocabulary?"

The sharp intake of breath practically sucked my ear off. "You've read my text messages you nosy bitch. I'll fucking *kill* you."

"Well, why not? That seems to be your answer to everything. Hopefully you'll get a bulk discount from your friend Billy."

"I . . . shit . . . I . . . You're fucking dead. Fuck . . . you've got to let me have the bag back. Please . . ." In the space of one sentence her voice changed from harridan to whiny six year old.

"No. Actually, doll, I don't have to let you have the bag back. I don't have to do heehaw." I shut the phone when the shrill voice started up again. I wondered whether Stewart was deaf. I'd been speaking to her for two minutes and that voice was really starting to grate on me. Some women give the rest of us a bad name.

I hugged my jacket closer to me and stared at the muddy Clyde as I thought about what I should do next. When I stole the bag it was a spur-of-the-moment thing. I'd been watching the woman for a while and when she put the bag down I just acted on impulse. Things had taken a surprising turn, but I was sure I could turn the situation to my advantage. I just needed to work out how.

The phone rang.

"Listen you fu . . ."

It rang again.

"Don't hang up."

"Then do try not to insult me. All that swearing is getting on my tits." I was enjoying this. It would seem though that poor Gillian would not recognize irony if it jumped up and bit her on the arse.

"Insult you? Where do *you* get off being so high and mighty? You're the fucking junkie, bag stealing bitch . . ."

She may well have been right, but I cut her off anyway. Besides, if we were talking about taking the elevator to the moral high ground, at least *I* was getting on it about half way up. I think adulterous, hitman-hiring shrews were roughly three floors below the basement.

"Please don't hang up."

"Better. Now, give me a good reason why I shouldn't."

"A hundred pounds."

"What is?"

"I'll give you a hundred pounds if you give me my handbag back."

I laughed. "Is that supposed to be a tempting offer?"

"Aye. Fuck . . . I don't know. It might save you sucking some guy's dick up an alley. What's the going rate for smack these days you . . ."

"Now now, Gillian. You know what happens when you start hurting my feelings. And if I hang up this time I'm going to take a wee wander up to Pitt Street and visit Strathclyde polis. I have an idea they might be interested in the contents of your phone."

"Oh, aye. That'll be right. I can just see you walking in there and saying 'Officers, here's a bag I mugged off of some wee wifey at Central Station.'"

"Maybe not, but I might just take one of these crisp twenties in your lovely flash handbag and buy some stamps. If I send it registered post it might even actually get there."

"Shite. How much do you want?"

I thought for a moment. I didn't want to come across as too cheap, but on the other hand, I didn't want to name a price that was so high that she would take the chance on me not going to the police. "Two thousand pounds."

"Two grand? You're kidding me, right?"

"Nope. I'm not smiling here. Two thousand. I think that's very fair. Tell me . . . just out of curiosity . . . does Tom know about your little plan to off your respective spouses?"

"Tom . . . ?"

"Yeah, you know, the poor misguided fool you're bumping uglies with."

"Of course he knows. It was him who gave me the idea."

"Really? Sounds like you're a match made in heaven."

Again, the irony was lost on her. "We are. We love each other. Can't keep our hands off each other. His wife is apparently a fat, frumpy bore, and my husband can't get it up any more."

"No wonder. You've probably sucked the life right out of him. And not in a good way."

"Oh shut the fuck up, you blackmailing bitch. When do I get my bag back?"

"Well, let's see. When can you get the £2,000?"

"Tomorrow."

Obviously I should have asked for more. "Do you know the Necropolis?"

"The big cemetery? I know of it, yeah."

"OK. Egyptian Vaults. 8pm tomorrow night. You can get a map off the internet. Oh, and bring your bit on the side. I'd quite like to see what all the fuss is about."

I shut the phone off before she could whine. I could tell from the noises on the other end of the phone that she was winding herself up to go off on one and, quite frankly, I'd had enough of her. She was mouthy, self-centered, trashy and shallow. Her plans proved that she was also dangerous and I didn't trust her one little bit. If I was going to meet her and Tom I needed some insurance. I opened the phone again and went to her contacts list. The phone was answered after one ring.

"Aye?"

"Billy? I want to buy a gun."

The Necropolis was locked up at dusk, but it's easy to get in, and so huge that it's impossible to ensure that no one does. I'd arrived at seven p.m., crossed the Bridge of Sighs, and made my way to the Egyptian Vaults via a circuitous route, just in case Gillian and Tom had planned a wee surprise for me. The place was not exactly welcoming during the day, but it was even less so after dark. Dilapidated and overgrown, it was a haven for junkies, wee neds drinking Buckfast and taking illegal substances, the homeless and the hopeless. Between some of the gravestones and in the sheltered spots beside the vaults were sleeping bags— as yet unoccupied—their owners perhaps at the soup kitchen on East Campbell Street, getting a little warmth and light before returning to this creepy place to sleep.

I wasn't worried about the dead. It was the living that concerned me, and I gripped the gun tighter. Billy had put me in touch with an acquaintance, who knew a guy, who had a friend who could possibly lay his hands on a gun. All very cagey, lots of ifs and buts, but I think Billy thought I was Gillian, since

I was ringing from her phone, so he opened a few doors for me. I guessed that the fifteen grand she had paid him would help. I assured him—as Gillian, of course—that I wasn't going to do a DIY job and cut him out. I just said I needed the gun for protection.

I met Billy's contact behind a pub in Possilpark. Just to be on the safe side I wore a blonde wig and sunglasses. I felt like Dolly Parton in a bad spy movie. The transaction had been quick and easy. The guy had turned out to be a man who could have been anywhere between forty and sixty. His cheekbones were prominent and angular and when he sucked at his cigarette his face turned into a skull.

"Do ye ken how tae use it?" Spittle came out of his mouth with every word. He had a set of false top teeth that he appeared to be breaking in for someone with a much bigger mouth, and no bottom teeth at all, which caused his face to cave in when his mouth was closed.

I nodded. I had grown up on a farm. "Aye." I held out the money we had agreed on and he passed over the padded envelope containing the gun.

He took one more drag of his cigarette. "Good luck, hen."

"Cheers, pal." And that was that. I don't know what I'd expected, but it was like going into the newsagents and buying the *Evening Times*.

I reached the Egyptian Vaults and chose a vantage point where I could see but not be seen. Just before eight o'clock I heard footsteps coming up the path.

"This woman's a weirdo. Why the hell did she want to meet us in this godforsaken place?" I recognized that shrill, whiny voice.

"Don't worry babe. We'll get the bag back and that will be that. These scumbags are only out for a quick score. I hope she's on time. Kate's expecting me home by nine."

I recognized *that* voice too. Cheating, murderous bastard. I stepped out of the shadows. "Don't worry, Tom. When you're not home by nine, I'll assume you have a good excuse."

"Kate?" Tom said.

"Kate?" Gillian repeated, looking at Tom and then at me. "You mean this fat junkie bitch is your *wife*?"

"Well, Tom? What do you say to that?"

"I . . . She . . . I . . ."

"Apparently Tom is lost for words Gillian. So, yes, I am the fat, frumpy bore married to your boyfriend. Not, however, a junkie. That was an assumption *you* jumped to. Understandable given the circumstances, I'll grant you that."

"How did you . . . ? What are you . . . ?"

"How did I know about your sleazy little affair, Tom? Well, let's face it, you're not exactly Mr. Discreet. And you look so guilty when caught answering text messages that are supposedly from your mates. So I followed you one day. And, well, not to get all Hercule Poirot about it, here we are."

Tom started towards me with his hands outstretched. "I'm sorry you had to find out like this, but let's just go somewhere and talk."

I raised the gun. "Just stop right there."

"A gun?"

"Ooooh, well *done*. That's exactly what it is."

"She's a fucking lunatic Tom. I told you what she was like on the phone. She . . ."

"Tom, tell her to shut the fuck up. This is between you and me right now."

"Don't you talk to me . . ."

"Gillian, just do as she says and shut the fuck up."

Gillian subsided into whimpering silence. It still sounded like fingernails scraping down a blackboard, but as long as there weren't any actual words, I could tune her out.

"So, did you go and see that divorce lawyer?"

"I . . . well . . . I . . ."

"No. The answer you're groping for is 'no' Tom. Because you chose a slightly more dramatic way out."

"It was Gillian's idea." His voice had turned from pompous to bleating and I could see him starting to sweat now.

Gillian's eyes opened wide. "You were all for it."

Tom ignored her. "It was easier for her because of the money. She would lose out on a fortune if she divorced Stewart. But I didn't want anything to do with it." A wavering smile appeared briefly as he tried to look sincere and honest. He looked about as sincere and honest as a politician caught with his trousers down in a brothel.

"You said it would be the best way. You lying bastard!"

We both ignored her. "I was caught up in it all, Kate. I wouldn't have hurt you. You've got to believe me."

This time it was my turn. "You lying bastard."

"Honest, Kate . . . I . . ."

"Tom, you wouldn't recognize honesty if it gave you a hug and called you mother." I could feel tears pricking behind my eyes. "Get your clothes off, both of you."

"What?!"

"Clothes off." I gestured with the gun. "Now. And fold them up neatly in a pile."

"Look, okay, you want to humiliate us, I understand." Tom hopped on one leg as he struggled to remove his jeans.

"Nah. I don't want to humiliate you. Now, lie down on the grass."

"I'm not doing—"

"Gillian, just shut it and do what I say. Lie down on the grass and put your arms around each other. Tom, you're looking decidedly unaroused. I've never seen it quite so shriveled and tiny. What's wrong? Lost your desire?" It was a cheap shot, but I couldn't resist.

They were on the ground, naked and shivering.

"Look Kate, this is just ridiculous. Let's go and talk somewhere like civilized . . ."

The shots were louder than I'd expected. And there was more blood. I pulled Tom's wallet out of his jeans and picked up Gillian's handbag. I would throw them in the Clyde on my way home, along with the gun. I wiped my prints off Gillian's phone and left it under the pile of clothes. If the police didn't think this was a mugging gone badly wrong, then maybe the text messages would lead them in Billy's direction. As far as he knew, Gillian had bought the gun. There was nothing to lead the police to me, and plenty to lead them away.

As I made my way out of the Necropolis and back to my car, it struck me that Gillian's handbag was another Prada. If nothing else, I'd saved Tom a small fortune in accessories.

Call me, I'm Dying

by Allan Guthrie

7:15 p.m.

Every year on the fifth of June we pretend we're married. This year is no different.

I look across at him, try to mold my face into the right expression.

"I'll get the soup," he says, getting to his feet.

Same menu as last year, I expect. And the year before.

I don't know, I'm guessing. I don't cook. I don't want to cook. I'm not paid to cook.

James likes to cook but he likes to play safe, too. Goes with the tried and tested.

Doesn't bother me.

I'm easy, so they say.

The food is a bonus.

Makes the sex easier.

7:16 p.m.

"You need a hand?" I ask him, knowing how he'll reply.

I'm dandy.

Sure enough. From the kitchen: "I'm dandy."

He's not that.

Supposed to be our tenth wedding anniversary and he's wearing a tatty checked shirt and jeans.

Could have made an effort.

We'll shower later.

I always insist on that.

7:17 p.m.

He carries the soup pan through. If it was me, I'd ladle it out in the kitchen.

It's not me.

If it was me, I'd have passed on the appetizer, gone straight for the main course. Takeaway pizza. Pepperoni and pineapple.

Each to his own, okay?

He places the pot on the table, takes off the oven gloves, removes the lid with a dramatic gesture and says, "*Voila!* French onion."

Now there's a surprise.

"Smells good," I say. And I shouldn't be harsh on him. It does smell good.

7:18 p.m.

"There we are," he says. "Shall we say Grace?"

I nod.

Then he hits me with this *you* or *me* thing, where he's just being polite 'cause we both know it's not going to be me. I grew up with it, and look how I've turned out.

"On you go," I say.

He nods, clears his throat, closes his eyes, adopts a tone somewhere between respectful and agonized. "For what we are about to receive," he says, "may the Lord make us truly thankful."

That's it. Good.

I blink. Pretending I've had my eyes closed too.

He's not fooled, but he joins in the game anyway.

It's all a game.

I always win.

I don't think he understands the rules. I'd ask him but I can't be bothered. I just want to get this over with.

I have things I'd rather be doing.

I'm liable to yawn and I don't want to upset him.

7:19 p.m.

"Nice?" he asks.

I pause, spoon halfway to my mouth. "Lovely."

"The key is to use plenty of butter."

That's it.

I lower the spoon, let it rest in the bowl. I'm not taking another sip. Butter. Plenty of it.

Is he trying to kill me?

I smile.

He smiles back. His hand edges across towards me.

"You don't mind?" he says.

Intimacy. Yes, I do mind. But I let him hold my hand anyway.

7:20 p.m.

"Your soup's getting cold," he says.

Fine by me.

"Not having any more?"

"Saving myself for the main course," I tell him.

"Oh," he says, disappointed but understanding.

Makes me want to smack a frying pan off his jaw.

At least he's let go of my hand.

I get a flash of him panting. In my ear. Sticky breath, getting faster and faster. I'm moaning, telling him he's the best, oh, yeah, the fucking best.

He likes it when I swear.

He comes and then he cries.

Wets my hair.

Every time.

Every year.

After dessert.

7:21 p.m.

He's talking. He's bought a boat. Not a fancy yacht, oh no. He laughs. Tells me about his boat.

I nod and smile, tuned out, wondering what I'm missing on TV.

White noise, his voice.

I smile from the heart, 'cause that rhymes.

Get a smile back, bless him.

I wonder if he'll be hard or if I'm going to have to play with him first.

7:22 p.m.

So excited babbling about his new boat, he spills soup on himself.

I grab a napkin, dab at his chin.

He likes that.

I wonder what precedent I've just set.

He excuses himself, says he has to change his shirt.

At least he doesn't ask me to do it for him.

I offer to clear the plates away.

He won't let me.

Always the gentleman.

7:25 p.m.

Back again wearing an almost identical shirt.

Took him long enough.

I heard the toilet flush, though. All that soup. Runs right through you.

Voila!

Must be the onions.

"You had enough?" he asks.

"Plenty," I say, only just managing to keep my hand from patting my stomach. A false gesture if ever there was one and I'm a better actress than that.

"Sure you don't want a hand?" I ask as he starts clearing away the plates.

"Just stay where you are," he says. "Keep looking beautiful."

7:27 p.m.

Still smarting from that comment.

Beautiful.

Bastard.

7:28 p.m.

The casserole dish is on the table, steaming.

Beef stew. Yep, same as last year.

Predictable, is our James the Sarcastic.

Smells good, though. I'm going to have to eat.

I don't want to. I want to punish him.

He might like that.

"Shall I be mother?" he says.

We know he's going to be mother. I don't know why he asks. "Yeah," I say. It's a role that suits him.

He slops some of the stew onto my plate. "More?" he says.

I nod. I hate myself.

7:29 p.m.

The beef's tender, melting into soft strings in my mouth. The sauce is sharp, peppery.

I swallow. Lick my teeth.

"Good, darling?"

Darling.

Have to play along. "Yes, *dear*," I say.

He puts his hand on mine again.

"This is nice, isn't it?" he says.

"Lovely," I tell him. Fuckwit.

7:30 p.m.

The phone rings. It's persistent.

He doesn't move.

"Answer it," I say.

"Not tonight," he says. "This is a special night. We don't want any interruptions."

So maybe you should have turned off the ringer.

"It's annoying," I say. And it is. Least he could have done was set up his answer machine to take it. At home, four rings is all you get. If I don't pick up by then, you're on to the machine.

Still ringing.

"You don't have an answerphone?"

"Yeah," he says.

"So how come it hasn't kicked in?"

"Dunno," he says. "Takes a while."

I lay down my knife and fork. "Go sort it," I say. "Turn it off."

He looks sheepish as he gets out of his seat. "May as well answer it, then," he says.

Course, by the time he gets there, it'll have stopped. I'd bet on it.

The phone's at the other end of the room. Amazingly it's still ringing when he picks it up.

"Hello," he says. Then gives his number.

Doesn't say anything else.

Just listens.

Then puts the phone down gently, like it's hurting.

7:31 p.m.

"Wrong number?" I ask.

He shakes his head, still standing there, hand on the receiver, receiver in its cradle.

"Not much of a conversationalist, then?" I say. "What did they say?"

He makes his way back to the table, silent.

"Well?" I say.

"You won't believe me," he says. He looks bemused, like a stranger just hit him with a fish.

"You'd be surprised," I tell him.

"It was a man," he says. "I didn't recognize his voice."

He stops. Bites his bottom lip.

"I don't have all night," I say. More to the point, *he* doesn't have all night. He isn't paying for that. Just till midnight.

"He said my name." He looks at me. Looks away.

"And?" I make a circular motion with my fingers to try to speed him up.

"He told me I had thirty minutes to live."

7:32 p.m.

That's weird, I have to admit.

"Why would anyone say that to you?" I ask him.

He doesn't answer, just sits at the table staring into his plate. He picks up his fork, holds it for a second, drops it. It clatters against the plate.

"Maybe it was a wrong number," I say.

He says, "He said my name."

"Maybe it was another James Twist," I say.

He doesn't bother to answer. We both know that's unlikely.

"It's a joke, then," I say.

That piques his interest. "You think?"

"Sure," I say. "A friend, a colleague."

"I don't think so," he says.

I spread my fingers, palms up. *Why?*

"I don't have any friends," he says. "And I haven't worked in ten years."

7:33 p.m.

Well, well.

"You're not an architect?" I ask him.

He shakes his head.
"Were you ever an architect?"
He shakes his head again.
"What did you do? What was your last job?"
"Postman," he says.
I can't believe I'm angry at him, but I am.
"You've been lying to me for years," I say.
"Sorry," he tells me.
"How can you afford to buy a new boat?"
He doesn't answer.
"That was a lie too?"
"Yes," he says.
"What about this place?"
"My mum pays for it."
"Oh," I say. "She didn't die when you were four?"

7:34 p.m.
It can't be helped, I suppose. The guy I didn't like wasn't the guy I thought he was.
Interesting.
"If it's not a friend or colleague," I say, "then maybe it's a member of your family."
"Just me and Mum," he says.
"And it wasn't her?"
"It was a man," he says.
"What happened to your dad?"
He pulls a face.
For a second, I don't know what he's doing, or why.
Then I realize it's involuntary. A spasm. I've never seen him do that before.
He does it again, his eyes screwing up tight, lips curling.
Like he just sucked a grapefruit.
And then it's gone.
"Your dad?" I remind him.
"He's dead," he says. Looks at me. "Honest."
"I'm sorry." I reach over and place my hand on his.

7:35 p.m.
He moves his hand so it's on top of mine. He squeezes.

We stare at our hands, don't look at each other.

Time drags past.

He strokes my hand. Over and over and over again.

I'm intrigued by the phone call. And by what I'm finding out about James.

"Your mum have a boyfriend, maybe?" I say, at last.

He tears his hand away from mine, swipes his plate onto the floor.

Don't fucking hit me. Don't you fucking dare.

He doesn't, although he looks at me like he wants to.

7:38 p.m.

He picks up shards of broken plate, lays the pieces on the table.

"I don't know why—" he says.

"I should leave."

"Please don't," he says. He sits, wipes his fingers on his napkin. "That call, it's thrown me."

I shrug. "Not surprising," I say.

"I'd like you to stay," he says. "I don't want to be alone."

"All right," I tell him. "But don't get violent."

"I won't."

"If you do," I say, "I'll kick the shit out of you."

He grins. Doesn't believe me.

He's never been aggressive before. I try to avoid men who are. But I've learned to deal with them just in case.

I can look after myself.

I teach self-defense classes when I'm not working.

I'm not scared of James.

7:39 p.m.

"We should clear up that mess," I say. "The carpet's a state."

"Just leave it," he says.

"It'll stink."

"That's okay."

"It'll stain."

He's quiet.

"You don't care if it stains?"

He shakes his head.

"Your Mum's carpet anyway," I say. "Her problem. That

what you're thinking?"

"No," he says. "I have other things to think about."

"Then let me do it," I say.

"It's our anniversary, Tina," he says. "You can't clean the floor tonight."

I sigh. If I can't clean the carpet, I might as well eat. "What's for pudding?" I ask.

7:40 p.m.

He thinks I'm joking.

I don't push.

He already looks like he might cry and I don't want to send him over the edge.

"Why did you stop working?" I ask him.

He looks at me, eyes dark and uncomprehending.

"You said you used to be a postman."

He nods. That's it, though.

I have to help him.

"Were you a postman for long?"

He plays with his fork again.

I anticipate another clatter.

"Five years," he says.

"Did you enjoy it?"

"Yeah."

"So what happened?"

"They let me go."

Another topic I shouldn't have introduced. I'm on a roll.

"I'm sorry to hear that," I say.

"Me too," he says.

And as I'm watching, he slams the fork into his hand.

Screams.

I scream too.

He wrenches the fork back out.

Blood's leaking out of the four holes he's made, running together, tracking down the back of his wrist.

"What the fuck?" I say. "What the fuck are you doing?"

His mouth's open and he's panting.

"He's after me," he says. "Don't look at me like that. He is."

"That's maybe so, James," I say. "But put the fork down and

let's see what you've done to your hand."

"It's okay," he says. "I feel better."

"It doesn't hurt?"

"It does," he says. "But it takes a little pain to let the evil out."

7:42 p.m.

Holy shit.

I'm torn between legging it out of here and making sure James is okay. He needs to go to the hospital. Leave him here on his own and God knows what he'll do to himself.

Between last year and now, he's turned into a headcase.

Presumably there was nobody on the phone. He made all that up about somebody telling him he only had thirty minutes to live.

This guy who was after him was a figment of James's fucked-up brain.

But the phone had rung. Someone had called.

I get to my feet.

7:43 p.m.

"Where are you going?" he says. "Don't leave me."

He's cradling his hand now.

"I'm going to check something out," I tell him. "I'll be right back."

I walk over to the phone. Punch in the code to find out who just called.

And hear: *You were called today at 7:30 p.m. The caller withheld their number.*

So much for that theory.

7:44 p.m.

"Let me take you to get your hand fixed," I say.

"No." He shakes his head hard.

"Then let me look at it."

He thinks about it. Then relaxes. Holds his hand out to me.

It's a bloody mess. The puncture wounds have coagulated, though. The blood's stopped flowing.

Not that deep.

Good.

He'll be okay.

"You got a first-aid kit?" I ask him.

"No," he says.

"Antiseptic wipes? Plasters?"

He looks vague.

"A clean cloth? Water?"

He grins. "Of course."

7:46 p.m.

So I've got the stuff and I'm cleaning his hand.

He winces like I'm scraping my nails on his heart.

"How come you had to do that?" I ask him.

For a moment he forgets to act pained. "Huh?" he says.

"Stabbing yourself. Seems . . . extreme."

He shrugs.

"You do that often?" I've never noticed any scars.

"My feet," he says. "The soles of my feet."

Ow.

"To let the evil out?"

"I wouldn't expect you to understand," he says.

Thing is, I do.

I do.

Me and razor blades, we go way back. Not that I'm going to tell James, though. None of his business.

He's my business, not the other way round.

I opt for, "You'd be surprised."

He gives me a look, winces again.

"You said he was after you," I say, dropping the cloth in the bowl of water.

"This is going to bruise." He flexes his fingers.

"I expect so. Who's after you?"

"I can't say."

"Maybe I can help," I tell him.

7:47 p.m.

His words come out slow and staggered. I'll summarize.

Started about a year ago when James began to feel he was being followed every time he walked home. Never spotted anyone, but just had the sense someone was watching him. Heard footsteps but couldn't swear they weren't echoes of his own.

And then he felt he was being followed whenever he left the house, too.

He started taking the car.

A vehicle always followed him. Not always the same vehicle, though. So it was sometimes hard to spot.

I wanted to ask him if he had surveillance cameras under his fingernails, and transmitters implanted in his brain.

I held my tongue.

He carried on. Told me how he was being watched all the time now. His stalker was close. Maybe watching him now. Him and me.

I say, "But if this is true, why does injuring yourself help?"

A textbook case of paranoia.

"Because of what I've done," he says.

Do I want to know?

"If you tell me," I say, "will you have to kill me afterwards?"

7:50 p.m.

"My uncle came back," he says.

He has an uncle?

"I thought you had no family," I say.

He says, "He's not really an uncle. He . . . went out with my mum for a while."

"Came back from where?" I ask.

"Disappeared a long time ago," he says. "Went off to Brazil. Never heard from him again. You assume the worst after a while."

"So you thought he was dead?"

He nods.

"And he's not?"

He nods again.

"And you stabbed yourself in the hand because of that?"

"No, no," he says. "It's a lot more complicated."

I expected so. I look at my watch.

"Maybe you better keep it simple," I say. "According to your uncle, you only have ten minutes to live."

A cheap shot, I know.

So I'm a bitch. What can you expect from a whore?

7:51 p.m.

"It wasn't him," James says. "I'd have recognized his voice."

"But you do think he's behind it?"

"Yes," he says. "No question. He's made my life hell since he's been back."

He flexes his fingers, a pained expression scrawled across his face.

"He must have hired somebody to make the call," he says.

"And why would he do that?"

"To scare me," he says.

"You think the threat's serious?"

"Definitely."

"James," I say. "What did you do to him?"

7:52 p.m.

He tells me.

It's not that bad. Not the sort of thing you'd kill somebody for.

Listen:

"I torched his car."

See?

"His dog was in it."

Oh.

"But I didn't know that."

Still.

"And he said he'd have to leave the country or he'd kill me."

"Why?" I ask.

"Because of the dog."

"No," I say. "Why did you torch his car?"

"Because," he says, and swallows. "He raped my mum."

7:53 p.m.

There's not much more to it.

Uncle goes out with Mum. Mum calls it off after a few weeks. Uncle returns and rapes mum. She won't go to the police, and who can blame her, the way we're all made to feel like it's our fucking fault. *What were you wearing?* As if that makes any fucking difference. Anyway, James torches dog and car. Uncle leaves country. Uncle returns several years later. Uncle's still angry.

But there's no way he's still going to be murderously angry. Not after all that time.

I say, "He's messing with you."

James says, "No."

"How can you be sure?"

"Cause I know him. I know what he's capable of."

"Well," I say, and I can't think of anything to add, so I say, "well," again and leave it at that. There's only one way to prove to James that it's all a hoax and that's to sit it out with him. I owe him that.

After all, he's paying for my time.

"I like dogs," James says. "Honest."

"I believe you," I say.

7:54 p.m.

Back in the sitting room, James keeps glancing towards the door.

He's shaking all over, poor soul.

No, I do feel sorry for him. I do.

He did something he shouldn't have. But he did it out of love. The dog was an accident.

But when I think about it, I can't imagine a dog not barking. They're territorial. A stranger approaches the car, close enough to set it alight, the dog would let him know it was there.

Wouldn't it?

James is lying.

But why?

Is he lying about the whole event? Or is he just lying about the dog?

7:55 p.m.

"You did it deliberately, right?"

"What?"

He knows what I mean.

I stare at him till he looks away.

He doesn't deny it.

But I have to say it: "You killed the dog."

He says, quietly, "It was an accident."

"So why do you cut yourself? What evil is it you're letting out?"

He makes that face again.

"Jesus," I say. "How long ago was this?"

"I was seventeen."

"Then it's about time you forgave yourself," I tell him.

"I can't," he says. "I can't, Tina."

"Well," I say. "I don't blame you, really."

"You don't?"

He starts to cry. Before long these horrible wracking sobs are jerking his shoulders up and down.

I put my arms round him, let him rest his head against my neck. His tears drip onto my neck, but what the fuck. I'm used to that.

"Thank you," he squeezes out between sobs.

"Shhh," I say, like he's a baby.

7:56 p.m.

He stops as suddenly as he started.

"How long?" he asks, wiping his eyes.

I tell him.

"I have to lock the door," he says.

He jumps to his feet, runs through to the hall where I can't see him any longer.

I hear him scrabbling about.

Then I don't hear anything.

For a while.

For too long.

I get worried.

7:58 p.m.

There's no sign of him anywhere.

He's not in the hall.

Not in any of the bedrooms.

Not in the bathroom.

He's gone.

Did he leave of his own accord?

If so, why didn't he tell me he was leaving?

Did his uncle sneak in, grab him, steal him away?

Sounds dramatic, and I don't believe a word of it.

I check the front door. It's locked. There we go.

It's crazy, I know, but I go back through all the bedrooms, look in the wardrobes, under the beds. I check everywhere, but he's definitely not here.

I'm feeling uncomfortable.

I get my things together.

I'm not hanging around here.

I'm going home.

8:00 p.m.

Outside, the traffic's busy.

Across the road, I see a face I recognize.

James.

He's wearing that screwed-up expression, the one I'd never seen until I mentioned his father.

He's standing by the curb, an older man in a long raincoat by his side.

I raise my hand, wave.

James stares right through me.

I shout to him.

The man in the raincoat thinks I'm shouting at him.

I can't say whether James is pushed in front of the bus, or whether he steps in front of it.

The impact is swift and brutal.

He never had a chance.

I wet myself.

After the shock passes, I remember the man in the raincoat.

But he's gone.

The bus has stopped.

The street is silent.

Nobody moves.

We're frozen like this, like a painting, and I wonder if James still has that expression on his face.

Everybody Loves Somebody

by Sandra Scoppettone

All my life I ran away from everything. When I was fifteen I made tracks outta Clinton, PA to the Big Apple fast as I could. I left my Mama, Daddy, brother Tom and my little sister, Beth Ann. I wrote a note tellin them not to look for me, I'd be okay. It wasn't that stuff was bad in my house, no drunks or my Daddy comin into my room late at night, or Tom haulin off on me. It was cause it was boring in Clinton and I didn't like boring.

I also left a guy. Wayne Preston. He was cool. But not cool enough. Good lookin. People was always sayin, "Look at the two of them, him with the blonde hair like Brad Pitt and her with that red hair like the gal on *CSI*" and "Wayne and Deb make such a cute couple." Guess we did. But I knew if I stayed Wayne and me would get married when he was eighteen and I was sixteen and I'd have a kid right away. We'd live in some fallin down house and Wayne would get a crummy job and then any fun we'd been havin would all go away. I'd seen it happen to more than one.

I left a note for Wayne, too, tellin him not to look for me. I told him Fran Karanewski had a big crush on him and he should take her out. They'd be good together. I figured it'd take Wayne about a week before he gave her a call.

When I got off the bus in the New York City terminal, I blew off the pimps who tried recruitin me and made my way to a subway. I had everything planned out so I knew where I could find a cheap room.

I found one all right. It was a dark place. The paint was comin off the walls and it smelled like old people. I hated it. But I couldn't afford nothin else.

I got a job same day in a coffee shop waitin on tables. That was the only job I knew how to do. The place was in the West Forties. It was your usual, with menus offering the world. The food stunk. A guy named Nick ran the joint. He didn't ask me to show any proof when I said I was eighteen. I looked it, but I think he knew and didn't give a rat's ass. The ass he cared about was mine.

The short-order cook, Buzz, found a way to rub up against my tits almost every time I passed him. I had the graveyard shift and was the only soup jockey there. So when there weren't any customers Buzz and Nick made my life hell.

It didn't take me too long to run away from that job. But every gig I got it was the same story so I ran away from one job after another. Until I met Edward.

"You live alone, Deborah?"

He wouldn't call me Deb.

"Yeah, I do."

"You like that?"

"It's okay."

"You like the place where you live?"

By then I'd moved to another room but it was just as gloomy as the first.

"Not a whole lot," I said.

"I think you should go out with me. I like your green eyes." He blew a perfect smoke ring.

I turned him down a lotta times until I got tired of the routine and I said I'd go. We went to a real fancy restaurant and he ate snails. It made me sick to watch him. He ordered for me and when the steak came it was runnin blood and looked like it was just cut from the cow. I could hardly get it down. Edward knew and I think he thought it was funny.

Afterwards, we went back to his place which was like somethin outta a magazine. I can't say I didn't know what was gonna happen 'cause I did. Me and Wayne had been doin it for a couple a years so I wasn't no innocent.

What I didn't know was Edward had plans for me.

He moved me into his place three days after that first time and treated me like a queen. Four weeks after that he started bringing home the men. I couldn't say no. I liked livin there and I liked not havin to sling hash for a livin.

"You do whatever they ask," he said.

"Okay."

"You understand this, Deborah?"

"'Course I understand. You think I'm a moron?" I lit a Marlboro Light.

"I think you're a beautiful girl and we can make a lot of money."

I laughed to myself. I knew I'd never see a penny and I didn't. I had my own room with a 32-inch Plasma TV and could order anything I wanted to eat, and Edward bought my clothes, but as for cash, nada.

After six months I took the cash I found underneath Edward's briefs in the top drawer of his dresser, some from his coat pocket and ran away. The money came to seven hundred and two dollars.

Funny thing about New York was it wasn't that easy to hide. I knew Edward would be lookin for me so I got on a bus and went to New Jersey. Waitress jobs were easy to get in Kearny. So were rooms.

My life went on like that, me runnin away from men and jobs and rooms and states even. By the time I was twenty I was livin in New London, Connecticut. That's where I met Julius all dolled up in his sailor suit. He was fine lookin, like a movie star.

"I got this garage, hon. An auto place. Me and my dad. We make good money there. And you wouldn't have to work no more."

"You'd take care of me?"

"You bet. I wouldn't want my wife to work."

"Wife?"

"Yeah, what did ya think?"

"I dunno. You proposin, Jule?"

"You want I should get down on one knee or somethin?"

"I just didn't know."

"Okay. How about you and me send our laundry out in one bag?"

Soon as he was outta the Navy we got married at City Hall and that afternoon we got a bus to Gary, Indiana, where he was from. I woulda gone anywhere with Julius.

His folks were okay. They drank a little more than I liked. And Jules, who'd hardly drank before, was knockin them back, too. I tried to keep up but I'd just get sick. We lived in an apartment over his folks' garage. Cindy, his mother, said I could decorate any way I wanted so that kept me busy for the first month. After that I didn't know what the hell to do with myself.

Then came the beatings. Jules would get drunk after work and come home late. That's when he found everything wrong with me and the place I thought I'd made so nice. He didn't like the slipcover on the couch, the curtains, the placemats, you name it. Especially, he didn't like me. He hated my freckles, my nose was too big, and my tits were too small.

He called me a bitch, a whore, a slut, a cunt, a liar and a thief. Always a thief. I never did find out what I was supposed to have boosted 'cause I didn't stay around after the twelfth time. I didn't know why I'd stayed that long, but I vowed I'd never do it again. So I ran away and I ended up in Detroit, Michigan.

It took me a bunch of rides and a bus to get there. Not sure I woulda stayed if I'd known I'd be cold all the time. Except summer. I was only good at one thing so I got a job at a luncheonette run by a dude named Randolph who everybody called Randy. And he was. Didn't take me long to find that out.

He wasn't a looker like Jules, but I told myself maybe the lookers were the worst ones. Randy kept his grayin hair in a pony tail and always wore a leather vest with silver studs over a black t-shirt, jeans and black boots he never cleaned. He kept a Harley out back and he spent most of his time workin on that hunk a metal. Least when he was romancin that thing he was leavin me alone. But when he wasn't foolin with the bike he was tryin to fool with me. And when he wasn't doin that he was dealin coke.

Finally it came down to the job or Randy. I figured I could get another job somewhere, but I knew there'd be another Randy. There'd always be another Randy. Besides, if it got too bad I could take off.

He had an apartment over the luncheonette and I moved in with him from a dingy room I had ten minutes away.

I figured this was what my life was gonna be. One waitress job, one lousy room, one dickhead after another.

His place was a mess so I cleaned it up, made it nice. After two days I saw the safe. It was in the wall of the bedroom closet behind his clothes.

That night I was lyin on the bed paintin my finger and toenails silver. Anything in the red line clashed with my hair. "Burglars come in here, Randy, that safe isn't gonna be hard to find."

"What fuckin safe?"

"The one in the closet. You got more than one?"

"You spyin on me?" Randy drank from his bottle of Bud.

"I was cleanin the closet." He hadn't said word one about how nice everything looked. "Anyways, it wouldn't be hard to find in there."

"Yeah, but burglars would have to know the combination."

"I thought safe crackers didn't need combinations. Don't they just listen to the clicks?" I lit a cig.

"You watch too much TV."

"But it's true. Safe crackers can get into any safe."

"Shut your trap."

I didn't let on I knew about his dealin and I figured he had a lot of cash in that safe.

"Whatcha got in there, Randy?"

"Wouldn't you love to know?"

"Yeah. That's why I'm askin." I blew some smoke outta my nostrils like the movie stars in them old black-and-white flicks.

He walked right up to the end of the bed where I was lyin. His face was red like a cherry. And if I hadn't known better I would've sworn steam was comin out of his ears like in a cartoon.

He pointed a finger at me and twirled it like it was on a ball bearing. "You listen to me, bitch. I don't wantcha askin about that safe or goin near it. You understand?"

"Sure. I was just kiddin around. No need to get so crazy about it."

Then he yelled. "I'm not gettin crazy. Don't ever say that again."

"Okay, okay. Everything's cool."

"It better be."

My life with Randy was mostly boring. On my days off I went to the movies. And when it wasn't busy in the luncheonette I read my mystery novels.

"Whaddaya read that junk for?" Randy asked, scratchin his balls.

"It's not junk. They're good stories."

"Lemme see."

I handed it over.

"*Elmore* Leonard?"

"What about him?"

"Sounds like a fag. Least you could do is read some of them guys like Spillane, or that other one."

"What other one?"

"You know."

"I don't."

"You know. What's his name?"

"Randy, I don't know who you're talkin about."

"McBain. Yeah. Ed McBain."

"I like what I'm readin."

"Faggot." He handed the book back. "Waste of time readin. Let's go for a ride."

I hated ridin on the back of that Harley. Scared me. But I knew if I said no he'd make my life miserable. Randy never hit me (I wouldn't put up with that again), but he'd sulk. Sulkin was the worst. I hated sulkers. Randy made the whole apartment black and soon I was depressed and ready to jump off a bridge.

So I put my blue and gold helmet on and hopped on the back of the goddamn Harley. I remember this day 'cause when we got back Bobby Mazard was waitin on Randy for the short-order cook job he'd advertised. Bobby was real good-lookin. Black eyes that matched black hair. A smile that brought out dimples and a nice full mouth. The body wasn't bad either.

Randy gave Mazard a hard time so I went upstairs. When I came back down I saw that Bobby had the job.

Bobby and me got to be friends right away. I never liked anybody so much so quick. Then one night when Randy was out dealin, and we were closin up, Bobby kissed me.

I was shocked. For two reasons: that Bobby would do that, kiss me just like that, and because I'd never felt that way before when I was kissed. I remember thinkin 'so this is what it's supposed to be like.'

I looked back at all the guys who'd kissed me and there wasn't a one made me feel like that. I knew I was in trouble. Big trouble. We started makin out and before I knew it we were on the floor of the kitchen and our clothes were flung every which way. And when I came it was like an explosion, like nothin I could've ever imagined.

We knew we had to be careful so we got dressed right away. Bobby kissed me goodbye and said real sweet, "Tomorrow, Princess."

That night when Randy came home I was wide awake in our bed, but I pretended to be asleep cause the thought of him puttin a finger on me made me want to throw up.

The next mornin I couldn't wait for Bobby to come to work. Randy said, "Why're you actin so fidgety?"

"I don't know whatcha mean. You give Bobby a key?"

"No. Ya think I'm crazy givin out a key after one day's work?"

"I'm goin down to open up." I went downstairs and saw that Bobby was waitin outside the door. I unlocked. Those black eyes made me melt. We pretended like nothin happened and I got the coffee goin while Bobby got the grill ready.

Weeks went by and whenever me and Bobby could be together we was. Sex got better and better. I couldn't believe what I'd been missin all those years.

I don't know why but one day I said to Bobby, "Randy's got a safe in the bedroom closet."

"What's in it?"

"He's a dealer."

"Yeah, I know. Weed?"

"Coke."

"You ever try it?" Bobby asked.

"No. You?"

"Tried it once. Made me sick. I'm not into it. I smoke a little weed now and then."

"Yeah, sure. Who doesn't?" Truth was *I* didn't. I didn't like it.

"So you think Randy's got product in that safe?"

"Maybe. But mostly money from dealin."

"How much?"

"Don't know, but I think it's a lot."

"Like what?"

I shrugged.

"Over ten thou?"

"Gotta be," I said.

"Sweet. How can we find out?"

I stroked Bobby's cheek. "Gotta get the combination."

"How?"

"That's the problem. Randy won't tell me. He won't even talk about the safe with me. Once when I asked him what was in there he went nuts."

"So there's gotta be mucho money in it."

"Yeah."

We talked about a lot of ways to get that safe open, but nothin we came up with was really gonna do it. Bobby said once we got the money we'd split this town and go somewhere warm. Like Mexico.

Sounded good to me.

The more days went by the more impatient we got and the more Bobby hated me sleepin in a bed with Randy. I couldn't stand it when he tried to touch me. I kept makin excuses, but I didn't know how long that would work. Least Randy wasn't the warm and fuzzy type, always huggin and kissin. But Bobby was, whenever there was a chance.

It was Thursday nights Randy opened that damn safe and put whatever he had inside. Bobby said that was when Randy made his deliveries and pickups. We figured we'd have to knock Randy out once he'd opened the safe. It was the only way.

Bobby was no safe cracker and me neither. And whatever the combination was it was in Randy's head and no place else, 'cause I knew that's how he was.

"You won't hurt him too bad, will you, Bobby?"

"Just a knock on the head that'll keep him out long enough for us to get the cash and beat it outta here."

We were gonna jump in the car, cross the border to Canada, drive across it and down to the West Coast where we'd buy a new car, then go all the way to Mexico. The good thing was Randy couldn't report anything to the cops.

When Thursday night came and we closed up, Bobby and me went upstairs. We made love and it was as good as ever. I especially liked doing it on Randy's bed. I had my suitcase packed and in Bobby's car.

About half an hour before Randy usually came home we took our places. I was in bed reading my mystery book and Bobby was hidin with a hammer at the far end of the closet behind my clothes I wasn't takin. The safe was in the middle.

It was nerve-wrackin waitin for Randy and I kept readin the same sentence over and over. Then I heard his bike, him parkin it, his feet crunchin the gravel. The luncheonette door opened and the little bell rang. I hated that fuckin bell.

I heard him walk to the apartment door then come up the steps. He crossed the livin room to the bedroom where I was waitin for him.

"Hey, Randy."

He grunted.

He was carryin his beat up briefcase, faded brown with a metal lock that didn't work. He went to the closet right away, opened the door, put the briefcase on the floor. His back blocked me from seein him turn the combination. That was the way he always did it.

I saw the safe door open and coughed twice. Bobby's cue. Randy looked to the side, surprised. Bobby hit him on the head with the hammer and Randy went down.

I jumped out of bed. Bobby kept hittin Randy. That wasn't in the plan.

"Hey," I said.

Blood was flyin all over the place, gettin on Bobby's shirt and face. And the back of Randy's head was so red with blood it didn't even look like a head.

"That's enough, Bobby. You'll kill him."

Bobby paid no attention to me and kept on hittin Randy.

Finally I screamed, "Stop it, stop, stop."

Bobby heard me then and stepped back from Randy's ruined head and limp body. I didn't want to get any closer to Randy, but I had to know.

Bobby was breathin like a horse. It was hard to look at the mess that was Randy's head so I kept my eyes on his arm and wrist. I leaned down and felt for a pulse even though I knew.

"You killed him, Bobby."

"It's better this way."

"Why? He couldn't of turned us in."

"Yeah, I know. But he could've tried to find us, sent somebody after us. We'd never be sure, lookin over our shoulders all the time."

"But now the cops will get in on this."

"They'll think it was a drug hit."

"Even if we're gone?"

"Don't worry about it."

I let it go.

"Look in the safe," I said.

"Jesus, Deb there's a lot in here."

"I told you," I said, as if that made all the difference. As if Bobby hadn't just done a murder.

We took the money from the safe and the briefcase, careful not to leave prints on those things. Our prints would be all over the place but that didn't matter.

I got Randy's old suitcase out of the closet and we both dumped the money inside. Then Bobby took a shower, changed clothes and I got dressed.

We turned off the lights and went downstairs. The creaking of the linoleum floor spooked me. When we got to the door Bobby turned and said, "Don't worry about nothin. I'll take care of you now." And then she kissed me.

Outside, we went around the corner where Bobby had parked her car. She opened the door for me like she always did and said, "We're on our way, babe."

And in another minute we were.

Working Girls, Tomboys and Girls Friday

Hungry Enough

by Cornelia Read

"I absolutely adore driving drunk," said Kay. "It's so damn *easy*."

The top was down on her little two-seater Mercedes—one of those burnished days, after a week of rain.

She surprised me by careening right onto Hollywood Boulevard, off Cherokee.

"Darling girl," I protested, "the Cahuenga Building went that-a-way. I'm an hour late as it is."

The wind was ruining our hair.

She plucked a strand of platinum from her lipstick. "One tiny stop, Julia. I have a few things for you at the house."

Kay'd offered me birthday lunch at Chasen's, her treat. I held out for Musso and Frank's so I had the option of walking back to work.

"You gave me your solemn oath," I said. "Only reason I agreed to that fifth martini."

"Wouldn't you rather arrive sober than punctual?"

"I need this job, Kay."

"You need a *husband*, Julia," she said. "You're twenty-five years old."

"I seem to recall having already suffered through this lecture. Somewhere between cocktails three and four."

"Honey," she said, "it's practically 1960 and you're dying on the goddamn vine."

"I happen to *like* the vine. Marvelous view. Fee fi fo fum, et cetera, et cetera . . ."

"Three years in Los Angeles, and what do you have to show for it?"

I had one ingénue turn on *Perry Mason* and a succession of glossy headshots to show for it, as Kay knew perfectly well. She, meanwhile, had a rich producer husband.

"Another Greyhound bus pulls into this town every five minutes," she continued, "packed to the gills with fresh-faced little mantraps—"

"—I cannot believe you're willing to be seen *driving* this tacky thing," I said. "Powder blue with white upholstery?"

"Says she who takes dictation from the man in a powder blue suit," said Kay. "Promise me you're not sleeping with him. He wears socks with *clocks* on them, for chrissakes."

"Promise *me* this color scheme wasn't your idea."

"Of course not. I found it in the driveway last week, complete with jaunty bow over the hood. Another little kiss-and-make-up incentive from Kenneth."

Kenneth, her rich producer husband, snared last year at a Sunday brunch swim party in Bel-Air. He'd been sunning himself on a raft in the water's shallow end. Kay sauntered up in a bathing suit and heels, crooked one finger, and said, "Hey you, out of the pool."

Tuesday morning, his third wife chartered a plane to Reno.

I caught her eye in the rear-view mirror. "Darling, this car practically *shouts* divorcée—"

"—A girl can dream, can't she?"

"For chrissake, Kay-Kay," I said, "If you're that unhappy, why not leave him?"

"Because I finally have some leverage, Julia, now that I've seen what that plate glass is for."

This was an inch-thick slab suspended above their bed on golden cables. Kay had recently discovered her husband lying beneath the transparent platform while baby-oiled young blond men wrestled one another atop it. Defecation earned them bigger tips at the end of the night.

"Did I tell you," she said, "that he actually thought I'd go down on him while those appalling creatures moiled around in their own filth?"

"Whereupon you told *him* he was out of his ever-loving mind and stalked out of the room," I replied, leaving out the part about how she showed up at my place that night with a bottle of Seconal, already half-consumed.

She turned to flash me a grin, then held up her wrist to flash something blue-white, flawless, and far more enduring. "Look what arrived with my breakfast tray, just this morning."

"Harry Winston?"

"Cartier," she said. "He's learning."

She hauled the wheel left again, shooting us down a palm-tree-lined boulevard.

I shrugged. "So you'll put up with it. You're one of the wives now."

"This year," she said.

I rolled my eyes. "And whose job it is to swab down the sheet of glass, afterwards?"

"Search me," she said, "but I hope to hell it's that little shit Carstairs."

Carstairs was Kenneth's secretary—a snippy little man who was still quite blond, possibly British, and ten years past earning his keep unclothed. He and Kay loathed one another. Trying to get him fired was her primary form of entertainment, after shopping.

We pulled up to a stoplight. The man in the Cadillac next to us wrenched his neck, getting an eyeful of Kay.

She ignored him with intent, one sly finger twisting the pearls at her neck. "I'm not ever going to be goddamn famous, now, am I?"

"'Course you won't," I said. "Fame is reserved for those fresh-faced little man-traps who can't go home on the Greyhound."

"I'm better looking."

"Fairest one of all," I said. "But you aren't hungry enough. You never were."

"And you're too goddamn *smart*."

"Have to be," I said. "I'm a goddamn brunette."

"Mere lack of will. Doesn't mean a life sentence."

"I prefer that collar and cuffs match, thanks ever so."

She stomped on the brakes and swerved right, bringing the car's powder-blue nose to a halt six inches shy of her driveway's cast-iron gates.

A uniformed flunky sprinted forth to swing them wide.

Kay checked her makeup in the side mirror, ignoring the man's salute.

She punched the gas before he was quite out of the way, spraying his shins with gravel.

I looked back and waved, mouthing a belated "thank you."

"I'm serious about your future," said Kay. "Had we but

known at Barnard you'd end up mooning over some cut-rate
detective—"

"—or that you'd end up playing beard for the man you
married?"

She laughed at that, rich golden peals that trailed behind us
till the end of her curving drive.

"What a monstrous pile it is," Kay said, cutting her eyes at
the Deco-Moorish façade she lived behind.

She walked away from the Mercedes without bothering to
close her door.

Someone would take care of it. Someone always did.

"I've got to call my service," she said, as we walked inside, our
heels clicking against marble and echoing back from the domed
entry ceiling.

"Why the hell do you have a service?"

"Because Carstairs manages to lose every message intended
for me."

She peeled off her white gloves, tossing them in the general
direction of a gilt-slathered side table. I kept mine on.

"I can't stay all afternoon, Kay."

"Go upstairs to my dressing room," she said. "I've laid out
some things for you to try on."

"I don't need your clothes."

"I spent the morning with that little woman at Bullock's,
picking out a few 'delightful frocks' for delivery here in your size.
Allow me that *one* small pleasure."

"And if I should happen to come upon Kenneth, ogling
something untoward above your marital bed?"

"Tiptoe past without making a fuss. I'll throw in a fur"

"For chrissake, Kay."

"*And* solemnly swear you won't have to kiss my ass for
a week."

"Make it two."

"Greedy guts," she said, as I started up the stairs.

As it turned out, her husband couldn't have ogled anything
at all.

There wasn't much left of his face, after the slab of glass had swung down to catch him under the chin.

The pair of golden cables at its footboard-end had given out. The closer one lay curled along the carpet at my feet. Three of its four strands had been neatly sliced, the last left to fray until it snapped.

Kenneth wouldn't have seen it coming, nor would his pack of wrestling boys. There were four sockets in the ceiling, little brass-lined portholes cut into the plaster. Two were now empty. The cables had been severed up in the attic, out of sight.

I lifted the phone on Kay's side of the bed, pressed the second line's unlit button, and dialed GLEnview 7537.

There was a click before my employer picked up on the third ring, grumbling.

"Philip?" I said. "I know I should have been back hours ago—"

"—This is why I never wanted a secretary," he cut in. "Too much damn trouble."

"It gets worse. I'd like to take you up on your offer of a birthday gift, after all."

"A little late to have something engraved."

"I'm with Kay. We need your help with a bit of a situation."

He took down her address when I explained what that situation was.

"Twenty minutes," he said. "Promise me you won't touch anything."

"I'm wearing gloves," I said.

"That's my girl."

Philip rang off, but I kept the receiver to my ear.

"Don't hang up just yet, Carstairs," I said. "Have Kay wait for me on the terrace. Fix her a drink so she'll stay put."

He exhaled.

I knew he hadn't yet called the police. The scent of ammonia was still too heavy in the room.

"After that," I said, "Come back up here with fresh rags. You missed a spot on the glass."

Philip walked into the library an hour later. I'd sent him upstairs alone.

"Happy birthday," he said, "though I'll hold off on wishing

you any returns of the day."

The room was all Gothic walnut, excised whole from some down-at-heel peer's estate—the dozen muddy portraits of faithful dogs and dead grouse included.

Carstairs made sure there was always a fire in the grate, air conditioning calibrated to offset its heat as needed.

"Nasty little scene to stumble across, upstairs," said Philip.

"Horrible," I said.

"Has it hit you yet?" he asked.

I shook my head.

He took my hand in both of his. Pressed it a bit too hard.

"It will," he said, "and I want you sitting down when it does."

He glanced over at Kay, stretched out asleep on a leather sofa. "Your friend seems to be bearing up rather well."

"I made her take a Seconal."

"Only one?"

"We had gin for lunch."

I let him pull me toward the fireplace.

"You're shaking." He put an arm around my waist, lowered me gently into a wing chair, then sat in its mate a few feet away.

"The boys are gone?" I asked.

"Carstairs handled it. He's had some practice."

"And you're sure they won't say anything?"

"Would you, Julia?"

I looked at the fire. "Of course not."

He nodded. "I've told him to phone Kay's doctor. Then the police. Then her lawyer."

My hands got jittery in my lap. "Philip, she didn't do this."

"I'm happy to believe that," he said. "You may have a bit more trouble convincing the detectives."

My gloves felt wet.

He looked at his watch. "Tell them that the pair of you came by the office before she brought you here. That was a little after two. I gave you the rest of the afternoon off."

"A little after two," I said. "What time did we get here?"

"You don't know. You called me the moment you found him, of course. I told you to let me handle it from there."

"Kenneth keeps some decent Scotch in that desk, if you'd like."

He shook his head. "Tell me how long you've known about the state of Kay's marriage."

"A month. Something like that."

"And how long had *she* known, before confiding in you?"

"Less than an hour. She drove straight to my apartment that night."

He thought about that. "Four weeks ago, Sunday?"

"I suppose it was."

"You called in sick the next day."

"I apologize for that, Philip."

"No need," he said.

"We were up all night." I looked to make sure Kay was still asleep. "She had a miscarriage."

"How far along?"

"Not very. She hadn't told Kenneth yet."

"Did she want the baby?"

"Even *after* she walked in on him," I said. "Maybe *more*."

"She thought it would help?"

"Women so often do, don't they?"

"I'm happy to report I have no personal experience in that arena."

"Lucky you," I said.

He rose from his chair and walked behind it. "What do you *really* think—was it Kay, or was it Carstairs?"

"I've already told you what I really think."

"So you have," he said.

"For God's sake, Philip, can you imagine Kay with a hacksaw?"

"I can't imagine Kay filing her own nails."

"*And* she's been with me since morning."

"I doubt it was done today," he said. "Could have been any time over the last month."

"All the more reason it had to be Carstairs, then."

"Not sure I'm following your logic."

"Philip, Kay *sleeps* in that bed—"

"—Still? You're sure about that?"

"I am," I said. "Yes."

"Any proof other than your say-so that she *hadn't* set up camp down the hall?" he asked. "Under the circumstances, one might presume she'd have wanted to ix-nay the arbor of connubial bliss with a stout ten-foot pole. Can't imagine they're short of alternate quarters, given the size of this place."

"Kay takes breakfast in bed every morning. Dry toast, black coffee, and half a grapefruit—broiled. I'm sure someone on staff could verify finding her there."

"Even so," he said, "those last strands looked strong enough to hold, as long as nobody put extra weight on the glass."

"But what if they *hadn't* been strong enough, despite appearances to the contrary? Philip, there's no way she could have been certain. The glass might've just as easily killed Kay and Kenneth both, while they slept."

"I suppose so."

He crossed his arms and leaned on the top of his chair, looking at the fire.

"Kay would have done it this morning, if at all," I said. "You know I'm right."

"And you'll tell the police she's been with you since breakfast? Helping out at the office?"

"She was at Bullock's," I said, "choosing dresses for me."

"Which left Kenneth free to pursue outside interests for several hours. Safe to say he had Carstairs make the arrangements, without help from the rest of staff. Boys delivered quietly at the service entrance, shuttled upstairs with none the wiser?"

"Carstairs must have brought the things from Bullock's upstairs himself," I said. "He wouldn't have let anyone else through to Kay's dressing room."

"Ducks in a row for Kay, then," said Philip. "Unless this was an elaborate suicide, Carstairs takes the rap."

It all hit me then—the bulldozed pulp of Kenneth's face and everything else, straight through to that moment.

I thought I would be sick, right there on the rug.

Philip wandered over to Kay, still asleep on the sofa.

"We'll make sure the police get a good look at her hands," he said. "Not a mark on them, and severing that cable must have been a bear."

He turned back toward me.

I peeled off my gloves and raised both hands, turning them slowly for his inspection, front to back.

Philip tried not to look relieved.

"I'll bring Carstairs in here," he said. "Make sure he's trussed up and ready to go."

He was wrong, of course. The cables had been a cinch to cut, four weeks ago Monday.

I'd chipped the polish on one fingernail, but the second fresh coat of red had been dry a good hour before Kay woke up, back in my apartment.

She'd have done the same to keep me from harm: without question, without hesitation and without my knowledge. Kay is my oldest friend, as I am hers. We take care not to burden each other with the onus of gratitude.

Conscience now clear in that regard, I turned from the fire to watch her sleep—my hands still, my nausea at bay.

Philip paused in the doorway, one foot across the threshold. We both heard the siren in the distance.

"Wouldn't hurt the appearance of things if you cried a little," he said, not looking back. "Plenty of time before they get all the way up the drive."

Sunny Second Street

by Charlotte Carter

I had been on my swollen feet for hours and now my size nines were talking nasty to me. I turned into Doc's Bar and took my usual stool with the slashed red leather seat. End of the working day. Time, as my buddy and coworker Portia says, to go postal. But Portia's not talking about a head case pulling out a gun and blowing away ten or fifteen people. When she uses that expression she means a bunch of mail handlers in a bar, gossiping and knocking back a Heinekens. I must have told her a thousand times there's no "s" at the end of Heineken, but she never seems to hear me.

All I know is, I'm mad with anybody who comes between me and my first long, cooling drink at the end of my shift. I am a bit of a beer fanatic, truth be told; a beer nut, if you will. There's this little deli on Second Avenue. I wouldn't trust the shrimp salad, but they have a damned impressive selection of beers from all over the world, and I'm slowly working my way through the whole inventory. I've been doing a little experiment, buying a different one every time I pass there. Baby, some of those Belgian ales! To die for, as my roommate Hal would say.

A bunch of us post office grunts meet just about every day at Doc's, the hundred-year-old bar off First Avenue. At night the youngsters come in by the truckload—kids with big bucks to spend on their clothes, on the over-the-moon rents being charged these days, and sure enough on booze. They love to get stinky drunk and act ugly in this neighborhood. But from about four to six every weekday Doc's belongs to us.

I was the first one in that afternoon. The rest of the gang would be along soon: Portia, Jonas and Earl. I ordered a Speckled Hen and got out my Morocco guide book. No, I'm not planning a vacation, except in my head. I've got a beautiful book about Rome too, another place I've always wanted to see. And of course there's Kenya, Nairobi, Venice, San Francisco. Don't the names alone just put you in another world?

Hal keeps pushing me to go ahead and actually book a flight somewhere. "You're one to talk," I always answer, "you never go farther than the lobby of the building. At least I got a passport. Just in case."

I put the book away when I saw Jonas walk through the front door. I wasn't in the mood for his teasing about my travel fantasies. Another thing he harps on: my living arrangements. Jonas has never met Hal, but he dislikes him anyway; something to do with Hal being, in Jonas's word, a homo—and white to boot. Well, Jonas's opinions cut no ice with me. Hal knew me only as Phyllis, the big-foot lady who delivered his mail in rain and shine and gloom of whatever. But when I got hit by that double disaster two years ago—marriage suddenly over, and then a house fire that left me with little more than the clothes on my back—he opened his home to me like I was a favorite cousin.

Know-it-all Portia says that Jonas would be set against anybody I lived with. She claims he has a thing for me. Now, that's ridiculous. I've got fifteen years and at least as many pounds on that Jonas. He is pretty, I give him that. Trouble is, when a woman doesn't fall at that guy's feet, he can't stand it. Anything in a skirt and over sixteen, she gotta be hot for him. It makes him crazy not to be wanted.

He took the barstool next to mine and right away started in with the usual *don't you look lovely today, Phyllis, and how about you put those suds down and let me buy you a real drink* crap. I played it off, like always, and a few minutes later the rest of the posse came in.

I let them carry the conversational ball. I was distracted, thinking about the evening ahead. The prospect of going out for a bite to eat and a couple of drinks doesn't faze most people; I mean, it's kind of the stuff of normal life. But tonight's planned dinner and drinks were going to be special. Why? Because Hal was going to be at the table. He was actually going to dress and go out to a restaurant.

My roomie is a beautiful human being, and nobody says any different while I'm in the room. But he is about as peculiar as they come. For years he has been all but a total shut-in. Fella about thirty-five—a real prime-of-life story—and he spends all his time indoors with his cats and his *projects* in the apartment, which is huge and blessedly rent-stabilized. If he's not repainting the dining room, then he's building shelves or putting in new faucets or tie-dyeing the coverlet on his bed. Hal might not get the sun on his face like he should, but he has made that old tenement apartment a mighty beautiful place to live, except for Forbidden City. That's what we call the big room at the rear of the apartment. He keeps making a start in there—patching the rotted sections of the ceiling, scraping down the swollen brown wallpaper—but he always loses heart and gives up on the mess. For the most part it is a graveyard for all our junk and a playhouse for the cats.

Just as Hal is always on my case to get out of the country, his friend Lucien is steadily on *him* to get a life outside of the house. Lucien is a sweetheart too, with scads of money and a social life that would kill the likes of me. When Hal needs new kitchen cabinets, Lucien calls his decorator. When uninsured Hal is yet again rushed to St. Vincent's because of that fearsome stomach trouble of his, Lucien will pay the bill with his pocket change, like he's springing for a cheeseburger or something. Which brings me back to tonight. Lucien has a new boyfriend he's been trying to introduce to Hal for months now. Finally Hal resigned himself to going out with them, and he has worked my nerves so bad that I signed on as well. We're supposed to meet Lucien and this new flame at 8:30 sharp.

I was suddenly aware that my crew had fallen silent. I looked up to see them all staring at me.

"You in some kind of daydream, Phyllis?" Portia asked.

"I guess I was. You say something to me?"

"Yeah. I said that gal was on your route, wasn't she? You used to talk with her sometime."

I didn't ask "what gal?" I knew. There had been a gruesome murder last week: Maggie Blaze, a young woman who lived on East Third, had been slashed in her basement apartment and left to die on the floor. I'd been delivering mail to her for years. The murder was no longer page one news but people were still buzzing about it because the cops hadn't caught the killer yet. Quiet as some people would like to keep it, there's still a lot of violence here on the Lower East Side, gentrified as we may be getting.

"You know she had to be messing with some kind of drugs," Earl said, shaking his head.

Portia was quick to agree.

"How do you know that?" I said. "Don't be so eager to muddy that child's name. She might not a been your cup of tea, but that didn't make her a dope fiend."

Earl shrugged. "You the one used to talk about how crazy she was."

In point of fact I had not called Maggie crazy—not exactly. I said that when she came out to chat with me as I sorted letters, she often looked like something out of a nightmare. You just never knew whether she'd be sporting green hair or an earring through her cheek, wearing a torn slip and combat boots or a sequined red gown. I guess she figured that telling me she was a "shock performance artist" would clarify matters. It didn't. She had given me a slew of flyers announcing her engagements, saying that I should come and see her work sometime. Of course I never managed one of them. And now that she was gone I felt kind of bad that I hadn't made the effort.

Jonas curled his lip, real nasty. "She call herself some kinda artist. Artist, shit. The chick was crazy. Done some of everything you can think of. Used to be a stripper too. A crazy stripper ho."

Mind always in the gutter, Portia laughed. "How you know about her business?"

He didn't answer.

"Did you hear what Portia asked you?" I said.

Jonas exploded then: "Forget you, Phyllis. None of y'all know half of what goes on around here."

I exchanged wary glances with Earl when Jonas turned up his drink and drained all the vodka out in one gulp.

Earl reached over and wrested the empty glass from Jonas, who looked as if he was about to crush it between his fingers. "What's the matter with you, boy?"

The grin had left Portia's mouth. She leaned into Jonas's face. "You was messing with her, wasn't you? You got you some of that stripper ho."

Again, he didn't answer. And didn't have to. All eyes were on him now.

Earl's voice shook when he spoke. "Goddamn, Jonas—you

don't know something about the killing of that girl, do you?"

"No! Back off me, motherfucker. And that goes for all y'all."

Earl dropped his face into his hands.

I got down slowly from my stool.

"Wait!" Jonas commanded. "Don't you go out of here thinking what you thinking. I did have sex with her, okay? A few times. More than a few times. I mean, I was seeing her off and on since you had the flu last year and I subbed for you. But I don't know anything about no killing. I'm telling you, I don't. You hear me?"

"Yeah, she heard you. We heard you too."

Nobody at the bar had a voice like that. So who had answered? Maybe Jonas was getting a message from Heaven.

Hardly. Standing behind him were two plainclothes cops from the nearby stationhouse. A black and white duo that I knew well enough to nod to when I saw them on the street. They weren't in here for the scotch and soda that often ended, or even kicked off their day. They were reading Jonas his rights as they pulled him through the front door.

* * *

Man, oh man. Jonas was in for it now. I had realized from the jump I'd better keep my dealings with him platonic, and damn if I hadn't been right. I had to wonder what else he'd been hiding from us all this time. The thing was—as vain and trifling a man as he is, I just couldn't see Jonas killing anybody.

One thing was for sure. When I got home and Hal asked me about my day, I'd have an earful for him. I turned the key in the lock and was greeted by the usual choir of mewls and rebukes. I filled the saucers on the kitchen floor with dry food and then jumped out of the path as the beasts stampeded in there and went to work on their grub.

I heard Hal's TV going. *Oprah*. I went to his bedroom and looked in. Sleeping is like a hobby for that man. I watched as he slumbered. I know no one else with his understanding of people, his generosity of spirit. Yet, his open heart aside, he has his secrets—and his bad dreams. I knew about his early life in Syracuse. I knew about his scholarship to art school in Rhode

Island, and that he had dropped out and come to New York City and found a job at the foundation that Lucien ran. The two of them became loving friends for life.

Too bad Hal's story didn't close out there. Something happened to him. No idea what it was. And as close as he and Lucien are, Lucien doesn't know either, not even to this day. He's told me that at some time in 1995 Hal collapsed like a cake in a cold oven. He checked out of life, cut all his social ties and holed up in the apartment for six months, lost twenty pounds and added twenty years of sorrow to his face. As time went on, he at least began to talk to Lucien again, read the papers a bit, show some interest in the living. But, Lucien said, he never came back to his old self.

I decided to grab a quick shower and change my clothes before waking him. I got myself ready and then went back to his room.

"Stop playing possum, boy. I know you're awake."

"I don't wanna go, Aunty Phyllis. Don't make me go."

"What are you talking about, fool? You're the one making *me* go."

"But I'm sick. I'm coming down with something."

"Hal, get yourself out of that bed. I gotta tell you some stuff happened today you won't believe."

* * *

People with googobs of money are geniuses at finding ways to waste it. Wave was the latest in a never-ending parade of trendy, outrageously expensive places to eat. They say there's usually a two-month wait for reservations. Count on Lucien to have an in. Hal, bless him, told me I looked hot in my new white dress, but I could see I was no competition for all the sexy young women downing mojitos and yellow rice on the black leather banquettes.

Lucien hugged us and presented us to his boyfriend, who stood up and kissed my hand.

"Hi, I'm Cary Newell."

Lord. Did he say Cary Newell or Cary Grant? Lucien had scored himself one gorgeous hunk of man.

Hal was getting a good eyeful of that beauty too. He couldn't stop looking.

"I know who you are," Cary said, "both of you. Lucien talks about you so much, I already know you intimately."

"No shit?" Hal said. "You'd think we'd remember something like that."

We were having a fine time. I'd never seen Lucien so happy. No mistaking that goofy behavior—the boy was in love. But when at last he pulled his eyes away from Cary and shifted them over to Hal, his expression changed in a hurry. "You're not eating, honey. What's wrong?"

"I feel like shit. Must be a summer flu, or maybe my kidney thing acting up."

I was stunned when I looked closely at Hal. He was sweating like mad even with the polar winds blasting out of the air conditioning vents and his skin was the same shade of green as those tea towels he had ordered from the Williams-Sonoma catalogue. I'd paid no mind earlier when he claimed he was sick. But now I could see he hadn't been faking. A minute later he excused himself and rushed into the men's room. When he came back to the table he didn't even sit down.

"I think I better beat it home before the dam bursts again," he said. "Lucien, I'm sorry."

"Never mind that. You're running a fever. I'm going to bundle you right into a cab."

I put my fork down, reached for my purse.

"No, no," Hal insisted, a hand firmly on my shoulder. "Stay and finish your dinner. I'll see you later. And don't come home sober, Miss Thing."

He and Lucien scurried away. "Take care of that cold," Cary called after them.

Not counting Hal's bad luck, the evening turned out pretty nice after all—a ton of crab cakes, spicy, just the way I like them, a fountain of fancy wine, and even a dessert with flaming bananas. Lucien ordered brandies for us, to cap off the night. But before the drinks arrived, Cary said he wanted to step outside for a smoke.

Must've been one of those all-day cigarettes. After thirty minutes, Lucien tried calling Cary on his cell phone. When there was no answer, he went looking for the man. He came back alone.

Can't say I ever saw Lucien that way before—at a loss, dumb-looking. "What happened to Cary?" I asked.

"I'd love to know."

Not ten minutes later, he got his answer, when a scream rang out.

There was a huge commotion at the entrance to the restaurant. We ran toward the front, thinking the place was on fire. The hostess was pointing at Lucien. The man who had dined with us, she said, had been killed. One of the busboys had just found him in the breezeway between the restaurant and the building next door.

Lucien burst out of the door, with me on his heels.

Cary's throat was sliced open. The jagged neck of an Amstel Lite bottle, covered in blood, glittered on the ground. While Lucien knelt next to the dead young man, I could only stare at the broken bottle in that pool of black-looking blood. I never really liked Amstel Lite, I thought, stupidly enough, but I do buy it once in a while—when I'm watching my calories.

All around us there was shouting, gasping, even some chatter about a serial killer. In another minute the sirens were roaring. I don't think Lucien heard any of it. Beneath the horror on his face, he still wore that expression of stupefied hurt and disbelief. I can't imagine I looked any better.

* * *

Life is all about routine—for people like me, at least. But then something'll happen, *bang,* and everything comes undone in a single day. All upside down. Jonas rousted out of Doc's on suspicion of murder and Lucien's friend killed less than eight hours later. Had everybody gone insane?

It was nearly two a.m. when the cops finished with us. Home at last, I began to strip out of my dress.

Then I remembered: Hal. After Cary's disappearance, I hadn't given another thought to poor Hal. No lights on in his room. As ever, life and death going on outside while this child slept behind closed doors. Maybe there was something to be said for that after all. If Lucien didn't call to tell him what had happened, then neither would I. I'd wait until morning to break the awful news.

I sat on the edge of my bed for a long time, too exhausted to put on my night things, too downhearted. I was thinking about Cary, and about Maggie Blaze; thinking about all young people, really, everywhere in the world, and what a robbery it seems for them to die before their time. Better pay more attention to time, I thought bitterly. See now, how it can end on such short notice? Maybe I'd stop dreaming about vacations and actually take one.

I went over to the reading desk and opened the drawer where I throw stray buttons, souvenir matchbooks, and whatnot. I was looking for the business card of the Greek woman who ran the travel agency on First Avenue. Maggie Blaze had handed me a dozen flyers over the past couple of years—those announcements of her doing her act, whatever it was that she did, in some of the local clubs. I had stashed a bunch of them in the desk drawer as well, but I didn't see them either.

I began to search for the card. That's when I heard the noise.

At first I thought it was one of the cats. Once in while the big orange one with the torn ear, Nestor, will get himself a spool of thread to play with. When that happens he can keep you up half the night frolicking. I went out to settle his hash before he woke Hal up.

The door was shut, but the light was on in Forbidden City. Nestor didn't do that. I pushed into the room. Hal was sitting on a milk crate, sobbing, and trying to stifle the sound.

I rushed toward him. "You know about Cary?"

He lifted his head, and as his body shifted I saw what was in his right hand. A jagged green shard from a Grolsch bottle. Good stuff. I'd bought that last week.

I couldn't speak for a minute there. When I did get a few words out, I didn't sound like myself. "What you doing with that, Hal?" I tried to laugh. "That's not for me, is it? Maybe that spooky movie we rented gave you some bad ideas."

"Don't even dream of it, Phyllis. You know I love you."

"Okay." I waited.

"That's not his real name."

Whatever he was talking about, it sure came out of nowhere. "Whose name?"

He could barely make the sound: "Cary."

"How do you know something like that?"

"That's not his name! And he ain't who he says he is." He turned on the crate then, and I could see his left wrist was cut, but not all the way open, a red stain on his striped bathrobe. "People used to call me by another name too. Steven. As in Steven Harold Major. Nobody calls me Hal except Lucien and you. Remember? He didn't call me Hal and I didn't call him Cary."

"Okay." I was right, earlier: everybody had gone crazy.

His next words came out in a snatching cry. "He didn't even recognize me, Phyllis. You get what I'm saying? He erased me."

I steadied myself, wet my lips. "What are you telling me here? You saying something terrible went on between you and that man."

"I wish it had been terrible. Terrible wouldn't have been so bad."

I tried to lift his chin, make him meet my eyes, but he wouldn't let me. "When you got . . . sick. In '95. It was because of something he did to you, wasn't it?"

He looked through me.

"And tonight," I said, no sense in stopping now. "After Lucien put you in the cab. You didn't take it home."

"No."

"Just tell me why, baby. What did he do to you?"

"I can't."

"Yes, you can, Hal. No matter how bad it is. Don't keep it on your heart anymore."

He shook his head slowly.

I would have gone on pleading with him to tell me all of it, except that I realized there was a brightly colored piece of paper stuck to my shoe. One of Maggie Blaze's flyers. Several others were on the floor at his feet. I felt my heart boom against my ribs. "What you doing with these?" I spoke as if I had caught him with my underwear on.

I repeated the question, except that second time I was screaming.

After a minute, he answered. "I wasn't going to let Whatshisname suffer for it. Not for very long, anyway. I'm going to clear your friend before I check out."

"*My* friend?"

I waited while it sank in. He meant Jonas. He was telling me he killed Maggie Blaze.

"Have mercy." My knees gave way and I fell onto the Chinese stool Lucien had claimed from his dead mother's apartment. I began to wail, tears running like May rain on a wall of flat rocks. "Oh, honey. Oh, Hal. Let me pray with you. Please."

He wiped at my face. "No praying," he said. "I'm not asking to be forgiven."

"You have to."

"No." He put one arm around me. "But I do want you to know—"

"What?"

"I don't know. That I wasn't always this pitiful wreck. That I was beautiful once. Believe it or not. I was young and—and nowhere near as sharp as I thought I was. In fact I turned out to be about the dumbest asshole that ever lived, because I loved that phony bastard.

"He and Maggie worked together in those days. She was supposed to be his little sister. Like I said, I thought I was pretty smart. But I wasn't. I was easy pickings for that pair. I let them talk me into doing some very bad things."

"Criminal things?"

"Let's just say shameful. The three of us scammed people, extorted them, hurt them. I knew how wrong it was, but I couldn't help myself. See what I mean? There's a whole lot of stuff I got no right to ask forgiveness for. Then Cary came up with this job that was going to bring us a bunch of money, and leave somebody dead. I told him no way. I just wanted out. But you know what happens when you give your soul over to somebody. Maybe you do wake up and realize you have to get out, but there's no getting it back. When I said no for the last time—well, they thought I was going to call the police into it, see. They panicked."

"Did you take a beating?" I said. "That what your kidney trouble's about?"

His eyes closed.

"What? They had somebody try to kill you—left you for dead somewhere?"

"Don't. I can't tell you. Not ever. The important thing is, they left. They disappeared. I never knew what became of them. Until I needed string one day, a couple of weeks ago. I went looking for some in your desk drawer and found those flyers. One of them had her picture. You'd even mentioned a woman on your route who lived on Third Street, a weird actress or something. I never gave it a second thought. But after I saw those announcements, I went into a kind of trance. Like I was acting out a script, everything all written down and determined for me. All I had to do was follow it.

"I figured if she was back in New York he couldn't be far behind. I trailed after you on Third for a few days, until I saw her. The hate was so powerful, I couldn't breathe. I ran back home, grabbed the nearest bottle and drank until I calmed down. Then I started to plan. What they took from me, I'll never get it back. The only way I could even begin to get it back was to obliterate them. Like they'd done to me.

"I made up my mind to force her to tell me where he was. And if she didn't, I was going to—"

"Hush, don't say it." I suddenly covered my eyes. I was seeing kind Hal choking with rage, slashing at that girl, killing her. I tried to push the horror back out the other side of my head.

"She fought me, cursed me. But she wouldn't tell. I got her to admit she wasn't his sister, though. They played me even about that. Laughing at me under the sheets, I guess."

"But if she never cracked, how did you know Cary had taken up with Lucien?"

"I didn't."

"You didn't?"

"That's the final joke, right?" he said. "Maggie died for nothing. I didn't need her. Even if I'd never seen those flyers, I would have met him tonight. I go out to dinner for the first time in I don't know how many years. So I can meet Lucien's new guy. And that bastard stands up and shakes my fucking hand. He's just standing there, grinning. Mister Life Is Good and You Look Like a Sad Little Eunuch But I'm So Pumped and Charming. I wanted to put a knife in him right there. Oh, Jesus, Phyllis. I'd rather die than see Lucien hurt. But I knew what that monster was capable of. He'd do something horrible to

Lucien. Just a matter of time. I only wish I could kill him all over again."

I understood what he was saying. Still, God knows, that wasn't what I wished. If I could have been granted a wish or two, Maggie Blaze would be performing in Milwaukee and Lucien would be ga-ga over a lovely churchgoing fella. Hell, as long as I was dwelling in the realm of the impossible, I wished that 1995 could have been rubbed out of history. I was scared to death about what would happen to him, of course I was, but I wanted Hal to know that he hadn't been erased, no matter what had been done to him; his sweetness and loyalty to Lucien and to me was proof of that. Surely by now he had matched every ugly deed he'd ever committed with a lovely one.

No, Hal wasn't asking for forgiveness. I'd have to do that for him, and I would, every day for the rest of my life. I took the shard of glass from his fingers and we talked quietly for a while, mostly about the distant past. His snowmobile, for instance, when he was a little boy; my favorite aunt's falling-down house in Alabama. Mostly, I think, we just needed to act like the sun wasn't rising up at us through the dirty windows that looked east to Clinton Street.

Finally, I agreed I'd make the call to the police—that, and anything else he needed me to do. We stopped talking then.

I don't know how much longer we sat there in silence before Nestor came in and started one of his routines with a pink felt mouse.

Hal looked down at him and took my hand. "You're going to look after them forever, aren't you?" he said. "Even though you were never a big fan of the cat?"

"Yes."

"And you'll look after my Lucien forever too?"

I was crying hard again, so I just nodded.

"You believe I love you dearly and you'll be with me. Forever."

"I know it."

"See there, Miss Phyllis? I did pray—sort of. And you answered me, girl."

Interrogation B

by Charlie Huston

The Bitch can't stand her.

Well, that's a given. Her sitting on that side of the desk, she's not going to like anyone on this side. But The Bitch does have a special hate on for her.

—Date of birth?

—Fuck am I gonna tell you that?

Second question. Second question on the damn form and The Bitch is already giving her shit. This after she already gave an obvious alias on the first question.

Betty Crocker my ass.

It's like this already with this shit, what's it going to be like when she asks The Bitch about her priors?

—Just met you, gonna tell you my fucking birthday? Next you be asking my weight, some other shit. Fuck that. Fuck you.

—How's it going, Borden?

She looks at Daws.

Why are so many male cops such clothes horses? Not just the dicks either. See them on the beat. Uniforms take their stuff and have it tailored. Not just hem the pants, bring up the cuff. Beat cops having their blues custom made. Daws, when he was a cadet, no doubt he was taking his grays to some chink tailor, having pleats put in, a break in the cuff if you please.

Lady cop tried to get away with that, wearing something even looks designer on The Job, she'd get the treatment for a year. Pictures from fashion magazines taped to her locker. Stories about cheek implants emailed to her. Name put on contact lists for fucking modeling schools. Assholes in the bullpen pointing at the Victoria Secret's catalog and asking why she didn't make the cut.

Guy like Daws hits the Barney's sale every six months and brags about the deal he got on his Versace and boys are treating him like he caught fucking Son of Sam.

She pictures him naked. Decides it's a bad idea. Way he always

keeps his jacket buttoned, he's hiding something in there. Gut like an ape no doubt.
—What's up, Daws?
—Game tonight?
—I'll be there.
     The Bitch clears her throat.
—What, motherfucker, come over here, invite to a game, got no invite for me?
     He points at The Bitch.
—This her?
     Borden nods.
     Daws folds his arms.
—She throwing attitude?
     The Bitch raises her eyebrow.
—Don't be talking 'bout me like I ain't here. Show you *attitude,* motherfucker.
     She hawks up a ball of pack-a-day phlegm, rolls her tongue into a tube and scores a bull's eye on the square toe of his left shoe. Borden taps the space bar on her keyboard a couple times.
     Daws looks at the thick brown gob on his toe. He slides his foot under Borden's desk and scrapes it clean on the bottom of one of her drawers, leaving a shiny streak down the middle of his shoe.
—How 'bout you let me take her off your hands, Borden?
     Borden hits the backspace key, deleting the empty spaces on her monitor.
—I got it.
—Hey, I'm not saying I want the collar, just let me finish processing the bitch for you.
—*Bitch?* Who you callin' *bitch*, motherfucker? Show you *bitch*.
     She coughs up another winner and nails the crotch of his slacks.
—Bitch! Fucking bitch!
     He sweeps his open palm across her face, ready to bring it back across and rake her with his knuckles.
     Borden snags the sleeve of his jacket.
—Cool it, Daws. Don't fuck up my collar.
     The Bitch covers her face with the hand not cuffed to her chair.
     Daws jerks his hand free.
—Fucking bitch!
     Borden takes the box of Kleenex from the top of her desk and

offers it to him.
—Clean that stuff off.
  He snatches three tissues and wipes at the dripping brown wad on the pale gray wool.
—Goddamn. Goddamnit! Gonna stain. Fucking bitch!
  The Bitch is rubbing her cheek.
—Looks like a shit stain. Looks like you been shittin' out your dick.
  Daws points at the stain.
—C'mon, Borden, give her to me. Look at this shit. Slacks cost me two bills. Give me five minutes with her.
  Borden leans back in her chair.
—Go to the john, Daws, put some cold water on that.
  He balls the Kleenex and throws it in The Bitch's face.
—Stain doesn't come out, I'm gonna find you in holding, bitch.
—Your mama's a cum stain, motherfucker.
  Daws nods.
—Uh-huh. OK. OK. I'm gonna deal with your AIDS-infected spit, then I'm going to holding and tell the matron about you. Gonna make an announcement to all the mamas in there about what we got your ass in for, bitch. See how fucking amusing you are when they get done with you.
—Your mama's a cum stain and your daddy's a shit smear.
  But Daws is already out the door. The Bitch's smile disappears with him.
  Borden rocks her chair back and forth. Detectives, uniforms and city employees in the bullpen getting back to work now that the show looks to be over.
  The Bitch probes the inside of her cheek with her tongue.
—Dick.
  Borden nods.
—You got that right.
  The Bitch grunts.
  Borden leans in.
—Only reason he stops by my desk, I lost a button from my blouse one day, he saw some tit. Now, every day, he stops by. Doesn't even work homicide. Works upstairs. Fucking narc. Comes by because he thinks I lost that button special for him. Comes by like it's a titty bar here waiting to happen. Worst part?

—Hn?

—Worst part is, dick doesn't even bring around a few singles to stick in my g-string.

The Bitch looks her over, nods.

—Yeah. Alright. You OK. Twelve. Ten. Eighty-one.

Borden taps a couple keys.

—Date of birth. December ten in nineteen and eighty-one. Got it.

She looks at the door. Looks at The Bitch. Nods to herself and stands up.

—Let's get out of here.

She takes a key out of her jacket pocket.

—Hold up your hand.

The Bitch offers her cuffed wrist and Borden leans over and frees it; unlocks the other bracelet from the steel chair and drops the cuffs and key in her pocket.

—Come on. Before he realizes that shit's not coming out and comes back to give you a dry cleaning bill and look at my tits some more.

The Bitch stands and stretches.

—Fine on me.

Borden takes an old paper form from her desk and leads The Bitch to Interrogation B. The Bitch sits and Borden takes the cuffs from her pocket, looks at them, weighs them on her palm, and sits, placing the cuffs on the table.

—So. Name: Betty Crocker. DOB: twelve, ten, eighty-one. How about place of residence?

—Shit, you should know, you picked me up there.

—Uh-huh, so you're saying that was your place?

—Not my place, my sister's place. But that's where I was keeping my ass.

—Uh-huh. And, so, not to get ahead of myself, but that was your sister in the tub with the hair dryer?

—Shit. *Not to get ahead of yourself.* Bitch, yes that was her. Always hogging the fucking bathroom. One fucking bathroom in the place. Bitch always soaking in that damn tub. Meanwhile, I'm the one got her moneymaker out on the street earning the rent.

Borden twirls her pen, ignores the form in front of her.

—Had a roommate like that once.

—A roommate.
—Yeah.
—College, I bet. A fucking roommate. Uh-huh.
—No. Army.
—Army? No shit. You in the Army?
—Straight out of high school.
—No shit. I served.
—No shit?
—Two years. Be in now, they didn't kick my ass to the curb.
—What for?
—Hustling. Sold a piece to a second looey. Ask me is he still in.
—Is he still in?
—Fuck, you know he is. Not a fucking mark on his record. Probably a major now. Hope his ass in Iraq.
—No surprise if it is.
—You a MP, I bet.
—No surprise. Here I am.
—Yeah. Sure. But I'd know anyway. That shit about having a roommate. MPs got them a dorm, rooms to share. Grunts in the barracks.
—Hell, why you think I went after the MPs? Got me out of the barracks. Twenty, thirty chicks all living together. After the first couple months, all hitting the rag the same week. Had to get away from that madness.
   The Bitch leans back and uncrosses her arms.
—Can't blame a bitch for wanting out of that shit.
   Borden drops her pen and leans forward, resting her elbows on the table.
—Almost as bad with my roommate. Never thought someone could get away with being a slob in the service. Chick threw her shit everywhere. Inspections, I got dinged right along with her. *Disordered quarters.*
—I hear that shit. Fucking sister, bitch was the same way. Her and the fucking kid.
—The kid hers?
—No, he mine. But he a pain in the ass. Cryin'. Whinin' all the time. Boy could have kept his mouth shut, I never lay much of a hand on him.
—But he was a whiner.

—Got that right. Boy a crybaby. *Auntie, auntie! Get out the tub, Auntie! Mama! Help auntie out the tub!*
—He freaked out, huh?
—Freaked like the pussy he was.
—That when you pushed him in the tub with your sister?
—Fuck yes.

Borden loops the fingers of her right hand in the closed bracelet of the cuffs and whips the open hook of the other bracelet across The Bitch's face.

The Bitch falls out of her chair, hands covering the eyebrow half ripped from her forehead.

Borden goes around the table, snapping the open bracelet closed and fitting the twin hoops of steel around her fist. She grabs The Bitch's hair and pulls her head back and punches her in the face four times. She lets The Bitch flop to the floor, opens the cuffs and snaps them around The Bitch's wrists, bangs her own forehead against the edge of the table twice and walks out of Interrogation B.

* * *

Daws tosses a twenty in the pot.
—Saw that bitch's face when they rolled her out on the gurney.

Borden watches the other police at the table as they fold out of the hand.
—Uh-huh.

She calls Daws and raises another twenty.

He looks at his cards.
—Twenty, huh?

She doesn't look at her cards.
—Yep.

He points at the scabby lump on her forehead and the eight stitches running across it.
—Hurt much?
—Itches like hell.

He looks at his cards again.
—Twenty, huh?

She doesn't move.

He tosses a twenty on the table.

—Call.

She lays down the winning hand and rakes the pot.

The other guys grunt and shake their heads, get up and wander to the deli tray and booze bottles.

Daws fingers her cards.

—Didn't figure that.

She stacks the cash.

—No, you didn't.

He shakes his head.

—Poker face like yours, Borden, you should go pro.

She pulls the cards together.

He gets up and comes around to the seat on her left.

—Good lookin' out on that bitch. Fucking kid killer. Probably doesn't know that's as easy as it's gonna get for her. She goes inside, they're gonna cut slices off her just so there's enough to go around.

Borden knocks the edge of the deck against the edge of the table.

Daws taps the green felt table top with his index finger.

—Still gonna be looking to get a shot at her myself. Kids of my own. Show her a thing or two about abuse.

Borden shuffles the cards.

Kid killer. Like killing a kid is worse somehow than killing anyone else. Like a five year old getting pushed in a tub full of water with his dead aunt and a plugged-in hair dryer is worse than some dealer putting a bullet in his rival's back. Like she gives a shit who kills who. Like how old the corpse is or how it's related to the killer makes any fucking difference to how the job gets done or how you get paid. Fucking killing like this, no cash coming from any angle. Dealers start pulling triggers, there's always some scratch to be made.

Kid killer. Waste of fucking time. And time is money.

And The Bitch did worse than waste her time. Bitch fucked with the police. Bitch spat on police.

In her precinct. No one gets away with that shit. No bitch, no cocksucker. No one makes police look bad in her house.

The other guys are coming back to the table, plates full of sandwiches, hands full of highballs.

Daws moves back to his seat and winks at her.

Fucking asshole.

She thinks about setting the deck. Giving him a winner, letting him get cocky before she cleans him out. But no, it'll be better doing it cold. Watching him get angry as he picks up loser after loser, always thinking he's due a winner. Going heavy in the pot, trying to get even. Losing straight through.

See how many $200 pairs of slacks the motherfucking titty peeper buys when she's done with him.

She places the deck in front of the cop on her right, watches him cut, takes the deck and looks at the loser across the table.

—Yeah, well, the bitch shouldn't have done what she did.

The End of Indian Summer

By Stona Fitch

After the lunch rush, Kate Hands walked along the Beeline, pausing beneath billboards and next to guardrails to pick jonquils, daisies, and Indian paintbrush. She sorted the spring flowers on the picnic table down by the town lake, murky as a cow pond. Some flowers were bound for the coffee shop, others for her motel room. She trimmed off the brown leaves and failed blossoms with scissors.

Winter-pale high school couples lay on the shore in swimsuits and pretended it was already summer, but the breeze sent them huddling under towels. Their new Chevrolets gleamed in the parking lot. Kate Hands walked by the showroom in town every day and knew the new colors by heart—Moonlight Cream, Empire Red, Mist Green, two-tone Falcon Gray.

A truck trailing black smoke drove up the lake road, turned into the parking lot, and skidded to a stop. Kate Hands watched the driver swing down from the mirror to the gravel. He stripped, threw his jeans and blue workshirt on the hood of the truck, walked toward the lake in his unlaced black boots and underwear. At the water's edge, he kicked off his boots and dove in. He surfaced once, shook his head like a dog, and swam across the lake, strong arms flashing, legs churning the oily water.

The high school kids quit making out and sat on their towels watching the lake, alive now, as if an ancient, powerful creature slapped from one side to the other, trapped by the shoreline. He did the military crawl, the backstroke, and finally joined his hands together and hammered the water in front of him, which sent him slapping across the glimmering surface.

After, the driver walked through the shallows to the beach, his broad chest dripping. He reached down to pull one of the teenager's towels from the dirt and wrap it around him. A boy rose up and said something, but the stranger just put his hand on the boy's face and shoved him back down toward his friends.

The driver looked up and squinted in the sun. Kate Hands

picked up her scissors, pretended to go back to work. He caught her stare and gave a wide-open smile. His blond hair and pale blue eyes reminded her of an actor, but she couldn't remember the name. He raised his hand to wave, strode up the hillside path in his unlaced boots.

He stopped at the edge of the clearing. "Live around here, Princess?"

She said nothing.

"Nice flowers you got there."

She nodded.

He walked closer and his shadow fell on the table. He reached for the flowers and his hand darted toward her blouse. She poked the scissors at his palm. He jumped back with a yelp and held his hand up to his mouth.

"Wildcat, are you?"

"Take a couple of steps back and we'll be just fine." She used the hard voice she used on drunks but it quavered.

He held out his hand. "Now see what you did?"

She tucked her long black hair behind her ear and looked at the driver's hand. It wasn't more than a scratch, barely bleeding. Tattooed on his palm was a dark black +, smeared a little as if rubbed with a diesel rag. He opened the other hand to reveal a second tattoo, a – sign.

"Positive and negative," he said. "Worked with high explosives when I's in the service. Me and some sailors got drunk one night in Ostend—it's in Belgium, a port town—and had ourselves tattooed up for fun. Came in kind of handy sometimes so we didn't blow ourselves up, you know, when we was on a mission."

She trimmed the red tips off a handful of Indian paintbrush.

"How come you're doing that?"

"Something to do," she said.

"I'm sure we could come up with something to pass the time." The driver stepped toward her.

Kate Hands pointed the scissors at him and he stopped. He dropped his towel suddenly and jumped up to grab a thick tree limb with both hands. As he did a dozen pull-ups, his damp underwear glowed in the sun.

He dropped down and wrapped the towel around his waist again. "I know'd you was looking at me," he said.

"Was not."

"Not now. When I was down there swimming." He pointed at the lake. "I could feel your eyes on me, them beautiful dark eyes." He smiled. "What are you, anyway?"

"My mother was Cherokee. Dad was part Cree."

"Two kinds of Injun, that's a laugh."

"Ain't laughing."

"Name's Tarlin. Tarlin Williams." He stretched out his hand but she just nodded.

"What kind of name's that?"

"Okie. I think they was kind of trying to come up with something else but couldn't spell it right. And what'd they call you?"

She told him.

"Hands. That's a nice one. Say, I'd like to get my hands . . . "

She shook her head slowly. "I heard that one a million times from every customer from here to Dallas."

"Waitress, are you?"

She nodded. "At a coffee shop off the highway."

He snapped his fingers. "Redskin, place down on the Beeline, right?"

She nodded slowly.

"I seen it, driving in. I pass through here every Friday on the way back from Dallas."

"Why'd you want to go to Dallas?" Texans were the worst customers—loud, rude, low tips.

"I bring lumber coming down. They can't build houses fast enough down there. And I take a load of pipe back to Bartlesville, where they got a bunch of new wells coming in. Whole town's slick with crude."

"Well you might think of stopping in," she said. "When you ain't busy swimming."

He turned serious. "Got pie there?"

She nodded. "Pecan. And lemon."

"Ever have apple?"

"Sometimes. Apples are pricey."

"That's my favorite."

"I'll remember that."

"You're from around here, ain't you?"

"Born and raised not a mile away." She pictured the dusty gray-board house on the edge of town where her mother lived. A couple of months had passed since she moved out, but it seemed like years.

"You think if I leave my rig parked here overnight I'll get any trouble from the law?"

"Why'd you want to do that?"

"Boss gives me a five-spot to stay in a motel and I'd just as soon keep it and sleep in the rig."

"Might as well try," she says. "Worse that could happen is that you'd get tossed in jail." She stood up and gathered the flowers.

He smiled. "Wouldn't be the first time."

"Figured as much." She walked away from the picnic table and the handsome stranger in his stolen towel.

"Leaving so soon? We ain't hardly got to know each other."

"Got the rest of my shift coming up."

"Redskin Café, ain't it?"

She was already walking toward the Beeline.

"I'll see you there, sometime, Princess," he shouted after her. "You ain't seen the last of me."

* * *

At the coffee shop, Kate Hands tied her black apron around her waist. She put the flowers in milkglass vases, spread them out along the counter and on the tables next to the windows. Mid-afternoon, no customers—it was her favorite time of day. The frycook had the hillbilly station out of Little Rock turned up loud. She sat at the counter reading the *Daily Oklahoman*.

The bell on the main door jingled and the cook looked out from the kitchen and turned down the radio.

"Afternoon." Mr. Peixotto touched the brim of his cowboy hat but didn't take it off. By the time he sat down at the far corner table, Kate Hands already had his iced tea and pecan pie on a tray.

She set the pie in front of him and handed him a long-handled spoon before he could ask for it. He upended the sugar pourer over the tea and let sugar drain into his glass until it covered the ice cubes. He stirred the tea carefully and left the spoon in the glass, holding it out of the way with his thumb so it didn't poke him in the eye. No reason to ruin a napkin with a wet teaspoon.

He noticed Kate Hands standing next to his table. "What're you waiting for? Don't you got something you're supposed to be doing?"

"I was wondering if we might have apple pie next week."

"Why?"

"Customer asked for it special."

"Regular?"

"Comes through all the time," she lied, straightening her apron.

"Apples are high now, cheaper come the fall."

"I'll cut the slices slim the way you like."

Mr. Peixotto looked at her for a moment. Beneath the brim of his hat his face was creased like a wadded-up piece of brown paper and his eyes were gray and empty as sky. He looked around, reached out to run his hand under Kate's apron, feeling around like a clumsy doctor. His boney fingers pushed against her soft cleft and almost made her scream.

"Apples it is," he said. "I like to keep my squaw happy, else she'll put a tomahawk in my head."

* * *

Kate Hands moved slowly through the coffee shop. She took orders, carried platters of food, cleared tables. The dinner crowd treated her better—no jokes about a redskin working at the Redskin Café, no wandering hands. It wasn't so bad, she thought. Her mother did sewing by the piece until it twisted her fingers. Her grandmother was a gleaner who pulled spade-marked potatoes from the red mud. Her great-grandmother walked all the way from Georgia to Oklahoma Territory in the wintertime.

When her arms and legs ached from a long shift, Kate Hands remembered these stories and considered herself lucky.

She stood at the head of a table, notebook in hand, while a clean-scrubbed family told her what they wanted to eat. The mother spoke slowly, as if Kate Hands might not understand

English. It was worse when tourists stared at her like a museum display, tried to slip a crumpled dollar into her apron.

Kate Hands looked at the bouquets at the center of each table, red-tipped flowers lost among the clutter of plates and glasses. Marked by the blood of the Cherokees as they walked past—that was what most people knew about Indian paintbrush. From what she knew, the dead didn't bleed. They fell frozen like statues along the Trail of Tears, four thousand in all, the rest driven further west, where the settlers hated them.

Now Kate Hands served the settlers' descendents Salisbury steak and mashed potatoes, the meatloaf special with stewed okra. When she thought about how she ended up in the Oklahoma flatlands rather than the pine forests of Georgia, Kate Hands thought it was kind of funny. She wasn't one to worry, get angry, let something bother her. She was even-tempered and reliable, the best waitress ever to work the Redskin Cafe. Mr. Peixotto told her this all the time.

* * *

Tarlin walked in on a blazing Friday afternoon when the parking lot was crowded with rigs churning the gravel. The screen door slammed and Kate Hands looked over at the door, shaded her eyes against the midday sun. The radiant air around Tarlin swarmed with specks of dust and he filled the coffee shop as he had the lake, his arrival noted by the regulars and every teenaged girl.

She didn't speak to Tarlin at all on this visit or the next, just filled his coffee cup and walked away. When he came back a third time, he had passed some kind of test. They talked long after everyone had left, past closing time even. When the cook showed up to get breakfast started the next morning, they were still talking, Kate Hands behind the counter, Tarlin sprawled on the other side, red Mexican boots up on a chrome stool.

* * *

"Ever seen a bridge blow up?" Tarlin lay naked on Kate Hands' bed at the Ranch-O-Tel, smoking a Winston.

Her ear pressed against his chest and she wore only his unbuttoned blue workshirt. The hot wind blew the gray lace curtains back and forth. "No, can't say I have." Her voice was slow, underwater.

"After you press the detonator, the whole thing holds in the air a second, even though the bomb's already gone off. First the middle drops, then both sides." He made a bridge with his fingers, nails black crescents, and let it fall.

"Sounds beautiful," she said.

Tarlin gave her shoulder a gentle push. "Damn, Kate. You're the first person I ever met that said that."

"Maybe it's true. There's plenty of terrible things that look beautiful if you look at 'em the right way."

"You think them bombs is beautiful?" He pointed toward the arched doorway between the bedroom and the kitchenette, the wood crowded with pictures cut from *Life*—Little Man and Big Boy and the new Russian bomb called Joe.

"I suppose I do. All shiny and such. Round like a peach. Or skinny like a lipstick. There's worse things to look at."

"Who're them people?" Mixed in were photos of movie stars and men from the newspaper.

She shrugged. "Just people. People whose faces I favor. Like yours." The breeze blowing through the room riffled the clippings like leaves.

He leaned over and kissed between her breasts, then picked up his cigarette, balanced on the water-stained nightstand.

"When I was in the service, I saw it all. People blowed to bits, boots with feet still in 'em. Crows peckin' at dead Krauts' eyes."

Kate Hands touched his face. "I'm sorry, baby."

"I keep it pretty well stowed away. Sometimes at night, though, I have some awful dreams."

She smiled. "I'll help you sleep."

"Every time I stay here I sleep like a dead man." He kissed her, ran his oil-marked fingers down her shoulder, stopped at the round, pale welt just above her elbow.

"Got burned on something, didn't you?"

"Ain't nothing. That's from a long time ago."

Tarlin squinted into her dark eyes. "You can't fool an old fooler, Kate."

She paused. "My daddy liked to smoke a cigar now and then. If we didn't move fast enough, he'd stick it to us. He was good-looking, though. I got his picture up there with the rest of them." She pointed at the doorway.

"Jesus H," Tarlin said. "If I ever saw him do that, I'd let him have it right between the eyes." He grabbed his nickel-plated pistol from the nightstand and pointed it at the kitchenette. "Just like that."

"That'd be fine with me," she said. "And with my mamma too."

"What happened to him?"

"Left town one day. Went away on a trip."

"Coming back?"

She shook her head slowly. "Don't think so."

"You tell me if he does."

"I will."

"Cause I want to take good care of you, Princess. I ain't never found a better girl."

"You talk so nice, Tarlin," she said. "Keep going. I do like to hear it."

* * *

Tarlin's rig pulled in front of the Redskin and raised a cloud of gray dust. Kate Hands watched from inside the coffee shop as another man swung down from the cab. His red hair was cut short and his belt disappeared beneath a belly that stretched his western shirt tight. He sat at the counter and ordered steak and toast. When he was through and drinking his coffee she walked over to wipe the counter in front of him.

"Ain't that Tarlin Williams' truck?"

He looked up. "You innerested in trucks?"

"No."

"Didn't think so," he said. "It's Boomer Trucking's rig. But yeah, Tarlin drives it most days. Boss has him running a load of pipe up to Sedan, just over the Kansas line. Some kind of 'mergency."

She nodded, turned to go.

The new driver grabbed her elbow and made her drop the coffee cup she was carrying back to the kitchen. The ranchers eating at a window table looked up, went back to their dinners. "You a friend of Tarlin's?" His voice turned low and urgent. "'Cause any friend of his is a friend of mine. He and I go way, way back."

She shook off his hand and picked up the coffee cup. "You in the service with him?"

The new driver smiled. "Told you he was in the service, did he?"

She nodded. "Said he served in Europe."

"I'll tell you something." He leaned as close as his gut would let him. "Tarlin ain't never left Oklahoma 'cept to go to Texas." He pointed to one end of the counter. "Or Kansas." He pointed to the other end. "That much I know for sure. And he couldn't enlist on account of his habit of getting arrested every so often. He mention that?"

Kate Hands shrugged. From her mother, she knew that handsome men lied the most. "If he weren't in the service, how'd he get them tattoos on his hands?"

"Ran electric lines out to drill rigs for a couple of years before he stole himself a Ford pick-up." He turned his head, squinted. "Say, how'd you know about them tattoos?"

"I seen 'em."

"Must have been pretty close to see them. You two friends? I mean boyfriend and girlfriend like?"

"Guess so," she said.

"Well I'll tell you one thing, sweetheart. If being in the service is what it takes to get your clock runnin', I was the feller hauling that flag up at Iwo Jima."

Kate Hands drifted down the counter, wiping away smears of butter and egg yolk. The new driver laughed so hard that he started to wheeze over his coffee cup.

In the kitchen storeroom, lined with cans of green beans and sacks of flower, she reached behind a tin of cinnamon and found the Mason jar, shook it, watched the bits of red flower swirl in the water, beautiful now, like pink lemonade.

* * *

The summer rose and faded, came back again radiant and

golden only to leave for good. Bales of hay dotted the fields and disappeared into barns. The drive-in theater shut down and the kids went back to high school and football games at night. Kate Hands watched the lights streaming along the Beeline from the front door of the coffee shop, smelled burning leaves. She shivered in the cool evening air, went back to cleaning the tables.

She hung her apron on its hook and locked the front door, walked across the gravel lot to the Ranch-O-Tel. Tarlin's rig was already parked behind her room. It was almost like they were married now, she thought. Married one day every week.

When she walked into the room, Tarlin grabbed her around the waist and threw her on the bed.

She raised her arms up, let him tie her to the bedposts the way he liked. Only tonight he pulled the ropes tighter and said nothing.

"That hurts, Tarlin."

"Supposed to," he said. "Name Jackson Dawkins mean anything to you?"

She shook her head, saw his flush, twisted face.

"Red-haired. Fat as a pig. Drove down here last month when I was on a special run."

"Yeah, I recollect him."

"Says he and you did it right here, that you were nothing but yard trash."

"I didn't do anything with him at all, Tarlin. Just asked him where you was."

"You gave him that note with your room number on it—I seen it. Didn't you?" He took a pinch of her shoulder between his fingers and squeezed hard.

"I didn't do anything like that, Tarlin."

"How come he knew your damn room number?"

"I don't know." He must have waited in the parking lot, watched her walking to the motel. She wondered why anyone would do something so cruel, then Tarlin pinched her hard and she screamed.

He wrapped his fingers over her mouth. "Shut up, you damned Indian bitch. I should've known better. Everyone warned me." He lifted his other hand.

She shook her head free. "I didn't do nothing, Tarlin. I swear it."

"What good is that?"

"I ain't a liar. Not like some people."

He pulled back his fist but paused in mid-swing. "What'd you mean by that?"

"You wasn't in the service, was you? Just working as an electrician. All them stories you told about the war? About how you blew up trains? Them're all lies, ain't they?"

"That what Fat Jack told you while you was both lying here in the bed afterwards?"

She shook her head. "I don't know him at all. We just talked at the counter for a bit."

"Who you gonna believe, a stranger or me?"

In his pale eyes, Kate Hands saw who had lied. She knew none of Tarlin's smooth talk could change it.

"Like I said," he shouted. "Who you gonna believe?"

She said nothing.

He reached toward her neck with both hands, tightened his strong fingers around it. She struggled against the rope, tried to shake Tarlin's hands loose. But he held on, letting her go only after her eyes rolled back in her head.

Tarlin pointed at his underwear, damp and slick. "See what you did? Made me finish up before we even got started."

She wondered if this was the night she would die at the tattooed hands of Tarlin Williams.

"No matter." He looked around her room. "There's other things we can do."

* * *

Tarlin walked into the coffee shop, dragging his bootheels, smiling. He pulled his leather jacket around him against the morning chill.

"Morning, fellers." He nodded at the regulars. "Coffee and pie, Princess," he said.

Kate Hands stared at him from behind the counter, wondered how someone so cruel could look so normal. Tarlin hadn't untied her until sunrise, until her skin bore teethmarks,

bruises, and rope burns. He carved his name across her back with
a penknife as if she were no more than a pecan tree.

Pain made her walk like an old woman. Her hands shook so
much that she could barely bring coffee to the men crowded the
length of the counter. Mr. Peixotto said she had better get a move
on, but she couldn't. She felt wrong and bright drops of blood
fell from beneath her apron. When she bent down to wipe them
up with a dishtowel, the room darkened as if a cloud passed over
the sun.

She cut the slice of apple pie narrow so Mr. Peixotto wouldn't
complain and walked through the kitchen to the storeroom. She
leaned against the cans for a moment and closed her eyes, opened
them again when the frycook slapped the bell over and over. Her
orders were up. She reached her hand behind the spice cans and
pulled out the Mason jar.

Her mother taught her that the strongest poison came from
the most beautiful flowers. A month in a jar with water, alcohol,
and a couple of pennies turned Indian paintbrush into devil's
arrow. Her mother always kept some devil's arrow around the
house, just in case, like a shotgun leaning in the corner. A few
drops made a man feel strange. More than that sent his mind
speeding toward the horizon. Kate Hands splashed the slice of
pie with the pink water, opened the Kelvinator, and spooned
whipped cream over the plate.

In the restaurant, she could hear people shouting, asking
for more coffee and their checks. She walked back toward the
counter, pie in one hand, gleaming fork in the other. She knew
Tarlin wouldn't leave a bite. Apple was his favorite.

* * *

Kate Hands stood at the front door to the coffee shop,
watched Tarlin pull his rig out onto the Beeline. He had a full
load of oil pipe bound for Kansas but he would never make it
that far. Somewhere outside of Okmulgee or Beggs the road
would start to rush toward him, then race even faster. Devil's
arrow sent her father on a journey. Now it did the same for the
stranger who had shared her bed on Friday nights for a summer.

She shut the door and sat down at the counter, opened

the newspaper to take her mind off the pain with news items about cattle sales, wheat prices, the legislature coming back into session. Some days there were stories about wrecks and pile-ups on the Beeline, so crowded, fast, and narrow. When Kate Hands read about Tarlin, she would cut his picture from the paper and paste it among the beautiful and dangerous bombs, the handsome men who told lies.

Kate Hands turned the page. Her mother, who was wise about many things besides flowers and the ways of men, told her once that there were really only two stories in the world. In one, a stranger comes to town. In the other, someone goes on a journey. Her mother said they were just two sides of the same dime.

Blooming

By Sarah Weinman

Mina bent over to smell the roses in her garden, her hand reaching out to stroke the red petals. She pricked her palm on a thorn and laughed. It was hopeless. Gardening didn't suit her disposition.

She got the idea after watching one of the new American movies playing at the local cinema. The picture proved forgettable, but the cartoon preceding it struck a chord. Something about a bull named Ferdinand who wanted nothing more than to sit nice and quiet and smell the flowers. Mina did, too. She'd earned it.

Grasping the bleeding hand, she ran back into the house to wash the cut and salve the wound. She was becoming careless of late, injuring herself nearly every time she tended to the flowers. But it made her happy to do so, even if most of the flowers would die soon. They were still hers and hers alone.

Emphasis on alone.

Mina frowned at the sight of her hand. Not because the cut wasn't healing, but because this was the most exciting part of her day so far. She chose this life because it would be slow, undemanding, unfulfilling. But time was taking its toll. The silver streak in her hair had spread more in the last five years than in the previous twenty.

Maybe she simply needed to go out more. Pay attention to her neighbors and their petty little problems and squabbles. Perhaps she needed to take a lover; it had been a while. Most had been mediocre, others distasteful.

Or maybe she needed to stop hiding.

Satisfied that the gauze had stemmed the wound's blood flow, Mina fetched a bucket and filled it with water. She stepped outside, the sun in her face, and moved to the right side of the garden. She kept clear of the roses, but the daffodils still needed attending.

"Plants, Mina? I'm amazed."

She stopped short. Not just because she hadn't heard her true name in over a decade and a half, but because of that voice. A harsh, guttural voice that still haunted her dreams.

The sun shifted and she stopped squinting. He'd aged more than she had expected. The lines around his eyes, the sprinkle of gray in his temples and the yellowing of his teeth caught her unawares.

"How did you find me?"

His shrug aped the Gallic customs he so admired. "Come, Mina, you know better than to ask such a question. A better one to ask is why others haven't."

Her blood went cold, but she refused to betray any trace of emotion. "Let them find me," she said lightly.

"Bullshit. They find you, and that's the end. That's why you fled."

That's just one of the many reasons, she thought.

"What do you want?" She caught herself before she uttered his name. Bad enough he used hers, but she wouldn't return the favor.

"What you should have done last time. Most of us don't get second chances. One is often too much. But you were always one of the lucky ones, Mina. Gifted by God, some said, though I never thought so. More that you had so much talent and were easily impressionable."

"I'm certainly not now," she retorted.

"Prove it. I know you can do this."

Her heart pounded double-time, then triple-time, but not for the reasons she expected. It wasn't fear that gripped her, but exhilaration. It seemed she'd been waiting for the opportunity all along.

But she had to keep him at bay. Capitulating wasn't part of the process. "I'm rusty," she said, feigning protest. "I spend my time on my garden, for god's sake. I'd need practice, I—"

"So you'll practice," he interjected. "I *know* you, Mina. I created you out of nothing. There's no one else to finish this but you."

"You can't be serious."

He ignored the comment. "Better I found you," he said, dropping his voice. "But I don't have to keep my mouth shut if there's a reason."

A shudder rippled down her back. She could not remember. She *would* not remember. "I'm not what I used to be." She took a step back and steadied herself against the nearby apple tree.

He smiled, though his eyes remained dead. Familiar. "No you're not. You'll be better." He walked slowly through the garden, his boots setting indelible impressions into the soil. He was marking his territory, making the garden his property. Marking Mina, once again, as his territory.

She let him. There were other choices, chances to resist, but he was right. The flowers would die regardless of what she did, even if the taste in her mouth had turned distinctly sour.

The taste worsened as he ambled through the garden, taking his time, smelling each flower one at a time. Then he faced her, eyes locking onto hers. It was an old technique of solidarity to show that they were together in their tasks, no matter what transpired afterwards.

"Three days," he intoned. "Then he moves to the next city."

"That's it? You expect me to be ready by then? That's barely enough time!"

"Perhaps too little preparation will work when too much did not."

Mina shut down and dropped her eyes to the ground.

"We'll meet in two hours and go over plans," he said, assuming acceptance. "You were the best, Mina. You still are."

"I was an innocent, Leonid," Mina spat out, rage forcing her to blurt out his name. "I grew up."

Their eyes locked once more. "Not completely," he said, and walked out of the garden.

Not completely, she brooded throughout the rest of the day. And that might be the bigger problem. Years ago she had no concept of right or wrong. It had been her greatest asset. Then she learned to understand. That had been her downfall.

That was why she failed.

Mina leaned against the apple tree, running a hand through her hair, and prayed she could rediscover her old instincts.

* * *

"You still have it," Leonid said with more than a trace of wonder.

No one was more surprised than Mina. Forty-eight hours of worrying, then disgust over her fears, then preparation, had led her to this moment of rediscovery in an abandoned warehouse three miles from her house. She hadn't asked Leonid why or how he had procured the isolated place. She simply fell back on the old instructions: never question, always follow.

Three weapons and seven targets—each depicting a different member of the Romanov family—awaited her at the warehouse, but the choice was obvious. The moment she picked up the Luger, the years she spent erasing her memories slipped away. It felt so right in her hands, and her aim was still true. One shot, then several others in quick succession, all but one hitting the chosen target dead center.

She pursed her lips at the sight of the Alexei target, where the bullet missed its chest by three inches.

"Let it go, Mina. You won't miss next time," Leonid reminded her.

"How can you have such confidence in me?"

He didn't face her directly, as before. Instead he went around from behind, wrapping his arms around hers, stroking the gun in an almost obscene fashion. Mina didn't flinch because she knew she wasn't the attraction. His desire was fully in his work, in the successful completion of such.

A trait she wished she didn't share.

"Because I made you who you are," he purred into her ear. "And when you disappeared, you turned me into something I never thought I would be."

Mina squirmed. She'd thought of Leonid off and on over the years but not as a person, as a living being. He'd been her handler, the man to shepherd her into a world she'd barely chosen, and to think of him as human would be to give in to the rage she didn't want to feel.

She opened her mouth, but Leonid cut her off. "Forget it. You're not interested in what my life was like, and truthfully, I'm not interested in yours. All I care about is that you keep shooting with the same accuracy."

She turned around, eyes flashing. "At what cost?"

He laughed. "Who thinks of cost? It's the end result that matters."

"Then why don't you kill him yourself? He was your enemy, not mine."

Leonid blinked, thrown by the fact that she had departed from whatever script he had concocted. The moment was brief. "I won't even dignify that with a response," he said, his voice returning to the haughty tones that haunted her dreams, "because it hardly requires one. But you've been out of the game for a while. Perhaps you need reminding—"

"Don't patronize me," she snapped, raising the gun for emphasis.

He smiled. "Yes. Never threaten a lady with a loaded weapon."

"Another rule you taught me."

"And I'll remind you of one more before we leave," he said, his voice returning to normal. "Never let emotions get in the way of a good hit. I kill him, it's a disaster. You do, it's a job. Plain and simple."

Mina didn't respond. She'd had her opening, her chance to explain why she had left, and it had passed. She readied the weapon and emptied the chamber into Alexei's chest.

* * *

The night before the job, Leonid sat at her kitchen table, noisily slurping up a plate of spaghetti. Mina watched, musing at how domestic the scene appeared. A father figure eating what was offered by his would-be child.

He looked up at her and frowned. "Eat something. It's better if you do."

"All these years and you're still giving me instructions."

Leonid made a face. "You never used to chastise me so much."

"Need I point out how much things have changed?" She waved her hand around the room. "This house. The garden outside. My life. I craved simplicity. I needed silence."

"You fidgeted every time you weren't working," Leonid interjected, punctuating the statement with a final slurp. "Have you looked in the mirror? Have you seen your eyes glowing? You want to do this more than you've ever wanted to do anything."

Damn him for being right, for Mina had looked in the mirror the previous night. Practicing at the warehouse and going over the plans had kindled something within her she'd thought long dead, and each day that passed only inflamed her desire to do what he'd asked. To exorcise the ghost.

"But you won't be able to carry it out if you don't tell me the truth," Leonid remarked, keeping his tone dangerously light.

She gripped the edge of the counter. "I couldn't lie to you."

"You've told me many true things, I'll give you that. But the whole truth? Not even close."

Her grip on the counter tightened to the point of agony. Once Leonid had his mind set, he would not relent until he had what he wished. But she had learned about clinging to her own convictions during her time of isolation, and she would not yield to him. Not on this.

His smile sent a chill through her. "I'll find out one way or another," he said, pushing the plate to the opposite end of the table. It slid off, its crash making a horribly dissonant sound that both of them ignored.

"Perhaps I'm on the wrong job," Mina uttered under her breath.

Leonid may have aged, but his reflexes were still very much intact. Before she could react he'd pinned her against the counter, his face inches from hers and a furious shade of red.

"You ungrateful bitch," he said, spittle hitting her cheek. "Would you rather I have left you to die, or worse, to be raped by those rampaging Cossacks? Would you rather have suffered the same fate as your family? Think of them." She turned her face away but he forced her to look at him. "Think of them!" he shouted.

"What the hell do you think I've been doing every day of my life?" Mina fired back. "Why do you think I ran away? I couldn't be that girl. Every time I killed someone, a part of me died along with them. A part of me that never had a chance to grow into womanhood. And then you asked me to kill *him*." She couldn't bear to say his name, could barely eke out the replacement pronoun "Because you couldn't muster up the courage to do so yourself."

She wanted him to move closer, throttle her, cross over the precipice. Her heart thudded in anticipation. But when Leonid drew back, Mina remembered her folly. He never lost control. This was as close as he would ever get.

And now that she knew it, he smiled more genuinely. "You'll need some of that fire tomorrow. Eight o'clock, at the bottom of the hill."

He didn't have to ask if she'd be there. Once again, Leonid knew her better than she knew herself.

But he didn't know everything.

* * *

Later, Mina wondered if the entire morning had been her mind's invention, a strange replay of the previous time. She could not shake the feeling of repetition, of going through a chain reaction dictated years before.

She arrived at the bottom of the hill thirty minutes early, and Leonid was already waiting. He wouldn't stay long, he said. It was up to her to aim and shoot.

"You came here to remind me of something I already know?"

A shadowy look crossed Leonid's face. "Perhaps I wasn't entirely certain you knew."

She didn't have time to decipher the statement. Now that she was here, she was itching to begin.

He retreated from sight, and Mina was alone. The plan was shockingly easy: her target jogged every morning, the same route each time. Up the hill on the far side then down the hill nearest to where she was stationed, continuing in a straight line for five-hundred meters until he reached his house.

She knew the route by heart because she had traveled it many times herself. Most of the time she hadn't admitted why, but now she faced the truth: she had been waiting for this moment.

Mina crouched down, gun in her left hand. She still hadn't decided whether to use it, but she wasn't keen on direct contact. It had never been her style, and even though she was proficient with the small dagger strapped to her thigh, it would take too long to unclasp it for use.

All was quiet until she heard the sound of one foot moving after another. He was going up the hill. It would take five minutes. Five long, slow, agonizing minutes for him to reach the other side.

Five minutes to keep her mind sharply focused on the now instead of retreating into the past.

Five minutes to ignore the well of rage bubbling up inside her that she'd gone back to her old life.

Five minutes to indulge a tiny pinprick of what might come in the future.

The running sounds increased, and Mina sensed his approach. He was coming straight towards her. She felt nothing, and it surprised her. She had expected the old rush to strike her as it had every time, so many years ago. But she didn't miss the childlike glee. She needed adult wiles.

She moved into a half-crouch, now able to see him clearly. Two seconds passed where her entire world rotated on its axis, enough time to process how time had changed him. Of course he'd grown older; she could hardly expect him to stay the young man she had known, had grown up with and trained with, the one she harbored vague thoughts of loving someday, if and when she was capable of such feelings.

And when he looked directly at her without recognition, not even registering the fact that she had a gun raised to his chest, she felt the last trace of the old Mina die completely. The years she'd spent suppressing her grief over a path not taken, her fury at Leonid for his unwavering yet cowardly quest to obliterate all rivals to power, and her shame over the impulsive decision to flee him all crumbled away in the face of a single stark realization:

Leonid's son did not know her.

The last vestige of connection demolished, Mina did what she could not do at the age of twelve, when she'd suddenly discovered the difference between right and wrong, and when the promise of hope seemed tantalizingly within reach.

Shoot straight and true.

* * *

Leonid found her in the abandoned warehouse, firing at

the practice targets. She didn't expect him to be surprised that she had been up all night shooting round after round with coolly perfect accuracy in an attempt to rid herself of oncoming memories and unshed tears. Nor did she expect him to be surprised when, instead of greeting him, she turned around and aimed the gun at his chest.

He didn't have any final words, not a single explanation or excuse. He took the two bullets to his heart with the mixture of silence, stoicism and ironic humor she knew all too well.

Mina wrapped his body in tarpaulin she normally used to cover the flowers during the frost. It wasn't the best, but it would do.

"I created you," Leonid had said to her so many times. And he had been right. Without him, she would have suffered an unimaginable fate.

Mina grinned, stashing Leonid's body in a nearby incinerator. She was still young, only twenty-seven, and she had so much time ahead of her. All the time in the world to sit back, nice and quiet, and smell the blooming flowers in the field just outside the warehouse. They were so pretty, she thought, and without a single thorn to prick herself on.

She'd earned it.

Hellcats, Madwomen and Outlaws

Round Heels

by Vin Packer

When I met Millie, Kate Wilde was managing Six Steps Down. I was a junior copywriter at Marshall Advertising by then, making sixty dollars a week. It was a lot more than many were making. Kate Wilde was impressed, and she'd sometimes talk with me at the bar, and even buy me a drink if I was running a big tab.

This was the early Fifties. We weren't calling them "gay" bars yet. When I came from college to New York City all my friends were straight. I had to ask a cab driver where queer bars for women were. I told him I was a reporter out to get a story about female homosexuals and he said, "Sure, sure," with a little smile. He'd probably taken young girls like me to bars like that before.

This bar became my favorite. It was in Greenwich Village, way east, long before there was an area called the East Village. The exteriors of these places were always dimly lit with outside signs you could hardly see. Some girls would get out of cabs blocks away and walk until they were sure no one was around who'd know them.

The lowest-denominator Mafia guy manned the door. He stamped your wrist as you entered, and that purple tattoo was good for one drink. There was always some broken-down woman sitting by the Ladies'. Her job was to give you a few sheets of toilet paper, and to make sure two girls didn't go in there at the same time. Inside the floors were usually wet and there was always a plunger near the toilet.

The night I met Millie I nearly fell off the bar stool when she came through the door. I was twenty six then. I'd had my share of lovers, even lived with one for two years. But I had never seen anyone who looked like Millie. Long black hair that shone like coal and fell past her shoulders. I had never seen a thin girl with breasts the size of hers. I had never seen a girl in a lesbian bar who looked so feminine, who had such style. She was wearing a tight black sweater, with a rope of pearls, a tight black skirt with a long slit up the side, three-inch high heels, and a worn Burberry raincoat over her shoulders. To top it off, she was carrying a copy of the *Saturday Review of Literature*. A beauty with brains

I took a deep breath and said, "Oh my God!"

"Don't even think about it," Kate said. "That's Mildred Cone. She's a round heels."

I'd been in New York City for three years by then, but I still didn't know all the jargon. I knew that the guys who stood outside at closing and wagged their tongues at you were called "fish queens." I knew that a "kiki" was neither feminine enough to be labeled a femme, or masculine enough to be called a butch. I was a kiki like most of my friends.

"What's a round heels?" I asked Kate, watching Millie look the room over while the Mafia fellow was stamping her wrist. Then she flicked back a strand of her hair with these long fingers, and looked our way.

Kate said," A round heels won't stay with you. She'll turn right around to the next female . . . and this one is light-fingered, too."

Kate wore pants, a sports jacket, and a spanking clean white shirt with a little ascot at the neck. In some queer bars you had to wear a skirt, but not many were like that, and none in the Village were. Kate was close to butch, but her pants weren't fly front, she wore lipstick, and her shoes were well-polished loafers, not lace-ups.

We watched Millie come toward us. I actually felt my knees go weak.

Kate said, "Get your change off the bar, Lark."

"Hello, Kate!"

"Hello, Mildred."

"I don't think we've ever met," Millie said to me.

Kate introduced us and Millie looked all over my face and said, "Are you as sexy as your name, Lark?"

"Same old line, same old Mildred," Kate said, and then she excused herself, saying she'd seen police walking back and forth outside. She'd better check on it.

Homosexuals didn't feel any entitlement in those days. If we could find a place that would have us for customers we'd play the game. We knew the Mafia paid off the police to let us be there. We knew there might come a night when those of us the police could catch, would be hauled off to the nearest precinct to be body-searched for dope. That was the way the police had of telling the Mafia they were serious about demanding more payoff money. Scare the hell out of the customers, and grab a few free feels getting them into the paddy wagon.

After Kate walked away from us, Millie said, "Kate doesn't like me at all. She doesn't think I'm a good person."

"Then why do you head for her the minute you arrive?"

"I was heading for you, Lark."

"You were probably heading for the bar."

"No," she shook her head. "I don't drink like most of them in this dump."

We were all kinds, all ages. We were secretaries, radio producers, actresses and musicians, lawyers and brokers. Some of us even had husbands we'd left home sleeping.

It was true that a lot of the customers drank too much. For some it was the first time they had ever been anywhere that served only women, and only women who wanted other women. For others it was the only place to have a drink with someone like yourself. There was a tendency to drink too much because you were nervous, self-conscious, not used to somewhere it was okay to flirt, to ask for a phone number, or a date.

Millie told me she worked for her father. He ran an antique store over in Brooklyn where she lived.

"I know what you're thinking," she said. "You're thinking I'm this nothing who still lives with her family. But I just moved back temporarily. I broke up with someone."

I said, "I wasn't thinking you were this nothing. I was thinking I'd ask you if you wanted to go to Reiss Park tomorrow. Do you like going to the beach?"

"Even if I didn't, I wouldn't tell you. I wouldn't want to miss a date with you, Lark."

And so it began: me with fair warning, wet palms and a pulse way past one hundred. Millie with her sly grin, her green eyes, a 36-D, size four, wearing fuck pumps, the bookmark in her magazine in the middle of an article on Elizabeth Bishop.

That Sunday morning when we went to Reiss Park, I hadn't finished work on my FreshSure account. I needed a new heading by Monday. A heading is like a slogan. You lead off your print ad with it, but you can also use it for radio, and to start a new campaign. The assignment was to think of a sentence that would sell a face cream to someone on the beach, or on the ski lift. A cream for warm weather and cold weather.

I doubted I'd ever think of anything that day. I had too much distraction, thigh-to-thigh with this long-legged, soft-skinned lady in a two-piece swimsuit, the bottom half beginning below her belly button. She was an outie.

I explained my problem to her. Tell me how I made any sense at all, smelling the scent she wore—Celui—and Millie looking at me, that way of hers, welcoming you with her eyes, a smile, an occasional brush against you with an arm, a leg. I was already a goner, falling, falling. They were right, whoever they were, when they said you FALL in love. It's a descent, isn't it?

Millie listened to me, and then she stretched out and closed her eyes, while I told myself, "Laura Larkin, how could you get this besotted so soon?"

After a while, Millie sat up and said, "I've got it!"

"Aren't you quick," I teased, wondering if she'd accept the fact no one became an overnight copywriter. It took years of experience.

"You don't think I'm very intelligent, do you?"

"It isn't a matter of intelligence; it's a matter of training."

"Want to hear it?" she asked.

"Go ahead."

"Out There You'll Need Me."

It took a beat for me to realize it was perfect.

So was she.

One of those two feelings I had that Sunday on the sand was dead on.

Millie and I lasted a year and a half. We loved each other intensely, foolishly, terribly and truly. She moved into my one bedroom apartment on West 13th Street off Sixth Avenue. She came up with the heading that helped me win an account for Drum, a new men's deodorant. SOME MEN DON'T NEED DRUM, and there would be a drawing of a skier off in the mountains by himself.

One night when I read her a Wallace Stevens poem she confessed that she didn't "get" poetry, that the *Saturday Review* she was carrying the night I met her was a "prop."

"I know you educated people read the stuff, but that's another way I don't measure up."

I said, "A lot of people don't like poetry."

"The people you know do. I'm not in their class and you know it. You shorten my name and now all your friends call me Millie. That's not very respectful." Her eyes were narrowed with anger. "It sounds like someone no one takes seriously, some little fluff without a job."

I said, "When the person becomes dear the name becomes dear."

"Are you saying I don't like myself?"

"Don't read so much into everything. Just be yourself. Just be Millie."

But since it bothered her, I began to call her Mildred.

I went with her to a family dinner. Her father looked like the Mafia bouncer at Six Steps Down in his double-breasted, pin-stripe suit, the zircon ring on his little finger, the cigar in his mouth when he talked. Her mother was like a servant in the apartment, hurrying food in and out of the kitchen, never sitting at the table, so fat she had to wear carpet slippers, calling Millie "my little bunny." Her two older brothers flirted with Millie, and looked me over with big grins and hand gestures I didn't want explained. They knew what we were. Could everybody tell what we were? It was always on my mind because Millie was so openly affectionate. I was glad my family lived way off in Ida Grove, Iowa.

My friends and I had a saying back then: "Out of the closet and into the unemployment line." Employment was something Millie longed for, so she claimed. She didn't know how to type or take shorthand. It was almost impossible in the '50s to get a job in publishing or advertising without those two skills. I'd tell Millie that and she'd say she didn't want to be a secretary.

"I'm more intelligent than that," she'd say.

"That's how I started, Mildred. I got $32.50 a week when I started, and I was just your age: twenty-three."

"My father pays me triple that."

"Then don't complain."

But she always did. A few days a week she took a subway to Brooklyn and worked in her father's antique store. One Christmas she gave me a very expensive watch someone had sold, asking me if I could imagine anyone selling something with that inscription on the back: *Thou hast my heart.*

How well advertising has taught me the importance of words. You can always get the picture with words.

These were some of mine when I was with Millie:

"There are a lot of jobs you could get if you don't want to be a secretary. You could work in a bookstore, or clerk someplace chic like Cartier's or Bergdorf Goodman. What about becoming an airline hostess?"

"Mildred, those are my friends, sweetheart. You can't take their things."

"No one has ever made me feel this way, either."

"Do you mean your father's a fence? All that antique jewelry is hot? Not the watch, too?"

"Let me pay for a shrink, darling. You need help."

"You have to take it back to Saks! Tell them you don't know how it got into your purse!"

"Who's the girl who always calls you?

"No one at the party will look down on you, sweetheart. Just be yourself; just be Millie!"

Then there were Millie's words:

"All I want is to be respectable, like you, Lark."

"Since I met you, I'm a completely different person. Thanks, Lark."

"I fully intended to pay for it. Then I saw that I had no money with me."

"How can the shrink help me? I lie to him all the time."

And finally:
"She's nothing to me. I met her at the movies. She was buying popcorn, too, and we started talking. That's all."

After Millie left me for the girl at the movies, I didn't see her again for seven years. I had taken a summer off, renting a small house in New Hope, Pennsylvania, hoping to finish a novel. As far out of Manhattan as New Hope was—mostly antique stores, real estate offices, restaurants and a busy summer theater—there was Aymon, a new gay bar. (Yes, by the sixties we were calling ourselves gay.)

When I heard Kate Wilde was managing, I went to Aymon first thing.

"Well, well, well, it's like old home week," said Kate. "You know who's living here? Your ex. Mildred Cone."

"I heard she was living somewhere with a realtor."

"She was living here with Adele Stein. Then, you know Mildred. A vase from someone's house-for-sale was missing. Guess who'd taken it?"

"And she's still here?"

"Mildred had passed the vase on to her father. It was returned, and Adele left town. She wouldn't press charges." Kate shook her head, offered me a cigarette and lighted one for herself. "Mildred rents our kitchen. She has this little catering business and afternoons she cooks here. She's gone by six. We don't do dinners. The bar is our gold."

"She couldn't cook when I was with her."

"She can now. She gets so angry when her customers don't call her and say the meal was delicious. Remember her temper, Lark? I saw her key someone's Jaguar outside one of my clubs once. She thought the woman who owned it had snubbed her."

I remembered a time she'd knocked a flower vase over when I was working too many times past midnight She'd

complained that my work always came first. My typewriter was
waterlogged, wrecked. She blamed it on my cat, who never
knocked anything over.

I asked Kate, "Is she living alone now?"

"Please tell me you're not still carrying a torch for Mildred."

"I'm not. You'll meet Carrie one of these nights.
She comes every weekend. But I think I'll always be curious
about Mildred."

"Well, this time she's really lucked out."

It wasn't another woman. It was a middle-aged couple,
the Starrs. They used to own Aymon until they won big money
in a lottery.

"You know the type, Lark. They're these underdog-
lovers, I guess because they felt like underdogs themselves, they
were poor for so many years. They're lovely people, serious art
lovers, ready to work for most liberal causes, very well liked in the
community. They took Mildred under their wing shortly after
the vase incident. She's always with them. They taught her to
cook on our fancy Hotpoint Electric Range. I'm told she's a good
cook. Now she's staying at Fenwick while they're in France."

"What's Fenwick?"

"It's Raymond and Lil's pride and joy. Fenwick is one of
the oldest houses in Bucks County. It's one of those historic
places. The original owner wouldn't sell it until he found buyers
he trusted to keep it as is. It overlooks the canal, and it's one of
our landmarks."

I wrote best in the afternoons. I'd walk to town for breakfast
first, read the *Times* and drink coffee while all sorts of people
came and went. But Millie wasn't one of them. I'd never asked
Kate if Millie knew I was there. Kate would read something into
it, a longing instead of curiosity.

One Saturday night Carrie and I went to Aymon for burgers
and a bottle of wine.

Kate said, "Mildred claims her phone's been ringing off the
hook with people raving about her bouillabaisse. She's all excited,
says she's turning over a new leaf, going into business full time
somewhere no one knows her. She's waiting for the Starrs' to
return to Fenwick."

"Let's put an order in some night," Carrie said. "Let's surprise her. I'm dying to meet Mildred."

"I'd like to see her again, too."

"She's a big bluffer," Kate said. "Give her time. She'll steal something or run off with someone's girl."

Carrie said, "Give her a break, Kate. Maybe she has turned over a new leaf."

"Just don't say I didn't warn you, Carrie. Lark should know by now that someone like Mildred doesn't know how to turn over a new leaf."

I'd heard about a new leaf long ago, after Millie and I went to dinner at friends and I'd discovered she'd swiped a gold-link Cartier bracelet from one of our hostesses. I got it back before they found out. She wept copiously in the cab going home, swearing she was going to start over . . . again.

I could never become angry with Millie. There was something so vulnerable about her. When she was in trouble her face would get this pinched expression, on the verge of crying, or cursing or both. I always thought that getting her over her destructive habits was like trying to teach a kitten to mind.

Then one morning I looked up and she was lighting up a cigarette, right across from me in Dan's Diner.

"Hello, Lark! It's me!"

"Long time, no see." This from Marshall Advertising's hotshot writer!

"Why didn't you ever call me? Kate told me you were here, and I waited and waited."

"I'm trying to write a novel."

"I thought you maybe hated me, or didn't want people to know we even knew each other."

"I think I maybe loved you," I said, smiling across at her. She was so easy to like and so eager to be liked.

While I told her about Carrie, and then a little about my book, she clapped her hands silently and held them against her breasts saying, "I knew you'd make something of yourself, Lark. I knew you'd be Someone one day."

"Millie, Mildred, I haven't even sold my book."

"You can call me Millie, Lark. I'm not that self-conscious little nothing I was once. Remember you told me if I liked myself

I'd like my name?"

"Something like that."

"Lark, guess what! I'm a gourmet French cook now! I can make *frogs' legs provençale* and *moules marinère*! I can make lots of things, Lark. I can even speak a little French. *Un petit pas.*"

I was enjoying her. She was so familiar to me, her little quirks of speech—"I thought you maybe . . ."—and still aboard: the Ghost of Being Nothing.

"When the Starrs get back from France, I'm going to open a catering business over near Princeton."

"How come Princeton?"

"I'm not going to be too fancy or too expensive. I'm going to appeal to the boys studying there—they can order in—and I'll cater to professors and their wives having other academics to dinner. Have you ever seen Princeton? It's such a beautiful little college town, Lark. I can do all the hoity-toity stuff: go to concerts there and theater.

She told me Lil Starr read the poet Kenneth Patchen to her.

" . . . and I understood it, Lark! I love this Kenneth Patchen! I like poetry after all it seems. I've changed, Lark!"

The last thing Millie had to tell me she said with a frown on her face, and that little spark beginning in her eyes when she was upset.

"I just hope the Starrs aren't planning to stay in Europe much longer!" she said. "They're what-do-you-call-it? Francophiles! They've already stayed a month more than they said they would!"

"Look at all the plans you've made, though, Millie. Maybe you needed the extra time to figure it all out.

"Thanks, Lark. You always made me feel better about myself. I just hope they . . ." She didn't finish the sentence.

I holed up and worked hard, seeing my numbered days coming to an end, thinking sometimes of Millie planning to leave Fenwick and strike out on her own. One weekend Carrie and I drove down Fenwick Drive and saw the house sitting at the top of the hill. It was made of gray shingles with gingerbread and Gothic Revival touches, all the shutters, steps and trim bright blue and white. It looked like a cake that had been iced and decorated. I remembered Kate telling me it had been built in 1793, and except for the modern plumbing and necessary repairs, they had kept most of it unchanged.

The night before Carrie and I were going back to New York, we visited Aymon to say goodbye to Kate and have a few glasses of beer. It was early. The boys were having dinner. We always called them the boys and they called themselves that, too, in the unenlightened past. There were very few of the girls then in Bucks County. Their time would come. The boys always discovered the gay playgrounds first.

Aymon was quiet and Kate sat with us for a while. We were talking about New York, telling Kate where the new bars were, trying to convince her to come into town and stay with us, see all the changes. She knew the Mafia still ran most places, but she didn't know that many of them had new paint jobs, much more lavish Sunday afternoon buffets, better entertainment and few of them charged to get in now. Gay liberation wasn't really in force, but things were better for us.

Suddenly people from the streets came in, shouting that there was a raging fire on the hill.

"Fenwick is burning!"

We all ran to the windows. You could barely see Fenwick from there, but off in the distance were great clouds of gray smoke licked by bright orange flames.

"Let's go!" some boys yelled, and ran for their cars.

"You can go if you want to," Kate said to Carrie and me, "but there'll be a traffic jam, and the fire trucks don't need that."

We shook our heads.

"I hope Millie got out okay," I said.

Kate said, "When you set a fire, you make sure that there's a way out beforehand."

"She wouldn't have set fire to Fenwick," Carrie said. "Why would she do that?"

"She was mad at the Starrs," Kate said.

"For not coming back yet," I said, never intending to say it outloud. I didn't want to believe it, but I remembered the look in her eyes the last time I saw her . . . and how her voice trailed off after she said, "I just hope they . . ."

In a town that small news travels fast, and before the night was over the boys were coming into Aymon with the news Fenwick had burned to the ground—all of it. Nothing left.

Firemen reported the house looked "torched." Someone probably set the fire. The only one there at the time was Mildred Cone . . . and then she wasn't there.

She had left the Starr's car in town. A cabbie said that he had taken Mildred to the Trenton railroad station, where she could catch a train to New York.

"You're not surprised, are you, Lark?"

I couldn't answer Kate. I walked out of Aymon with tears behind my eyes, and Carrie said, "I'll drive, honey."

The next day we went home. I still had to finish my novel, and Carrie was overworked as usual, looking through law books, handling any case she could, bucking for partner.

But there was a soft center in my insides hurting for Millie.

A few weeks later, Kate sent the local newspaper with an update on the fire and an old photo of Mildred when she had been questioned about the missing vase.

MYSTERY OF FENWICK SOLVED

The Starrs came home the day after Fenwick burned to the ground. The taxi they hailed to take them from the train station took them directly to the police station. There they were informed that where Fenwick had been there was nothing but the ground it had stood on. Typically, Raymond and Lil Starr asked first if Mildred Cone was all right.

In the hours before Fenwick burned, as a welcome-home surprise and a thank you for the Starrs' hospitality, Mildred Cone had impulsively decided to paint the kitchen. It was seldom used. She knew the Starrs wanted it painted. Cans of Mason and Mugg Flat White were in the cellar. Raymond Starr was always intending to use it, but it was postponed when they went abroad.

Mildred Cone had never cooked there. She had always paid Aymon for the use of their kitchen. Not only was Fenwick too small, but she was afraid her catering business would leave unwelcome cooking odors in the elegant old house.

She could easily paint the little room herself. She chose an early evening when she had finished her work, and was not too tired. She turned on the radio and lay the newspapers down everywhere, ready to ascend the ladder and paint the ceiling first. But before she did that she decided to have a cigarette in the small gazebo out back. She sat there in one of the Adirondack chairs, facing the early evening sky as it darkened, watching the lights come on circling the Delaware.

What had escaped her notice was the pilot light of the old gas stove inside Fenwick. Mildred had been used to the electric Hotpoint at Aymon. It did not take long for the small flame to reach the newspaper covering the stove's top.

By the time Miss Cone walked back to begin her work, Fenwick was in flames. She could not reach the telephones inside, and there are no neighbors near the estate. Miss Cone drove the Starr's Buick to get help, but she knew there was little anyone could do.

What Miss Cone did next was run: horrified, fearful, in deep despair, she went to her family's home in Brooklyn, New York.

Then in the early morning hours she went to the 76th Precinct to talk with police.

She was not charged with a crime; she was charged with leaving the scene of an accident. The investigating police reported there had been no crime.

The Starrs were in shock, but both agreed that a good turn went tragically bad.

There was no way Fenwick could be resurrected, the newspaper reported. The art collection containing many local artists, and several de Koonings, Hans Hoffmans and Gorkys, among others, was destroyed. So were the priceless old furnishings inside.

At last report, the Starrs intended to go back to Europe, and make their home there.

Miss Cone had no plans to return to the area.

I tried to reach Millie, even calling her family in Brooklyn to ask where she was. Her father said if I found out he'd like to know, too. I didn't know any of her friends. I wasn't sure that she even had friends.

Life goes on . . . and so it did with no word of Millie.

Then, one morning the next summer, while Carrie and I were bumping into each other dressing for work in our bedroom, each one trying to get clothes out of the closet, slide into heels and hose, munching on toast from a plate on top the bureau, pushing the cat's nose away from milk glasses, Carrie said, "That's her! Lark, look—that's Millie on television."

Now you see her, now you don't. It was at the end of a short interview in a week CBS was featuring Female Entrepreneurs.

Carrie exclaimed, "Oh, Lark, she is as gorgeous as ever!"

I laughed with happiness, relieved to finally know what had become of her.

"An entrepreneur!" I said. "A gourmet French cook!"

After the interview the camera zoomed in on the cubbyhole restaurant catering to Princeton University students and faculty.

We saw the sign above the door. JUST BE MILLIE.

Cherish

by Alison Gaylin

Watching him die, she fell in love.

She'd seen him fight battles and break codes and scale buildings in tights and a cape. She'd seen him make love to women who looked and spoke like she did, in her dreams, in her fantasies. So many times, she had gasped when the camera cut in close, when it offered up slices of him for her private consumption—his eyes, his lips, twenty feet high on the screen of the West Los Angeles theater where she worked—his chest, his hands, the warmth of his smile . . .

But it wasn't until the last scene of *Forgotten Son* that Myra Wurtz fell, truly *fell*, for Deacon Blaine. In it, Deacon was a football player with inoperable cancer and, as a result, he was in bed for most of the film. As she sat in the back row, gripping her flashlight and staring up at his beautiful, pale face, Myra envisioned herself under those clean white sheets beside him, begging him not to leave her alone in this cruel, cruel world . . .

Nothing unusual. Ever since she graduated from community college, Myra had worked as an usher. By this point, she must have seen around five-hundred movies—each one repeatedly, at least half starring men she fantasized about. But then Deacon looked straight at the camera, straight through the screen at Myra's face, and everything else disappeared. The cloying smell of hot butter, the coughs and whispered comments of the theater patrons, the dust flecks in the shaft of light projecting Deacon's image onto the screen—gone, as if someone had taken a vacuum cleaner to it all. It was then she saw the pathway, beaming out of Deacon's eyes and into her own. Her chest tightened. She bit back tears.

"I'm . . . scared," Deacon said. "Help me."

And Myra knew that some day, she would.

* * *

There are pathways, long and winding, that span between certain minds. They've existed since the beginning, since birth. God puts them there, but most of us can't see them. We spend our lives groping in the dark, without knowing what we're looking for. And only if we're lucky enough to bump into that pathway, to follow where it leads . . . we meet him. That Special Someone. We meet him and our souls merge. Forever.

Myra's pathway connected her with Deacon Blaine, and if she hadn't gone off her meds and watched him die on-screen, she never would have known about it. He was a movie star and she was an usher. He was 35 and she was 25. He was married, and she'd never had a real boyfriend. He was extraordinary, born to be stared at. And she was a born audience member—especially on those awful meds, which dulled her out like an old eraser. But the pathway existed. There was no mistaking it.

The night she watched Deacon die, Myra went home to her South Pasadena apartment, where she sat down and wrote him a long letter, explaining all of this. *We were meant to be*, she told him. *I know it. I've SEEN it.* Somehow, she knew that he would understand. She knew he would come to her. She made a copy of her key the next day, placed it under the welcome mat outside her apartment, addressed the letter to Deacon Blaine, c/o his agent, and put it in the mail. She then drove to work, watched *Forgotten Son* one more time, drove home and flushed the rest of her pills down the toilet.

One week later, Deacon Blaine started sending her signals. Two weeks later, he used the key.

* * *

Deacon had told her to watch him on Letterman. At least, she was reasonably sure he had. At this point in their connection, Deacon Blaine so filled her thoughts, so occupied her dreams, that Myra was beginning to wonder if maybe she'd imagined some of the things he had told her between the sheets of her bed at those odd hours of pre-dawn when nothing seemed real to begin with. *Watch me,* she had heard Deacon whisper. *It helps me survive to know you're out there, watching.*

But . . . what kind of a movie star would say something like that?

By morning he was gone, leaving nothing behind but the feel of his breath in Myra's hair, the soft memory of his voice saying, *It will be all right. I promise . . .*

So Myra would watch, just like she always did whenever Deacon was interviewed on TV, in magazines, on the web. She'd look for the signals, and those signals would prove Deacon was not a dream. They'd prove Deacon really did use the key Myra left under the welcome mat—even if he did always place it in the exact same spot when he put it back. They'd prove Deacon Blaine, *the* Deacon Blaine truly did cherish her. Because cherish was not a word usually found in Myra's vocabulary. Maybe she had imagined Deacon. But could she have imagined that word? Was she capable? Even off her meds, Myra did not come up with words like *cherish*.

Myra closed her eyes for a minute, tried to transport herself to . . . when? When had Deacon said that? Two weeks ago? Three? Myra had been losing track of time lately. It seemed to melt in her hands. She'd been showing up late for work, so deep was she in Deaconworld, talking Deaconspeak, having her Deacondreams.

Just yesterday, the theater manager had given her a warning. "There was a line," he had said. "A long, angry line, Myra. Remember, one loose gear can wreck the entire machine, and. . . Why are you smiling at me like that?"

"Sorry."

"Well cut it out. It's giving me the fuckin' creeps."

She was always asleep when Deacon showed up, always in a half-dream state when the door creaked open and she heard those footsteps, moving across the cheap carpet in the living room so softly, like a ghost. Her heart would pound, but she dare not move, dare not speak—not yet—for fear Deacon, like time, would melt away.

But that word. That word was said to *her*. That word was *real*.

I cherish you. Myra had been aware, so very aware of Deacon's bare stomach, pressed up against the small of her back, of Deacon's strong, smooth hands, gripping her shoulders

She'd been aware of Deacon's soft lips, moving on her neck. Deacon smelled of cigarettes and coconut oil and this was not a dream, it was not.

I cherish you. You. Are. My.

"What? I am your what? Please . . ."

My only real inspiration.

Letterman was finishing his Top Ten List . . . a list Myra hadn't paid attention to at all, lost as she was in her own head. He was announcing Number One now, shouting to be heard over the thundering drum-roll. "What, no kielbasa?"

The crowd went wild.

Myra didn't get it.

"Next up, Deacon Blaine." Myra got that one. Bad. Her heart swelled to bursting, just at the sound of the name. She leaned forward, and when Deacon walked out on stage, she was so close to the screen she could see the multi-colored pixels that comprised his face. But she couldn't see the pathway. It was always so hard to see the pathway on TV.

*   *   *

Deacon didn't mention his wife during the interview. Her name, Claire, was usually one of the first words out of his mouth. But that never bothered Myra, not now. Deacon and Claire shared three homes and a dog, nothing more. He had told her that himself. (A tender whisper between her shoulder blades. *Claire and I share three homes . . .* But when? Two weeks ago? Five?)

And why did he always hold her from behind?

Deacon talked and talked. About stunt work and emotional preparedness and the sailboat he'd bought that was more trouble than it was worth. He talked about his sheepdog Frieda and his wacky neighbors and the good people of Hanna, Wyoming, where his new film, *Meltdown*, had been shot.

Myra didn't catch a signal. Not one. Maybe she and Deacon had been nothing but a dream after all. Maybe Myra should go back on the meds, go back to that therapist—the one who told her she needed to accept her own limitations because that's what made her human after all and . . .

"Your leading lady is a lovely young woman," Letterman said.

Myra didn't know why that snapped her to attention, but it did.

"Yes. Her name is Grace Ryan. And she's . . . what can I say?" Deacon paused a moment, and gazed at the camera. "She's an inspiration."

For longer than was comfortable, Myra stopped breathing.

* * *

Three days later, close to dawn, Deacon was whispering in Myra's ear. "I need you."

"You . . ."

"You are my one true inspiration. I need you . . . to get rid of the false one."

"You mean—"

"You know what I mean," he said. "There is a gun dealership on North Lake Street. Buy a Walther P22. It is perfect for you. Ladylike, but powerful. Make sure to get it fit with a silencer." He ran his hands down the length of Myra's arms, kissed the back of her neck. "Check the *Meltdown* website. It will tell you where and when you can find Grace."

"And then . . ."

"Then our pathway will be clear."

"You want me to—" she started to say. But for the first time, he turned her over onto her back. He slid on top of her and looked her in the eyes and the words died in her throat. *You want me to kill Grace Ryan.* Moonlight seeped through her bedroom window, turned Deacon's hazel eyes into warmed honey. When he kissed her lips, kissed them for the first time, he kept those eyes open. Myra saw the pathway—how short it was now, how bright—and she knew she'd never say that sentence aloud.

* * *

Grace Ryan usually wasn't one for ultimatums. But she usually wasn't one to sleep with married men either, and desperate times. . . you know the rest. The night of *Meltdown*'s wrap party, she'd pulled Deacon aside and said in his ear, "If you don't tell Claire, I will."

At first, it had seemed to work. "I'll tell her as soon as I get home," Deacon had said. Then he'd taken her into his trailer and made love to her in front of the full-length mirror for an hour.

Well, it had been more than eight weeks since then—Christ, the movie was opening in just a few days—and still he hadn't told Claire. "Try to get this," he had said during their last phone conversation. "There was no prenup. She could take everything."

Grace had breathed into the receiver for a good half-minute, feeling almost as if she were warming up for a scene. Then she'd said it, calm and slow as she could: "What part of 'If you don't tell her, I will' *don't* you understand?"

The following night, she'd spotted Deacon and Claire, dining at Orso. "How wonderful to see you both," she had said, watching the color drain delicately out of her leading man's face. She'd given Deacon a hug, slipping a note into his jacket pocket that she'd written on a cocktail napkin and folded into quarters.

Deacon,
I am pregnant. It is yours. Tell Claire or I will.
—Grace

Grace was thinking of that note as she exited the offices of KTRA radio after completing a promotional interview with a sweaty, shouting deejay called Hogman. She was walking out of the building with *Meltdown*'s publicist, Loren Weiss, but really, she may as well have been alone for all the attention she was paying to whatever it was he was saying to her. *No response to the note. Not even a text message. What kind of person doesn't respond to a note like that?*

"Penny for your thoughts," Loren said.

"Believe me," Grace replied. "They aren't worth it."

"Well, I happen to think the interview went well. You handled those boob job questions wonderfully. Hogman seemed to respect you."

"Now, there's a sentence you don't hear every day."

He smiled. "Lunch?"

"Nah," she said. "I think I'll just go home." The word *lunch* made her queasy, which reminded her of her condition, which made her queasier still . . .

Grace knew she'd never tell Claire. She couldn't hurt anyone like that—especially someone unfortunate enough to be married to a self-absorbed prick like Deacon Blaine. She'd have the baby, but she'd tell the world that the father was Abel, her stylist. Abel was a good guy. He'd go along with the story long enough for the tabloid news cycle to be over, and then they'd stage a break-up and Grace would move on with her life.

That's what movie stars do, isn't it? They move on.

Grace's eyes were starting to well up, so she said goodbye to Loren quickly, and hurried through the station's parking lot, in search of her car. *You were always so careful. Why did you let your guard down? How could you have done that, for someone like him?* By the time she reached her car, she was actually crying.

"Miss Ryan, might I have a word?"

Grace wiped her eyes with the back of her sleeve. When she turned around, she saw an obese woman in dark pants, a white shirt and a bowtie. "I don't need a valet," Grace said.

"I'm not a valet. I'm an usher," said the woman. "Do you . . . You know Deacon Blaine, right?"

A fan. A strange emotion flooded Grace's brain—an irritation so strong, it crossed over into anger. *How dare she say his name to me now?* Maybe it was the hormones, but Grace was struck by an urge she'd never had before—the urge to slug this woman, this stranger, in the face and . . . God, the woman was smirking at her!

Grace would have done it, would have hauled off and socked another person for the first time in her life—if the obese woman hadn't reached into the pocket of her dark pants. If she hadn't pulled out a gun, and aimed it between Grace's eyes. If she hadn't pulled the trigger before Grace had time to think of another word, ever.

* * *

The shooting part, Myra had mastered. She'd gotten good at it, keeping both eyes on the sights and her thumbs to one side of the loaded magazine and her arms held straight as plywood, immune to kickback. After a few rounds, she was hitting the paper target again and again between the eyes. Even the store owner had been impressed with Myra. She'd scored perfectly on the written test, and he'd believed her when she told him that her neighbor had been robbed and she needed the gun for her own protection—believed her enough to wave the ten-day waiting period and let her walk out with the Walther P22.

So when Myra showed up in KTRA's parking lot—early enough in the morning to be sitting behind her wheel when Grace Ryan pulled her white Land Rover into one of the VIP Guest spaces and met a skinny, bespectacled man at the station's front door—she thought she had come prepared.

But she hadn't known what the bullet would do. She didn't expect all the blood, the way the face seemed to shatter. She didn't expect the thick yellowish substance that seeped out of the hole, either, or the sound that came out of her mouth, just before she fell—that wet gasp. Grace Ryan was not a paper target, she was . . .

"Deacon?" Myra said. Almost all the time these days, she'd been hearing Deacon's voice in her head. But now there was nothing in there but silence . . . the kind that shrieks.

Myra slid into her own car. Somehow, she got out of the parking lot and on the freeway and into her apartment, but she didn't remember the journey.

She never would.

* * *

For most of the afternoon and evening, Myra lay on her living room floor, listening hard as she could for Deacon's voice. It never came. At one point, she got up and turned on the TV, but the TV was full of Grace Ryan's murder, so she turned it right off, then on again, then off . . . . When she next turned it on, Deacon's face filled the screen. Her breath caught in her throat, until the camera cut to Grace's face, and she realized it was the trailer for the new movie, *Meltdown*.

"I cherish you," Deacon's character told Grace's. "You. Are. My . . ."

"No," whispered Myra.

"Only real inspiration . . . It helps me survive to know you're out there, watching. It will be all right I prom—"

She turned off the TV. Had they shown the trailer before *Forgotten Son*? Was that when Deacon had said all those things—the one and only time? Myra couldn't trust her mind to remember. "No, no, no, no, no . . ."

She took off her shirt and pants, and rolled her body on the carpet, hoping to catch the slightest hint of Deacon's scent, a tiny, discarded fragment of him—a strand of blond hair, a coin from his pocket . . . Nothing.

No, no, no, no . . .

She ran into the bedroom and buried herself in her sheets, tried to smell the coconut oil. But all she could smell was her own sweat, her loneliness. She got on the floor, squeezed her head and neck under her bed, rubbed her face and belly and hands on the rough carpet until finally . . . finally she found it. A bit of him. It had to be, or else . . .

She held that bit of him between her breasts so her heart could beat against it. And then, only then was she able to sleep.

* * *

At three o'clock in the morning, Myra was awakened by a crashing knock on her door. "Deacon?" she said. But she knew it wasn't Deacon. He never knocked. She was still wearing her underwear and bra, so she threw on her usher's uniform. "Hello?"

"LAPD." She opened the door on two men in grey suits, one short and squat, one tall and loping.

"Are you Myra Jane Wurtz?" said Short.

"Yes."

Tall told her that the parking lot surveillance camera had captured her shooting Grace Ryan. Then he started reading Myra her rights, just like in the movies, and when they brought her outside and helped her into the police car, there had to be at least a dozen photographers outside her small apartment, flashing her picture. *That's why Deacon didn't come tonight. He was scared of the press.* Realizing this, Myra felt an odd sense of relief. As they drove to the station, Myra said, "Deacon Blaine is going to be mad at you."

Short gave Tall a meaningful glance. "You think you know Deacon Blaine?"

Tall shushed him.

"I *do* know him," Myra said. "He'll tell you that."

Tall shook his head, but Short spoke anyway. "Deacon Blaine called us two months ago, gave us a fan letter from you. He told us to keep an eye out for you. He was afraid you might be dangerous."

"You're lying."

Short turned around and stared at her. His face was very red. His nose reminded Myra of a rotten piece of fruit. "What's the matter?" he said. "You don't see a pathway coming out of my head?"

Myra's throat closed up. Her cheeks went numb and clouds rushed into her eyes and she wanted to scream and scream and never stop. She opened her mouth, but no sound came out. But then a voice in her brain said, *Calm down!*

It wasn't Deacon's voice. It was a new one, soft and female . . . Grace Ryan.

The piece of Deacon you found on the floor, said Grace's voice, just as Myra felt it—the small square of tissue paper between her breasts. *Don't just sit there. Take it out. Look at it.*

Myra did as she was told. It was a napkin from Orso. She unfolded it, read what Grace had written inside . . .

With a shocking calm, she handed it to Tall, telling him Deacon had left it in her apartment. And as she watched Tall's eyes go wide at the neat writing on a napkin from a restaurant that would never admit the likes of Myra, as she watched him hand it to Short with the same stunned reverence people usually reserved for movie stars, Myra knew that, no matter what happened, her name would be connected to Deacon's, forever.

Because, as it turns out, some pathways are stronger than the souls they join.

Cutman

by Christa Faust

Just because I'm a cutman, doesn't mean I'm a man. It might take you a minute to figure that out from looking at me, but you can take my word for it. Fighters call me "sir" all the time, but I don't really mind. In a way, it's better. When guys say they like two chicks together, you can bet they don't mean me. Sure, they love to see skinny college broads making out in bars or fake-titty porn stars poking their tongues into each other for a paycheck, but the idea of somebody like me having a pretty woman, it just makes them sick. Or mad. Or both. Well, if you got a problem with the fact that I unbuckle my dick when I'm done, then to hell with you. You can just sit there and bleed.

I learned the cutman trade from my daddy. A cutman is the person in a fighter's corner whose job it is to stop cuts from bleeding. Sometimes the fighter's regular cornerman'll take care of that job. Other times, like for a real important bout or if the fighter's a heavy bleeder, they'll bring in an ace, like me. I don't coach, water, massage, cheerlead or make the decision to throw in the towel. I just do cuts.

It sounds pretty simple, but there's a real art to it. Every fighter is different. Not to mention the fact that everybody is counting on me. If I can't stop the blood, they stop the fight. There's nothing a fighter hates more than stoppage on account of a lousy cut.

My daddy was one of the best cutmen in the state, but he's been dead six years now. Respect for him is the main reason people are okay about letting a big ugly dyke mess with their fighters. Daddy never treated me like a girl so no one else does. That's the way I like it.

I guess you heard about what happened with Mia. Christ, who hasn't? I had cops and nosy reporters all over me for weeks afterwards, but I kept my mouth shut. I never really told my side of the story. Not until now, anyway.

They called her "Tinkerbell." Mia "Tinkerbell" Ortega. She had this wild black hair that wouldn't stay braided. Strong shoulders. Thighs that could snap you in half. A stone-cold opening bell staredown that gave me goosebumps every time. She wasn't real pretty in the face. Hell, she was a fighter, what do you expect? She had that flattened, broken nose that all the pugs get. Wary dark eyes and acne scars across her high Indio cheekbones. She had a tough face. She wasn't pretty, but she was beautiful.

She fought at 122, so she just barely made featherweight soaking wet. She was ambitious like that. She liked to go after bigger opponents. She was a real dancer, so light on her feet, it looked like she was floating an inch off the canvas. That's where she got the nickname "Tinkerbell." She would flit around the ring like a little fairy and you'd be all caught up in how cute she was, then that left hook would come around the corner like a speeding truck and knock you on your ass. It hurt my heart to look at her.

Of course she went for men. Not like I'd have had a shot anyway, with a mug like this. Still, I can dream, can't I? I still do sometimes, even after what happened.

My girl Stacie had up and left me about four months earlier. Stacie was an exotic dancer. People used to ask if that bothered me, her shaking her stuff in front of all those men. It didn't. After all, I was the one she went home with at the end of the night, right? When my friends asked why she left me, I told them I had no idea. That was a lie. I knew exactly why, I just didn't want to talk about it.

You see, I'm kinda shy in bed. I don't like to take off my undershirt and shorts. I'll do anything a woman wants to make her feel good, but it takes me a really long time to get comfortable enough to let her touch me back. Even through the shorts. Stacie was always on me about that. She said she needed to express her love in a physical way, to give as well as take. I really wanted to let her do those things, but in the end I just couldn't. So she left me for a chick she met on the internet, some vegetarian photographer with a lot of tattoos and political bumper stickers on her Volvo.

One of the things that made me fall so hard for Mia was that she was shy, like me. She wouldn't shower or even change in front of the other fighters. A lot of the girl boxers have bikini shots all over the internet and like to fight in the skimpiest possible outfit to get the guys all worked up. Not Mia. She always wore the long trunks and a thick tank top. There was a rumor going around that someone had touched her when she was little. Maybe that's why she became a fighter.

It's pretty embarrassing to admit it now, but I had this whole corny fantasy going about Mia and me. How I was gonna romance her real slow and old fashioned. How I would give her plenty of time to feel safe, to open up slow and beautiful like a Christmas amaryllis. No man could ever be as good to her as me, because I understood her like no man ever would. But she never gave me the chance. She didn't want someone to be good to her. She was the kind of girl who went for men who hit her.

When I heard Mia was in the hospital, I knew what I had to do. It was that simple. There were a bunch of different stories about what happened to Mia, but I knew in my heart it was Santiago Diaz who put her there.

Diaz: good fighter, bad person. A handsome light heavy with an iron chin. Cocky as fuck. I worked his corner a few times and he always treated me like a necessary evil. Life support for the enswell. Still, he knew better than to make any cracks to my face. You know that list of people you don't want mad at you? Your cook. Your computer guy. Your gynecologist. Well if you're a fighter, put your cutman on the top of that list.

Diaz didn't love Mia. He just wanted to piss on her. To own her and make sure everybody knew it. He would talk shit all day long about her. How she liked it in the ass. How she couldn't get enough of what he had. He kept leaning on Mia to retire because he didn't like women boxing. Said it was unnatural. He told her that she'd better pull out of the McDougal fight if she knew what was good for her. She obviously didn't know what was good for her. She knocked Carrie McDougal out in the first round and the next thing I heard, Mia was in the hospital with internal bleeding. Car accident they said. Or maybe she fell. Yeah, right.

You'd think it would be this big moral dilemma, deciding to kill a man. To me it seemed like the obvious response, as natural as reaching for one of the cotton swabs behind my ear. I decided to put cyanide in the Avitene.

Now, you're probably wondering where I got that cyanide. Well, you're just gonna have to keep on wondering. I don't care if the whole world finds out about what I did, but I don't want to piss off the person who hooked me up. You wouldn't either, if you knew who I meant.

Anyway, I knew that would be the best way to do it. The latex gloves they make us wear now would protect me. All I had to do was make sure I didn't put a swab between my teeth after I touched the poison. I got that bad habit from my daddy, and it was a real hard habit to break.

I knew I was probably gonna go to jail for what I planned to do, maybe even get the needle, but it didn't matter. All I could think about was Mia. I hoped maybe she would write to me, thanking me for saving her from that scumbag boyfriend of hers. Maybe she'd even visit.

The deciding was easy, but the waiting was nothing short of hell. Diaz had his regular guy, a real control freak named Alvarez who usually took care of everything. Even though he was older than dirt and sometimes looked like he was gonna keel over dead in the corner before the end of the first round, he didn't want anybody else to lay a hand on his fighter. He didn't miss a single fight for what felt like a hundred years. Then, finally, he had some kind of problem where the doctors needed to open him up and poke around his insides. I got booked to round out Diaz's corner for the upcoming title fight against Jamal Benjamin.

When I finally got my chance, I thought maybe I wouldn't be able to get it up after all. I thought maybe I was crazy to do something like this for a woman I barely knew. But then I'd see Mia working the heavy bag at the gym and her sweaty shirt would lift up a little on one side, giving me a quick flash of the ugly bruises across the curve of her hip and lower back. I would see her like that and it would all make perfect sense.

I'll admit I was nervous. The night before, I couldn't sleep for shit. I kept on wondering what would happen to my stuff if I went to jail. Not like I had much, but I did have some photos of my daddy and me and some cool old fight cards that were maybe worth something. I didn't have any family. My mother had died trying to squeeze out my big ugly head and my daddy had been an orphan, raised by the state. It had just been the two of us, until the emphysema finally killed him. I didn't like the idea of my landlord tossing all my stuff in the trash, but I couldn't let stupid sentimental thoughts about old pictures keep me from staying focused on what really mattered. What mattered was Mia. I just knew that she would love me back if she could see how far I was willing to go for her.

That morning I called up an old friend and asked her to take Gypsy Rose, the scrappy old cat that Stacie had left behind. That cat was plain gray and not very friendly, but we got along. In a way, it's like we both got dumped. Anyway, it was nice to have someone to come home to. I couldn't worry about photos and stuff, but I did want to make sure that cat would be okay.

The day passed as slow as the night, but it did pass. I kept on looking at flowers and sparrows and the sparkly sign on the ice cream parlor and thinking, *Is this the last time I'm ever gonna see that?* Eventually, it was time to head over to the venue.

Once I got there, it was better. The raw, animal sound of the crowd. The fighters' wordless language of grunts and heavy breath and the dull slap of leather against flesh. The smell of sweat under hot lights. These things were as comfortable and familiar as my favorite jacket. They made it seem like it would work.

I stood outside the ropes, watching Diaz from his corner and thinking, *Christ, what if he knocks Benjamin out? What if he goes the distance and doesn't get cut?* But Benjamin kept on peppering him with these fast, surgical jabs all through the third round and finally, it came. The red stuff that I'd been waiting for.

The bell rang and Diaz hit the corner, squinting against the blood. I reached into the ice for the cold metal enswell and pressed it against the growing mouse beneath his eye while my other hand rolled an epinephrine-soaked swab in the open cut. I gave the cut some steady pressure for a few heartbeats, then mopped the rest of the blood away with a wad of clean gauze. When the cut above his eyebrow was as dry was it was gonna get, I tossed the swab and the gauze and packed the cut with the Avitene flour and cyanide mixture. He hissed and swallowed a curse, trying to be a man about it.

I didn't feel nervous anymore. My hands moved automatically, like they always did. They squeezed and spread the lips of the cut, testing to see if the blood had stopped. It had. I tossed the enswell back in the bucket, slapped a smear of my daddy's special formula cutsalve across Diaz's eyebrow and then nodded to the ref. The chief cornerman shoved Diaz's mouthpiece back between his teeth, throwing out some last minute advice in Spanish and smacking his ass as he stood. Diaz tipped his head from side to side, shifting his weight and shaking out his arms. He looked as solid and confident as ever. No sign that he was feeling the effect of the cyanide.

When he TKOed Benjamin less than a minute later, my heart filled with a cautious excitement. If Diaz dropped dead right there in the ring, the cops and the Athletic Commission would have to get involved right away. If he felt weak, dizzy and confused after the fight, everyone would think he was just punchy. They'd tell him to go home and sleep it off. He would never wake up, but I could be across the border before anyone thought to look for me. Of course, that's not how it happened.

I hadn't seen Mia all through the fight. She made a point of being there for all Diaz's fights, even though he was never there for hers. I thought it was a little weird, her not being there, but I just figured she was late, or maybe she finally had enough of him. I had other things on my mind and so I didn't give it a second thought. I was pretty surprised to see her standing there in the aisle after the final bell, but not nearly as surprised as I was when I noticed she had a gun.

Her hair was all wild and coming out of her braid the way it did when she fought. She looked beautiful just like she always did, except something was different. It was her eyes. Her eyes were black and dead.

She raised the gun and shot Santiago Diaz in the face while the ref held up his gloved hand in victory. Then she shot herself.

It was big news, of course. You'd think we were in Madison Square Garden with the number of people who claimed to have been there. Diaz's family was very religious, so they refused an autopsy. Besides, it's not like there was any question about what killed him. No one ever found out about the cyanide.

I still have bad dreams about what happened. I keep seeing her empty, hopeless eyes and the way all those little frizzy licks of hair puffed out around the place where the bullet came out of the back of her head. I keep thinking I could have done it different, somehow. I keep thinking if only I had acted sooner, maybe I could have saved her.

I would have done anything for that girl, but I'll tell you what. Every time I drive past that sparkly ice cream parlor sign, I'm glad to see it.

The Grand Inquisitor

by Eddie Muller

Reaching for the doorbell, heart hammering, Lulu scolds herself to *calm down*. Five times during the past week—sometimes morning, sometimes night—she had parked across from this house, to observe who came and went: no one. Yesterday, Lulu finally was convinced that the only person living here was Hazel Reedy. *An old woman all alone,* Lulu reminds herself. *There's nothing to be afraid of.*

She rings the bell.

For long moments Lulu steadies her pulse by staring at her shoes: the cream-colored sling-back leather pumps are the best she's found in ten years of second-hand salvages. Superstition made her wear them today. She'd bought these shoes the same day, in the same store, where she'd discovered the books. Half those books now filled the bulky purse weighing down her aching shoulder. Two months ago, on that fateful Sunday, she'd assumed these shoes were the day's big find. That was before she examined the books more closely.

Sunday church bells toll in the distance. Otherwise, the neighborhood is eerily quiet. Lulu nervously smoothes the pleats in her dress. An actual Alfred Shaheen, picked up for fourteen dollars at a St. Vincent De Paul thrift. White cotton twill with subdued floral pattern, square bodice, pleated shoulders. Mid-fifties, barely worn. And the shoes: not marred by a single crack or scuff. She wondered why some vintage clothes had little or no wear: what had happened to the original owner? A change in taste? Size? Or something sudden and dreadful?

Lulu's imagination could gallop away if she didn't grip the reins. Tougher now, off her meds.

She hears a deadbolt unlatch but sees no one behind the front door's veiled window. A key turns in a lock, followed by a metallic snap. After a moment another bolt slides back. Then a different deadbolt unlocks. Four locks, total.

Lulu isn't the only one afraid.

The door opens a crack, revealing a slender woman in her late sixties, wearing a simple blue housedress. Her striking features have been wizened by age and veined by alcohol. Lustrous waves of white hair, fixed with jeweled barrettes, frame her gaunt face.

—Yes? May I help you?

—Good afternoon. I have some things I believe may belong to you, Mrs. Reedy. You are Hazel Reedy?

—Yes. What things?

The woman gives Lulu a suspicious head-to-toe inspection.

—Some books.

Lulu pats the purse. *Don't get specific out here. Make her invite you in.*

—Books? I don't read. My eyesight is going.

—They belong to your husband. At least I think they did. I was hoping you might be able to tell me for sure.

—My husband is dead.

—I know. I'm sorry. Mrs. Reedy, I think these books are important. Vitally important. If I could just have a minute of your time, I think you'd be able to clear up a lot of things.

—How did you find this place?

—I'd be happy to explain. May I come in?

Hazel Reedy leans out to look past the young woman on the stoop, and Lulu notices a milky white mass in her left eye. The woman seems to be dimly gazing beyond the begging foliage in the overgrown yard, beyond the weathered houses across the street, beyond even the dark flat-bottomed clouds gathering over the horizon. Lulu blanches in embarrassment when she realizes she is staring at the flawed eye.

Several silent seconds crawl by before the old woman finally says something, too softly for Lulu to comprehend.

—Excuse me?

Hazel Reedy steps back inside, leaving the door, not quite plumb, to slowly drift open on its own.

—Come inside.

—Thank you, Mrs. Reedy. I'll try not to take too much of your time.

Lulu enters a foyer murky and silent and still. Hazel Reedy closes the door and turns a key to re-lock one deadbolt. She leaves the rest untouched. The place reminds Lulu of Aunt Joan's and

Uncle Jim's after their children died in the boat accident. A pall of grief descended on the rooms and hallways, until it felt like misery itself was holding the house together.

Lulu scans the foyer for photographs and personal mementoes. *Evidence, any piece of evidence.* All she notices are huge stacks of newspapers, going back months, maybe years. Recycling hasn't reached the Reedy residence.

—I didn't get *your* name.

—Lulu.

Hazel Reedy leads her guest to a small living room, where every piece of furniture is at least forty years old.

—That's your birth name? Lulu?

—No, it's really Heather. But I hate Heather. Too many Heathers in the world.

—There are? How about that. I've never known a Heather. Or a Lulu, for that matter. You know, I was very fashionable once, like you. I like that dress. It's lovely. Come, sit down.

—Thank you. It's vintage.

—I still have lots of them. Closets full, upstairs.

The chesterfield breathes out dust when Lulu sits. Motes swirl in the afternoon light that angles through a gap in the drapes.

—Excuse the gloom. I never have visitors and rarely open the blinds. I don't want the upholstery to fade.

—You have a lot of lovely antiques.

Hazel Reedy clicks on a floor lamp beside the chesterfield.

—Is that what they are? I've made myself a pot of tea. May I bring you a cup, as well?

—Um, sure. That would be nice.

Lulu needs a few moments to gather herself. Watching the old woman walk to the kitchen, she notices Hazel Reedy's hands seeking out familiar landmarks: a chair rail, the edge of the dinner table, a stretch of wainscoting. Her bad eye is obviously blind.

Glancing around, Lulu notes full ashtrays stationed on every flat surface. Stale cigarette smoke, decades worth, thickens the air. Hung on nicotine-stained walls are dingy landscapes familiar to Lulu from every antique store she's ever been in. "Grandma's Guest Room Art," she calls it. No photographs are displayed anywhere. No trace of any husband, relatives, children.

Lulu steels herself, opens the purse, and begins removing

books. She stacks them on the coffee table in front of her.

Hazel Reedy returns moments later carrying one saucered cup, which she carefully sets before her guest.

—Aren't you having some?

—Could only carry one at a time.

—I'm sorry, I should have asked if you needed help.

—I'll get mine in a moment.

—Let me get it for you.

—Sit down. In a moment.

Hazel Reedy lowers herself onto a straight-backed chair, its green velour seat worn to a shine.

— Are those the books you wanted me to see?

—Do you recognize them?

—No. But I'm curious why you think I should.

Lulu separates from the pile an exhausted volume: *The Synonym Finder* by J. L. Rodale. The broken-apart hardcover is missing the front signature and the cover boards are held tenuously in place by a patchwork of masking tape. Lulu delicately places it on the table and flips it open to a random page. The margins are filled with miniscule notes in various colors—cribbed comments running vertically up the side, across the head and foot, sentences underscored with heavy pen lines, certain words and phrases highlighted with yellow marker.

—Look familiar?

—It looks like the work of a crazy person. Your hairdo is very old-fashioned, dear. I'm trying to think of that actresses' name. My memory–

—It does look that way at first. But when you look closely, you see it's not really crazy. It's not disorganized or random. It's more like the work of someone whose mind won't shut off. There's a thesaurus I didn't bring that's 1,289 pages. There are notes like this on every page. He's trying to grasp everything. Account for everything. And struggling not to lose control.

Hazel Reedy silently lights a cigarette, her movements so stealthy Lulu doesn't notice the lighter striking.

—You think you're describing my husband? From this book?

—Well, I'm asking: were these your husband's?

—John did study a lot, I'll say that. If that was his, I wouldn't be surprised. I'd like to get my tea now.

—Your husband was a brilliant man, I'm assuming. Being a teacher and all.

—Hmm.

Hazel Reedy's good eye gazes through a plume of exhaled smoke as Lulu places a 1946 *Encyclopedia Brittanica*—Volume 16: Mushroom to Ozonides—atop the Rodale. The young woman opens it to a bookmarked section midway through the volume.

Hazel Reedy says softly:

—You don't mind my smoke, I hope.

—Of course not. Here's a long entry in this encyclopedia regarding "Numbers." Notice all these marked-up and highlighted sections pertaining to cuneiform numerals and hieroglyphs; all this stuff here about the development of numerals through the symbolic, decimal and cipher stages . . .

—And your reason for showing me this?

Hazel Reedy reaches for an ashtray at the end of the table and moves it closer. She taps ash into it, never taking her eyes off her guest.

—I'm getting to that. Um, I'm sure you remember many years ago there was a man, a man who killed some people and boasted about it by sending letters, letters and messages in code, ciphers, to the newspapers.

—You came here because you think my husband was Zodiac.

—Am I the first?

—Yes, you are. You certainly are.

—I know this is a terrible thing to suggest and I'm sorry. But I need to show you what's in these books . . . then maybe you can tell me something, anything, that will prove I'm wasting my time. You'd be doing me a favor. Here, look at this–

Lulu hands Hazel Reedy a musty paperback entitled *Haunted Mesa*, by Donald Bayne Hobart.

—This is one of a series of westerns about a vigilante gunfighter with a secret identity. There were several "Masked Rider" novels in with these other books. Look at the last page . . .

Hazel Reedy's bony fingers, balancing a dwindling Pall Mall, absently turn pages. Her gaze, however, stays on Lulu's face. A flush rises from Lulu's chest to her cheeks. Her heart begins racing. She'd expected a different reaction: anger, or at least annoyance. Shaking slightly, Lulu takes the book, riffles to the end, and replaces it in Hazel Reedy's passive hands.

—See what's there?

Below the final line

He disappeared into the night, heading for the hideout where he would wait for Blue Hawk.

is a series of numbers, arranged to form a code. Beneath that: a crudely etched circle bisected by two crossing pen slashes.

—What am I supposed to make of this?

—Doesn't that symbol mean anything to you?

—I suppose you'll tell me.

—It's a gunsight. It's the symbol Zodiac used to sign his letters. Flip through that book, any of these books. That symbol is all over the pages.

Across a vast stretch of years, the two women stare at each other.

—Don't let your tea get cold.

Parched by her nervousness, Lulu swallows gulps of tepid tea.

—Lulu. If you thought this all amounted to something, you wouldn't have come brazenly knocking on my door. You'd have taken all this to the police.

—I have.

—And did they laugh at you?

—No. No, they did not.

Laughter would have been preferable to the dismissive looks Lulu got from the San Francisco cops when she'd proudly presented her findings. Or the condescending come-on she endured from a Vallejo PD detective who actually came to examine the books at her apartment. After a few cursory glances at the pages he asked if "a good-looking girl couldn't find better uses for an over-active imagination."

Lulu cannot help looking into Hazel Reedy's bad eye, as the woman says:

—If the police saw something in all this, why aren't *they* here?

—Because there's nothing in these books they can act on. It's barely circumstantial. But when I learned that John Montgomery Reedy was married . . . well, it seemed obvious that his widow was the person who could settle this. You're the one who can provide the evidence that will blow my whole crazy theory right out of the water.

—Or I could just admit that my husband was a murderer?

—Or that.

—You have a lot of guts, young lady. I'll say that for you. We called it moxie, in my day.

Hazel Reedy stands up again and starts toward the kitchen, trailing cigarette smoke. She pauses beside a small desk situated between living and dining rooms. Her fingers absently move some envelopes around, then she flicks a precarious ash into a waiting ashtray.

—Dear, the things in these books, aren't they simply what you'd find in any teacher's reference books?

Lulu stands up and approaches Hazel Reedy, a slip of paper clutched in her hand.

—This was used as a bookmark. It's a bank deposit slip: J. Montgomery Reedy, 25 Fairlawn Drive, Riverside, California. Were you married then? In Riverside?

—Yes. I was married to John Montgomery Reedy from the time I was twenty-two years old. A very naïve twenty-two year old. How old are you, dear?

—Twenty-six.

—You weren't even alive then. What possible interest could you have in those horrible crimes? For God's sake, look at you. You're still a child. You've got a life ahead of you. I envy you. Why are you pursuing something like this?

—I know someone who was murdered.

—I'm sorry . . . were you close?

—I barely knew her.

Hazel Reedy's eyes focus on something distant. She steps into the dining room, where on the lace-covered table yet another ashtray awaits.

Lulu observes her slumped figure for a moment, then persists.

—Your husband taught in Riverside for two years, at Harbor Avenue Junior High School. Isn't that right?

—Yes. He taught English. The notes in those books, they're just things a teacher does. The musings of a fertile mind.

Lulu crowds Hazel Reedy.

—Some of these books were purchased in Riverside. The receipts are still in them. Zodiac's first documented murder was in Riverside: Cherie Jo Bates.

—We moved here in 1967. So that seems to–

—Cherie Jo Bates was killed in 1966. The records at Harbor Avenue Junior High show that Mr. Reedy quit three months after her murder. He immediately got a job up here in Danville, teaching at Monte Vista High School. But you *lived* in Vallejo, where the Zodiac killings started again in 1969. Neither school has a single photograph of Mr. Reedy on file. He's the only employee in either school system with no photo on file. How would you explain that?

—John didn't like having his picture taken.

—Any particular reason?

Hazel Reedy has no response other than a long drag of her cigarette. Lulu dashes to the living room, and is back before Hazel inhales again.

—Let me show you something else: It's from a book called *An Experience in Literature*. I made copies of these pages because I couldn't carry the whole book with me. But look at this . . . this is your husband's writing here, isn't it?

Hazel Reedy crushes the butt in the ashtray and accepts the stapled pages as if they are a dead thing. She moves back to the chair and resigns herself to it, perusing the pages silently. Lulu kneels beside the old woman, their arms touching.

—This is an excerpt from Dostoevski's *The Brothers Karamazov*, a section called "The Grand Inquisitor."

Lulu guides the suddenly mute woman through pages she has endlessly studied, making sure that Hazel Reedy's eyes follow her finger as Lulu traces the intricately-inscribed notes that fill every available space in and around and between Dostoevski's prose. Lulu's finger points out highlighted words: God, death, free will, enslavement, Good/Evil—and she lingers on the violently underscored phrase, Through Suffering Victory Over Flesh.

—All these references appear in Zodiac's letters to the press. I've read every word of these books, Mrs. Reedy—the ones

---

printed on the pages and the ones written in by your husband. There's a manifesto in the margins of these books. I have a very strong sense of the man who did all this.

—You do.

—He scares me. Just on the page, he scares me. Did he scare you?

—Why did you come here?

Lulu sits opposite the old woman, leaving "The Grand Inquisitor" in Hazel Reedy's trembling hands. She looks up into the old woman's good eye.

—Why haven't you asked me to leave? If my suggestion is so outrageous, you'd have run me out by now.

—There's no proof these books belonged to my husband. And even if they did, maybe he bought them second-hand, maybe the writing was already in them. How could we know? And how did you come to have them?

—I found them in an antique store, all boxed up together. These and more I didn't bring. The dealer bought them all at a church bazaar at St. Isidore's, just down the road from here. I went there and they remembered these books being donated by a long-time parishioner. The books had belonged to her late husband, who passed away eight years ago. Sister Joan told me that your exact words were, "Someone else needs to have these now." It's odd she'd remember that. Those exact words.

—I didn't go to St. Isidore's very much by then. Yes, they would have remembered.

—Did you know what these books were? Did you *want* them to be found?

Hazel Reedy draws a deep wheezing breath, which doesn't fill her deflated frame. Lulu presses on.

—Why didn't *you* take the books to the police? Why send a message in a bottle? After eight years?

Hazel Reedy finds no more Pall Malls in the ragged pack.

—I left my cigarettes in the kitchen. Come with me.

—Mrs. Reedy, if you can disprove the things I've suggested, please do. Any of them. Look, here—how the writing on this side of the page slants to the left. Yet in the other margin it leans to the right. From all the police reports and research done over the years, the belief is that Zodiac was ambidextrous, that he could write with either hand, which would account—

—Don't believe that. That's ridiculous.

Hazel Reedy rises from her chair.

—Was your husband ambid–

The old woman holds up her hand, like a reprimand. She glares at her young inquisitor.

—The person who wrote all this . . . madness . . . was not ambidextrous. What you see in these pages is more like schizophrenia.

Lulu's chest tightens. Her arms tingle.

—Follow me. I want to show you something.

Hazel Reedy feels her way through the dining room, her figure disappearing through a doorway. *She's an old woman living alone*, Lulu reminds herself. *There's nothing to be afraid of.*

She faintly hears the sounds of a cabinet opening, a faucet running, a cup being rinsed. Then Hazel Reedy's voice, calling:

—Dear, please. Come in here.

Lulu is surprised how unsteady she feels, wobbly in the knees, feet slightly numb. She is more afraid than she realized.

Stepping through the doorway between the dining room and kitchen, Lulu is startled to see the empty liquor bottles. Dozens and dozens of them, marshaled on the tile counter, collected in boxes on the floor, precariously poised atop the refrigerator. Gin, vodka, anything and everything. Even given years, it doesn't seem possible that the woman standing before her, wiping her nose with a tissue and lighting another cigarette, could have by herself consumed this ocean of alcohol.

Lulu notices several wastebaskets inside the kitchen door. They are filled with empty prescription drug containers. Hundreds of them.

Hazel Reedy turns from the sink to face Lulu. She urgently draws down the cigarette, lengthening the ash.

—Louise Brooks.

—I'm sorry?

—That's who I was trying to think of before. She had a hair-cut like yours.

—That's why I took the name Lulu. After her movie.

—You're too young to know that. And too young to be my daughter, I'm afraid.

Lulu isn't sure she's heard right. The words sounded distant, faint. Her head feels strange. She tries to ignore it, asking:

—You have children?

—No, thank God. That's one prayer He answered. Making me miscarry.

—What? I'm sorry. I thought you said something about a daughter. Sorry.

—Stop apologizing. It's not necessary.

—I'm . . .

Hazel holds up her hand again, hushing Lulu. She drags deeply on the cigarette again and lets the smoke out in a long, luxurious breath.

—That's it. My last one.

The butt is tossed in the sink. Hazel Reedy straightens to her full height.

—Lulu, listen to me. There isn't a lot of time. What if I told you you were right? What would your reaction be? Would you hate me? The way I hate myself?

Lulu tries to answer, but her tongue is too thick to let words out.

—Look at me, look at this place. I have been ill my whole life. I couldn't do what needed to be done. That's why I needed you. And you answered. *You* answered my prayers. Not God. *You*. You knew. Look at you. I'm so glad it's going to be you. You're young and bright. I wish you were my daughter. I'd have something to be proud of. You were born after those girls died. You came here for *them*, that's what I think.

It takes incredible effort for Lulu to get the words out:

—It's not your fault. God forgives.

—I don't want God's forgiveness. All this pain is His fault, I fear. Where is God when the damage takes place? Why hasn't he eased my conscience after all the years I've spent praying for help? Why would he let it happen, any of it? I don't want God's forgiveness—I want *your* forgiveness. Look at you, such a beautiful girl, so full of promise. Like the ones that died. The ones he killed.

—The ones he *may* have killed.

Did I say those words? It sounded like someone else, muffled, maybe in the next room.

—What, now you're going to argue the other way? I was here. I know what he was capable of. He'd take off for days at a time and not call. He became another person and I became a stranger to him. When he came back, he'd burn his clothes in the trash. I saw him do it more than once. But it would pass, you see. It wasn't always like that. But then he decided I couldn't be trusted. He realized that I knew. At first he drugged me. He did things to me when I was helpless, to scare me into never saying what I knew. I lived in terror.

—Oh my God, I'm so sorry. I am *so* sorry.

—Lulu, look under there.

Hazel Reedy points to a banquette in the corner of the kitchen. The tabletop is pink-and-gray speckled Formica. Lulu sets a hand on it to steady herself. She leans over, peering under it.

She doesn't see anything.

Lulu feels dizzy, like she might be sick. The walls are moving.

—Kneel down.

Hesitantly, Lulu lowers a knee to the floor, bends over, and cranes her neck to look beneath the table. Attached to the underside is a foot-long butcher's knife, its handle wrapped in black electrician's tape. It is held loosely in place by a pair of custom-made wire hooks.

Lulu stands up too quickly; her head reels, tiny black dots swirling and exploding all around her. *Get out. Go now.*

—He had them hidden all over the house. Clubs too, in secret places. That's the only one left. I don't know why, but I had to keep one.

—I need to leave now. I don't feel well.

—You'd better sit down. Use that chair.

—I don't know what's happening.

—I put drugs in your tea. It took so long for you to finally get here, I didn't want you running away.

Lulu pitches back against the banquette, clutching it to stay upright.

Hazel Reedy stands beside Lulu and touches her damp face. Both women have tears in their eyes. Hazel points to her bad eye.

—He did that. You asked before if he scared me? He

paralyzed me. He controlled every minute of my life from the day we met. He owned me, every moment I was alive. I had no one to help me, no one to talk to. But that's not an excuse. I *let* it happen. He was such a horribly sick man. In some ways he couldn't help himself. But *I* could have done something. John did evil things, but I am guilty too, as much as if I'd held the gun or the knife. This is what I've lived with my whole life.

—No!

It is a moan more than a word; it is all Lulu can muster before her limbs go slack. She wants to scream, *Why are you doing this?* but she cannot.

Hazel catches Lulu as she sags, cradling her gently. The older woman is surprisingly strong. Lulu can feel smoky breath on her face as she is lowered onto the chair.

—Here, let's get this off. It'd be a shame to ruin it.

Lulu's eyes fight to stay open. They beg for mercy. She feels the zipper slide down her back and the dress spread open. Gently, Hazel Reedy slides the dress from Lulu's shoulders, to her waist. She balances the young woman against the banquette and tugs the dress down her hips and off. She folds it expertly and sets it on the seat at the banquette's far end. Hazel notices Lulu's foot twitching. She realizes, glancing in the young woman's eyes, that Lulu is making it happen.

—I wasn't going to forget,

Hazel Reedy says around the rising lump in her throat.

She slips off Lulu's shoes and carefully places them on the dress.

—There are things a girl like yourself shouldn't have to know. You see, to make sure I never left him, John made me his accomplice. How could I possibly betray him then? He was brilliant, as you said. But I wrote everything in those books, Lulu, not John. All the ciphers, all the letters. I wrote them. For him. With him.

Hazel spreads Lulu's knees apart and kneels between her bare legs. She reaches her right hand under the table and pulls the hidden knife free. With her other hand she caresses Lulu's face, tilting her chin gently upright.

—Can you still hear me? I'm sorry to put you through this, Lulu . . . but I am guilty of terrible sins. God won't forgive me.

I don't want him to. I could have stopped it, but I didn't know how. I can't forgive myself. But you, you can forgive me, Lulu.

The old woman sits back on her haunches, her face streaked with tears.

—Please, my dear . . . try to understand. That's all I want. It's what I've waited for all these years. I need to look in your eyes and see your forgiveness. Will you forgive me?

With what little will she still possesses, Lulu holds her head up and looks into Hazel's eyes. She nods. She won't remember doing it, but she nods.

—Thank you so much for coming, my dear. Thank you for being so smart. And for hearing my confession. God hates me, Lulu, but He blesses you.

With a fast deep cut, Hazel Reedy pulls the blade across her own throat. The remains of her life spill into Lulu's lap. The knife clatters to the floor as Hazel Reedy, shuddering convulsively, clutches Lulu around the waist and hugs her, more tightly than she has ever held anyone.

Uncle

by Daniel Woodrell

A cradle won't hold my baby. My baby is two-hundred pounds in a wheelchair and hard to push uphill but silent all the time. He can't talk since his head got hurt, which I did to him. I broke into his head with a mattocks and he hasn't said a thing to me nor nobody else since. Uncle is Ma's evil brother and there never was a day when I wasn't afraid of him, even when he gave me striped-candy from his pocket or let me drive the tractor in the yard.

Before Uncle became a baby, when he was a man, myself and Ma both tried to never be alone inside with him, tried to never even stand too close outside, as he was born with a pair of devils in his chest and the one just eggs on the other and neither ever rests, and last fall he seen my undies on the clothes line moving in the wind and said to me kind of joyful and mean, Old enough to bleed, old enough to breed.

I was waiting on him ever since, the slide-in move under my quilt as I slept, the whiskery rub on my cheek, the fingers riding roughshod over my skin like cowboys hunting an Indian to blame. Ma always was scared to chase him off, or even let on she noticed the things he done.

The day I come across the mattocks in the shadows and swung down on his head and rendered him into my own big quiet baby, there was a girl. The girl was yelling high-pitched the way they did, out there in the old barn where Uncle took them. The barn sets near where the house was once, long ago, a good ways down the cow pasture from where the house is now, and the wood hangs at a tilt on the sides of the barn, all dried up and flaky from sun and rain and freeze since two grandma's ago, and the roof had fallen open in a bunch of spots but there's some hay put by inside, pitched around loose, and a shock of old garden tools leaned in the corner, and small birds black as pepper come and go from the slanted rafters. This one screamed louder than most, and screamed loudest in between sentences she said, such as, There's no need for this! Get off of me! Stop! Stop! Please, stop!

Uncle culled these girls from down on the river, which they come here for, and flows just yonder over our ridge and down a steep hill. They come here from where there are crowds of people bunched in tight to loll along our crystal water in college shirts and bikinis, smoking weed and drinking too much, laughing all the way while their canoes spin on the river like bugs twirling in a spider's web. Mostly they don't know what they're doing, but the river is not too raging or anything. Everybody thinks they can do that river when they stand looking at it up at Heaney Cross, where they rent the canoes and the water is smooth. Uncle dicks them when he catches them, on the smelly damp hay in the old barn, with the open spots above leaking light on his big behind bouncing white and glary on some girl whose eyes won't blink anymore.

But this yelling girl was giving him a tussle, clawing at him and such as that, scratching him under his eyes so blood laid a narrow path down his face and dropped from his chin onto her chest and bare boobies, and Uncle dicked her even harder in his own blood. She had brown hair that was bright blond on top in perfect streaks, which looked pretty and special, something I might ought to try, and stopped yelling because he had his hands on her throat.

Uncle stood once his own breaths slowed, stood and hooked his bibs up and left her lay there, and then is when I slunk into the barn and knelt.

Let's get you out of here, lady. Sometimes he comes back.

I hauled her up and made her move, trying to get her to the spring pooled under our ridge where her canoe would likely be waiting. Uncle looked for loners, mostly, and understood that the law here ain't eager to come into our woods after him, so he was bold as an idiot sometimes, when he smoked powder or drunk a bunch. I held hands with her down the trail, which switches back and forth and is steep, with little rocks slippery underfoot, and she didn't say a word. Get in the spring, I said, and when she didn't, I pushed her. The cold water shocked her face into a different cast, brought color to her skin. The water in the pool shimmered like glass and you could see the polish on your toenails standing in there. I made a shallow cup of my hands and sloshed what water I could onto her skin, which had tanned, and she wore earrings I liked, the kind that hung low from the ears but didn't flop around all spaz every time your head moved, with purple glass in the low part, my favorite color. Her body had got to be one big goose bump, plump and trembling, her lips pressed together and mumbly.

There was a bird book in her canoe that put a name to all of them it looked like, with inked pictures. I said, Come on, lady, get the hell away from here. And, listen, if you run to the law, well, he'll know, and pretty quick he'll know where you live, too. You won't want that. Nobody wants that. She got into the canoe, and I gave it a strong shove out to the main current and waved goodbye. She didn't raise a paddle, even, until she was near gone from sight.

Back in the pasture, he said to me, She leave anything good?

Didn't she have on a necklace, I said. Seems like there was a skinny golden one around her neck before she laid down on the hay. Must be it flew off or broke loose.

You might be right, he said, and headed for the barn. I think maybe you are. He started staring at the messed straw and dirt and bird puddles on the ground. Golden, was it?

I said, Just there, I think. She laid just there. Then I eased to the dark nearby corner and let my hand drop to the mattocks handle. Maybe you could find it best with your fingers, feel for it. He got on his knees to feel the dirt for gold and I hoisted that mattocks overhead and slammed down like I was busting the cow pond ice open in winter, so the whole herd could drink.

There was a good deal of blood, and his arms and legs and fingers and all shook pretty jittery for a spell. His face was to the hay and the blood built a creek down his backbone. He messed himself so I could smell it strong standing back from him a distance.

I had sat down and started poking him with a stick by the time Ma got home from work. He wasn't shaking that much anymore. She screamed, yanked on her hair, called for an ambulance, and asked me, Who did this? I said, The last girl he was after done it. She said, Oh, my, if he don't die what'll we do?

Ma works, so he became my baby to take care of once they turned him out of the hospital. He was there almost all summer, s'posed to pass away any ol' day, but he never. Doctor said, He'll need constant care, like a newborn. Ma said, I got a job already—he's yours, hon.

You finally get an ogre under your thumb and you can't hardly keep from torturing him some at first. That's how it started with my baby, torturing him a little bit now and then, but his face hardly twitched and his eyes just stayed focused on something over yon behind the clouds that he couldn't look away from, so it wasn't as much fun as you figure torturing an ogre should be. I wheeled him out to the yard in thunderstorms and left him set there in his metal chair. Rain beat on him and blown leaves stuck to his face, but he never caught pneumonia or a lightning bolt. I poured bird feed into a bread pan and set him along the treeline with the pan on his lap. One day I put him in a frilly pink dress Ma had and did his hair up in a french bun and used the whole bucket of Ma's make-up on him—eyeliner, rouge, lipstick, and wheeled him out front to the road and left him sit all day beside the mailbox, for every passing neighbor and stranger to see, until Ma found him and wheeled him back to the house. Then she and me spent the evening curling his hair like Shirley Temple and laughing, hooking bras on him, drawing movie star moles on his cheeks, searching for just the right spot until he looked like a disease had got him, trying all the shades of lipstick on his sagged mouth, and cherry red worked best, we figured, with his complexion.

I had to feed him pabulum with a cereal spoon and squirt water into his throat so his pills would go down. He could chew, which must be the last reflex to shut off in a body, or something. Once I rolled him all the way around on the paved road to the river, and shoved him into the water up to his neck. He made a picture, with only his head poked up for turtles to rest on, while tiny white waves lapped at his jowls, and the chair scooted slightly in the current. I left him there for fate to find him easy, and floated away to the bridge where I dove and dove for tourist treasure that might've washed down from all the canoes that take spills upstream, and let the sun dry me after, then dawdled back to where he waited. He wasn't exactly where I left him, but was fine, cold but fine, and I had a terrible awful time wheeling such a big fat wet baby uphill to home.

Twice a day I slid the thunder pan under him and wiped his butt, and every three days I shaved his face with an old straight-razor in case my hands shook and he got cut to ribbons by accident. I wiped the drool from his chin when he slobbered, which was always, spent most of my time with him, and in about a month I caught myself singing at him, "You are my sunshine . . ." and such, baby music, the kind you coo more than sing. I puked out the front door, catching myself that way, the first time. It was awful, awful, singing happy words to a baby that had done so much bad in this world, but soon it started to happen again, about every day, and I got used to catching myself singing to him, accepted it as a human thing of mystery.

He was helpless, and I took to wondering if Uncle was still evil now that he'd become a helpless baby. Do babies learn evil in the run of their days, or bring it with them from the other side of all that you can see? He drooled and I held a rag to his lips, and wheeled him outside into the fresh air and bright light, shoved him along the driveway, to and fro, singing.

It was coming up on Halloween when I first caught my baby's eyes following me across the room. Then it got to where every time I spun around quick his eyes were on me, and not on my face, neither. Uncle was yet alive inside that big old baby, and his eyes was wanting what babies don't even know about. When he raised a hand to swat a fly, I peed down my legs and ran around the house seven times. Come morning I shoved him to the paved road and around to the hill and down to the bridge. The air hung gray and cool and I could see fish in the water, still in the flow with their noses pointed upstream. I wheeled Uncle to the far edge of the bridge, where a drunk in a truck had torn away the railing, and pushed him to the edge. I dabbed the slobber rag to his mouth, then looked into his eyes and saw how babies do change so fast. I tossed the slobber rag into the river and it made a small shadow over the fish before the current whisked it past.

I'd been making him well, now I needed to make him right.
My baby ain't meant for this world.

Undocumented

SJ Rozan

None of the snakehead's men could say with certainty that Wei An-Lin was behind the women's revolt. Still they scowled and cursed her, the more because their maledictions bounced off her like arrows striking rock.

Though for all the men's spitting and scowling, it was hardly a revolt: just a co-ordination of the single women, those with no husbands to protect them. A schedule of waking and sleeping, of cooking and going on deck and using the toilet in groups of four, of six. A system that made all accountable for each, left none alone, unwatched, unguarded.

For the snakehead's men, access to the women was an expected recompense for the long, hard months at sea. Their quarters were little better than the cargo's, nor their food, and the weather and the boredom and the rolling of the ship were the same. As always, when collecting the cargo they'd taken note of the meek, the frightened. The ones who came from farthest, and came to the wharf alone. These were the promising ones. No man had counted Wei An-Lin among them. Flinty, one said. Another said stringy, like a laying hen too old for eggs but still cackling. Wei An-Lin wasn't old, though she'd likely seen thirty, but they all understood, and they all laughed.

So when, not a week out to sea, they were met with a new, if tentative, defiance even from the most timid women, the men erupted in anger and confusion. These were strong and brutal men: they resolved disputes with force. No matter how organized, of course the women could never have withstood an equally organized assault by the men. Some of the men argued for it, as a lesson to future groups if nothing else. But the enforcer forbade it. Victory was assured but so was damage to the cargo. The men were being well paid. The cargo, on the other hand, were expected to work off their passage once they reached America. As a matter of loyalty to the snakehead it was the men's duty to deliver the cargo whole. A matter of loyalty, a matter of a paycheck, of future prospects, and in the end, of their own good health.

The men grumbled but did as told, especially after Xu Zhao vanished. He'd been the most angry, the most vocal. The most likely to disobey the enforcer. And one morning he was gone. Had the enforcer, unable to control him, gotten rid of him? Was the brown stain on the deck his blood, was he far behind them now, riding the gray sea? Many agreed that must be what had happened. Though some said the enforcer would never have denied it, if he'd done it; on the contrary, he'd have boasted of it. And others claimed to have seen a gleam of steely triumph in Wei An-Lin's eyes.

The enforcer took no action against Wei An-Lin for leading the women, or for anything else. It was a quiet voyage, better than most. No rowdy demands for more food, more light, more cooking fuel; as for water, the women in their groups emerged on deck in each rainstorm like earthworms from the ground. They brought cooking pots, thermos bottles, even, it seemed to the enforcer, thimbles. They carried the water below, where other women waited with cloths to dry them and warm them. They stored the fresh water, bathed in it, washed clothes, boiled tea. They shared it with the couples and the single men.

After two weeks at sea the cargo in the hold might have been one village, all uprooted and come together. They cooked together, helped each other, fashioned gongs from pots and taught each other peasant songs. One of the married men was chosen spokeman. He approached the enforcer with respect but not subservience when problems arose, but these were few, as they dealt with most within themselves.

The enforcer, as was his duty and practice, made frequent descents into the hold. On most crossings these visits were required for intimidation. This time he felt as an official from the capital might in a rural village: eyes followed him, but he was walking through a vibrant life in which he had no part. On other voyages he'd dreaded these descents, more so as the time stretched on and the hold grew rank. Now, he found it less necessary to steel himself. Because water was abundant the smells of people pent up for weeks never grew as potent as they might. Even sometimes he imagined he caught a whiff of an aroma from memory, something appetizing as meals were cooked. He learned it was not memory: Wei An-Lin, in her single poor suitcase, carried paper-wrapped packets of spices, herbs, dried roots. The packets were not labeled; Wei An-Lin could barely read or write. But certainly, she could cook. Her herbs, shared with the others, transformed the rice and vegetables on which the cargo subsisted into tempting stir-fries and stews. The enforcer found himself irritable in the presence of the ship's cook, who produced for the crew meals of more substance but less enticement.

On his trips into the hold the enforcer saw that Wei An-Lin was everywhere, almost always in conversation with a group, a couple, a man or woman. Often she was intent; sometimes her eyes held the steely glint. Only rarely did he find her sitting alone; twice he saw her poring over a letter whose creases were soft-edged, so many times had it been opened and refolded. Laboriously, she traced each character with a finger. She wasn't reading it, he realized: she'd memorized it, and was learning the characters that went with the sense she already knew.

One day he spoke to her. "Where do you come from?"

"Goose Creek Village. In Fujian Province."

"Goose Creek Village. I've heard of it."

"You've emptied it. Many are gone; all who leave go through Snakehead Ma Guo."

He frowned. "You know the snakehead's name?"

"Yours also, Lu Rong."

"How is this?"

Her smile held a sharp edge. "A full jar, an empty jar, both are silent when shaken. It's the jar half empty that sounds. Goose Creek Village is half empty now."

He was troubled by her knowledge, but went on. "What you've done on this ship, it eases the voyage."

"If it eases it for you, for the snakehead's men, that's your luck, not my goal."

"What is your goal?" The enforcer was curious.

"These people's hopes are high, but will be crushed. Their lives in America will hold more misery than they know. Why should they suffer more than they must?" Every word Wei An-Lin said was true, though there were words she didn't say.

"More misery than they know," Lu repeated. "But you know. Yet you go to America, also. Are your hopes high?"

"No."

He held her in a quiet look. "You go in search of work?"

"Why else would I go?" Although it was a real question, and had a real answer, Wei An-Lin did not expect Lu Rong to understand that.

He did not. "What you've done here you could do on other voyages," he said. "I'll speak to the snakehead. In one year, your passage will be repaid. If you stay beyond, you could earn a good wage."

"You'd offer a job to a woman?"

"I never have before."

But Wei An-Lin refused.

Her years in the sewing factory—or the brothel—in America would be far more than the one the enforcer was offering: four or five to repay the passage price. Yet he understood. Lately, he himself had begun to wonder if it wasn't time to leave this dreary existence, ferrying miserable human cargo to Gold Mountain.

The ship didn't dock; that would be folly. As always, the cargo was unloaded onto small craft in the dead of night. Men and women who'd spent two months in the cramped, closed hold shivered toward shore over open water. Enforcer Lu watched the boats dwindle, then sent the men below to make sure the hold was empty. He shook his head as they scrabbled through the poor belongings these poorest of people had left behind. When he was assured no one, out of sickness, terror or change of heart, had remained, he gave the order. The ship came slowly about and plowed into the dark.

Wei An-Lin found work immediately in one of the snakehead's factories, behind a sewing machine. The sewing women were paid piecework. Most worked long hours, each dollar translating into minutes, eventually days and months of freedom after their passage debts were settled. Wei An-Lin was not lazy, but she did not seem driven, either. Her work was neat and true, though, and the snakehead—to whom all reports were brought—was satisfied. If she served six years in his factory to another woman's four, that was her choice, and made no difference to him.

And he had no other use for her. Snakehead Ma personally inspected all his arriving cargo. It was one reason for his success. Some snakeheads didn't bother with the cargo at all. Some watched it load and washed their hands. But Ma Guo smuggled himself into the U.S. to meet each ship. By air, of course, and first class, of course. The smuggling of people was the business of snakeheads, and he laughed at the others, whose fear of the American authorities kept them in Hong Kong, Guangzho, Taipei. So he'd seen the women, and made his assignment: go here, go there. He'd kept Wei An-Lin himself because he could see no one would pay for her, and he sent her to the factory because he judged that in a brothel she'd be worthless.

Though he was wrong.

Enforcer Lu could have told him, but the snakehead would not have thought to ask. The enforcer was one of his most long-term, loyal men. Ma Guo relied on his judgment without question. If Lu chose a woman from the hold to take his comfort with, that was his privilege. Even if the snakehead had known the woman was Wei An-Lin, he'd have done nothing but raise a bushy eyebrow. Perhaps, if he'd been aware the choice had been made by Wei An-Lin more than by the enforcer, his response would have been different. But that was something even Enforcer Lu didn't know.

The enforcer was also unaware of the extent to which, in the warm time between spending himself and finding sleep, he had taken a different comfort. Senior man on this voyage, senior also among the snakehead's three enforcers, Lu had no one with whom to share his growing heartsickness, his exhaustion with the sea. Wei An-Lin heard him out, not as though she were bound to, but with quiet, even kindly interest. She neither coddled nor blamed him as he spoke of his nights and days, his work, the dark deeds he'd been forced into. It was yet another reason to regret that she'd turned his offer down. But the allure of America, he reasoned, made these people leave their villages, travel in wretched circumstances toward certain unhappiness, in the hope of future joy. A pull that strong was something with which he and his cold ship could not compete. He thought little more about it as he headed back to sea.

Wei An-Lin thought about Enforcer Lu, however. And many other things. For one, she thought about the brothels. She knew Snakehead Ma thought she'd be useless to them, and she was gratified, for it was her intention that he think so. When Ma Guo lumbered into the Brooklyn warehouse to inspect his cargo, Wei An-Lin scowled before him with unwashed raggedy hair, blunt-nailed filthy hands, stooped shoulders, cold steel eyes.

All this was manufactured in service to her purpose. All but the steel in her eyes. In the village they said she'd been born like that.

For weeks Wei An-Lin drew fabric through the whining machine in the crowded, dusty factory, slept in a tiny basement room with four other women, shared her poor meals with those poorer and talked with those around her. She inquired about people's villages, their voyages, their relatives and hopes. One day she asked about the brothels.

Some of the sewing women had served in them. Some had been allowed out, to sew instead, and some were ordered out. The young and the beautiful were made to stay.

"I'm looking for someone," Wei An-Lin told a group of women. "Young and beautiful."

She told another group of women, and another, and another. In this way she found her little sister.

Most of the sewing women worked seven days a week. Two reasons were behind this. Foremost, the desperation to pay their debts and be free. But also, a machine idle too long or too often would find another operator the way a fertile hen would always find an owner. All the women worried over an idle machine because it usually meant a double calamity: a woman too ill to come to work, and soon to be without work at all.

But after two weeks and many conversations, Wei An-Lin began to be absent. Not for a full shift, but an hour or an afternoon. The other women grew concerned—they all liked her, for her generosity and her sympathetic interest in their lives, these women to whom no one listened—and at first they tried to cover for her with lies. But they saw this was not needed, because of two strange things. Wei An-Lin, it became clear, was giving Foreman Wing red-envelope gifts in appreciation of his forebearance. And Wei An-Lin was increasing her production, so that her daily output remained the same.

The women thought this odd. If Wei An-Lin was capable of such speed, why not work like that from the beginning, to be free sooner? And to take the few dollars from her miserly wage that were hers to keep and pass them to Foreman Wing—what could explain such odd behavior? Wei An-Lin, approached in the most oblique and respectful manner, offered the women smiles, and hot tea, and no explanation.

Some of the sewing women, with relatives in America or other auspicious attributes, hoped to become legal residents. They had gone to lawyers for help. Those pleased were eager to share their good fortune (and those dissatisfied, to share their grumbling, to which Wei An-Lin listened with her usual kindness). During one of her absences from the factory, though none of the women knew it, she kept an appointment with the lawyer who interested her most.

He listened to her story, her request. He asked, "Why did you choose me?"

"I've been told you are honest, and bold."

"This may not be easy. It may not be possible."

"I understand."

The lawyer accepted her as a client. She gave him cash borrowed from Moneylender Chang against her family's remaining fields in Goose Creek Village. Though the loan was necessary for the voyage, she was unlikely to repay it; she and Chang both understood that. By the time she'd worked off her passage in hours and years, this small debt would have grown into an unclimbable mountain. When Wei An-Lin boarded the rickety bus to begin her journey, Moneylender Chang became a landowner in Goose Creek Village.

Wei An-Lin also gave the lawyer a letter in her own hand. Though not long, it had taken her some time to write. Of all Wei An-Lin's regrets—and they were few—her slowness in reading and writing was the greatest, though she understood that this weakness was responsible for her excellent memory. The letter she'd received in Goose Creek Village that had started her on her crossing to America had been read for her by Letter-writer Chu; she'd memorized it word for word after his second reading. She would have trusted him to write this one for her, even given what was in it; but in America she knew no one she could trust, except her lawyer. When she started to tell him about it, though, he stopped her.

"I can take care of it for you, but I can't know what's in it."

Strange country, America, but her lawyer knew best. So she wrote it herself, inking clumsy characters, hoping they conveyed her meaning.

Wei An-Lin was not absent from the factory the next day. But late that night, she sat over a cup of tea in the glare of a grimy McDonald's. Some of Ma Guo's brothels were in Chinatown, but not all; two were in midtown. To them the snakehead sent the most delicate, pale girls, the ones who'd appeal to *lo faan*. The enforcer had told her that.

The tea was undrinkable. She didn't drink it, but spent a dollar on another cup when she felt the counterboy's eyes. For an hour she stared through the window as men—some white, some black, none Chinese—entered and left the building that housed her sister's brothel, greeted and seen off by the fat jiggling auntie at the door. From then on each night found Wei An-Lin paying for bitter tea, watching out the window. She came to recognize some of the men.

Over the next two weeks she spoke to the lawyer many times. He told her what could be done, what might be done, what could not be done.

"I don't think there's a chance of political asylum," he said.

Wei An-Lin repeated, "No asylum."

Because the lawyer had been very clear, very practical, she was not surprised when the men came for her. The lawyer had suggested she come to his office. She was paying him for his advice, so she followed it. The men were there when she arrived. Government men, she knew immediately. They were not Chinese: one was white, one was black; but the faces of government men always look the same.

She went with them. The lawyer came also, explaining in Chinese what was happening, what might happen next. At the government office an interpreter was waiting. Wei An-Lin asked the lawyer if this meant the authorities didn't trust him to interpret impartially, and if he was in trouble because of that. He told her he was her lawyer, so it was his job not to be impartial.

In America the authorities respected that.

Strange country, America.

The government men asked questions, looking directly at Wei An-Lin although speaking English. At first Wei An-Lin faced the interpreter—she was speaking to him, after all—but soon decided in America it must somehow be polite to look into the eyes of a listener, even when making nonsensical sounds. So she did as her questioners did, and met their gaze when she replied.

A few times she consulted her lawyer, as questions came she did not want to answer: where she lived in America, where she worked. "This does not concern the sewing women," she said, "or Foreman Wing."

In English her lawyer told the government men, and they frowned but moved to other questions.

After a time her lawyer, with a raised hand, ended the discussion. He spoke to the men, then told her in Chinese what he'd told them: "That's enough. Now we'll wait."

One of the government men argued with the lawyer, but without passion, and soon left the room. The interpreter poured tea, and they drank in silence until the door opened and the government man returned, in the company of another.

Wei An-Lin recognized the second man. She'd seen him going into her sister's brothel.

She started to speak, but again her lawyer stopped her. He spoke to the new man in English. The interpreter told her what they were saying. "My client will not continue on your assurance. I'm sorry but we must see for ourselves."

The new man left the room, and returned with Wei An-Lin's little sister.

Pale, thin, with wide and frightened eyes, her sister cried out when she saw Wei An-Lin. There were kisses and tears; the men all looked away. Wei An-Lin sat her sister in a chair, smoothed her hair and whispered she must stop her sobs. She gave her sister tea, resumed her own chair and nodded to her lawyer.

For three days Wei An-Lin spoke to the government men. Her sister never left her side as she told everything she'd learned about Snakehead Ma Guo: his smuggling routes, his ships, his lies and promises. Each person in the cargo hold, each sewing woman had a different story of contacts, payments, paths; of imprisonment, betrayal, fear. Enforcer Lu had had stories, also. Wei An-Lin told their stories, and her own. And her sister's, which had come to Wei An-Lin in a letter six months after her sister, with such high hopes, had left for America.

Wei An-Lin was slow in reading and writing. But because of that, she had an excellent memory.

Patiently she answered every question, balking only when her lawyer told her that the government men still wanted the location of the factory, of the room she'd shared.

"I told them about the brothel because the women were slaves. But the sewing women have hope." That was all she'd say.

After the third day, Wei An-Lin, her lawyer, and her little sister sat in a hotel room with the government man outside. They ate dumplings, good, but not as good as Wei An-Lin could make. They watched the television news and saw Snakehead Ma Guo's buttons strain over his prosperous stomach as his wrists were handcuffed behind him. He scowled darkly as he was led from the airport's first-class arrivals lounge. His scowl made Wei An-Lin's little sister tremble.

"There'll be a trial," the lawyer said. "You'll stay until it's over. The government will hide you. We call that 'protective custody.'"

"But then . . . ?" the little sister asked anxiously.

"I said from the beginning, there will be no asylum."

"But we must stay in America. The snakehead's men will kill us if we return!"

Wei An-Lin said, "Hush. There is nothing to worry about," and the lawyer agreed.

Though eight months later, after the trial, conviction and imprisonment of Snakehead Ma Guo, after the arrest of twenty-seven other men on two continents, the freezing of nine accounts in four banks and the seizing of three ships, Wei An-Lin was no more. Her little sister vanished also.

But well-fed and radiant, Chen Li-Ling and Chen Yu-Yan stepped from an airplane in Shanghai. Their Chinese passports were real, though new. The little sister, Yu-Yan, was pale, delicate, and properly deferential to the elder. The elder sister, Li-Ling, carried in her single new suitcase cinnamon, dill, jalapeños: herbs and spices she'd discovered in America.

The sisters were met by a government man—government men always look the same—who gave them keys to a flat where six months' rent was already paid. That would be more than enough, the older sister had determined, to find a job in a restaurant kitchen, now that they had papers to prove they were legally in the city. The little sister would work there, too, washing dishes and waiting tables until she learned to cook. And perhaps they'd find a tutor. The older sister wanted to improve her reading, her writing. It had taken her much too long to ink the letter she'd given her lawyer in America when they'd first met.

Whether the awkward hand in that anonymous letter had been recognized, she didn't know. But as the American and Chinese nets had tightened together around Snakehead Ma's empire, as more arrests were reported daily, her wish that the warning in that letter would serve its purpose turned to certainty that it had. Among the names of those ensnared, one that never appeared was Enforcer Lu's.

She hoped he would find peace in his new life, away from the sea.

APPENDIX

Women in the Dark:

An array of authors, booksellers, critics and film aficionados pay homage to favorite noir writers, characters and performers.

CHRISTINA BAILEY: REMEMBER ME
by Woody Haut

Though her on-screen life lasts only ten minutes, Cloris Leachman as Christina in Robert Aldrich's adaptation of Spillane's *Kiss Me Deadly* (1955) is, as far as I'm concerned, noir's most memorable female character. Within those few minutes, the trench-coated, frightened Christina kick-starts the narrative and rips to shreds the misogynist Mike Hammer (Ralph Meeker). In fact, her repartee is a virtual critique of an era in which paranoia regarding the bomb, communism and the role of women is rife. It's hardly surprising, given her sexual politics, that Christina should be institutionalized and quickly killed off. Not only does she know about *the great whatsit,* but her attitude threatens the male-dominated culture Hammer and his cohorts represent.

Leachman's lines come courtesy of A.I. Bezzerides, whose ingenious screenplay alters the book's politics, turns the nameless woman into Christina and what had been a discussion about the woman's mental state into something more significant:

Christina:
I was just thinking how much you can tell about a person from such simple things. Your car, for instance.
Hammer:
Now what kind of message does it send you?
Christina:
You have only one real lasting love.
Hammer:
Now who could that be?
Christina:
You. You're one of those self-indulgent males who thinks about nothing but his clothes, his car, himself. Bet you do push-ups every morning just to keep your belly hard.
Hammer:
You against good health or something?

> Christina:
> I could tolerate flabby muscles in a man if it'd make him
> more friendly. You're the kind of person who never gives in a
> relationship, who only takes. Ah, woman, the incomplete sex.
> And what does she need to complete her? One man,
> wonderful man!

Here for once the woman delivers the most incisive lines, while Hammer is left to fathom Christina and her desperate exhortation to *remember me*.

It's a brilliant performance—incredibly, Leachman's first screen appearance—equaled perhaps only by Marie Windsor's dressing down of Elisha Cook in *The Killing* (1956) and Stanwyck and MacMurray's verbal jousting in *Double Indemnity* (1944). A different kind of femme fatale, Christina is neither narcissistic nor out for material gain. Despite her vulnerability, she uses her intelligence and wit to unravel the tough-guy perspective while remaining cognizant of the deadliest kiss of all.

Noir historian and journalist WOODY HAUT was born in Detroit in 1945, grew up in Pasadena, California, attended San Francisco State University and has lived in Britain since the 1970s. His books, Pulp Culture: Hardboiled Fiction and the Cold War, Neon Noir: Contemporary American Crime Fiction *and* Heartbreak and Vine: The Fate of Hardboiled Writers in Hollywood, *are published by Serpent's Tail. His blog covering noir fiction and film can be accessed at woodyhaut.blogspot.com.*

ELLEN BERENT
by Stephen Whitty

In a shadowy world of dark corners and rainswept streets, Ellen Berent is a slash of vibrant color, her red mouth set in a crimson line, the world around her full of bottomless blue lakes. She stands in the painful yellow sunshine, fists clenched, intense and alive.

And that makes her all the more real, and all the more dangerous.

As played by the gorgeous Gene Tierney in 1945's *Leave Her to Heaven*—fresh from *Laura* (1944) and still a decade away from slipping into her own midnight pool of mental illness—Berent starts the film as a conventional heroine, in love with a conventional hero, played by Cornel Wilde.

But Berent is a creature of pathological jealousy. ("Hers," explained the posters, "was the deadliest of the seven sins.") She will not share her new husband—not with his crippled kid brother, not even with the unborn child soon growing inside her. She will do anything to have him to herself, alone.

And so she throws herself down the stairs to abort the child she already resents, and calmly watches her young brother-in-law drown, her face impassive behind dark glasses.

We expect our noir heroines to be hard, pumping bullets into Fred MacMurray or doing in nice Cecil Kellaway. But killing little lame boys? You'd have to go back to Euripides to find such chilly feminine evil. Although the title advises us to reserve judgment, it's difficult to repress a shiver of distaste.

Occasionally *Leave Her to Heaven* veers perilously close to camp. The story's melodrama is accentuated by Fox's usual overripe Technicolor, and by director John M. Stahl, who had spent the '30s making three-hanky classics like the original *Imitation of Life*. Wilde is thick and ordinary, too, an unworthy focus for Tierney's obsession.

But Tierney herself is astonishing, and so is the character she creates. Ellen Berent is violent, she is vivid, she is unrelenting. Even death cannot vanquish her. And in the sometimes pallid world of noir, she stands out like a red rose on a tombstone, a splash of blood in the dirty snow.

STEPHEN WHITTY is the film critic for The Newark Star-Ledger *and the current chair of the New York Film Critics Circle. In addition for writing for magazines from* Cosmopolitan *to* Entertainment Weekly, *he has published fiction and made short films. He is proudest, though, of once winning First Prize in an annual Raymond Chandler parody contest.*

BOND GIRLS
by Harley Jane Kozak

I was never a Bond Girl.

I wanted to be. I was an actress working in Hollywood from 1985 (*A View to a Kill*) onward, but I never caught the eye of the producers and my agent considered it a peculiar ambition. No matter. I was nine when I found *Dr. No*, and forever after my psyche, if not my career, was shaped by Ian Fleming's brand of noir.

Not that there's a lot of noir in celluloid (versus literary) Bond. The lighting is too bright, the locations too sunny. Everyone's healthy. The darkest element, until *Casino Royale* (2006), is 007's well-cut suit—and the women: cynical, often corrupt, always *fatale*.

I was raised in Nebraska. Women in my world didn't frequent casinos, carry guns in their handbags, kill without compunction and have pre-, post- and extramarital sex for reasons beyond romance. Bond Girls had pasts. Love gone bad. Betrayal. But their back-story got only a moment of screen time, so they remained mysterious.

"Mysterious," I thought. "That's what I want to be when I grow up."

And, of course, beautiful. I dreamed of being Ursula Andress, not Lotte Lenya, but it was attitude, not pulchritude, that mattered most. Even the most wooden actress among them exuded independence, and if the Bond Girl ultimately needed 007 to save her life, she as often saved his. She came into the movie at a flat-out run. No shrinking violets. No wounded birds. She exploited her feminine wiles, but she also knew the value of a kick to the groin. She'd sleep with James, but when it was over, she wouldn't weep into her Dom Perignon. For her, there was life after love. There were other fish in the casino.

My Bond Girl years came and went. On the big screen I shot guns, threw punches, and endured torture, often in evening gowns, but never in the company of 007. Just as well. I'm kept in the dark, in my seat in the Cineplex, eating popcorn, and Bond's kept his mystique. I still know who I want to be when I grow up, but it's not the Girl anymore. These days it's M.

HARLEY JANE KOZAK, a sometimes actress, lives with her family in Los Angeles. Her debut novel, Dating Dead Men, *won the Agatha, Anthony and*

Macavity awards. Its sequel was Dating Is Murder, followed by Dead Ex. Her short prose has appeared in Ms. Magazine, Soap Opera Digest, The Sun, The Santa Monica Review *and the anthologies,* Mystery Muses *and* This is Chick Lit.

LEIGH BRACKETT
by Bill Crider

Long years ago, I discovered Leigh Brackett and her work in the science fiction field. She wrote dozens of short stories and a number of entertaining novels, including her series about Eric John Stark, and one genuine classic, *The Long Tomorrow* (1955). Later she wrote the screenplay for *The Empire Strikes Back* (1979). What I didn't know at the time was that she had also written crime fiction, including a hardboiled private-eye novel called *No Good From a Corpse* (1944).

According to Hollywood legend, when Howard Hawks was getting ready to direct the screen version of Raymond Chandler's *The Big Sleep* (1946), he told his secretary to call "that Brackett guy" to work on the screenplay along with William Faulkner. Hawks had read *No Good From a Corpse* and thought it had been written by a man. Today that wouldn't be considered a compliment, but Brackett must not have minded. She went on to work with Hawks on a number of other films, including *Rio Bravo* (1959) and *El Dorado* (1966).

Hawks wasn't the only reader impressed by *No Good From a Corpse*. Anthony Boucher praised it when it was reprinted in 1964, and Bill Pronzini says that the novel is "so Chandleresque in style and approach it might have been written by Chandler himself."

So why didn't I know about this book? Well, for one thing, it's had an erratic publishing history. From 1944 until 1964 it was out of print. I picked up the Collier edition around 1965 and thought it was terrific, but it didn't stay in print. It disappeared until 1989, when Blue Murder published it. It dropped out of sight for ten more years. Then Dennis McMillan brought it back. Now, thanks to the Internet, used copies are easy to find, and there's even a print-on-demand version available. If you haven't read it, I'd suggest that you can find a copy. You're in for a real eye-opening treat.

BILL CRIDER is the award-winning author of the Sheriff Dan Rhodes, private eye Truman Smith, Professor Carl Burns and Professor Sally Good mystery series. "Cranked," his story in Busted Flush Press's 2006 anthology Damn Near Dead, *was nominated for the Anthony & Edgar' Awards and won the Derringer Award. He lives in Alvin, Texas.*

GLORIA-ANN COOPER
by Wallace Stroby

Her name is Gloria-Ann Cooper—"Glory" to the folks back home in Greer County, Oklahoma. She's big, blonde and beautiful—and hell on wheels with a straight-edge razor. She's the avenging angel of Bob Ottum's 1976 novel, *The Tuesday Blade*.

In synch with a mid-'70s pop culture zeitgeist of ultra-violence and vigilante fantasies, Ottum, then an editor at *Sports Illustrated*, briefly hit the bestseller lists with *Blade*, which took a classic noir femme fatale and made her the central character of a blacker-than-black comedy of urban paranoia and women's liberation.

Twentysomething Glory has come to New York to live with a childhood friend and make her way in the big city. But only a few minutes after arriving at Port Authority, she's approached, charmed and eventually abducted by an upscale white pimp, who keeps her in a drug-induced haze at his Park Avenue apartment for the entertainment of his "party guests." In a moment of clarity, Glory finds a set of expensive straight razors in his bathroom, one engraved for each day of the week. When the pimp returns for a little post-party loving, Glory leaves him curled on the bedroom floor, less of a man than he used to be, and causing one jaded cop to muse, "You forget how much stuff is all crammed inside your body until you see one all laid open like that."

Soon Glory learns that Manhattan is full of pimps of varying racial and economic makeups. She declares war on them in the name of women everywhere, stalking and killing them in their tricked-out purple Cadillacs or four-star hotel rooms. At the same time, she's trying to keep two romantic relationships going—one with a police sergeant investigating the murders—

and maintain a career as a researcher at *Time* Magazine. She's also trying to get a handle on her intimacy issues and inner rage, seeing a female therapist who encourages her to "loosen up" and explore her own sexuality. When she tries to, picking up a silky older man at the Americana Hotel across from Penn Station, things go south quickly. And even though the police are closing in on her, she can't seem to keep that blade in her pocket . . .

Given the tenor of the times, when New York's crime rate was near an all-time high and *Death Wish* (1974) and *Dirty Harry* (1971) ruled the box office, it's almost a certainty that *Tuesday Blade* was optioned for film at one point or another. Why it was never made is a mystery. Ottum died in 1986, but in *Tuesday Blade* he left behind a vivid time capsule of New York in the 1970s, rooted in real-life locales and laced with an undercurrent of hysteria that brings those Bad Old Days instantly back to life.

WALLACE STROBY is the author of the novels The Heartbreak Lounge *and* The Barbed-Wire Kiss, *which was a finalist for the 2004 Barry Award for Best First Novel.*

PHYLLIS DIETRICHSON
by Meg Gardiner

Barbara Stanwyck plays the original noir blonde in *Double Indemnity* (1944): Phyllis Dietrichson, the cunning wife who maneuvers Walter Neff (Fred MacMurray) into killing her husband. She sounds like silk, looks like she's been poured from whole cream, and has a face and a heart like a rock. She lures MacMurray into murdering her husband for an accident insurance payout—the double indemnity of the title.

Double Indemnity is the archetypal noir film. A man on the edge jumps off, for the sake of a femme fatale. Written by Raymond Chandler and Billy Wilder from James M. Cain's 1935 novel, it's set in a Los Angeles that's always dark and always raining. And from the moment MacMurray's car roars through a stop sign, disaster looms. Insurance salesman Walter Neff is an easy target for Phyllis, his customer's unhappy wife. Bored and cynical, Walter is a wisecracker but not wise. Once Phyllis saunters toward him, fingering the top button on her dress, he practically leaps into adultery, fraud and murder. He fails to see that it isn't just the insurance company that's being scammed. So is he.

Phyllis is a classic James M. Cain dame. She drinks bourbon, trades double entendres and cries "softly, like the rain on the window." Stanwyck underplays her every word and move—the feistiness, the vulnerability, the betrayals. When Walter breaks her husband's neck, she quietly relishes the moment. When the scheme goes wrong, she tells him why he can't escape the consequences: "You planned the whole thing. I only *wanted* him dead." She's as smooth as broken glass.

Phyllis is bad—"rotten to the core," she confesses—but the script is so slick and Stanwyck's performance so subtle that, like Walter, we're played for suckers. We discover the extent of her treachery late in the game, and it hits us square between the eyes. It's a perfect shot.

MEG GARDINER is the author of five thrillers featuring Evan Delaney. A graduate of Stanford Law School, she has been a three-time Jeopardy! *champion and has taught legal writing at the University of California, Santa Barbara. She lives with her family near London.*

PHYLLIS DIETRICHSON
by Theresa Schwegel

". . . that's a honey of an anklet you've got there, Mrs. Dietrichson," says Walter Neff. Phyllis Dietrichson uncrosses her legs and pinches her knees together—probably not the first time she's simultaneously offered a guy both a yes and a no.

At the film's end, we know Walter Neff isn't the first guy she's ruined, either. Fascinating to watch it happen, though: Neff doesn't buy the lies about Phyllis' mean husband or her unfair life; then again, he doesn't seem bothered by the way she paces and plots, keeping her real plans tucked in somewhere deep—somewhere he thinks he can get to. "We're both rotten," she says. "Only you're a little more rotten," he says back.

If Neff had a little man tugging at his moral insides, he was no match for the raw appeal of Phyllis' hard beauty—hot from the ankle up, and cold to the core.

THERESA SCHWEGEL was born and raised in the Chicago area. In 2006, her book Officer Down *won the Edgar Allan Poe Award for Best First Novel. Before her books were published, Schwegel worked as a personal trainer, a director's assistant, a freelance writer and a bartender. Today she writes full time, which is most likely better for all those trying to get into shape, make movies or to get drunk. Her third book,* Person of Interest, *was released in November 2007.*

I RE-DREAM MRS. DIETRICHSON
by David Corbett

There are only two books I've ever picked up and not put down until I reached the final page: *Double Indemnity* (1935) by James M. Cain, and *Tell Me* (2000), a book of poems by real-life femme fatale Kim Addonizio. A National Book Award finalist, Kim is one of those poets who fuses passion with craft so deftly you never see the slap coming, and despite an often confessional tack she never loses her cool eye, her brutal self-honesty, often conveyed in sorrowing tirades or craving whispers—which she somehow manages to craft into diamonds.

I think of her as an unholy twin, half Anna Akhmatova, half Patti Smith—or better still, a heroin-haunted Anita O'Day, singing "Murder, He Says" in front of Gene Krupa's orchestra, Roy "Little Jazz" Eldridge slamming the high notes behind—a raven-haired queen of the night, complete with strategically placed tattoos (how she loves nudging down her skirt to show you the winged figure at the small of her back), a talent for blues harmonica (the woman's got a wicked mouth), and a gift for livening up stuffy literary gatherings (like the time she stripped down to her underwear for a dip in a San Francisco hotel lobby fountain). A poet, yeah, down to the bone.

I was underwhelmed by Cain's ending to *Double Indemnity*—too hokey, too misogynist—and though the Wilder-Chandler film version improved that considerably, I like to imagine my own ending, with the inimitable Kim cast in the part of Phyllis Dietrichson, knowing that this final tête-à-tête with Walter ain't gonna end well, but still mustering that peerless sang froid, as she tells him, in a line from her poem, "For Desire":

> *I want to lie down somewhere and suffer for love until*
> *it nearly kills me, and then I want to get up again*
> *and put on that little black dress and wait*
> *for you, yes you, to come over here*
> *and get down on your knees and tell me*
> *just how fucking good I look.*

DAVID CORBETT is the author of three critically acclaimed novels: The Devil's Redhead, *which was nominated for the Anthony and Barry Awards for Best First Novel of 2002;* Done for a Dime, *which was named a* New York Times *Notable Book and was nominated for the Macavity Award for Best Novel of 2003; and* Blood of Paradise, *which was published in 2007. To learn more, go to www.davidcorbett.com.*

ALAN FARLEY: A WOMAN'S WORK IS NEVER DONE
by Kevin Burton Smith

Given the era's perhaps-understandable tendency to obscure gender behind initials and pseudonyms, a roll call of women writers of the hardboiled pulps doesn't exactly roll off the tongue. A case in point is Alan Farley who was, according to E. R. Hagemann's *A Comprehensive Index to Black Mask, 1920-1951*, the pseudonym of (Mrs.) W. Lee Herrington. Biographical information is scarce as hell—we don't even know what her real name was. But we know that her husband, W. Lee Herrington, was a fellow pulp writer (and a 1952 Best First Novel Edgar[*] nominee for *Carry My Coffin Slowly*), and that they may have occasionally collaborated, possibly sharing his byline. Or maybe they didn't. Maybe *she* was also W. Lee Herrington.

Still, we do know that as Farley she had at least a couple of stories published in *Black Mask* in the forties. They're solid, enjoyable efforts that held their own, as I recall. But it was a short string of stories that appeared in *Dime Detective* featuring Mike Tyre that really knocked my socks off.

Tyre wasn't a private eye, per se—he just acted like one. Instead, he ran a rather peculiar employment agency that proudly boasted that "No job is too odd for Tyre to fill." And odd the jobs were—and of a surprisingly domestic nature for the pulps, which rarely acknowledged a world much beyond the mean streets. In the aptly titled "Death Burns the Beans" (September 1945), for example, Mike's hired by a housewife to turn off a pot of beans left simmering on a stove and in "Malady in F" (June 1946) he must escort a young musical prodigy to a recital—hardly the typical duties of most pulp-era detectives. Mind you, murder would always soon rear its ugly head, but Tyre proved to be an engaging and more-than-competent shamus with more than a few tricks of his own (and some top-notch wisecracks) up his sleeve.

But what really made the stories so entertaining and oddly compelling—beyond the quick wit and screwball nature, reminiscent of fellow pulpster Norbert Davis's Max Latin stories, and the refreshing attention paid to the day-to-day concerns of the harried housemakers who made up Tyre's client base—was the Chandleresque sense of bruised romanticism and compassion with which 'Alan' somehow invested them:

I stood and watched her go down the stairs and out the dirty door. After that I went back and did what I had to do. My face felt cool for a long time where she had touched it.

Tyre appeared in at least one other story in *Dime Detective* for sure, and there may be a few more lurking out there in the shadows somewhere, just waiting to be discovered.

God, I hope so.

KEVIN BURTON SMITH is a Montreal editor, author, critic, essayist and blogger currently stationed in the peculiar state-of-mind known as Southern California. His writings on crime fiction, music, film, bicycling and sundry other topics have appeared in web and print publications all over the world, including Details, Blue Murder, The Mystery Readers Journal, Word Wrights, Over My Dead Body, Crime Time *(Britain) and* Crime Factory *(Australia). He also writes an occasional column, "Crimes on .45" for* Crime Spree Magazine, *that combines his love of both crime fiction and music.*

GINNY FABLON
by Brian Thornton

Ross Macdonald's major contribution to crime fiction was his series sleuth Lew Archer. Though Macdonald's work was hardboiled, Archer was not your typical tough-talking, hard-drinking, vaguely misogynistic private investigator. When accused of having a "secret passion for justice," Archer replies: "I have a secret passion for mercy. But justice is what keeps happening to people."

Is it any wonder that the author of this passage brought both compassion and insight to the vividly drawn female characters in his stories? Before Macdonald arrived on the scene, women in noir fiction tended toward the two types Hammett gave us in *The Maltese Falcon* (1930): the femme fatale, and the taken-for-granted, spunky girl Friday.

But like Shakespeare before him, Macdonald liberated "his" women. In fact, most of his truly memorable characters were female. In groundbreaking works such as *The Chill* (1964), *The Galton Case* (1959), and *Black Money* (1966), Macdonald set the hardboiled standard on its head.

Typical of Macdonald's complex female characters is the indomitable child-woman Ginny Fablon from *Black Money*, Macdonald's conscious homage to F. Scott Fitzgerald's *The Great Gatsby* (1925). Long an admirer of Fitzgerald's writing, Macdonald held up *Black Money* as his personal favorite among his own works.

In *Black Money*'s climactic scene, Archer exposes a love triangle between a married college professor named Tappinger, his former student Ginny Fablon, and Ginny's recently murdered husband, the Gatsby-like Francis Martel. Ginny and Tappinger had conspired to have Ginny marry well, divorce quickly and use a generous settlement to run off to Paris together. As it turns out, Ginny ends up falling in love with the patsy, Martel. Instead of waiting to rip him off for a divorce settlement, Tappinger murders Martel in a fit of jealous rage. Other murders follow. In their final confrontation, Ginny is iceberg cool while eulogizing her own lost innocence:

She looked at him scornfully. "You're not even a man. I'm sorry I ever let you touch me."

He was trembling, as if her shivering chill had infected him. "You mustn't talk to me like that, Ginny."

"Because you're so sensitif? *You're about as sensitive as a mad dog. I doubt that you know any more about what you're doing than a mad dog does."*

He cried out: "How dare you treat me with disrespect? You were an ignorant girl. I made a woman of you. I admitted you to the intimacy of my mind—"

"I know, the luminous city. Only it isn't so luminous. The last dim little light went out Monday night, when you shot Marietta."

His whole body leaned toward her suddenly, as if he was going to attack her. But the movement was inhibited. I was there.

"I can't stand this." He turned away abruptly and almost ran into the sitting room.

"Be careful of him," Ginny said. "He has a gun in there. He was trying to talk me into a suicide pact."

The second coming of Daisy Buchanan, Ginny Fablon is not. Ross Macdonald could write women.

BRIAN THORNTON's first paying writing gig was doing a weekly opinion column for beer money back in college at Gonzaga University. His short fiction has appeared in Alfred Hitchcock's Mystery Magazine, Shred of Evidence *and* Bullet UK. *He is also the author of several full-length works of non-fiction, including* 101 Things You Didn't Know About Lincoln *(Adams Media 2005). His historical articles and book reviews have appeared in* Columbia: the Magazine of Northwest History *and* The Pacific Northwest Forum. *Mr. Thornton makes his home in the Seattle area and is Northwest Regional Chapter President for the Mystery Writers of America.*

LUISE FISCHER
by Jeff Abbott

I shouldn't like Luise Fischer. But I do. She's the heroine of Dashiell Hammett's arguably least important work, *Woman in the Dark* (1933), an awkward novella with a most unpromising subtitle, "A Novel of Dangerous Romance." Luise lacks the calculated smarts of Brigid O'Shaughnessy and the elegance of Nora Charles; bless her heart, she's just not as memorable those icons of crime fiction, watered down by Hammett's too-shallow experiment on bringing "romance" into noir.

We first meet Luise stumbling on a road in a red party dress, with a sprained ankle and cut knee, penniless, escaping the Boyfriend from Hell, all without a plan. She doesn't do a thing for herself—not tend to her own injuries; not escape from her crazy boyfriend when he catches up with her; she doesn't beg her rescuer, an ex-con named Brazil, for help. Mostly she remains stoic and plays at being coy, a bargain-basement Marlene Dietrich.

But Luise, clever lady, wins me over by running the whole show.

She serves as the single catalyst for all action; the story is her quest for freedom. Even when she is simply sitting still, whether having her injuries wrapped or being ogled by gossiping restaurant patrons, she commands the room. The men, both good and bad, in the story are all besotted by her; not because she is flirtatious; but because she is cool and distant and unknowable, the way the men wish they could be. The men's weaknesses are on their sleeves; Luise keeps hers bound in her own heart. When she is told her boyfriend is "screwy," she laughs: "All men are."

I love Luise's self-awareness. Her best line in the story is when she tells her tormenting boyfriend, "But I am not afraid of you. You should know by this time that you will never hurt me very much . . ." Luise is comfortable with her fear. She proves it later by an act of sacrifice to save an innocent man. (She also shows us that a cigarette can be a weapon; and she alone identifies the key to the story's mystery and therefore takes control of the fate of every major character.)

Woman in the Dark is a bit bizarre: it's noir with a happy goodbye kiss. But I like Luise too well to begrudge her an ending that brings her out of the shadows.

JEFF ABBOTT is the internationally best-selling author of Fear, Panic *and several other suspense and mystery novels. He is a three-time nominee for the Edgar° Award. He lives in Austin with his family.*

GILDA
by Bonnie Claeson and Joe Guglielmelli

Indulging in a vice of the middle-aged, we are watching *Turner Classic Movies* on a 32-inch flat-screened television mounted to our bedroom wall. In crisp black and white, two tuxedoed men stand outside a Buenos Aires boudoir. One is elegant and sinister with scars and a sword cane, the other is all-American tough guy with a worried expression. "Gilda, are you decent?" With a head toss, a beautiful face framed by long curled hair fills the screen. "Who? . . . Me?" By the sheer power of this iconic film moment, we are, for an instant, transported to a majestic movie palace watching *Gilda* on a big screen in 1946.

Even with its Hollywood ending unspoiled by malevolent fates, *Gilda* is quintessentially noir as Gilda (Rita Hayworth), her former lover Johnny Farrell (Glenn Ford) and her husband/his employer Ballin Mundson (George Macready) wield sex and desire as mortal weapons. With her physical appeal and her power over men, Gilda should be the archetypal femme fatale. Gilda tortures Johnny with her promiscuity for his past sins, which the film wisely keeps vague. She forces him not only to watch her with other men but also to keep her secrets from Mundson, who may or may not have been Johnny's lover. After Johnny briefly gets the upper hand in this sadistic and pathological game, the film's most famous sequence—a striptease to "Put the Blame on Mame" in the strapless black evening gown—is the culmination of Gilda's efforts to punish Johnny.

But listen to the song's lyrics, which recount the exploits of legendary deadly dames in comic fashion, and look at the joy in Gilda's performance. The dance demonstrates that Gilda has not let life turn her into a murderous cynic such as Phyllis Dietrichson in *Double Indemnity* (1944) or Elsa Bannister in *The Lady from Shanghai* (1947). Gilda remains the odd mixture of realist and romantic who knows that she can get a man to take care of her but needs a man to love her. As a femme fatale, Gilda will put a man in the ER, but she won't put him in the morgue.

BONNIE CLAESON and JOE GUGLIELMELLI owned the Black Orchid Bookshop in New York City from 1994 to 2007. Thanks to Joe & to Turner Classic Movies, Bonnie is reveling in the glories of black & white movies.

GG: MY GIRL
by Robert Ward

There have been tons of tomes written about lusty and busty MM, and thousands of trees have been cut down so that French critics can write existential, epistemological treatises on BB, but neither of these beauties ever lit up the screen like GG. And what does she get? One halfway decent little biography called *Suicide Blonde* (1989).

Ok, I'm playing a little game with you, Dear Reader. You know that MM is the great Marilyn Monroe, and of course BB is fabulous Brigitte Bardot. But GG? How many of you have any idea who I'm writing about?

My guess? Damned few of you. And yet when I write her name, you'll remember her at once . . . that is, if you've seen any of her pictures.

Indeed, if you're like me and are a fan of noir, she will be your girl like she's mine. Truth be told, I never cared a hang for MM. Always thought she was too moony-eyed, too flabby, too blonde and dumb. And then there was the little matter of the movies she was in. I hated most of them. *Gentlemen Prefer Blondes* (1953) . . . yawn. *The Seven Year Itch* (1955) . . . snore. The only flick that I ever really dug her in was *Niagara* (1953).

Now BB . . . well, she was another type altogether. Sex kitten, awesomely beautiful. Yeah, I lusted after her, but her movies were even worse than Monroe's. I remember sneaking into the Rex Theatre in Baltimore to see her in lame stuff like *And God . . . Created Woman* (1956). Yeah, I got hot, but in the end the movie was a drag. Dumb French soft-core trash.

But GG, she was different. I dug her movies the most! They were smart and, though she played tramps and hookers, it was obvious that she was smart too.

By now maybe some of you already know who I mean. GG is Gloria Grahame, the greatest yet often forgotten actress of the '40s and '50s. Think of any actress of the time . . . Jane Russell, Greer Garson, Joan Crawford, Anne Francis, Bette Davis . . . the list of actresses who were more famous than Grahame is endless. But none of them were any better.

She was the kind of soft/hard, dumb/smart blonde with killer eyes, lips that you wanted to kiss forever. The kind of woman I thought . . . no, *knew* would dig me back.

She made movies I not only loved as a kid but still watch over and over again. Like the great noir classic, *The Big Heat* (1953), in which she played gang moll Debby Marsh, a woman who gets boiling coffee thrown in her face by her hoodlum boyfriend Lee Marvin. Then, her fabulous looks ruined, Debby turns into a real human being, and bravely helps hero Glenn Ford bring down the men who killed his wife. Though Ford is the steely-eyed star of the film, it's Grahame who makes the biggest impression. She's tough, cynical, romantic, and totally vulnerable all at once. Any scene she's in, she's impossible not to watch. She plays half the movie with her face a mass of scabs, and she still kills you.

Then there's the great noir film (with a social conscience) *Crossfire* (1947), in which GG holds her own with the best men stars of the period, the three Roberts, Mitchum, Young and the great Robert Ryan. In *Crossfire* her part is small. She plays a hooker who has a heart of gold and lead. One minute she's helping an in trouble GI, letting him sleep in her pad, the next she's laughing at Paul Kelly, an older man who adores her, and who pathetically sniffs around her apartment just to stay in her shadow. She makes Ginny Tremaine the realest person in the picture, at once tender, paranoid, angry and sweet. A tense thriller, most of the character parts are standard good-guy, bad-guy stuff. But Gloria's turn as Ginny Tremaine is what acting is all about. She takes what easily could have been a nothing part and makes it a fully realized portrait of a troubled, complex woman. Both victim and victimizer.

The best part she had in her tragically under-developed career was in the great noir classic *In a Lonely Place* (1950), opposite Bogart. Based on a terrific novel by Dorothy B. Hughes and written for the screen and directed by Nicholas Ray, *In a Lonely Place* is the perfect vehicle for Grahame. She plays Laurel Gray a woman who helps her screenwriter neighbor, Dix Steele (Bogart) get off a murder rap. They soon fall madly in love, and their affair is tender, sensual and moving. And adult. But Laurel soon finds out that with the tortured, often sadistic Steele love isn't going to be nearly enough. In this film GG has a role that call forth all her brilliance as an actress and her heartbreaking portrait of Laurel Gray is something that Monroe, or Bardot, couldn't have begun to pull off.

Gloria Grahame died at 58 from cancer, her best days behind her. They say she was difficult, argumentative, and in her private life she managed to alienate even liberal Hollywood insiders by marrying both Nick Ray and then later his son. In short she was a piece of work.

And that's the kind of women she played to perfection on the screen. The kind you wouldn't bring home to mama. The kind you should see only once because you know she'd drag you down with her. The kind maybe you wanted to kiss and slap at the same time. The kind that would slap you back. And make you like it.

A bad girl who would be nothing but trouble. But the kind of trouble that you couldn't afford to turn down. The kind of trouble you'd see just once and couldn't get out of your head, forever.

ROBERT WARD has published eight novels, including Shedding Skin, *which won an NEA Grant,* Red Baker, *which won the PEN WEST Winner for Best Novel of 1985, and his latest,* Four Kinds of Rain, *which has been nominated for the 2006 Hammett Award. He has also served as co-producer of the classic television series* Hill Street Blues *and co-executive producer of both* Miami Vice *and* New York Undercover. *Currently, he can be seen playing himself in the ESPN miniseries,* The Bronx Is Burning. *He lives in Los Angeles with his wife, Celeste Wesson, and his son.*

THE TALENTED MS. HIGHSMITH
by Lisa Unger

In some ways, I suppose I've always felt a bit alienated by noir fiction, although I have always *adored* that smoky, mysterious atmosphere—the hourglass-shaped dame half in the shadows, the cigarette dangling from pouting lips, the impossibly virile man with a gun and a low ball of whiskey.

My early exposure to the genre was mainly film, classics such as *The Postman Always Rings Twice* (1946), *The Maltese Falcon* (1941), and *Strangers on a Train* (1951)—the film adaptation of Patricia Highsmith's first novel, of course, though I didn't know it at the time. As for noir fiction, however, I often found the characterizations shallow, the prose too spare, the portrayal of women two-dimensional and flagrantly misogynistic. As a young female writer, being neither good girl, nor vixen, nor deranged man-eater, I wondered if the noir greats had much to offer me. Rather than being forged as a writer from this kind of fiction, I came to the party late.

My discovery of Patricia Highsmith (1921–1995) changed the way I thought about noir. With her dense characterizations and her subtle, deliberate ratcheting of suspense sentence by sentence, Highsmith captivated me. Her characters—Thomas Ripley, David Kelsey, to name two—are truly haunting, utterly sick and twisted, and yet strangely sympathetic. They're mentally ill, they're killers; you *really like* them anyway.

Highsmith's carefully evoked images and the desperately unhappy people who populate her novels linger long after the book is closed: In *This Sweet Sickness* (1960), David Kelsey is so in love with a woman who rejected him that he creates a home where he retreats and pretends they live there as a married couple. Meanwhile, he stalks her. Very, *very* creepy. In *Deep Water* (1957), Vic is so desperate to hold on to his loveless marriage to Melinda that he allows her to have affairs, all the while sick with jealousy. Driven to the edge of his sanity by their arrangement, he tries to win her love by inventing a tall tale of a murder he's committed –one that soon comes true. *Unbearable* suspense.

Like most noir, Highsmith's prose is lean but it packs a one-two punch; it's both beautiful and deep. Highsmith had a strong interest in abnormal psychology and spent a great deal of time reading case studies, making her psychological portraits as realistic as they are disturbing. In her novels, we are on the inside looking out.

Highsmith peeled back the layers of the mundane and the familiar to explore a dark heart of obsessive behavior, dangerous appetites, and mental instability. She was a keen and non-judgmental observer of all the folly and cruelty of the human existence. Largely unrecognized prior to her death in 1995, Patricia Highsmith was a true master of noir fiction. Her work caused me to rediscover and fully appreciate the entire genre with fresh eyes, to finally see it in all its richness and originality. I strongly suggest *This Sweet Sickness*, *Deep Water* and *The Talented Mr. Ripley* (1955), just to start.

LISA UNGER is the New York Times *and internationally best-selling author of* Beautiful Lies *and* Sliver of Truth *(Crown/ Shaye Areheart Books).* Beautiful Lies *was chosen as the International Book of the Month.* Beautiful Lies *and* Sliver of Truth *will be published in 25 countries. She lives in Florida with her husband and daughter. Unger also has a series of novels featuring true crime writer Lydia Strong published by St. Martin's Minotaur under her maiden name Lisa Miscione. Read more at www.lisaunger.com.*

DELORES HITCHENS
by Kevin Burton Smith

"If you are going to generalize about women, you'll find yourself up to here in exceptions."

Dolores Hitchens said that, and you've got to figure she knew what she was talking about.

In a long and varied writing career that stretched from the thirties through the sixties, she wrote plenty of what women of her era were expected to write: gothic romances, traditional whodunits and cozies.

You know, girl stuff. Like her series featuring crime-solving, mild-mannered Professor A. Pennyfeather, or the one starring Miss Rachel and her cat. Just about what you'd expect.

Except . . .

Delores Hitchens was someone who didn't like to be pigeon-holed. By occupations or pen names or genres or even husbands.

She was born Julia Clara Catharine Dolores Birk in Texas in 1907 and her first book, *The Clue in the Clay*, as D.B. Olsen (her first husband's name) in 1938, after having already worked as a nurse and a teacher. She eventually wrote over fifty novels under an assortment of pen names. And she was one hell of a writer.

She had two children by Olsen and she co-wrote five excellent and unapologetically tough procedurals about a team of railroad detectives with her second husband, Bert Hitchens. She pulled off a pretty solid western,

Night of the Bowstring (1962), and even her cozies were often touched by a sly humor and dark wit. More than a few of her books were picked by France's prestigious *Serie Noir*.

But it's two books she wrote as Dolores Hitchens, *Sleep with Strangers* (1955) and *Sleep with Slander* (1960), that most warrant her inclusion here. There's nothing lightweight or "girly" about these novels—they're the real deal, gloomy hard tales of working class grit and a world of hurt. Long Beach private eye Jim Sader is ex-Army Intelligence, a reformed alcoholic whose brassy idealism has been hammered down by life until it's brittle and paper thin. Post-war he specializes in finding missing persons. But if the notion of a P.I. carrying the weight of the world on his broad, if slightly-stooped, shoulders (and the prose style itself) seem straight out of Chandler, the intricate Byzantine plots of the Sader novels are pure Ross Macdonald, full of nasty family secrets that refuse to stay secret.

Sleep With Slander is particularly effective, a missing child case that soon turns tragic—and stays there; its themes so disturbing a few libraries actually jerked it off their shelves when it first came out. Yet it's drawn heavy praise over the years from everyone from Anthony Boucher in his *New York Times* review to Ed Gorman and Bill Pronzini who, in his much-quoted entry in *1001 Midnights*, called it "the best hardboiled private eye novel written by a woman—and one of the best written by anybody."

Not bad for someone whom most modern mystery readers probably know, if at all, for her cat mysteries

KEVIN BURTON SMITH is a Montreal editor, author, critic, essayist and blogger currently stationed in the peculiar state-of-mind known as Southern California. His writings on crime fiction, music, film, bicycling and sundry other topics have appeared in web and print publications all over the world, including Details, Blue Murder, The Mystery Readers Journal, Word Wrights, Over My Dead Body, Crime Time *(Britain) and* Crime Factory *(Australia). He also writes an occasional column, "Crimes on .45" for* Crime Spree Magazine, *that combines his love of both crime fiction and music.*

ELISABETH SANXAY HOLDING
by Maria DiBattista

I am a lover of dames, even when they are toxic and glow in the dark, as they do in noir films and novels that expose the underlit realities lurking beneath the gleamy surfaces of American life. So I am a goner when I come across a passage like this: "The shades were up and he could see her. She was sitting alone at a table spread with a lace cloth, with four candles in silver holders; she wore a green dress and her red hair glittered. She looked lonely, but she looked all right."

This is a glimpse into the heart of noir, when we know that everything looks all right but is all wrong. Such scenes, which never lie but never tell the truth either, are the stuff Elisabeth Sanxay Holding's waking nightmares are made of. Holding is expert in the dread that seeps through the meshes of the everyday, disarranging the neat look of things.

I first read Holding after seeing *The Deep End* (2001), a film adapted from her psychological thriller, *The Blank Wall* (1947). I wanted to see whether the judgment that dogs so many women mystery writers—that the movies men make of their books are better than the originals—was justified in this case. How many times have I heard that Nicholas Ray's *In A Lonely Place* (1950) was better than the Dorothy B. Hughes' noir classic on which it was based? The film is wrenching, but the book is pitiless; Ray didn't have the nerve that Hughes showed in getting inside the head of a psychopath and staying there.

Even Hughes, though, hadn't the staying power of Holding. Her books are about panicked states of mind (1929's *Miasma*, 1945's *Net of Cobwebs*) and the moral innocents (*The Innocent Mrs. Duff*, published in 1946, and the young bride of 1942's *Lady Killer*) who naively believe their "normality" exempts them from disaster. My favorite remains *The Blank Wall*, Holding's story of a mother who frantically attends to her household chores even as she schemes to cover up the accidental killing of her daughter's lover. Holding knew how it felt to be lonely and desperate but want everything to look all right. It is a feeling that she brought home to her readers with relentless cunning—and with a lethal malice toward the everyday. The malice is as intense, but more subtle than Patricia Highsmith's, and makes her an equally great writer of noir.

MARIA DIBATTISTA, who teaches English and Comparative literature and film at Princeton University, is the author of Fast Talking Dames.

DOROTHY B. HUGHES
by Jamie Agnew

When someone tries to tell me women can't write hardboiled fiction, I just wave Dorothy B. Hughes's *Ride the Pink Horse* (1946) in front of their face. It's one of the most hardboiled books ever—charbroiled really—something that's apparent as soon as the reader discovers that the protagonist's name is simply "Sailor." All the classic elements are there—the exotic setting of Santa Fe during Festival, the haunted, hunted man with a shady past, the innocent female in the midst of corruption, and an overwhelming atmosphere of inevitable doom leading to a final line worthy of Samuel Beckett, "Blindly, he stumbled on." And of course the result of all this darkness is an absolutely enjoyable read.

Hughes began as a poet and kept her lyric touch throughout a long and varied career. None of her other books are as perfectly hardboiled as *Ride the Pink Horse*, but her remarkable talent for creating character and generating suspense is apparent in all of them. Her first novel, *The So Blue Marble* (1940), is a delicate, somewhat fey confection, but, like many noir novelists World War Two seemed to darken her vision. Her war novel *The Fallen Sparrow* is a tightly wound spy story, featuring the chilling, unforgettable villain "Wobblefoot," determined to bring the fascist terror he perfected in the Spanish Civil War to the United States.

Hughes captured the postwar spirit of paranoia and disillusionment in the harrowing *In a Lonely Place*. The anti-hero, Dix, is an ex-flyer who misses "the feeling of power and exhilaration and freedom that came with loneness in the sky" he knew in the service, and who is having a hard time blunting the sharp hyper awareness of combat enough to adjust to the dull reality of civilian life. And then there's his troubling obsession with that elusive strangler who's been preying on the women of Los Angeles. *In a Lonely Place* is the masterful portrayal of a man and a society in which the defeat of an external enemy has only served to unleash the darker spirits within.

As the golden age of noir wound down so did Hughes's productivity. She continued to be a faithful member of the mystery community and wrote sporadically, her last novels exhibiting the same prescient sensitivity towards minorities and social inequality as her earliest. From the beginning Hughes championed the thriller as a worthy vehicle for serious writing, and her impressive body of work more than proves her point.

JAMIE AGNEW and his wife ROBIN own and operate Aunt Agatha's New and Used Mystery, Detection and True Crime Books in Ann Arbor, Michigan. He is no relation to Kitten Agnew, murder victim in Hughes's Dread Journey.

DOROTHY B. HUGHES
by Sarah Weinman

Countless lists of the best crime novels have appeared over the years. You know the usual suspects: Hammett, Chandler, the unrelated MacDonald/Macdonalds, Cain, Christie, Allingham. Any list will leave off a slew of equally deserving writers—by dint of being out of print, forgotten, dated or whatnot—but one of my favorites, Dorothy B. Hughes, has the unfortunate label of "unsung heroine" attached to her name and work. Part of it's my fault; it's the title of an essay I wrote about her three and a half years ago (from which some of this piece is adapted.) But you'd think in that intervening time more people would have embraced the subtle, ahead-of-her-time quality of Hughes' fiction and its prophetic predictions of genre trends decades in the making.

I was first introduced to Dorothy B. Hughes when the Feminist Press reissued her 1947 novel *In a Lonely Place* in late 2003. The novel served as the basis for the movie of the same name, and even though Humphrey Bogart turned in a stellar, disturbing performance, his Dix Steele was not what Hughes had originally envisioned. The 1950 movie kept the dark suspicion of Steele's criminal culpability (adding the wonderfully turbulent chemistry between Bogart and Gloria Grahame's knowing turn as Laurel) but eliminated any possible suspicion that he might be responsible for the brutal murders of several co-eds.

That suspicion hangs over the book, and even though it becomes increasingly obvious what Dix is up to, Hughes never spells it out, making the novel's progress all the more suspenseful and chilling. Instead of a straightforward whodunit, Hughes creates the prototype of psychological thriller that predates Jim Thompson's *The Killer Inside Me* (1952) by half a decade, with arguably more insight into the deranged mind.

In Dix Steele, Hughes paints a portrait of a man who fits many of the traits now commonly attributed to a sociopathic personality; Dix has an unusually strong hatred of women, he takes an extra beat to react to horrible news, and he often adopts feelings of love and friendship instead of truly feeling them. He also demonstrates additional traits befitting modern serial killers; he has an unhealthy interest in following the murders in the newspaper, and delights in asking police detective (and erstwhile friend) Brub Nicolai questions about the investigation—questions that Nicolai is all too happy to answer. By insinuating himself into the investigation, Dix manages to throw suspicion off him for the longest time.

And then, Hughes turns the tables, making Dix's new ladylove Laurel and Brub's suspicious wife Sylvia the real heroines of the story. Previously depicted as just another housewife—primarily because that's how Dix chooses to view her—Sylvia shows surprising toughness and mettle in her final confrontation with Dix. At the novel's close, Dix is reduced to a crying mass, but Sylvia remains cool under fire. It's a neat role reversal, made especially significant because of the time and circumstance of the novel's publication. Instead of creating a dashed-off, throwaway pulp, Hughes offers a searing social commentary on the disintegration of personality, how a sociopath is made, not born, and how a person is always ultimately responsible for his or her actions.

Based solely on *In a Lonely Place*, Hughes deserves a permanent place in crime fiction's canon. But she wrote many other novels where women are the instruments of their own fate, plunging headlong into adventures of murder, mayhem and espionage and emerging, if not always triumphant, with dignity and personality intact. Hughes did not care to create victims; true heroines of a subtle, understated quality were far more interesting. Her work is a direct and indirect model for almost every crime writer following suit.

SARAH WEINMAN is the Baltimore Sun'*s crime fiction columnist, writes "Dark Passages," a monthly online mystery & suspense column for the* Los Angeles Times Book Review *and is the proprietor of* Confessions of an Idiosyncratic Mind *(at www.sarahweinman.com), hailed by* USA Today *as "a respected resource for commentary on crime and mystery fiction." Her short fiction has appeared in* Ellery Queen's Mystery Magazine, Alfred Hitchcock's Mystery Magazine *and several anthologies, including* Dublin Noir, Baltimore Noir, Expletive Deleted *and* Damn Near Dead.

CLAUDIA KINCAID
by Alafair Burke

Claudia Kincaid is a pretty hardboiled kid. At first glance, the protagonist from E.L. Konigsburg's *From the Mixed-up Files of Mrs. Basil E. Frankweiler* might not cry out, noir, but she is a young version of the classic femme fatale. At just twelve years old, Claudia was certain of little besides her need for adventure, far from her unadventurous family and outside the confines of female domestic life. When she ran away to the Metropolitan Museum of Art, she took her smart-aleck little brother in tow, but only for his money. By the end of the book, Claudia had pieced together not just a puzzle about a marble statue of questionable provenance, but also the diverse pieces of her own identity. A runaway who yearned to be different, she found her own sense of self—and a way to feel special in a sometimes mundane world—in a place where she first hid to find anonymity. When I started writing my first novel nearly twenty-five years after meeting Claudia, I named the protagonist Samantha Kincaid. Perhaps unintentionally, I set a very high standard for her indeed.

ALAFAIR BURKE is the author of Dead Connection *and the successful Samantha Kincaid series. A former deputy district attorney in Portland, Oregon, she is now a professor at Hofstra Law School, where she teaches criminal law and procedure. She graduated with distinction from Stanford Law School, completed a judicial clerkship with the Ninth Circuit Court of Appeals, and serves as a legal and trial commentator for various radio and television programs. She lives in New York City.*

ROSE LOOMIS
by Jonathan Santlofer

Niagara (1953), a B-minus movie with one A-plus attraction, and it ain't the falls. Rose Loomis, Marilyn Monroe, aged twenty-five and looking older, riper than she had any right to, from the first incredible indelible shot—nude under the sheets, pretending to sleep, dreaming of her lover while her battle-scarred, cuckolded husband whispers her name—to what should have been the fade out, when he finally kills her. After that, do we really care if Jean Peters goes over the falls or Joseph Cotton is arrested?

Marilyn never played another bad girl; the studio bosses, the public, weren't interested in her dark side. They wanted cotton candy and Sugar Kane Kowalczyk sweetness. She campaigned to play *Baby Doll*, Tennessee William's slatternly nymphet, but lost; was slated to play Lola Lola in a remake of *The Blue Angel*, but that never happened. Two losses. *The Misfits* (1961), her last role, was a misfire that might have ignited if Arthur Miller had written some dark and dirty dialogue for his then wife, not the banal poetry, Roslyn, his idealized Marilyn, is forced too recite like some narcotized rescuing angel.

Thank God we have Rose, stretched across a Cinemascope screen in a dress "cut down to her knees," a smoldering two-timing woman with enough raw sex appeal to excite every man in the audience and embarrass every woman. Marilyn/Rose: every man's dream, every man's nightmare.

JONATHAN SANTLOFER is a highly respected artist whose work has been written about and reviewed in the New York Times, Art in America, Art News, Arts *and* Interview *and appears in may public, private and corporate collections such as Chase Manhattan Bank and the Art Institute of Chicago. He is the author of four novels:* The Death Artist, Color Blind, The Killing Art *and* Anatomy of Fear. *He serves on the board of Yaddo, one of the oldest artist communities in the country. He lives and works in New York City.*

IDA LUPINO: HER WAY OR NO WAY
by Reed Farrel Coleman

Ida Lupino, are you kidding me with that name? It lands on the ear with the grace of a cluster bomb. I used to wonder how she managed to get through her first audition with such an incredibly ugly name in a town obsessed with beauty and myth. That she did and that she persisted for six decades in that same town where careers are usually measured in glances and afterthoughts, is testament to everything about Ida Lupino.

It was never a love thing between me and Ida. I never had a crush on her the way I did on the young Patricia Neal. To this day I think of Patricia Neal in that black lace and silken slip she wore in *A Face in the Crowd* (1957). And trust me when I tell you that if I had played Gort in *The Day the Earth Stood Still* (1951), Michael Rennie would have stayed dead. If Patricia Neal had whispered *Klaatu barada nikto* to me in that deep, throaty purr of hers, I would have given the phrase a whole new interpretation.

No, Ida Lupino's black-and-white youth in movies like *They Drive by Night* (1940) had escaped me. I met Ida on '60s TV, a plump woman with impish eyes who looked more like she should be playing Mah Jongg with my mom and Aunt Sylvia rather than doing bit parts on *Batman* or *Columbo*.

Then I saw *High Sierra* (1941) and things changed for me and Ida. It still wasn't love, but it was something. Can you fall in respect with a woman?

Her portrayal of Marie Garson to Bogart's Roy Earle is a revelation. She's tough and vulnerable in the same breath. She's fiercely loyal, fiercely loving, but achingly quiet in rejection. Her face was my first lesson in the pain of unrequited love. But it wasn't her acting, which earned her the title of the poor man's Bette Davis, that I so admire. It was her determination.

Rather than moping around after being suspended by her studio, Ida took it as an opportunity to study directing. In 1949, with *Not Wanted*, she became one of the first female directors. In 1950 she tackled the volatile issue of rape in *Outrage*. And in 1953, she became the first woman to direct a film noir with *The Hitch-hiker*. She was the second female admitted into the Directors Guild and she continued directing in TV, doing work on *The Twilight Zone, 77 Sunset Strip, The Untouchables, The Fugitive* and many more. I no longer wonder about how she kept that ugly name.

REED FARREL COLEMAN is the former Executive Vice President of Mystery Writers of America. His sixth novel, The James Deans, *won the Shamus, Barry and Anthony Awards for Best Paperback Original of 2005. It was also nominated for the Edgar*, *Macavity and Gumshoe. He was the editor of the short story anthology,* Hardboiled Brooklyn. *His short stories appear in* Damn Near Dead, *Wall Street Noir,* This Gun for Hire, Dublin Noir *and many other publications. He lives on Long Island with his wife and family.*

ADELAIDE FRANCES OKE MANNING
by Barbara Peters

As I exited the movie theater after *Casino Royale* (2006), I couldn't help reflecting on my very favorite British agent, the Double-Oh of his day though no number was assigned. Thomas Elphinstone Hambledon of the Foreign Office. No good at cards, no womanizer (rather bashful, actually), probably very ordinary looking, was just as invincible as James Bond, just as daring, just as dogged, just as lucky. But better at teamwork. And for his day, quite handy with gadgets.

Although Tommy technically makes his first appearance in *Drink to Yesterday* (1940), I never could get into it and recommend you skip it. You'll learn the story anyway when you read what I think is the real series' start, a gem entitled *A Toast to Tomorrow* (also 1940) which has the alternative title *Pray Silence.* I won't give away the central premise which is truly daring, but I can say that the portraits the authors, Adelaide Frances Oke Manning (1891–1959) and Cyril Henry Coles (1899–1965), neighbors in East Meon, Hampshire who wrote together as Manning Coles, draw of the key Nazis molded my perceptions of these figures for all time. And have proved to be spot on from the historical record.

It is the brilliance with which Manning Coles illuminated character that makes the Tommy Hambledon novels so outstanding, though the plots are fun. By character I don't mean just the spy guys, but the whole range of cohorts and bad guys. Who could forget Herr Professor Ulseth, the scummy scientist of *Green Hazard* (1945, written with the knowledge that the Allies were winning), arguably the funniest of the Hambledons (he goes undercover in the lab as Ulseth's assistant to thwart development of a Nazi super weapon)? Or the murderous sidekicks Forgan and Campbell?

Skip the disastrous 1961 effort *Search for a Sultan.* If anything is needed to prove that Adelaide was the key partner in Manning Coles it is this wooden book. Hers was the voice (I suspect Coles did the major plotting) and when it was stilled, so was the soul of the series, one I reread to this very day. It never grows stale nor fails to delight with its use of language (the German, French, Spanish is flawless), its pace, and its cheerful assurance that, with Hambledon at the helm, Britain cannot fail.

Librarian/lawyer BARBARA PETERS founded the Poisoned Pen Bookstore in 1989 and, with her husband, Poisoned Pen Press in 1995. For more information, see www.poisonedpen.com and www.poisonedpenpress.com. She's a voracious reader of everything, though one can tell in A Hell of a Woman *she has favorites.*

KATHIE MOFFAT
by Shannon Clute

Maybe she doesn't have the make-you-stupid sex appeal of Gilda (Rita Hayworth) or Kitty (Joan Bennett), or even the wicked bite of Vera (Ann Savage). But Kathie Moffat (Jane Greer in 1947's *Out of the Past*) has an arsenal just as deadly: a starry-eyed, up-from-under look that makes you fool enough to think she needs your help; a carefully tooled affectation of virginal innocence (yeah, you know that's impossible, but you let yourself believe it anyhow); an ever-ready excuse that bad men forced her to do the awful things she did, but deep down she never betrayed you. And when all else fails, she has a trigger finger twitchier than a Mexican jumping bean. Maybe the combination isn't unheard of, but you'll swear you've never seen anything so fresh, so bedazzling, so real. Soon you'll be flip-flopping allegiance as fast as she does—a blob of Mercury on the teeter-totter of Life. You'll feel smooth, fast and deadly, but every time she rises you'll fall, 'til you're disoriented and deathly sick. So you'll try to get away. You'll pile the miles and years between you, and build a new life—out of sand.

You see, Kathie's not the sort of woman you leave behind: with a whisper like surf, and the nocturnal shimmer of waves rolling, she'll casually wash your castle away. Then you'll remember the first time you kissed her, on the beach, by the light of the moon—framed by endless nets. You were caught the second you said it, but you'll say it again: she'll present her excuses—ask if you'll trust her one more time—and you'll mutter, "Baby, I don't care." Together you'll go fishing with the soft lure of her limbs, and it's your soul that'll get hooked.

Greer's Moffat never goes away. Maybe she meets her demise in the film, but her quicksilver blood spills out of the frame and gets in yours—poisoning you forever. Hell, she's the reason I do what I do.

SHANNON CLUTE's first manuscript—a Chandleresque tale of greed and corruption entitled The Mint Condition—*was selected as one of ten semi-finalists in the Court TV "Next Great Crime Writer" contest. With Richard Edwards, he co-produces two podcast series: "Out of the Past: Investigating Film Noir" and "Behind the Black Mask: Mystery Writers Revealed." Together, Clute and Edwards are also co-authoring a study of film noir. Clute holds a Ph.D. in Romance Studies from Cornell University, and has taught French literature, great books, and the history of mystery fiction and film noir in various universities. He currently lives and works in Atlanta.*

CAY MORGAN
by Charles Ardai

When Hard Case Crime began, our goal was to revive the look and feel of the post-war paperback crime novel, while reissuing not typical but exceptional books from that era. Now, anyone who has seen a typical post-war paperback knows the most visible role women played: They were the imperiled damsels or the imperiling femmes fatales painted pin-up style on the cover in too much makeup and too few clothes. Between the covers, women's roles were, for the most part, similarly circumscribed. Good girls were weak; strong girls were bad. Submission to men was celebrated. Sexuality was feared. Hair color was a good predictor of temperament, and not a bad one of moral probity.

But there were exceptions. One of the most noteworthy was Wade Miller's 1952 novel *Branded Woman*. The title character, Cay Morgan, is a blonde, but she's neither a good girl nor weak; at the same time, while she's a jewel smuggler on a mission to kill the man who wronged her, she's not exactly a bad girl either. What she is is a distinct rarity for the 1950s (and, some might argue, not as common as you might wish even in today's crime fiction): a strong, willful, self-possessed and self-aware female lead, a woman subject to her passions but neither their victim nor their slave. She tracks down the object of her vengeance with a single-minded determination that would make her the envy of any male assassin, but she does it without ceasing to be a distinctly female character, and a distinctly sympathetic one.

Oh, there are moments of sexism in the book—no 1950s novel lacks them utterly. And some bits of business have dated awkwardly, to the point that they now read as parody (I think, for instance, of the "judo chops" Cay uses to fight off an assailant). But overall the book is a remarkable one, particularly for the time, notable as much for its revolutionary female lead as for the effectiveness of its suspense scenes or the intricacy of its very satisfying plot.

When, at the book's climax, Cay faces down her nemesis across a pit in the jungle, sweaty and filthy and toting a gun, and not about to take any shit from any man—well, it's in that incredible, Sigourney Weaver-worthy moment that you realize Wade Miller did something remarkable for his time—and something very exciting for readers of both genders.

CHARLES ARDAI is an Edgar Award-winning crime writer and the founding editor of Hard Case Crime, in which capacity he has had the privilege of editing the work of authors such as Madison Smartt Bell, Lawrence Block, Pete Hamill, Stephen King, Ed McBain and Donald E. Westlake.

EVELYN MULWRAY
by Jonathan Santlofer

"My sister . . . My daughter . . . She's my sister and my daughter! My father and I . . . understand, or is it too tough for you?"

Evelyn Mulwray to J.J. Gittes, Chinatown, Roman Polanski's 1974 neo-noir thriller; incest, a shocking theme at the time, and Polanski made it sting.

Evelyn Mulwray: rich, beautiful, doomed. Faye Dunaway at her peak, all Marcel waves and penciled eyebrows, hand trembling as she lights her cigarette, tremulous voice uttering lies—or so it seems—begging Jack Nicholson's Jake Gittes to "trust me this much."

A Technicolor film in black and white, costumes, cars, the arid California desert, everything about the movie bleached of color, parched, dying of thirst. The ill-fated heroine, etched with not quite enough ink, there, and not there, in her stylish monochrome suits. We don't know her until it's too late.

Mrs. Mulwray, I think you're hiding something.

Indeed. Under those cloche hats and dotted veils Evelyn/Faye is not your ordinary femme fatale; no conniving Lana Turner or Barbara Stanwyck. Evelyn is a wounded, quivering peacock: "You know my f-father?" she asks Jake, shielding her naked breasts, shame twisting her features.

Evelyn/Faye: all starts and stops, tics and stutters, half truths and lies to protect a secret—"my sister, my daughter"— that will be her ultimate demise.

If only she would tell the truth; if only he would believe her. What we, the viewer, keep thinking, hoping for, a good ending that will never be.

JONATHAN SANTLOFER is a highly respected artist whose work has been written about and reviewed in the New York Times, Art in America, Art News, Arts *and* Interview *and appears in may public, private and corporate collections such as Chase Manhattan Bank and the Art Institute of Chicago. He is the author of four novels:* The Death Artist, Color Blind, The Killing Art *and* Anatomy of Fear. *He serves on the board of Yaddo, one of the oldest artist communities in the country. He lives and works in New York City.*

NAUGHTY BOOKSTORE GIRL
by Charlie Huston

She's just so damn naughty.

From the moment Bogie drifts in the door and starts asking enigmatic questions about repeated lines in the sixth edition of *Ben Hur,* you can see it in the eyes behind her wire rim glasses, the Acme Bookstore Proprietress is a naughty girl.

Such an unbecoming screen credit: Acme Bookstore Proprietress. So anonymous. Like she's just another of the femmes fatale littering the ground at Philip Marlowe's feet, having thrown themselves unsuccessfully at him in one scene or another of *The Big Sleep* (1946). But that anonymity of title belies the truth; she's the one.

She's the one who got him.

Oh, Bacall may have walked away with the prize at the end of the final reel, and in real life, but it was the Acme Bookstore Proprietress who got there first.

So naughty.

Suggesting that Mr. Marlowe, "A private dick on a case," might be more comfortable casing the bookstore across the street from inside her own shop, and out of the rain. And oh so eager when he informs her of the bottle of rye he happens to have in his pocket—"I'd much rather get wet in here," indeed.

From there, it doesn't take her but a moment to close the shop and lower the window shade. Soon after, cocktails are served in paper cups handy in her desk, and only a moment after that, those glasses are being slipped off and the hair is coming down.

Much to Marlowe's delight. "Well, hello."

Don't be fooled by the discreet cut away, or by how unmussed and fully clothed the two of them appear when we return to the action. Listen instead to the romantic soundtrack backing their farewell. Look at the longing in her glance as he slips from the store and into the taxi at the curb. Don't be fooled into thinking it was a more innocent age, that things like that didn't happen, and that if they did, they most certainly were not on display in the cinema.

It happened, just the way you think it did.

Marlowe, with the bookstore girl, amongst the shelves, in the middle of a rainy afternoon.

The Acme Bookstore Proprietress. If you've seen the movie, you knew exactly who I was talking about without being told. She makes that kind of impression.

Her name, her other name, is Dorothy Malone. She won an Oscar for playing the spoiled-rotten rich town tramp in *Written on the Wind* (1956), and her star is on the Walk of Fame at 1718 Vine.

CHARLIE HUSTON is the author of the Henry Thompson trilogy (Edgar⁻-nominated Caught Stealing, Edgar⁻– and Anthony-nominated Six Bad Things and Anthony-nominated A Dangerous Man), the Joe Pitt Casebooks, including Half the Blood of Brooklyn *(December 2007), and the suburban noir,* The Shotgun Rule. *He lives in Los Angeles with his wife, the actress Virginia Louise Smith.*

HELEN NIELSEN: HUNTING FOR HELEN
by Christa Faust

"The whole thing started with a dream, a cockeyed, crazy dream . . ."

It was the author shot on the back cover of a dog-eared copy of *Dead on the Level* (a.k.a. *Gold Coast Nocturne*, 1951) that originally ignited my crush on Helen Nielsen. Under the caption "Mystery Writer on the Rise" there was a small black and white photo of this tough, confident woman looking right into the camera. She had short dark hair and minimal make up. She looked more like a lady wrestler than a writer, like she could take any one of her male contemporaries in a fair fight. (Okay, maybe not Mickey Spillane, but she could've made Richard Prather, Day Keene or John D. MacDonald eat canvas without cracking a sweat.) I was intrigued. I had concocted this whole elaborate fantasy about who she was long before I ever read the first page.

The novel was nothing new. A fast-paced, pulpy tale of a man who is offered five grand to marry a woman he meets in a bar. Needless to say, noirish complications ensue. The thing that was different about this one was the addition of a very strong, unconventional female in a secondary role. Of course there's the standard blonde femme fatale, but in the "good girl" role there's this quirky artist who defies society's standards for female behavior by living alone and wearing short hair and taking in strange men in the middle of the night. She "smells of turpentine and tobacco" instead of fancy perfume and isn't conventionally pretty but the hero falls for her anyway because of her intelligence and her wry sense of humor.

I started seeking out other books by Nielsen. *The Kind Man* (1951), *Detour* (1953, not to be confused with the earlier film noir of the same name) *Seven Days Before Dying* (1958). The more I read, the more curious I became about Miss Helen Nielsen. Never "Mrs." Just "Miss." Who was she, this steely-eyed, apparently unmarried woman who wrote in a lowbrow, traditionally masculine genre, but always with this subtle, proto-feminist twist?

I tried to forget who I wanted her to be and set out to find out who she really was. I trolled the internet and dug deep at the Downtown library but there were hardly any solid details to be found. Just tantalizing scraps that painted a portrait of very private and fiercely independent woman. She grew up in the Midwest and attended the Chicago Art Institute. She later moved to Southern California and eventually Arizona. She had been a draftsman during the war, working on designs for B-36 and P-80 aircraft. She had an interest in Democratic politics and Norwegian Elkhounds. In addition to her novels, she also wrote for television, including shows like *Perry Mason* and *Alfred Hitchcock Presents*.

What I couldn't find was information about her private life. Her parents are mentioned, but no one else. No "survived by" in her obituary. No children and no mention of any husband, lover, or long time companion. Nothing at all. The deeper I dug, the less I knew about her. Everything I found pointed back to the writing, away from the writer.

Sitting there in the Downtown library with a scant handful of clues and that single, compelling photograph, I felt this crazy compulsion to keep on digging. I had the address of her literary agent and her last address in Southern California. I knew the name of the Arizona town where she had died back in 2002. I had a list of contact information for local Norwegian Elkhound clubs and rescue groups. I knew I would eventually find someone who knew her. Someone who knew her secrets.

But what was I really after? Did I want to "out" her, to prove to the world that she was queer, like I wanted her to be? Did I want to know who she really was or did I just want to validate my own fantasy version of her as this tough, two-fisted dyke writer who did as she pleased and never had to answer to a man?

As a mystery writer and reader, I like resolution. I want to find out whodunit at the end of the story. But I walked away from the hunt for Helen. I decided to let her remain a mystery, a cold case that will never be solved, because that's obviously the way she wanted it.

CHRISTA FAUST is the author of nine novels including Hoodtown, *the award-winning novelization of* Snakes on a Plane *and* Money Shot *(Hard Case Crime, 2008). Faust will be the first female author published by Hard Case. She lives and writes in Los Angeles.*

MILDRED PIERCE
by Laura Lippman

As a child of the '60s and '70s, I often encountered the parody before the source–in *Mad* magazine, or cartoons such as *Rocky and Bullwinkle and Friends*, where I think 90 percent of everything that happened in Frostbite Falls sailed over my head. (I was almost in my 20s before I stopped to think about the local college's name, Wassamatta U.) *The Carol Burnett Show*, in particular, was instrumental in my early education, introducing me to classics such as *The Godfather* (1972), *Gone with the Wind* (1939) and *Mildred Pierce* (1945). Logically, this should have spoiled the originals when I finally caught up with them, but it never seemed to work that way, particularly in the case of *Mildred Pierce*. Perhaps that's because the film is a steaming pile of crap.

It's possible, easy even, to champion the novel *Mildred Pierce* (1941) without lambasting the film, but I have insatiable urge to try and eradicate the latter from public imagination. Forget the hokey murder story, which inverts James M. Cain's deliciously nasty novel, where no murder occurs.

Forget Joan Crawford, who played Mildred as a selfless, lip-quivering sap. And forget the post–World War II era in which the film was set. Of all the inevitable book-to-film changes, I think I dislike that one the most because *Mildred Pierce* makes no sense once it's removed from the early years of the Depression, an era in which a too-proud man might cope with his inability to provide for his family by decamping altogether.

Abandoned thusly, Mildred becomes a "grass widow," an ordinary-looking young woman with great legs. She uses her legs and home-cooking to try and recruit a replacement for her feckless husband. When that fails, she resigns herself to finding a job. A waitressing gig leads to a prosperous pie-baking sideline, then a whole chain of restaurants. Her ambition is fueled by her desire to impress Veda, the oldest of her two daughters. In fact, when Mildred's younger daughter dies from a strange and sudden fever, Mildred admits guiltily to herself that she's grateful her favorite child has been spared.

According to Cain's biographer, Roy Hoopes, one of Cain's friends supplied the idea for *Mildred Pierce*—the old story of the woman who uses her wiles to achieve her ends. But it was Cain's idea to focus Mildred's attention and energy on her daughter. Not a man, not a job, not money. Everything is for Veda, who openly loathes her mother, but can be seduced by cash and the trappings of class. At one point, Mildred is so desperate to reconcile with Veda that she marries a man she doesn't love, a Pasadena playboy. Veda moves home—and embarks on an affair with her stepfather, even as Mildred flirts with embezzlement to maintain the pair's expensive lifestyle. When she discovers them together, she leaps at her daughter and attempts to choke her. (The quick-thinking Veda turns the attack to her advantage.) Yet there's a glimmer of a happy ending for Mildred, who reunites with her first husband and—at last—sees her daughter for the monster that she is. "Let's get stinko" may not be the greatest final line ever written, but it's always felt valedictory to me.

Mildred Pierce lives not just in the shadow of its film version; it also suffers by comparison to Cain's first novel, *The Postman Always Rings Twice* (1934). It's hard to argue that there's any injustice there—*Postman* is pretty much perfect—but I've always had a soft spot for Mildred.

She is Cain's best female creation, perhaps because he had to see the world through her eyes. Cain understood how pragmatic women are, how bracingly unsentimental they can be in pursuing their goals. Maternal love is generally presented as a good thing in literature; we reserve our scorn and horror for the Medeas of the world. Cain realized that a mother can love not wisely, but too well. Mildred, the grass widow, is a precursor to the scary soccer mom, the hypercompetitive mother who barrels through the suburbs in her SUV with the "My child is a honor student" bumper sticker. Don't ever get between her and what she thinks is best for her offspring. Mildred lives!

LAURA LIPPMAN has written thirteen novels—ten in the award-winning Tess Monaghan series and three critically acclaimed stand-alones, including What the Dead Know, *a* New York Times *bestseller. A collection of her short stories will be published in late 2008. A former reporter, she lives in Baltimore.*

ELLA RAINES
by Peter Spiegelman

Smart girls have always slayed me. It's something about the competence, the self-sufficiency, the geeky glamour (if they wear glasses, I'm done for), and the whole still waters running deep thing. It started in sixth grade, I think, with Cassie S., who had cropped blond hair and mistaken but rigorously reasoned views on the Vietnam War that we argued over in the lunchroom (her hawkishness did not dim my crush). I won't bore you with the choppy progress of my love life from that point, but suffice it to say that when I first encountered Ella Raines, starring opposite Brian Donlevy in *Impact*, an often overlooked 1949 film, I was destined to fall hard. And so I did.

She plays a small-town gas station owner in the film, a plucky war widow, and we first see her from behind—a slender figure in dirty coveralls, head bent beneath the hood of a Kaiser sedan as she hammers away on its engine. Donlevy says something and she looks into the camera. Her smudged face is squarish, with a pointed chin, a strong nose, heavy brows, and a wicked widow's peak and, grease stains notwithstanding, her features are not as delicate or chiseled as those of other leading ladies of the day. She's saved from severity by an opulent mouth, a sexy overbite, and by those eyes.

They're startling. Pale and wide-set beneath the dark brows, they can switch in an instant from welcoming, to appraising, to daunting with just the subtlest narrowing, and only the slightest tilt of the head. Whatever their arrangement, there's always a sense of kept counsel in Ella Raines's gaze— something knowing, skeptical, surprisingly hip and smarter than you are.

Such frank intelligence is rare, I think, in the personas our screen deities serve up, in Raines's era or in our own (IQ doesn't sell tickets). Rarer still is that Raines's smarts are never mixed with arrogance or hauteur. Rather her intellect is buoyant, optimistic, and enthusiastic—and somehow never naïve.

Competence, optimism and loyalty are at the center of her role in *Impact*, where she becomes, in succession, Donlevy's employer, love interest, defender, and finally his savior, uncovering (with the help of detective Charles Coburn) the evidence that clears her man. She proves more worldly than she at first seems, and she cuts a dashing figure as she rushes through the streets of San Francisco in pursuit of witness Anna May Wong. She favors berets and suits with fitted jackets in that film—a vaguely martial look that looks good on her athletic frame, and that strengthens the impression of an alluring, grown-up Girl Scout.

Her part in *Impact* is a watered-down version of her more famous part in 1944's *Phantom Lady*, the Siodmak/Schoenfeld adaptation of Cornell Woolrich's classic 1942 novel. *Phantom Lady*, like *Impact*, is part rescue fantasy, with Raines as the rescuer. She plays a supremely loyal, supremely competent woman, out to clear her boss (Alan Curtis) with whom she happens to be in love, and who's been convicted of killing his wife. As in *Impact*, Raines proves to be more worldly than we initially assume (far more so), but with no hint of the Girl Scout.

Raines's *Phantom Lady* character is more passionate and dynamic, and she's often in peril. She rushes headlong into the role of amateur detective, stalking a bartender whom she's certain knows more than he's saying. Her hounding is instrumental in the man's death, though not before they share tense moments on an elevated train platform. Raines has trailed the man through sultry nighttime streets, and he's sweating from heat and guilt. Alone with Raines, he nearly turns to violence, creeping up behind her as a train approaches, raising his arms and leaning in—and stopping short as another passenger steps on to the platform. It's a harrowing sequence, and the cinematography is stunning—the wet, steaming streets, the shadowed station, and Raines, slim and luminous in a diaphanous white raincoat. She's poised at the edge of the track, aware of the threat behind her, but outwardly unconcerned. Her stillness is almost provocative—all but a challenge to the desperate man.

Of course, no scene in *Phantom Lady* is so memorable as Elisha Cook Jr.'s drum solo. Cook plays a coked-up musician—another shady character Raines thinks knows the truth behind Curtis's frame-up—and Raines disguises herself as a party girl (complete with cheap clothes, costume jewelry, chewing gum and a fake beauty mark) to get close to him. He takes her to a jam session in a basement, and ushers her into an orgy of smoke, booze, and jazz. The sexual imagery is blatant: trombones, clarinets, and trumpets are brandished like phalluses in a Beardsley drawing, the musicians leer, hunch, and heave over their instruments like incubi, and there are close-ups of Cook's crotch and Raines's breasts. Cook takes a seat at the drums and the music grows louder and more fevered; the very air is throbbing as he ogles Raines. Raines is apprehensive and disoriented; she appears not to recognize her own reflection in a mirror, and it seems that at any moment she'll be overwhelmed. And then she undergoes a curious change—Raines seems suddenly at home in this cellar Sodom. Her manic grin matches Cook's own, and as she urges him on to a frenzied (musical) climax, her laugh is mad and taunting. Now, it is Cook who's nearly overwhelmed, and Raines who's calling the shots.

Ella Raines is smart enough to keep her head in *Phantom Lady*, even when she's in over it, and she goes on to unmask the deeply creepy Franchot Tone as the killer who has framed her boss. But intellect isn't enough to protect her character from the fate that the film—and the conventions of the time—have in store for her. She saves Curtis's hide and captures his heart in *Phantom Lady*—just as she does with Donlevy in *Impact*—but in both cases the prize diminishes her. Neither of the male leads is worthy of the vital characters Raines portrays, and in winning their love she's demoted from action hero to employee (in *Phantom Lady* she's last seen swooning over Curtis's voice on a Dictaphone), or worse—unpaid domestic laborer. It's the raw deal—the sad betrayal—at the heart of so many Hollywood endings, and Ella deserved much better.

PETER SPIEGELMAN is the Shamus Award-winning author of Red Cat, Death's Little Helpers *and* Black Maps, *all of which feature private detective and Wall St. refugee John March. Peter is the editor of* Wall Street Noir, *a collection of short fiction set at the darkest end of The Street, and his short stories have appeared in* Dublin Noir *and* Hardboiled Brooklyn. *Prior to becoming a full-time writer, Peter spent nearly twenty years in the banking and financial software industries. He is a graduate of Vassar College, and aside from a brief stint in L.A., he grew up in and around New York City. He currently lives with his wife and children in Connecticut, where he is at work on another John March novel.*

ANN SAVAGE
by Tribe

From her first appearance at the side of the road in Edgar G. Ulmer's *Detour* (1945) you know Ann Savage is why hitchhikers have a bad name. All skin-tight sweater, wind-swept hair, an icy look that should freeze over the hellish desert landscape, venomous sneer, she plays Vera with all the subtlety of Kali, the Hindu Triple Goddess of fertility, death and regeneration.

When she suddenly turns to face schmuck Al Roberts (Tom Neal) for the first time in the middle of his soliloquy, you fully expect her to sprout another set of arms, stick her tongue out to her navel, rip his head off, and have her way with the corpse. That's the mojo she radiates in *Detour.*

Sex and death.

Robert Graves knew it. Once in proximity to the Queen Bitch, you're touched forever. Besides, Kali ultimately kills everyone in the end.

Is it really a surprise that actor Tom Neal would shoot his real-life wife in the back of the head with a .45 twenty-years later?

TRIBE fancies himself a critic and writer, but obviously does neither terribly well. Tribe has had short stories published in various print and internet sources including Plots With Guns.

ANNA SCHMIDT
by Daniel Judson

There are many reasons why I keep coming back to Sir Carol Reed's *The Third Man* (1949): A flawless script by the great Graham Greene; Orson Welles, as the slick but lethal Harry Lime, making one of the best entrances in film history; a soundtrack comprised entirely of Anton Karas' solo zither, haunting and strange and completely unforgettable; and an final scene, silent and downbeat but with the ring of truth, that would please anyone with a taste for the noir. And, of course, let's not forget Joseph Cotton, as a down-and-out author of pulp-westerns, uttering one of my all-time favorite lines: "I'm just a hack writer who drinks too much and falls in love with girls." Ah, self-esteem! I smile just a little knowingly every time I hear those words.

But, to be honest, what really keeps me coming back again and again is Alida Valli as Anna Schmidt, a beautiful woman as completely shattered by the loss of her lover as the city of Vienna, in which she lives as a Czech refugee, was shattered by the war.

I first saw *The Third Man* on television as a teenager, then studied it a few years later in a film course in college. Valli was stunning, yes—dark-haired, exotic, alluring, a kind of slightly-less-than-wholesome Ingrid Bergman—but it wasn't really her looks that caught the attention of my young and impressionable mind as it was her fierce loyalty. Orson Welles' Harry Lime, Anna's dead lover, was the worst kind of man, and the more that is revealed about him as Joseph Cotton's Holly Martins investigates his mysterious death, the worse Harry Lime seems. But Anna doesn't want to hear about it; she loves Harry, and that's all she knows. Perhaps in post-war Vienna, destroyed by Hitler and then sliced into allied-controlled pieces by Roosevelt and Churchill and Stalin, Harry Lime, a callous leader of the black-market, isn't any worse than—at least not any different from—the rest of mankind. Or perhaps, as Anna herself says when confronted with the truth about her lover, "A person doesn't change because you find out more." She is in love with Harry, dark side and all. And, really, who wouldn't want to be loved like that?

Anna Schmidt, disturbingly enough, became a kind of ideal woman for me. (Again, I was young and impressionable when she first came into my life.) Creatively, I have been drawn to strong-minded, melancholy women. And, alas, I've been drawn to them romantically as well. This interest has served my novels well; as for my personal life . . . well, that's another story. Still, it has been an interesting ride, and all, I can safely say, because of Valli's portrayal of Anna Schmidt—devoted, defiant, and desirous, for better and for worse, of the whole man, the devil and angel at war in all of us.

DANIEL JUDSON is the author of the Shamus Award-winning The Poisoned Rose, *the Shamus- and Barry-nominated* The Bone Orchard *and* The Darkest Place, *a 2007 Shamus-nominee for Best Hardcover. His next novel,* The Water's Edge, *will be published by St. Martin's Minotaur in June 2008.*

THERESA SCHWEGEL
by Richard L. Edwards

Theresa Schwegel's stories feel like they are written on a Chicago Police Department typewriter. Typewriters don't word process, they slam into paper and carbon with an intention, leave a mark. And the actual typewriter is not a machine at all, but a beat-weary cop, trying to get down a version of the events as they really happened (is there ever anything but a version of events?). And through Schwegel's skillful prose, we become witnesses to situations that spill out of the squad room into the all-too-real lives of rookies and officers of the CPD who do indeed "serve and protect," but the question is whom and for what reasons? Like Officers Samantha Mack and Ray Weiss, wryly known among their fellow cops as Smack and Vice, we find ourselves caught between duty and human nature, and we find that the ties that bind are frequently tied too tight. In her novels, we struggle to make sense of procedures that are meant to preserve our sense of law and order. And while we can debate—at a safe distance—if her characters are doing right or wrong, they still have a job to do. Smack and Vice are the types of cops you can imagine bumping into in a diner—sitting prominently in the large front window on Western Avenue, eating great food that does nothing for your cholesterol count—one of those places that has been around for a long time, doesn't look like much on the outside, but always seem to have a patrol car or two parked out in front regardless of the time of day—because, well, *you know*. And if we craned our ears from one booth over and listened to their stories, problems, loves and concerns, I imagine it would be a lot like reading Theresa Schwegel.

RICHARD L. EDWARDS received his Ph.D. in Critical Studies from the University of Southern California's School of Cinema-Television. Currently, he is an Assistant Professor of Media Arts and Science at Indiana University's School of Informatics. With Shannon Clute, he is the co-host of two hardboiled podcasts, "Out of the Past: Investigating Film Noir," and "Behind the Black Mask: Mystery Writers Revealed."

CARMELA SOPRANO
by Jason Starr

When Megan asked me to write about a favorite female noir character from film, TV or books the first two words out of my mouth were Carmela Soprano. I wasn't the only one who picked Carmela and I'm grateful that I got first dibs.

Carmela isn't a femme fatale, like Phyllis in James M. Cain's *Double Indemnity* (1935) or Sherri Parlay in Vicki Hendricks's *Miami Purity* (1995). She doesn't have a sinister agenda of her own, and she doesn't coerce or manipulate a mate into committing depraved acts. She functions entirely outside of the criminal world, and yet she's as sinister as any femme fatale in the noir canon.

Despite their surfacey marital problems, Tony and Carmela Soprano are a perfect couple. Tony needs a woman in his life who will blissfully look the other way and won't question his criminal behavior and Carmela fits that bill perfectly. In season six, Tony comments that he has a "Don't ask, don't tell policy" with Carmela regarding extramarital affairs, and yet this attitude could describe their entire marriage. Carmela will never ask Tony if she's cheating on her the same way she'll never come out and ask Tony if he had anything to do with disappearances of several of her close friends. She knows, yet she doesn't want to know, and it's this terrific lack or self-awareness and ability to compartmentalize that makes her so fascinating.

Carmela's view of herself is a sharp contrast from the way we view her. She doesn't see herself as the wife of a psychopathic mob boss. She sees herself as a deeply religious person, and a devoted wife and mother. She may posture about leaving Tony, but she never will. Shared guilt is her great comfort zone. She will never fire a gun or bury a body, yet in the end she is just as accountable as her husband.

For me, Carmela Soprano is fascinating to watch and she is a constant inspiration. She reminds me of my other favorite delusional, dysfunctional noir heroines, and is a perfect example of what makes this genre so compelling.

JASON STARR is the author of eight crime novels published in ten languages, including Barry Award-winner Tough Luck *and Anthony Award-winner* Twisted City. *He has also co-written two novels with Ken Bruen for Hard Case Crime—*Bust *and* Slide. *His latest novel from St. Martin's Press is* The Follower. *He lives in New York City and Paris.*

HELEN WALKER
by Don Malcolm

Her pale hair was straight and she wore it drawn into a smooth roll on the nape of her neck. It glinted like green gold. A slight woman, no age except young, with enormous grey eyes that slanted a little.

The grey eyes seemed as big as saucers, like the eyes of a kitten when you hold its nose touching yours. He looked at the small mouth, the full lower lip, carefully tinted but not painted. She said nothing.

This is how William Lindsay Gresham introduces noir's most cunning, clinical femme fatale, Dr. Lilith Ritter, the aptly-named avenging demon of *Nightmare Alley* (1946). In noir as elsewhere, the eyes have it: comparing this description to the on-screen presence of star-crossed actress Helen Walker, we see the simultaneous power and peril of inspired casting.

The power is in the performance: Walker has less than ten minutes of screen time, but her cold-eyed precision and assurance is breathtaking. The peril is in the real-life story: a young actress whose talent and beauty was just a little too cold to play in 40s Hollywood, and one terrible misfortune that hastened a downward spiral.

Walker was the toast of New York in the spring of 1942: just 21, she was a sensation as the love interest in *Jason*, an otherwise uneven play by Samson Raphaelson (best known for a series of incandescent collaborations with Ernst Lubitsch). Scooped up by Paramount, she was immediately cast opposite Alan Ladd after his breakout role in *This Gun For Hire* (1942).

That film, *Lucky Jordan* (1942), a gangster-joins-the-army piece of wartime hokum, gives Walker about ten minutes to command the screen before backing away from a character arc that would make Lauren Bacall a star two years later. Nevertheless, in those first ten minutes you can see what Helen Walker had—and, up until *Nightmare Alley* (1947), you can see that no one got close to it again.

Walker raised enough ruckus about her plight to get cut loose by Paramount in 1946; she landed at Fox—in part because Raphaelson recommended her to Lubitsch, and Lubitsch had Darryl Zanuck's ear. She had a small but showy role in 1946's *Cluny Brown* (Lubitsch's last film) later that year.

Fate (or some other mysterious force) intervened at this point, however. On New Year's Eve, Walker was returning to Los Angeles from Palm Springs: she gave a lift to three returning servicemen. Halfway back to LA, she lost control of her car, hit a median, and flipped the car over. One of her passengers died; the other two were seriously injured (Walker sustained a broken pelvis).

There was an investigation, there were lawsuits. A cloud passed over Walker's life, and it never went away. Her once-convivial drinking took a more "therapeutic" turn.

Her great performance as Lilith Ritter, the woman who chewed up and spit out Tyrone Power, did not advance her career: *Nightmare Alley* flopped, primarily because it gave Zanuck the creeps.

Though Walker was exonerated when the merry-go-round of litigation came to a halt in 1948, her career was dead in its tracks. She was dropped by Fox; freelance work was so dicey that she had no choice but to do pale variations on Lilith to pay the bills. Watching her as the disgruntled trophy wife in *Impact* (1949), one senses a different source for the contempt she directs at stolid, hapless Brian Donlevy.

Her final screen appearance is her most affecting: as Alicia, the discarded wife of mob boss Mr. Brown in *The Big Combo* (1955), her years of drinking evident, Walker is heartbreakingly vulnerable, her once-regal voice cracking under the cumulative strain of dissipation and abandonment. It's clear that this is a woman Walker understood all too well.

A few years later, her North Hollywood home burned to the ground.

Five years after that, she was diagnosed with cancer.

She was only 47 when she died.

So whenever you find yourself bemoaning your fate, think of Helen Walker. She is proof that things can always get worse—much, much worse.

DON MALCOLM is currently Managing Editor of the Noir City Sentinel, *the newsletter of the Film Noir Foundation. His book,* As Dark As It Gets: The 100 Darkest Film Noirs, *is in preparation and is slated to appear in 2008.*

HONEY WEST
by Robert Randisi

Actually, I'm not all that sure this is an appreciation of Honey West, as much as it is an appreciation of Anne Francis *playing* Honey West. But there I was, all of 14 years old in 1965 when Honey West hit the small screen. I thought then Anne Francis was the hottest, sexiest thing I'd seen on TV—and I still pretty much think so.

Well, by the time Honey was cancelled after a single season I had found the books, the Pyramid editions with Anne Francis on the covers, and I was hooked again. It was later I found out that G.G. Fickling was actually husband and wife Forrest E. "Skip" and Gloria Fickling. They were friends with Shell Scott creator Richard Prather, and decided to create a sort of female version of the swinging, white-haired P.I. Instead, Skip Fickling admits that he had both Mike Hammer and Marilyn Monroe in mind, and mixed parts of the two together liberally. (Gloria said in an interview that Skip thought of Hammer, and she thought of Monroe.)

Miss Francis fell just short of Honey's magnificent 38-22-36 attributes, but only by a couple of inches and not so you'd notice when she strutted onto screen with her hour glass figure clad in a tight dress, or a Mrs. Peel-type jumpsuit (although she pre-dated. Emma Peel in the U.S.)

Honey West was the first leading lady P.I. in either print or TV and staked her claim to the position in grand, over-the-top fashion. (An argument can be made for Erle Stanley Gardner's Bertha Cool, but she shared billing with the diminutive Donald Lam.)

Now Overlook Press is bringing Honey back. They've already reprinted the first two, *This Girl for Hire* (1957) and *Kiss for a Killer* (1960), and I believe the plan is to publish them all—although, for my benefit, they only need to do the first nine. There was a seven-year hiatus between the publication of *Bombshell* (1964) and *Honey on Her Tail* (1971), during which time Honey went from P.I. to spy.

The first nine books are well worth picking up for anyone interested in the history of the P.I., or if you simply love the P.I. genre. These books are a piece of genre history and, make no mistake, they are a guilty pleasure. No one ever claimed they were great literature, least of all the Ficklings. For my money, though, they're an important part of the genre, as are Honey West *and* Anne Francis.

There are plenty of websites about Honey, and Anne Francis has her own personal site. They can all be found by googling "Honey West." Skip Fickling died in 1998 from a brain tumor, and as recently as 2004 Gloria was still around. Gary Warren Neibuhr wrote a lengthy appreciation of Honey for *Mystery Scene Magazine*, which you can also find on the web.

On the other hand this appreciation of mine is short and sweet, and I'm leaving now to reread *This Girl For Hire*.

Here are the titles, including the 10th and 11th spy books. Enjoy.

- *This Girl for Hire* (1957)
- *A Gun for Honey* (1958)
- *Girl On the Loose* (1958)
- *Honey in the Flesh* (1959)
- *Girl on the Prowl* (1959)
- *Kiss for a Killer* (1960)
- *Dig a Dead Doll* (1960)
- *Blood and Honey* (1961)
- *Bombshell* (1964)
- *Stiff As a Broad* (1971)
- *Honey on Her Tail* (1971)

ROBERT RANDISI *is the author of over 400 books, 50 short stories and the editor of 30 anthologies. He is the author of the* Miles Jacoby, Nick Delvecchio, Joe Keough *and* Rat Pack *mystery series and the co-author of the* Gil & Claire Hunt *series. His most recent anthology is* Hollywood & Crime *(Pegasus Books, 2007). His next novel will be his* Rat Pack *book,* Luck Be a Lady, Don't Die *(SMP, 2007). He is the founder of the Private Eye Writers of America, creator of the Shamus Award and co-founder of* Mystery Scene Magazine.

ALABAMA WORLEY
by Sean Doolittle

"You got a lot of heart, kid," the hit man played by James Gandolfini tells the ex-hooker played by Patricia Arquette in the 1993 film *True Romance*. This line comes after a sequence so brutally violent that I've never been able to watch it without flinching, but by the time we hear it, there's no doubt in the room that the hit man is right: Alabama Worley has a lot of heart. And also a corkscrew. Both of them in the right place.

In some ways, Alabama—formerly Whitman, a call girl not a hooker, and not what they call in Florida "white trash"—is the antithesis of the conventional femme fatale. Here's a girl who hitches her wagon to a kung fu fanboy whose adolescent notions of comic book chivalry can only bring her trouble. "But if I'm with you," she tells him, "then I'm with you." She's a promise of sunshine in the midst of a drab Detroit winter for our hero Clarence, quirky and endearing as Patricia Arquette's eye teeth, and when it comes to relationships, she's one hundred percent.

Plenty has been written about the iconic fatal woman of classic noir, her dual role as both quivering male fantasy and the embodiment of masculine anxiety. I won't argue with any of that, but I'll spill a gender secret. Here's the real male fantasy: the girl sitting beside you on the couch at the brink of doom. It's all your fault. She passes you a note that says, "You're so cool."

SEAN DOOLITTLE's latest novel, The Cleanup, *was nominated for the 2007 Barry Award, the 2007 Anthony Award, and was named Favorite Book of 2006 by the readers of* CrimeSpree Magazine. *His next novel,* Safer, *will be published by Bantam Dell in 2008. He lives in Omaha, Nebraska with his wife and kids.*

Contributors

Lynne Barrett, recipient of the Edgar* Award for Best Mystery Short Story, is the author of *The Secret Names of Women* and *The Land of Go*. Her stories have been published in the anthologies *Miami Noir*, *A Dixie Christmas*, *Mondo Barbie* and *Simply the Best Mysteries*. She is co-editor of *Birth: A Literary Companion* and *The James M. Cain Cookbook, Guide to Home Singing, Physical Fitness and Animals (Especially Cats)*, and wrote the libretto for the children's opera *Cricketina*. She lives in Miami where she teaches at Florida International University.
Photo credit: Michele Baker

Charlotte Carter is author of two highly praised mystery series. The Nanette Hayes series—*Rhode Island Red*, *Coq au Vin*, *Drumsticks* (Warner/Mysterious Press)—features a leggy young jazz-loving sax player whose sense of adventure inevitably lands her in the middle of murder. And the Cook County series—*Jackson Park* and *Tripwire* (Ballantine/One World)—narrated by precocious black hippie Cassandra Lisle, is set on Chicago's South Side during the volatile Vietnam era.

Walking Bones (Serpent's Tail, 2002) is her dark novel about the intersecting lives of six New Yorkers brought together by the twists inherent in love and sex, alcohol and violence, and, inescapably, race. Winner of the Chester Himes Mystery Writers Award, she has also been published in many anthologies in England and America.

A long-time New Yorker, she has worked as a part-time teacher and an editorial grunt, and has also traveled and lived in North Africa, England and France. She currently lives with her husband on the Lower East Side.

Christa Faust is the author of nine novels including *Hoodtown*, the award-winning novelization of *Snakes on a Plane* and *Money Shot* (Hard Case Crime, 2008). Faust will be the first female author published by Hard Case. She lives and writes in Los Angeles.
Photo credit: Jim Ferreira

An entertainment writer by day, **Alison Gaylin** is also the author of the Edgar*-nominated *Hide Your Eyes* and its sequel, *You Kill Me*, both of which came out in 2005. Her standalone, Hollywood-set thriller *Trashed*, debuted in September 2007. And she is currently at work on her next novel which will come out in 2008. She lives in upstate New York with her husband, daughter and dog.
Photo credit: Jennifer May

Sara Gran is the author of the novels *Dope*, *Come Closer* and *Saturn's Return to New York*. Born and raised in Brooklyn, New York, she now lives in California.
Photo credit: Robert Urh

Libby Fischer Hellmann is the author of the award-winning suspense series featuring video producer and single mother Ellie Foreman. Libby grew up in Washington D.C., but has lived in Chicago for 30 years. She is also the editor of *Chicago Blues*, a dark crime fiction anthology, which was released by Bleak House Books in October 2007. Her next novel, *Easy Innocence*, a stand-alone PI novel, will be released in 2008.

She blogs at "The Outfit" (*www.theoutfitcollective.com*) with six other Chicago crime fiction authors, including Sara Paretsky, Barbara D'Amato and Marcus Sakey.
Photo credit: Sean Chercover

Vicki Hendricks is the author of noir novels *Miami Purity*, *Iguana Love*, *Voluntary Madness*, *Sky Blues* and *Cruel Poetry*. She lives in Hollywood, Florida, and teaches writing at Broward Community College. Skydiving, SCUBA and travel adventures often provide atmosphere and plot for her writing.
Photo credit: Jennifer Feebeck

Naomi Hirahara, born and raised in Southern California, is the Edgar* Award-winning author of the Mas Arai mystery series, which features a Japanese American gardener and atomic-bomb survivor. A previous editor of *The Rafu Shimpo* newspaper, she also has produced seven nonfiction books on local horticulture and Asian American history. Her short stories have been published in various anthologies, including *Los Angeles Noir*. Her middle-grade book, *1001 Cranes*, will be released next summer by Delacorte. Her website is *www.naomihirahara.com*.

Annette Meyers was born in Manhattan, grew up on a chicken farm in New Jersey, and came running back to New York as fast as she could. With her long history on both Broadway (assistant to Harold Prince) and Wall Street (headhunter and NASD arbitrator), she is the quintessential New Yorker.

All of her books—the eight Smith and Wetzons (contemporary), the two Olivia Browns (1920), the standalone *Repentances* (1936)—are set in New York.

Using the pseudonym Maan Meyers, Annette and her husband Martin have written six books and multiple short stories in *The Dutchman* series of historical mysteries set in New York in the 17th, 18th and 19th centuries.

Her own short story "You Don't Know Me" was included in *Best American Mystery Stories* (2002).

She was the 10th president of Sisters in Crime and is current president of the International Association of Crime Writers, North America.
Photo credit: Donna F. Aceto

Donna Moore was a crime fiction fan from a young age. She decided that she wanted to be one of Enid Blyton's Famous Five and fight crime with the aid of only a basket of cucumber sandwiches and a bottle of ginger beer. So, that summer she spent her spare time following mysterious strangers around the village—especially those with cockney accents and a couple of days' growth of stubble—until a complaint from the new local vicar put a stop to her sleuthing career. She decided instead to become a Superhero. So far, she has the tights and the cape.

Vin Packer, a pseudonym for Marijane Meaker, was one of the 1950s Gold Medal Books paperback crime writers. She also writes Young Adult novels as M. E. Kerr. She has won Lifetime Achievement Awards from The Publishers' Triangle, Lambda Literary and the American Library Association's Margaret Edwards Award. She lives in East Hampton, New York.
Photo credit: Zoe Kamitses

Rebecca Pawel was born and raised in New York City. She has published four books set in Spain, including the Edgar*-winning *Death of a Nationalist* (2003) and *The Summer Snow*, which was listed as one of *Publishers Weekly*'s best mysteries of 2006. She teaches in a public high school in New York, which at times feels like being a member of the International Brigades, and at times—given the climate at the Department of Education—feels like belonging to the Falange. She is currently working on a novel about Renaissance Flanders. Much of her social life revolves around tango, but she has always been too timid to participate in a birthday dance.
Photo credit: Marie-Jeanne Tavernier

Cornelia Read's first novel, *A Field of Darkness*, has been nominated for Edgar*, Anthony, Barry, Macavity, Gumshoe, Audie and RT Bookclub Critics Choice awards. She lives in Berkeley, California, with her Intrepid Spouse and twin daughters.
Photo credit: Robert M. Greber

Lisa Respers France is a writer and editor living in New York City. A native of Baltimore, she is a former reporter at *The Baltimore Sun* and *The Los Angeles Times*, an ardent reader and a proud graduate of Western High School. Her work has also appeared in the anthology *Baltimore Noir*.
Photo credit: Mary Reagan

SJ Rozan, the author of ten crime novels, is a life-long New Yorker. Her novels and short stories have won the Edgar*, Shamus, Anthony, Nero and Macavity. SJ is a former Mystery Writers of America National Board member, a current Sisters in Crime National Board member and ex-President of the Private Eye Writers of America. She is at work on a new Lydia Chin/Bill Smith novel, *The Shanghai Moon*

Sandra Scoppettone has published 19 novels, five of them for young adults. Two books have been made into movies for TV. She has been nominated for two Edgars* and won a Shamus under the name Jack Early, which she used for 3 books. She lives with her partner of 35 years in Southold, New York.
Photo credit: Linda Crawford

Zoë Sharp spent most of her formative years living on a catamaran on the northwest coast of England. She opted out of mainstream education at the age of twelve and wrote her first novel at fifteen. Sharp turned to writing crime after being on the receiving end of death-threat letters in the course of her work as a freelance photojournalist, and this led to the creation of her no-nonsense ex-army-turned-bodyguard heroine, Charlie Fox. The latest in this award-nominated series, *Second Shot*, was published by St. Martin's Press in September 2007.
Photo credit: Andy Butler @ ZACE Photographic

Sarah Weinman is the *Baltimore Sun*'s crime fiction columnist, writes "Dark Passages," a monthly online mystery & suspense column for the *Los Angeles Times Book Review* and is the proprietor of *Confessions of an Idiosyncratic Mind* (at *www.sarahweinman.com*), hailed by *USA Today* as "a respected resource for commentary on crime and mystery fiction." Her short fiction has appeared in *Ellery Queen's Mystery Magazine, Alfred Hitchcock's Mystery Magazine* and several anthologies, including *Dublin Noir, Baltimore Noir, Expletive Deleted* and *Damn Near Dead*. She lives in Manhattan, and would like to spend more time sitting nice and quiet and smelling the flowers.
Photo credit: Mary Reagan

Ken Bruen is the award-winning author of over twenty novels. He has a Ph.D. in Metaphysics. He lives in Galway, Ireland and is the proud father of Grace.
Photo credit: Reg Gordon

Stona Fitch's novels have been praised by Nobel Laureate J. M. Coetzee, Russell Banks and others in the U.S., U.K. and France. *Senseless*, his latest novel, is now a feature film from Scottish director Simon Hynd. He lives and writes in Concord, Massachusetts, where he also leads Gaining Ground, a non-profit organic farm.
Photo credit: Clark Quin

Allan Guthrie was born in Orkney, but has lived in Edinburgh for most of his adult life. He is married to Donna. His first novel, *Two-Way Split*, was short-listed for the CWA Debut Dagger and went on to win the 2007 Theakston's Old Peculier Crime Novel Of The Year. His second novel, *Kiss Her Goodbye*, was nominated for Edgar*, Anthony and Gumshoe awards. His third, *Hard Man*, was published in 2007 along with *Kill Clock*, a novella for adult reluctant readers. Allan is a commissioning editor for PointBlank Press and a literary agent with Jenny Brown Associates.
Photo credit: Mary Reagan

Charlie Huston is the author of the Henry Thompson trilogy (Edgar*-nominated *Caught Stealing*, Edgar*-& Anthony-nominated *Six Bad Things* and Anthony-nominated *A Dangerous Man*), the Joe Pitt Casebooks, including *Half the Blood of Brooklyn* (December 2007) and the suburban noir, *The Shotgun Rule*. He lives in Los Angeles with his wife, the actress Virginia Louise Smith.
Photo credit: Ray Coco Smith

Eddie Muller writes novels, movie histories, plays, short stories, films and biographies, including the recent national bestseller *Tab Hunter Confidential*. His fiction debut, *The Distance*, was honored by the Private Eye Writers of America as Best First Novel of 2002. He is a two-time Edgar® Award nominee and twice an Anthony Award nominee. He is also founder and president of the Film Noir Foundation, dedicated to "rescuing and restoring America's noir heritage." He has produced and directed a film version of his contribution to this collection, "The Grand Inquisitor," starring Marsha Hunt.
Photo credit: Ron Rinaldi

Daniel Woodrell has published eight novels and lives in an isolated neighborhood in an isolated town in the isolated Missouri Ozarks because there's something about the place he likes.
Photo credit: Bruce Carr

*   *   *

Megan Abbott is the Edgar®-nominated author of *Queenpin* (2007), *The Song is You* (2007) and *Die a Little* (2005), as well as the nonfiction study, *The Street Was Mine: White Masculinity in Hardboiled Fiction and Film Noir* (2002). She lives in Queens, New York.
Photo credit: Joshua A. Gaylord

Val McDermid is the internationally best-selling author of 21 novels, two story anthologies and one Edgar®-nominated work of non-fiction, *A Suitable Job for a Woman*. Her latest release is the fifth Tony Hill /Carol Jordan thriller, *Beneath the Bleeding*. Val divides her time between South Manchester and Northumberland. She has a son and three cats.

MIAMI PURITY
by Vicki Hendricks

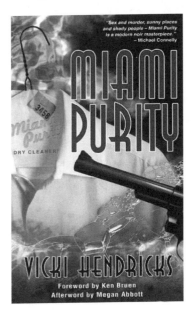

Now back in print!

New foreword by Ken Bruen.
New afterword by Megan Abbott.
Trade paperback. $16.
ISBN 978-0-9792709-3-2

"Sex and murder, sunny places and shady people— *Miami Purity* is a modern noir masterpiece."
—Michael Connelly

"*Miami Purity* is the toughest, sexiest, most original debut noir novel ever written, and instantly rockets Hendricks into the list of all-time great noir authors. Gripping, super-sexy, and unforgettably raw."
—Lauren Henderson

"Shocking and supercharged, both reverent and original, this is the novel that amped up a new generation of noir writers."—George Pelecanos

"The authentic heir to James M. Cain, Vicki Hendricks is the high priestess of neo-noir. A fierce and fearless talent."—Dennis Lehane

"*Miami Purity* is as sleek as a well-oiled weasel and tight as the Gordian knot. One of the best of its kind from a very fine writer."—Joe R. Lansdale

"Vicki Hendricks is a true original. She is undoubtedly one of the most important noir writers of the past twenty years, and *Miami Purity* is one of the best crime novels I've ever read, period."—Jason Starr

Busted Flush Press books are available from your favorite independent, chain, or online booksellers.

Visit www.bustedflushpress.com to see what's coming from BFP next. And while you're there, sign up for BFP's e-mail newsletter.

Coming soon...

Crime fiction reprints by Ken Bruen, Reed Farrel Coleman, Chloe Green, David Handler, A. E. Maxwell, Cynthia Smith, Mitchell Smith, and much more!

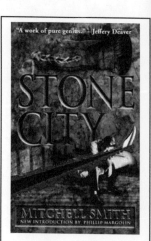

Mitchell Smith's *Stone City*... Available from Busted Flush Press in early 2008!

"Dense, authoritative, and written with a rare ferocity and grace, *Stone City* is undoubtedly one of the great crime novels in contemporary literature." —Thomas H. Cook

BUSTED FLUSH

PRESS

www.bustedflushpress.com